Scorned Justice

Other Books by Margaret Daley

Saving Hope
Shattered Silence
Severed Trust (coming October 2013)

SCORNED JUSTICE

Book 3 of Men of the Texas Rangers Series

Margaret Daley

Abingdon Press fiction
a novel approach to faith

Nashville, Tennessee

Scorned Justice

Copyright © 2013 by Margaret Daley

ISBN: 978-1-4267-1436-8

Published by Abingdon Press, P.O. Box 801, Nashville, TN 37202
www.abingdonpress.com

All rights reserved.

The persons and events portrayed in this work of fiction
are the creations of the author, and any resemblance
to persons living or dead is purely coincidental.

Published in association with the Steve Laube Agency.

Library of Congress Cataloging-in-Publication Data has been
requested.

Printed in the United States of America

1 2 3 4 5 6 7 8 9 10 / 18 17 16 15 14 13

To Steve and Jan for helping me with this book. I appreciate your support and time to answer my questions and help me brainstorm.

Dear Readers,

I've written the Men of the Texas Rangers Series because I'm so impressed with the law enforcement group, the Texas Rangers. They are dedicated officers who are highly skilled and experienced. *Scorned Justice* is the third book in the series (*Saving Hope* and *Shattered Silence* are books 1 and 2). I wanted to explore what it was like to want revenge so much you go too far. What does it do to you? To the people around you? God wants us to forgive someone who has hurt us or done something wrong to us. Revenge comes out of the ability not to forgive a person for a wrong done.

In the fall of 2013 *Severed Trust,* my fourth book in the series, will be out. It explores what the abuse of prescription drugs does to a community.

I love hearing from readers. You can contact me at either margaretdaley@gmail.com or P. O. Box 2074 Tulsa, OK 74101. You can also learn more about me and my books and sign up for my quarterly newsletter at www.margaretdaley.com.

Best wishes,
Margaret Daley

1

The pain in her neck and shoulders sharpened its grip on District Court Judge Rebecca Morgan as she left the courtroom. She headed for her office, welcoming the quiet in the corridor. Inside her sanctuary from the madness of this new trial, she shed her black robe and hung it up in the closet. Finally, the end of the day—the weekend was here and she could escape to the ranch. Two glorious days to spend with her brother and his family. She could forget for a short time the case before her—the murder of a businessman by a high-level member of the Russian mob.

With a sigh, she grabbed her purse and started for the door. The ranch was almost an hour away from San Antonio, and as it was, she would be in traffic for a while.

Before she could reach for the knob, the door swung open and her law clerk stood in the entrance. A frown etched deep lines in the forty-year-old woman's face.

Rebecca stiffened. "What's happened?"

"You got a delivery half an hour ago from a florist."

"I did?" She couldn't think of anyone who would send her flowers. It wasn't her birthday or any other occasion for a celebration. Then Rebecca focused on the deepening scowl on Laura Melton's face. "What's wrong with it?"

"I'll show you." Laura turned into her office, which connected with Rebecca's, and strode to her desk. Lifting the lid on a long white box with Blooms and Such stamped on its side, she tilted it toward Rebecca.

To reveal a dozen long-stem roses—all dead.

Rebecca gritted her teeth. "They are *not* going to succeed in ruining this trial the way they did the last one." The first trial, under Judge Osborn, had been declared a mistrial when it was revealed there was jury tampering. "This new tactic will not be tolerated." As she spoke, though, she tried to decide how she would handle this. "Is there a card with it? Anything to give to the police?"

"Just this box. It was sitting on my desk when I came back in here right before you ended the trial for the day. I called Detective Nelson. He's on his way over here."

Rebecca checked her watch. "I need to leave. My brother's birthday party is in less than two hours. Can you handle it by yourself?"

Laura's frown relaxed into a neutral expression. "Sure. Charlie has a special interest in this trial and wants to make sure justice is done here. And he isn't too bad to look at either."

Rebecca laughed. "Leave it up to you to turn this into checking a man out."

"I could always give you tips if you're interested."

"I appreciate the offer, but I'll pass." *Especially a cop.* She'd been married to a policeman who had died in the line of duty three years ago. She wouldn't go through that again. She made her way toward the door. "If Detective Nelson needs to talk to me, he can reach me on my cell. Otherwise, I don't want to deal with any type of business until Monday morning, when jury selection continues."

"Forget this place. I'll make sure the detective doesn't have any questions for you. I'll use my womanly wiles on him." Laura winked.

"You do that." As Rebecca hurried toward the elevator, she realized how fortunate she was to have such a good law clerk and friend in Laura. She made her life so much easier, especially now, with this difficult trial. She would have to take Laura out to dinner next week as a thank-you.

❦

When Texas Ranger Brody Calhoun let himself into his house, Dallas, his black Lab, greeted him at the door, wagging his tail and nosing Brody's hand. He stopped and knelt to pet Dallas, knowing if he didn't, his dog would hound him until he did it properly.

"Did you and Dad get along all right today?"

Dallas barked.

"So this was a good day, then?" Brody rubbed behind his ten-year-old dog's ears.

"Of course we got along okay, Son. I told you he was growing on me."

Brody looked toward the den, where his father was standing, instead of using his electric scooter. The deep lines on his face revealed a man who appeared to be ten years older than he really was. But three months ago, at sixty-eight, he'd had his second heart attack, and his recovery had been much slower than the last one six years before.

"Where's Ted?"

"Gone for the day."

"I must have just missed him."

"No, I told him to get out after lunch. I don't need anybody watching me take a nap. A waste of good money." His dad swept his arm down the length of his body. "See, I don't need my scooter. I'm capable of getting around under my own steam. You can turn it back in."

Brody rose slowly, using the time to suppress his anger. Why hadn't Ted called him to let him know what his dad had done? He pulled out his cell and . . .

"Put that thing up. I told him he'd better not call you. He works for me, not you."

A denial of that fact was on the tip of Brody's tongue, but instead of saying anything and causing yet another argument, Brody gritted his teeth and stuck his cell back in his pocket. "Ted is here to keep you company, make sure everything goes all right." *To give me peace of mind. I almost lost you.*

His father scowled. "As soon as the doc says, I want him gone. I don't need a babysitter."

Brody ignored his father's usual complaints. "Ted is a nurse, not a babysitter."

His dad's eyebrows slanted down even more. "I'm no fool. I know exactly why Ted is here. I've been taking care of myself for more years than you've been alive."

"Samantha is bringing dinner for you tonight."

"Where are you going?"

"To Thomas Sinclair's birthday party. It started out as a small affair, but it's turning into a big deal now that Foster Sinclair is coming. Although I'm not officially on duty, I'll be keeping an eye on the governor. Can't have anything happen to Foster at the same party I attend."

"There was a time when I would have been invited when Thomas's dad was around. At least Tom wasn't put out to pasture like I've been."

"Dad, Thomas would love to see you. Do you want to go with me?"

"No," his father quickly replied, "not until I'm back to being 100 percent."

"That's what I told Thomas when we talked about it."

"No reason to leave, especially like this. And for your information I don't have to have my granddaughter take over for Ted. I can put a dinner in the microwave." His dad swung around and shuffled into the den.

Brody followed him. "We've been over this. Until the doctor thinks you can stay by yourself, you need someone checking up on you throughout the day. I have to work and sometimes get caught up in a case—"

His dad turned up the volume on the television set. Its blaring sound negated any possibility of having a reasonable conversation with the man. Brody stared at him, sitting in his lounge chair in front of the TV with some game show on. His dad had gone from being an invalid part of the time to thinking he could do anything he had done before his heart attack.

Brody headed to his bedroom to change his shirt. He had come back to his hometown of San Antonio to fill a ranger's position in Company D because his father's health had taken a turn for the worse six months ago. Then he'd had a heart attack and his dad had required a lot more care than Brody, checking with him every day, could give him. When his dad was released from the hospital, he came to live with Brody.

And to test my patience every day since then.

As Brody finished dressing, the doorbell rang, the sound competing with the TV. He quickened his pace and let his niece into the house. "Are you ready for duty?"

Samantha clicked her heels together and saluted. "Aye, aye, sir. How is he?"

"I'm just peachy."

Samantha leaned around Brody and grinned at his dad. "Hi, Grandpa. Are ya ready for me to beat you at chess tonight?"

His old man snorted. "When the tropics freeze over."

"I'll leave y'all to hash out who's the best chess player in the Calhoun family. I can't be late for the governor."

"Don't worry about Grandpa, Uncle Brody." Samantha stood on tiptoes and kissed his cheek. "After I beat him at chess, I think a rousing game of dominos will be fun."

"In your dreams, Samantha," his father said with a chuckle.

Brody left, realizing his nineteen-year-old niece was just what his dad needed. Dad had a hard time resisting a pretty female. Maybe that was Brody's mistake. Maybe he should have hired a woman to nurse his dad back to health, especially now that he could get into and out of bed by himself. His dad was also walking more and only used the scooter when he got tired. Maybe he should think about returning the scooter they'd rented. To his dad it was a symbol of his invalidism. He'd also call the agency tomorrow and check into requesting a female nurse. He had to have someone who wouldn't let his father dictate what he did. Ted should have called him today and let him know that he had left hours before he should have.

❧

Rebecca parked next to her brother's F-150 and slid from her car as her two nieces flew out of the back door of the ranch house and raced toward her. Bracing herself, she hugged both of them to her.

"We thought you would *never* get here," Kim, her ten-year-old niece, said, leaning back to look up at Rebecca.

Aubrey still clung to her leg. At five, she did everything her big sister did. "Yeah, Aunt Becky. What took ya so long?"

She cringed at the name Becky. The only other one who used that name besides her nieces was her brother. Probably because she still called him Tommy to irritate him. "Traffic.

Everyone was leaving San Antonio for the weekend, all at the same time." She hugged them to her and started for the house. "Where are Tory and your dad?"

"Tory's in the kitchen freaking out about the food and the fact that Dad isn't here yet for his own birthday party." Kim reached for the door and opened it.

"He isn't? I imagine Tory is upset."

"Daddy forgets the time." Aubrey entered first.

Tory stood at the island counter, putting one hand on her waist. "And he must have forgotten his cell again. I can't reach him on it. Or his ringer is off. I don't know how many times I've told him to take it with him and have it on so he can hear it when it rings."

Rebecca chuckled. "You two still arguing about that?" Her brother wasn't a big fan of cellphones because he loved getting away for a while by himself to think, which was usually when he was riding his horse, Rocket.

"The governor is coming tonight, and Thomas is out riding the fences." Tory's gaze flitted from one stepdaughter to the other. "And you two need to go get your good clothes on. Go. I laid them out on your beds." Frowning, she waved her hand toward the doorway. "Now."

Rebecca kissed the top of Aubrey's hair and then hugged Kim before they scurried off to follow their stepmother's directions. "See you two later." When she turned to her sister-in-law, she continued. "You know, he does his best thinking while riding."

"Yeah, worrying about the drought and forgetting he's turning one year older."

Her older brother had hated his thirtieth birthday. His thirty-fifth had been even worse, and now he was thirty-seven. "He does know Foster Sinclair is coming?"

"Yes." Tory frowned, taking the decorated, Texas-shaped sugar cookies off the cookie sheet and placing them on a platter. "He's one of his cousin's biggest supporters, so this is a treat for him. I can't understand why he isn't back yet."

"Have you sent someone out after him?"

"The hands are in front helping set up the barbecue."

"Then I'll go out and try to find him. And I'll take my cell with the ringer on so you and I can communicate. Okay?"

Tory pointed her fingers at Rebecca. "You aren't dressed for riding."

"But I will be when I change. It won't take me five minutes. You know how I love to ride. As much as Thomas does. This gives me a reason to do it before tomorrow."

"That's one thing I've not gotten into since coming here a year ago." Tory held up both hands, palms outward. "I know. Thomas doesn't understand. But I'm not comfortable around horses. Thankfully, he loves me in spite of that flaw."

Hattie, her brother's housekeeper, rushed into the kitchen. "Everything is looking good out front. Why don't you let me finish up in here, and you go get ready for tonight?" The fifty-three-year-old woman, who had been with the Sinclair family for thirty years, edged Tory away from the cookie sheet and took the metal spatula from her hand.

"I think I will. Then I'll do one final check. I'm much better at planning and hosting a party than riding a horse." Tory left the kitchen.

Hattie watched Rebecca's sister-in-law until she disappeared, then switched her full attention to Rebecca. "Ever since Foster accepted the invitation, she has been a basket of nerves. You would think the president of the United States was coming, not the governor. Wait 'til she sees him arrive with his security detail."

"I'd better go find my brother. It would help if the man wore a watch."

"How many times have we heard Thomas say he can tell the time by the sun?"

"Too many to count. Do you think he is purposely staying away until the party has started? He hates anyone making a fuss over him."

"Then he really should have made that point clear to his wife," Hattie muttered as she finished placing the cookies on the platter.

After Rebecca retrieved her bag from the trunk of her Mustang, she quickly changed into comfy jeans, a casual shirt, and boots. Ten minutes later, she rode Angel Fire from the stables and headed in the same direction the foreman, Jake, said her brother had gone. The sun almost kissed the tops of the hills to the west, bathing the terrain in golden hues. Making a beeline for the fence line on the eastern edge of the property, she leaned forward and urged her gelding faster, the warm September breeze blowing her hair, put up in a ponytail. The scent of the outdoors, with its hint of sage, laced the air. She loved that smell.

All the worries of the new trial started to flee her mind. No gangland shootings. No vague threats. Nothing but peace. The presence of the Lord surrounded her as she let go of her worries and enjoyed communing with the natural beauty God had created.

But that didn't tell her where her brother was. Knowing him, he was probably taking care of some problem with the cattle. The ranch was his life.

In the distance, she glimpsed a black horse that was like the one her brother rode, riderless and galloping across the pasture toward her, his run odd-looking. *Where's Thomas? Did he fall off his horse?*

Rebecca urged her mount faster, her heart pounding as fast as Angel Fire's hooves against the hard ground.

Brody climbed out of his blue SUV and scanned the area in front of the Sinclair's large, two-story adobe house, where the barbecue would take place in less than half an hour. He'd come a little early to make sure security was in place for the governor's arrival. Although he wasn't officially a part of the security team, he couldn't *not* be a Texas Ranger and make sure nothing happened to Foster Sinclair. One area of his expertise for the Rangers was security. Having been trained by the U.S. Marshals and the Secret Service, he was often involved in the protection of people in need.

He was at the barbecue as a friend to the Sinclair family, especially Thomas. They'd reconnected when he moved back five months ago. They had grown up as best friends and only lost touch with each other when he moved to Amarillo, and then to Dallas as a highway patrol officer and later a Texas Ranger. He'd welcomed the change. He couldn't stay and watch Thomas's sister, Rebecca, marry another man.

Three waiters came out of the house with Hattie right behind them directing them in their duties. He approached the housekeeper as the young men left to take their places.

"My lands, Brody Calhoun, you have grown even taller than the last time I saw you. What, six feet four or five inches?" Hattie greeted him with a hug, his large frame dwarfing her petite one.

"Still six three."

"Are ya sure? What was it ten years ago?" She cocked her head to the side. "And why has it been ten years? One day you're around a lot, then all of a sudden you're gone."

"I became a highway patrol officer. They sent me to Amarillo."

"Why did you leave the San Antonio Police Department?"

"Because I wanted to be a Texas Ranger." *Because I was too late. Rebecca loved another.*

"How's your dad? Did he tell you I visited him a couple of times in the hospital?"

"Yes. We kept missing each other, but I'm glad you did. It brightened his day."

"I bet he gave you and his doctors a tough time about staying in the hospital. I imagine you've had your hands full corralling your dad, so I'll forgive you for not coming here until today."

Brody reflected back to that week, tension clamping around his spine. "You imagined right. He wasn't too happy being trapped in the hospital being a human pin cushion, as he put it."

Hattie's chuckle reminded Brody of the good times he'd spent at the Circle S Ranch. "That doesn't surprise me at all. He reminds me of my husband. He insisted on coming home to die. He wasn't going to stay in the hospital and have the last thing he saw be that room with its beige walls and every machine in the world hooked up to him. His words. I still miss him after five years."

"I didn't even know about him dying until a week after the fact."

"I got your letter, and it meant a lot to me. I had a small memorial service before I scattered his ashes over the land he loved so much."

"The Circle S Ranch?"

"Yep. He was foreman here for thirty years. He's the reason I'm here taking care of Mr. Sinclair's two adorable children. It doesn't look like my daughter is going to get married anytime soon and give me grandchildren."

Tory stepped out onto the front porch to survey the yard, from the lights strung up, to the tables set with red-and-white checkered tablecloths, to the grills set off to the side behind the buffet area.

Hattie leaned close to Brody and whispered, "She wanted a fancy party once she found out about the governor. Thomas had to put his foot down."

"Yeah, I can imagine. He's the least pretentious person I know. Besides, Tory must not know Foster well. He's a lot like Thomas." Brody pivoted toward Thomas's wife, who was walking across the manicured lawn.

She stopped beside Hattie. "Your daughter said the brisket is ready to come out of the oven."

"I'd better go and put the finishing touches to the food." Hattie clasped Brody's arm. "Don't be a stranger now that you live in San Antonio and your dad is getting better. I don't want it to be another ten years before you come back to the ranch."

As Hattie hurried into the house, Brody said, "I'd forgotten how much I love this ranch. I spent many days exploring this place with Thomas. Where is he?"

The corners of Tory's mouth twisted into a frown. "Out checking fences. I don't know what gets into that man's head—he knows he needs to be here when the guests start to arrive." She looked down the long drive and moaned. "Two cars full of guests who are here for his birthday. What do I tell them?"

"The truth. He had a situation he needed to take care of on the ranch, which I'm sure is what has kept him away. A lot of the guests are ranchers and will certainly understand. If he's not back in twenty minutes, I'll go out looking for him."

Tory's forehead grooved deeper. "You don't think he really ran into a problem?"

"Knowing Thomas, he's forgotten the time. I can gently remind him he has guests."

"Rebecca already went out after him." Tory started toward the two cars now coming to a stop. "Call her on her cell. You don't want to cover the same ground that she has."

"What's her number?" Glad Tory's back was to him, he doubted he was doing a very good job covering his reaction to hearing Rebecca's name.

Tory rattled off the number, then greeted the first set of guests while Thomas's daughters raced out of the house, dressed in their Sunday best. He wondered how long Aubrey would stay clean in her pretty white dress. According to Thomas, his youngest loved to don her fancy clothes even when going out to play in the yard. His gaze swung to Kim with her matching outfit, but her face reflected her discomfort. She was Thomas's tomboy and probably only wore a dress when Tory insisted.

Kim threw him a glance as she crossed to her stepmother. He smiled at her, only having seen her a handful of times in the past five months when Thomas brought her into town with him on the weekend. He'd only been around Aubrey once, when the girls went with their father to Sea World and he had tagged along. Aubrey was the very image of Thomas— and Rebecca. A picture of Rebecca materialized in his mind: medium height with just the right curves, auburn hair, thick and wavy, framing a beautiful face dominated by blue eyes that were the color of the sky on a clear sunny day.

As another SUV pulled up, the picture of Rebecca vanished, and he quickly oriented himself to the task at hand. He waved at two fellow Texas Rangers, then strode toward the barn while digging out his cell to call Rebecca. A thin film of sweat coated his forehead and upper lip. Listening to the phone ring, he swiped his hand across his brow.

Get over it, Calhoun. You knew she was going to be here.

Rebecca neared Thomas's stallion, who was coming up a small incline, his pace slowing. Rocket's ears twitched back and forth, independent of each other and his eyes were wide, their whites showing. His nostrils flared.

Something's wrong. What spooked him?

She slowed Angel Fire so as not to spook Rocket further and kept shortening the distance between them. When her cellphone rang, she gasped and pulled back on the reins with one hand while fumbling for her phone with the other.

Rocket came over the rise as she answered, "Rebecca."

"This is Brody Calhoun. I'm at the house and told Tory I would help you look for Thomas."

That was when she saw that Rocket was dragging a rope. Her gaze latched onto what the stallion towed. A scream erupted from deep in her throat, and the cellphone slipped from her fingers.

2

The sound coming from his cellphone curdled Brody's blood. He ran flat out toward the stables as he shouted into the phone, "Rebecca. Rebecca, what's wrong?"

Nothing but sobs came through the connection. Suddenly the line went dead. Still holding the phone, he quickly saddled the nearest horse and hoisted himself up onto it, then called Rebecca again. It went to voicemail.

Where are you? The ranch covered thousands of acres.

Scanning the yard, he spied Jake standing by a corral behind the stables and spurred his gelding toward the foreman, whom he'd met a couple of times in town with Thomas.

"Do you know where Rebecca went?"

"East toward the front of the property, by the road. At least I think so. I told her Thomas went that way."

"There's something wrong. I called her, and all I got was a scream and sobs."

"Rebecca?"

Brody nodded. "I'm headed that way."

"So am I. I'll be right behind you with some help. Most of the vehicles are out, but we've still got one four-wheeler here."

"Don't say anything to Tory or Hattie until I know what's happened. Bring a few men to help."

Jake ran toward the stables while Brody brought his horse around and headed toward the eastern part of the Sinclair ranch. Still a lot of ground to cover even with it narrowed down.

Setting his gelding into a gallop, Brody was vigilant for any sign of trouble, anything out of the ordinary.

❧

Thomas's horse slowed at Rebecca's urging. She hopped to the ground and made her way toward Rocket. "Easy, boy." The stallion snorted and moved a few steps to the side. "Whoa." Rebecca snatched up the dangling reins.

Rocket's extra couple of steps brought what the stallion had been dragging over the incline. Her hand tightened about the reins. She glimpsed the bloody body at the end of the taut rope tied to the stallion's saddle.

"No!" Sobs tore from Rebecca's throat. *It can't be Thomas.* Frozen, she maintained her grip on the leather strap to keep the horse from taking off again.

He could be alive.

That thought sent her into action. Trying to untie the taut line tethered to her brother's saddle while holding Rocket still, she couldn't loosen the knot. She didn't have anything to cut the rope, and there was no way she would release the horse with Thom—a man tied to him. When she started to back Rocket toward the body on the ground, hoping the stallion in its agitated state wouldn't step on the man, an idea popped into her mind.

"Easy, Rocket," she murmured over and over in a calm voice that didn't reflect how she really felt.

With the reins in one hand she unfastened the girth. Once the saddle slipped to the ground, she released the stallion. Now free, he shot forward while she raced toward the person caught up in the rope—hauled, no telling how far, by Rocket.

Rebecca knelt next to the body. Although his face was covered in blood and dirt, she instantly knew it was her brother by the brown curls she'd teased him about as a child. *How did this happen?*

She reached out with a shaky hand to feel for a pulse. Pressing her fingers against his neck, she looked into his face for any sign of life. A faint pulse beat beneath her touch. A flicker of relief fluttered through her.

He's alive.

She had to get help. Now. She dug into her pocket for her cell. Nothing.

"Where *is* it?" She had it in her hand then . . .

Bolting to her feet, she strode back toward Angel Fire, scanning the ground as she went. There in the dust lay her cell, smashed as if her horse had stepped on it.

Useless.

She hurried back to Thomas, checked again for a pulse and once more found a faint one. *Lord, help. I don't want to leave him. What do I do?*

She surveyed her brother's injuries to determine if she could do anything for him before she rode back for help. The leg that was caught in the rope was bent at an angle. Broken. His jeans were intact but his shirt was shredded, hanging off him in strips. Scrapes, cuts, and blood everywhere. He must have been dragged a good distance.

"What happened, Tommy?" She smoothed his hair away from his face, revealing bruises beginning to form and more scrapes and cuts from the brush and rocks on the ground.

It didn't matter at that moment. She had to get help. She rose and started for Angel Fire. In the distance, she glimpsed a rider coming toward her. Jumping up and down, she waved her arms to make sure the person saw her.

When he came closer, she saw that it was Brody Calhoun. She'd heard he was back in town and that he was coming to the party. Thank goodness he had called her on her cell before she had dropped it. The sight of him comforted her—help would be here shortly. She went back to Thomas, wishing her expertise were in medicine, not law.

For the third time, she made sure Thomas was still alive and then prayed her brother would be all right with only a broken leg and a few bruises and cuts.

Brody halted his horse only feet from Thomas and Rebecca.

"What happened?" he asked as he leapt from his saddle.

"I don't know. He's unconscious, but alive. My cell got stepped on and doesn't work. Call for help." As she spoke, Brody took his phone out and began punching in a number.

In the background, over the sound of Brody talking, Rebecca heard a four-wheeler coming toward them. She wasn't alone to deal with this. *You never are,* weaved through her thoughts, and she felt the hand of the Lord on her shoulder.

Brody finished his call. "Help is on the way, and I notified them back at the house."

Rebecca whispered a prayer as she examined Thomas's skull to assess the extent of his injuries. Several deep gashes on each side worried her more than the broken leg. His head must have bounced about, hitting the rocks that littered the ground in this part of the ranch. She was afraid to lift him to check his back, where the worst damage would be.

Hadn't she read somewhere not to move a person with a possible spine or neck injury? What else?

Keep him warm. She hurried to the saddle she'd removed from Rocket and grabbed the blanket that was underneath it, then returned to Thomas. She knelt next to him and covered him. She wanted to clean his wounds but had nothing to do that with. A couple of them still bled.

"I need something to stop the bleeding," she said over her shoulder to Brody.

While Jake drove up with Gus, a cowhand, Brody shrugged out of his shirt and gave it to Rebecca. Pressing the cotton material into Thomas's worst injuries, she continued her prayers for help to be here quickly because she didn't know what she was doing. Her hands shook as she went from one deep gash to another.

Having done what little she could, she sat back on her heels. Her heart continued to hammer so rapidly against her ribcage that it was difficult to draw in a decent breath. Jake crossed to Brody and said something she couldn't hear. If something was going on, she needed to know.

She pushed up to her feet. Too fast. She wobbled from lack of food; toast in the morning was the only thing she'd had that day. Before she realized it, Brody had wrapped his arm around her and steadied her.

"Okay?" he asked, leaning closer to her ear.

She moved away. "I should have eaten lunch but with the trial . . ."

"Yeah, I know you. You throw yourself into your job and forget everything else, even eating." He dug into his pocket and handed her a mint. "This will help your blood sugar. A helicopter is on its way to take Tommy to Mercy Memorial, so it shouldn't be long."

Jake stooped next to Thomas and assessed him. "We need to splint his leg. Gus, see if you can find a branch I can use."

While Gus scoured the ground for something to use, Jake removed his belt. Brody did the same with his, and assisted Jake as he used the straight tree limb Gus brought him to stabilize Thomas's broken leg.

Jake rose. "There isn't much else we can do until help arrives."

She wished she could do something more. She fought the helpless feeling inching over her. "This shouldn't have happened. Thomas is always careful." Her gaze fastened onto her brother lying on the ground with a blanket over him, his blood leaving a trail to follow.

Still kneeling next to Thomas, Brody peered up at her. "After we get him to the hospital, we'll talk about this. Riding accidents happen even when we're careful. Remember the time he broke his arm being bucked from his horse?"

"Because he was riding a stallion he shouldn't have been riding. Dad didn't let him forget that."

Brody checked Thomas's pulse, then stood. "Still not strong."

She lifted her gaze to Brody's face, shadowed by his cowboy hat. "He's going to be okay, isn't he?"

"I'm not going to lie to you. It doesn't look good."

Her throat closed, trapping any response she wanted to say. Not even the heat of the day still lingering in the air could warm her chilled body. Her brother needed her. She squatted beside him again and took his hand, putting her two fingers over the pulse in his wrist. As long as she felt his life force beneath her touch, she would be all right.

Vaguely she heard Brody and Jake whispering behind her again. She tossed a look over her shoulder. "What are y'all saying?"

"Just trying to figure out what happened, Miss Rebecca." Jake removed his hat and struck it against his jean-clad leg.

Dust flew off the black felt. Then he plopped it back on his head and headed toward Angel Fire while Gus took hold of the reins of the gelding Brody had ridden.

"After Thomas is picked up, Jake and Gus are going to track Rocket's trail to see where it happened. They're going to take our horses, and we'll use the four-wheeler."

"You think there's a cow stuck somewhere, or one trying to have a calf?"

"Thomas tied the rope around his saddle horn for a reason. Maybe he was trying to get a calf or cow out of a mess. Either way, while it's still light I'd like to know where this happened and possibly why."

"Can't it wait? The trail will be here tomorrow morning, or Thomas will wake up and tell us." She spoke with more confidence than she felt. She wasn't going to say out loud that Thomas might not make it. "Jake probably should get back to help Hattie. I imagine by now it's chaos at the ranch house."

"Probably so. Tory didn't take the news well at all. I told her we would be back there as soon as possible." Brody walked up to Rebecca and crouched beside her. "There's a good chance it's going to rain after midnight. I wouldn't want the hoof prints washed away without at least checking them now."

He wasn't saying that Thomas might not ever tell them what had happened. But the implication was evident in his strained voice and evasive look. "What if he can never tell us?" She asked the question he was probably thinking too.

"We'll deal with that if it happens. Right now, I want to gather as much information as we can. People will want answers. Tory. You. Foster. Okay?"

The lump in her throat swelled even more. She nodded, staring at her brother, thinking of all the times they had ridden over the ranch, raced to the fence line, and teased each other about who was the better rider. The sound of a helicopter invaded her memories. Bringing real life back in full force—where her brother was critically injured, barely hanging on.

When the chopper landed, the wind whipped up the dust, swirling it in the air. Jake and Gus held the horses' reins, but the animals jerked on them, prancing back away from the helicopter, its high-pitched, whirring sound overriding all others. Rebecca shielded her brother as best she could, using the blanket while Brody headed toward the chopper.

My life is about to change. A shiver rippled down the length of her body as the paramedics hopped to the ground and hurried toward Thomas, grim expressions on their faces. Rebecca fixed her gaze on Brody. Beneath his professional countenance, the glimpse of apprehension in his eyes reinforced what she'd known when she'd first seen her brother. Only prayer would help Thomas now.

❧

"We're almost there." Brody looked at Rebecca, dressed in one of Thomas's shirts and staring straight ahead, quiet for the past twenty minutes. Her grip on the edge of the seat in his SUV highlighted what she was going through.

"I appreciate your bringing me, but I could have driven myself. You didn't need to come."

"Really?"

She finally glanced at him. "Okay. Maybe I wouldn't have had my thoughts totally focused on driving."

"Which is to be expected. There was no way I wouldn't come, so there's no reason for you to drive yourself. Thomas is a friend. I'm here to help. I'll stay and take you back when you're ready."

"I saw you talking with the sheriff. What did he say?"

"He's going to ride out before it gets too dark and meet up with Jake."

"Do you think this is foul play?"

"I don't know. That's why I'm having the sheriff follow up with Jake and check out the place where it went down. Has Thomas angered anyone? Is there a reason you would think it might be foul play?"

Rebecca pressed her fingertips into her temples. "I don't think he has any enemies. But he owns or rather is part-owner of a large ranch. Maybe there's someone I don't know about. We usually talk business on Saturday afternoons when I visit."

"So other than that, you don't have much to do with the Circle S Ranch?"

"I may own half, but Thomas runs it. I trust my brother. He knows what he's doing. He had the best teacher."

"Yeah, your dad."

"I wish he were here right now." Pain laced each word as Rebecca went back to staring out the windshield.

"Your dad was the best. I miss him, too."

"That was an awful year for me. First, my husband was killed in the line of duty, then my father died from a stroke six months later. I don't want to ever repeat what happened three years ago."

He'd come back for both funerals but had stayed in the background, at least as far as Rebecca was concerned. Thomas and he had had lengthy conversations about transitioning the running of the ranch from father to son. He'd helped his friend the best way he could long-distance. "Any problems going on at the ranch?"

"Like what?"

"With hired hands? Customers? Neighbors?"

"No . . ." she twisted her hands together, "unless he was keeping it from me. I know he did that first year after Garrett was killed, but I called him on it when I realized what he was doing and I don't think he has since then."

"But you're not sure?"

She glanced at him. "I can't answer 100 percent. But I'm 90 percent sure."

Which left 10 percent, enough to bother him. Thomas had always been protective of Rebecca. If anything looked suspicious, he would check into what was going on at the Circle S, even if he had to do it quietly without Tory and Rebecca knowing.

Silence fell between them again. Brody concentrated on driving, going as fast as he dared.

"I'm glad Foster was there at the ranch to take Tory to the hospital. Hopefully she'll be there not long after my brother arrives at Mercy Memorial."

"And it never hurts to have the governor there to expedite anything that needs to be done."

"Foster does have a commanding way about him."

Heat from her gaze warmed his face. He locked his hands tighter about the steering wheel.

"I've missed you. I can't believe this is the first time we've really talked since you came home five months ago."

"I've been busy. Crime doesn't come to a standstill when you want it to."

"Tell me about it. My current case proves that."

"I heard you caught the retrial of Dmitri Petrov." Brody turned into the parking lot near the emergency room at Mercy Memorial.

"I was the lucky one. I know one thing—when the jury is finally selected next week, I'll be keeping a tight rein on them. No jury tampering this time around. We don't need to go through a third trial." Rebecca grabbed her purse from the floor and positioned herself as if she were going to fling the door open the second he came to a stop.

"It seems strange to have a Mexican-American gang going toe-to-toe with the Russian Mafia. If only we could sit back and let them duke it out."

"Kill each other off? That doesn't always happen. In this case, some innocent people got caught in the crossfire. A businessman in the community died."

"I know. I haven't been following the case, since it happened before I returned to San Antonio." Brody pulled into a parking space near the entrance to the hospital.

"It started as the usual payback for something done to one of their members."

"An eye for an eye."

"This Russian Mafia goes beyond that. They take out everyone connected to the person." Rebecca shoved open the door as Brody turned off his engine.

She was halfway to the door by the time he'd climbed out of his SUV. As he strode toward the entrance, the hairs on his neck tingled. He paused and scanned the parking lot.

Something is wrong.

Dusk had crept across the asphalt, throwing part of the area into shadows. Searching the murkiness, he didn't see anything out of the ordinary. Maybe it was his imagination. Maybe because of all the talk about gangs and the Russian Mafia. Or maybe someone had followed them to the hospital.

He laid his hand on the butt end of the gun in his holster and slowly turned in a full circle. Still nothing.

He continued his trek into the hospital as he placed a call. "Sheriff Overstreet, this is Brody Calhoun. Do you have anything yet on what happened to Thomas?"

"No, I'm almost to Jake. He found a calf trapped in a gully. That must have been what Thomas was trying to rescue when he got caught up in his own rope."

"Maybe, but Thomas has been riding and roping all his life."

"I'll go over the ground. I've got a deputy with me. We should be able to cover it before it rains. We both have high-beam flashlights, and if I feel we need to bring in extra lighting, I will."

"Call me when you finish."

"Will do."

Brody headed through the doors to the emergency room. A doctor entered the waiting room. Brody quickened his pace and walked in. Tory's face went white, her eyes large. She sank into the chair and covered her face with her hands.

No, not Thomas.

3

$\mathcal{J}$.R. sat across the street from the entrance to the emergency room at Mercy Memorial. The Texas Ranger had stopped and then made a slow circle as though he knew he was being watched.

Although J. R. was a hundred yards away, he'd ducked down in his car. They wouldn't be able to connect him to Thomas Sinclair, but there was no use taking chances. Later he'd go in and snoop around.

That Sinclair had been taken to the hospital meant he was alive. But would he survive? He needed that question answered. What had Sinclair seen when he'd turned to his right just before J. R. hit him with a rock?

Rebecca laid her hand on Tory's shoulder in the waiting room. "He's going to pull through surgery. He's alive, and these doctors will keep him that way."

Tory lifted her face, tears streaking her cheeks. "He's barely hanging on. How's he going to survive surgery?"

"With a lot of prayers on our part. They have to stop the internal bleeding."

Their family physician, Dr. Henderson, dressed in blue scrubs, stepped forward. "Mrs. Sinclair, we need your consent to operate. Time is of the essence."

"But what if he dies on the operating table? How can I . . ." Tory grabbed the clipboard the doctor held and scribbled her signature beside the X. As she gave it back, it slipped from her fingers and clanged against the floor.

Dr. Henderson picked it up. "I'll let you know what's going on with your husband as soon as I know."

Tory stared at him as he left the waiting room, then swung her gaze to Rebecca. "It doesn't sound good." Tears welled up in her eyes and spilled over.

Rebecca patted her sister-in-law's back but was at a loss about what to say or do. She wanted to cry herself, but glancing around the room stilled the sorrow deep inside her. She'd been taught never to display her emotions in public, and with the governor standing not far away with his entourage, her training came to the foreground. She should talk with Foster, but she didn't want to leave Tory.

When her sister-in-law rummaged in her purse for a tissue and then dabbed her face with it, Brody approached them. "Tory, Rebecca, can I get you something to drink? Coffee?"

Tory sprang to her feet. "What I need is to get out of here for a while. I'll go with you. Rebecca, can I get you some coffee?"

"Yes."

"We'll be down the hall if you need us." Tory and Brody left the room.

The second her sister-in-law disappeared into the hallway, Rebecca released a long sigh, raking her fingers through her hair—something she did when she was nervous or upset. Tory hadn't been able to contain how frightened she was, which only heightened her own sense Thomas might not make it. But she couldn't allow herself to think that. She had to be the strong one for the family.

How were Kim and Aubrey doing? Did they know? They hadn't when she'd left the ranch. She slid her hand into her pocket and grasped the cell the housekeeper had given her when she left the house to come to the hospital.

Foster came toward her and took the chair Tory had been sitting in. "How are you holding up?"

"I'm okay, but I don't know about Tory."

"She didn't say a word the whole way to the hospital. I was concerned. I'll be able to stay until we hear how well the surgery went. At least I hope so. I have a critical meeting I need to keep first thing tomorrow morning in Austin, but the meeting isn't too far from here."

"I appreciate your bringing Tory. I can make sure she gets back to the ranch when she needs to."

"Does Brody know anything? I heard the sheriff was called out to the Circle S."

After she told Foster all she knew surrounding what had happened to Thomas, she sat back, finally relaxing her rigid posture, which she couldn't maintain any longer. Her muscles twitched. Pain gripped her.

"So, no one knows anything?"

"That about sums it up, Foster. But I intend to get some answers as soon as I find out that my brother is going to pull through. I know how important the first few days of an investigation are."

"I guess you would, having been a district attorney and married to a cop."

"On a number of occasions Garrett bemoaned how slow an investigation was proceeding."

Foster covered her hand, which rested on the arm of the chair between them. "It's been a tough few years." He glanced toward the entrance. "I'm glad Brody is here to help. I know how close you three were growing up."

Rebecca looked up as Tory and Brody returned to the waiting room. "Yes, we were, but these last ten years we lost touch. At least Brody and I did. Not Thomas and Brody." Why had she let that happen? Probably because she had been a newlywed and had been caught up in her marriage to Garrett. Time passed. And then her husband died and her world fell apart for a while. She didn't want to go through something like that again.

Tory paced the waiting room while Foster sat quietly next to Rebecca. Waiting for word from the doctor.

Finally Foster stood, breaking the silence that had descended. "I'm going to have Brody work the case until he's satisfied it was an accident. I'll feel better with one of our rangers supervising what's going on. I'm sure Sheriff Overstreet won't mind the help."

"Thanks. I'll feel better having him work the case, too."

"Anything for family."

"That's how I feel."

As Foster closed the distance between him and Brody, Rebecca decided to go out into the corridor to place her call to Hattie. She didn't want Tory to overhear her—her sister-in-law had enough to deal with. She'd take care of what was going on at the ranch and let Tory focus on Thomas. That would be the way her brother would want it.

In the hallway, Rebecca placed her call, and Hattie answered on the third ring with, "Tell me Thomas is alive."

The desperation in her voice nearly undid Rebecca. She gripped the cellphone tighter. "Yes, so far, but he's in surgery.

The doctor isn't saying it, but I get the feeling it will be touch-and-go with Thomas."

"I don't wanna hear that."

"I know. You practically raised us when our mother died. How are Aubrey and Kim? What do they know?"

"Just that their daddy is at the hospital because he hurt himself. Aubrey wanted to know if it was like the time Kim jumped from the second floor of the barn into the hay and broke her arm. I told her yes. I don't have the heart to say anything else until we know more for sure."

"Good. No sense alarming them. I'll be back to the ranch as soon as Thomas is out of surgery and stable. I want to tell the girls."

"I'll be praying."

"Thanks. Me, too." Rebecca disconnected the call and turned to go back into the waiting room.

Brody stood in the entrance, his gaze on her. She hadn't realized until she saw him earlier how much she'd missed him these past years. As usual, she could count on him to be there for her. She didn't know what she would have done if he hadn't come along. Leaving Thomas out there by himself while she rode for help had been the last thing she'd wanted to do.

Brody moved toward her. "Everything all right at the ranch?"

"How did you know I'd called there?"

"A hunch."

"Hattie hasn't said anything to the girls. She's saving that for me."

"Not Tory?"

"Kim and Aubrey were excited to get a new mom, but I'm . . ." She realized what she was about to say and swallowed the last word. Tory and she weren't alike. She was still surprised that Thomas had married Tory, who was nine years yonger than her brother, but he was happy, so she was grateful to her.

"But you're family. That's kind of how I feel about Thomas. I had an older sister who didn't want to have anything to do with her bratty brother."

"Has that changed?" Lightness infused her voice for a moment when she thought of the times they had played pranks on his sister, Kathy.

"We've got a great relationship. I take care of Dad and she goes her merry way. Since Kathy got a divorce, we see more of my niece than her."

"I heard she got a divorce a couple of months ago. That has to be hard."

"Not according to her. She celebrated being free of her husband. I think it crushed her when she found out he had a girlfriend on the side."

She'd never had to worry about that with Garrett, only whether he would come home unhurt when he was on duty. She'd tried to persuade him not to be an undercover cop, but he'd loved the job. He wouldn't have been the same if he had changed departments. But in the end the work he'd loved killed him—or rather a drug dealer had.

"You okay?"

She mentally shook the thoughts away and focused on Brody, whose gray eyes had darkened with concern. "Thinking about Garrett. There's been too much death lately."

He clasped her arm. "I'm here if you need to talk. I didn't know Garrett well, but I heard he was a good cop. One of the best."

"Until the day he was murdered by a gang member who sold drugs. That's why the Petrov trial is so important to me. I want to send a message. Gangs, mafias, whatever you want to call them, are not welcomed here."

"Which reminds me. Governor Sinclair has asked me to look into what happened with Thomas to make sure it was an accident. He knows about the trial you have started and what's transpired with Dmitri Petrov's first one."

"You think what happened to Thomas could be tied to my trial?"

"On the ride here didn't you tell me you received a bouquet of dead roses today?"

"Yes, but . . ." Horror took hold of her and spread through her body in a flash. She laid a hand against the nearby wall as her energy drained out. "Thomas doesn't have anything to do with the trial." *I can't be the reason this happened.*

"Didn't you say the warring factions go after family, too?"

"They have with people who have crossed them."

"Your tough reputation on crime has preceded you. That probably has the defendant worried."

"Not much has happened other than I've been hearing pretrial motions and only a couple of potential jury members have been questioned."

"Maybe they aren't pleased they drew you as the judge. It's well-known what happened to your husband. Either way, your cousin is concerned and wants to make sure it has nothing to do with what happened to Thomas. I agree with him after what you received today."

Thomas's doctor went into the waiting room. Rebecca started toward him, saying, "We'll discuss this later when I'm not so tired."

When Rebecca entered, Dr. Mike Henderson was saying to Tory and Foster, "The surgery was successful as far as stopping his internal bleeding, and now we'll just have to wait and see if he comes out of the coma he's slipped into. His body has suffered quite a trauma. Besides the injuries to his head, there is spinal damage."

"How extensive is the trauma to his brain?" Rebecca asked, locking eyes with the doctor.

"I've always told you like it is, Rebecca. His head was bounced around when he was dragged across the ground. There were a couple of deep gashes in the back. There's swelling. Again, it's wait and see. There's a good chance he suffered some kind of brain damage."

"Will he remember what happened to him?" Brody came over to her.

"It's too early to say much of anything. He's still in critical condition and will be in the ICU until that changes." Dr. Henderson looked at the wall clock. "It's one in the morning. Go home. Get some rest. There's nothing you all can do here. I'm insisting."

Rebecca listened as the doctor spoke with Foster about what would happen in the near future with Thomas if he continued to improve, but the words slipped in and out of her mind so fast she didn't comprehend what was being said. Brain and spinal injuries. In a coma. He was alive, but for how long?

Brody slid his arm around her and leaned in to whisper, "He's a fighter, and we'll be here for him."

His roughened voice, raw and heavy, spoke of his pain at hearing the details of Thomas's injuries. His presence shored up her resolve to make sure her brother had every opportunity to recover—no matter the cost.

⁂

"How's Tory?" Brody asked when Rebecca stepped into the kitchen after checking on her sister-in-law.

The scent of coffee drifted over to her, and she headed straight for the pot on the counter. "She's sleeping." She lifted the coffeepot. "Want some more?"

"No, I just poured a new cup."

Rebecca trudged to the table and sank into the chair next to Brody. Exhausted beyond sleep, she tried to forget the past hours at the hospital. She couldn't, especially the prospects for her brother if he came out of the coma. Then, on top of that, as they neared the ranch with Brody driving both her and Tory home, her sister-in-law came out of her silence as though the lights of the ranch had flipped a switch in her brain and she had become aware of her surroundings. She'd begun sobbing. Her arms folded across her chest, she had rocked back and forth, her nails digging into her flesh, making it bleed.

"I'm glad the girls weren't up to hear and see us when we returned. Aubrey, who doesn't remember her own mother much, has begun to think of Tory as her mother. Seeing her like that when we brought her inside would have freaked Aubrey out. Usually Tory is poised and reserved." Cradling the mug between her hands, Rebecca stared at the dark brew. "I hate coffee. I don't know why I got this."

Brody grasped her arm to draw her attention to him. "Don't drink it. I can fix you some tea. I seem to remember you liked it."

"Still do." She slid the cup away from her, wishing he were still touching her.

He started to rise.

"Don't. I'm really not thirsty. Just tired."

Instead of sitting back down, he straightened to his full height. "Go to bed. Tomorrow is going to be here in a few hours, and it's going to be a long day. I need to leave anyway."

When he turned away to take his mug to the sink, she reached up and stopped him. "Please. As exhausted as I am, I can't sleep right now and I don't want to be alone. Hattie went to bed. She wants to be up early in case the children get up and want to wake Tory."

He settled into the chair again, cupping her hand between his palms. "I'm here as long as you need me."

"I still can't . . ." She swallowed the knot. She had to be here for her nieces.

"He'll have a hard road ahead of him."

The sound of Brody's voice, husky and pain-filled, caused her to look at him. A sheen glistened in his eyes. "He's always thought of you as a brother."

"I know. That's how I feel."

"He missed having you around."

"We talked on the phone."

"Not the same thing. The day he heard you were moving back to the area, he called to tell me how excited he was that you'd come to your senses and were returning home."

Brody pulled his hands away from hers and leaned back in the chair as though he were putting as much distance between them as possible. "I went where the job took me. I was still in Texas."

"San Antonio and Amarillo are eight hours apart. At least when you were in Dallas you were a little closer, but you hardly came home."

"I didn't know you kept track."

"Thomas would grumble about it from time to time."

"I see."

What did that mean? Her brain was like mush, and she couldn't seem to figure out the simplest things. He almost sounded as though he were hurt by what she had said. She couldn't blame Thomas for how he had felt. She'd felt the same. She'd missed the rides the three of them used to take years ago, especially when Brody had lived down the road from them. She'd been able to tell him things she could never tell another.

When she snatched up her mug, she took a long sip of the strong black coffee and nearly choked.

"I thought you didn't want any."

"I don't. I . . ." She set the cup down and asked the question she had been avoiding since she first came looking for Brody, "What did the sheriff say happened to Thomas?"

"He didn't see any evidence of foul play. There was a calf that fell into a gully and was carrying on when Jake came up. It appears that Thomas was going to hoist the animal out of the hole, but he must have gotten tangled up in the rope and Rocket was spooked."

"I don't believe that. I know that Rocket can be high-strung, but what would have spooked him?"

"It could have been a rattler. I've seen it happen with a hawk. From what Jake said, the calf was loud, so maybe he started carrying on when he saw Thomas and that scared Rocket. What your brother loved about Rocket was his feisty spirit. But that meant he was temperamental, too. A handful."

"I know. Thomas loved Rocket. He was a gift from his first wife." She collapsed back against the hard slats of the chair. "My brother is a risk-taker in all he does. And now he could be brain damaged and might not be able to walk—if he wakes up. I don't know how we're going to tell the girls tomorrow. I'm not sure Tory will be up to it."

"You'll be there for her. That'll help." He scooted his chair back and pushed to his feet. "But you're going to need your sleep. Tomorrow will be a hard day. I'm coming back first thing in the morning. I'll ride out to look at where the accident happened."

"You think the sheriff or deputy overlooked something?"

"Sheriff Overstreet is a good man. If he did miss something, it was because it was getting dark. In the light of day things may look different."

"If it doesn't rain."

She followed him from the kitchen, walking next to him toward the foyer. "You can stay the night here. You won't be at home long before you'll have to turn around."

"I need to check on Dad. Make sure he takes all his medicine. He complains a lot about all the pills he has to take."

"He's lucky to have you."

"No, I 'm the lucky one. He was always there for me. I have to be there for him now. He hates being sick and has been fighting me and the doctor about what he can and can't do."

"That sounds like Sean. Before he retired from the police department a couple of years ago, I saw him when I visited the station." When her husband was still alive and she had a reason to go there. Now she avoided it unless she had to because of her job, which rarely happened. The police came to her now that she was a judge rather than the district attorney. "Tell your father hi for me."

"I will. See you tomorrow morning."

After Rebecca shut and locked the front door, she leaned back against it and surveyed the large foyer of her childhood home. A wide staircase curved up to the second story, and a massive round oak table with a fresh bouquet in the middle of it dominated the area. Her mother had started the tradition of always having a vase full of flowers as the first thing people saw when they entered the house.

A symbol of life contining? But what kind of life would Thomas have if he couldn't walk, had difficulty doing the simplest tasks? Why, Lord? Why have You done this? Thomas is all the close family I have except my nieces. You've already taken my parents and my husband, and now this with my brother.

The vivid red and yellow of the roses blurred as she stared at them. She'd been careful to keep her emotions under control while Brody was here, but now sadness overwhelmed her. She slid down the door. Clasping her legs against her chest, she laid her head on her knees and cried for her brother, who had been there for her when her husband had died and then their father.

❧

"Dad, why are you up so early?" Brody said when he came into the kitchen to grab some coffee before he returned to the Circle S Ranch to ride out to the place where the accident had occurred—at least the evidence collected so far pointed to an accident. But this was Thomas. He had to know for sure it wasn't attempted murder—not just because the governor had asked him to, but because of his past with Thomas and Rebecca. He owed them.

Dressed in jeans, a short-sleeved shirt, and boots, his father finished putting the coffee into the pot, then switched it on. "I'm going with you to see the Sinclair family. Their father was a good friend. I need to help them as much as I can, and since you're going that way, I thought I'd hitch a ride." He grinned, which was really more like a grimace. "I know how you don't like me driving myself anywhere right now, so . . ." He let the unspoken threat hang in the air between them.

"I'm not sure there's much you can do right now."

"I imagine Hattie will have her hands full. I can help her."

"But—"

"It's either you drive me or I drive myself." His father lifted his chin and fastened his "I mean business" gaze on Brody. "Which will it be, Son?"

"It seems I don't have much choice."

"Yup, I agree." His father retrieved two mugs from the cabinet and set them near the coffeemaker, then folded his arms across his chest and lounged back against the counter. "Last night you didn't say much about yesterday. What do you think happened with Thomas?"

"Honestly, I don't know what happened. No concrete evidence either way at this time."

"No opinion?"

"You always taught me not to jump to a conclusion, to leave myself open to all possibilities, or I might overlook something."

"Yes, but I always taught you to err on the side of the worse-case scenario."

"So you think I should look at this as an attempted murder?"

His dad nodded and shifted to pour the coffee into both mugs.

"There's nothing specifically pointing to someone trying to kill Thomas. The sheriff said the scene doesn't indicate foul play."

"Did the doctors who worked on Thomas think there was anything that indicated foul play?" His father handed Brody a mug.

"I'll be going to the hospital later to see Thomas and to talk to the doctors and the staff."

"Let's go. I wouldn't mind taking a look at the scene."

"Dad, you're retired and recovering—"

"And what's that supposed to mean? That I've stopped thinking like a cop? That I'm no longer any use?"

"No, but you had a heart attack and nearly died. You need to take it easy."

"That was three months ago. I'm much better now. I'm not an invalid, so quit treating me like one. How many times do I have to tell you that?" His dad clamped his jaws together, a nerve twitching in his face.

"I almost lost you. Sorry if you don't like the fact that I worry about you."

"Worry is unnecessary. What good does it do you? Can you change anything because you worry? Trust the Lord. When my time comes, it comes. You worrying about me isn't going to change that fact, but it might raise your blood pressure."

"So you don't worry about me?"

"Nope, not anymore. I figure God knows better than I do. His will is so much better than mine."

"That's easier said than done. Our family is small. It's just you, me, Kathy, and Samantha."

Sipping his drink, his dad ambled toward the back door. "Well, you can always change that. Get married and give me some more grandkids."

"Don't start with that. You know how difficult it can be for an officer to have a good marriage, and that's the only kind I will settle for."

"Then quit your job. You have a lot of talents."

Brody glanced at his father. "This from the man who was a police officer for over thirty years."

"Your mom and me found a way to work it out." He clambered into the front passenger seat in the SUV. "I'm not saying we didn't have tough times, but we decided when we first got married that we would never go to bed mad at each other. We would stay up and figure out a way to compromise."

Brody could remember a few of those nights, listening to them talk for hours—sometimes in raised voices, but most of the time in low tones. Maybe that was the problem. He'd had a great example of what a marriage should be and hadn't been able to find someone to share that kind of life with. No, he'd found someone, but she'd fallen in love with another man, while he was only her brother's best friend. Now, after ten years, they were two different people—shaped by what had occurred to them these past ten years they had been apart.

"I'm thirty-seven. A little late to change now. Being a bachelor has its advantages." Brody backed his SUV out of his driveway and turned toward the highway that led to the Circle S Ranch.

"Name one."

"I can do what I want when I want."

"Really? You can?"

He ignored his dad's sarcasm, punched on the phone in his SUV, and called the ranch. When Hattie answered, he said, "I'm heading your way. Is anyone else up?" To the east the sun peeked over the horizon, painting the sky a rosy hue.

"Just me and Rebecca."

"Let me speak to her."

"She's gone."

"Gone? Where?"

"She rode out to where the accident happened."

"She did! How long ago?"

"Ten minutes maybe. I'm not sure."

"Can you connect me with the stables? Maybe someone is up down there, and they can stop her."

"Is there a problem?"

"I don't want her disturbing the scene."

"If it's an accident, and that's what Sheriff Overstreet said, then why should that be a problem?"

Brody pushed his foot down on the accelerator, not sure why he felt such an urgency to get to the ranch. "Hattie, don't patch me into the stables. Instead, please find Jake and get him to stop Rebecca."

"Sure. If he isn't in his office by now, I think I know where he is."

"I'm about thirty minutes out." Brody disconnected the call and concentrated on the ride in the light, early morning traffic. "She couldn't wait. She had to go out there first thing. She knew I was coming this morning to ride to the scene."

"Are you referring to Rebecca?"

For a second Brody had forgotten his father was in the car with him. "Yes."

"Why are you worried about her? She's used to riding alone on the ranch. Has for years."

"What if her brother's accident wasn't an accident at all, but attempted murder instead?"

※

Rebecca slowed Angel Fire to a canter and then to a walk as she neared the place where her brother had become tangled in his rope. There was so much that would have to be done today. No matter how hard she tried not to think about what happened yesterday, she had kept coming back to it—all night long. She had to see the place for herself. Try to visualize how it had happened. Be satisfied it was an accident.

The ground became rockier as she drew nearer to the streambed that was filled with water only in the spring. Even though the bottom of the sun still brushed the eastern horizon, the temperature had risen several degrees since she left the stables half an hour ago, when it was still dim—dawn not quite fully unfolded.

Usually this was her favorite time of day—right before everything started. But not today. A football field away, rocks littered the ground. Looking at the landscape near the gully, she saw a couple of places where someone could have hidden and surprised her brother—if that was what really had occurred.

Who would have a beef with Thomas? Everyone loved him. He was generous with his money and time, helping the closest town of Dry Gulch and its people wherever he could. No one with a grievance came to mind. No disgruntled employee. No feuding neighbor.

Intending to follow the trail to where she had found her brother, Rebecca guided her gelding in the direction Rocket would have run with Thomas—agony jammed her throat with that thought—being dragged behind him. The horrifying image snuck into her mind like a fox into a henhouse. Would Thomas ever wake up? Walk again? Fully recover?

"Will he, Lord?" she shouted in the early morning quiet. Anger surged up in her like an oil well gushing. "Why has this happened? He's a good man."

She'd read somewhere that yelling to release anger and frustration was supposed help. She released a scream, but it didn't help at all. When she found hoof prints in the dirt—more than what Rocket would have made—the reins dug into her palms. She began to systematically examine the ground for anything that might give a hint as to what had happened. Her survey halted when she noticed drag marks in the dust, the vegetation broken as her brother's body had plowed through it.

The sight flooded her with an overload of feelings—rage, grief, confusion. In the distance, she glimpsed a couple of people riding toward her. She couldn't tell for sure, but she thought one of them was Brody. Who else? She didn't want to be around other people. Later she would have to be. Not now. She thought of spurring Angel Fire toward the western part of the ranch, where she could seek some alone time, but knowing Brody, he would worry and follow her.

Shifting away from the galloping horses coming at her, she continued her search of the ground. Beneath a prickly pear, a silver flash caught her attention.

4

Rebecca swung her leg over Angel Fire's rump and hopped to the ground. Kneeling beside the cactus, she peered at a cellphone she was sure was Thomas's. She started to reach for it, but instead balled her hand and kept it at her side. It could be evidence.

She scanned the area toward the gully. It was obvious the phone came free while her brother was dragged by Rocket. And this explained why he wouldn't have answered anyone trying to call him.

The sound of galloping horses brought her to her feet. She spun around to see Brody and his father riding toward her. She hadn't seen Sean Calhoun in a few months. She'd paid him a visit at the hospital, hoping to also see Brody. But her childhood friend had left not twenty minutes before she'd arrived. She'd stayed even longer than planned in case Brody returned, but he hadn't.

Brody jumped to the ground and marched toward her. "What are you doing out here?"

She backed up a step, squaring her shoulders. "Riding."

"You should have at least waited until I came."

"Why? I often ride early in the morning before it gets too hot."

"We don't know for sure what happened to Thomas. You should stay close to the ranch house until—"

"Hold it right there. I don't have to account for my where-abouts to you." She leaned to the side and smiled. "Hello, Sean. It's good to see you again."

"You, too." He tipped his Stetson at her. "My son has a point. You should be cautious until we know if it's an accident or attempted murder."

Brody glanced at his dad. "We?"

"Yes, I'm here to give my expert opinion after investigating many murder cases in my thirty-two-year career as a police officer. Or have you forgotten?"

Brody grumbled and turned back to Rebecca. "Why did you stop here?"

She pointed at the prickly pear. "That looks like Thomas's cellphone, and just so you know, I didn't touch it. I'm letting the experts deal with it."

He thumped his chest. "Oh, you mean me."

"Yes. If this isn't an accident, I want the chain-of-evidence strictly adhered to."

He strode back to his gelding and withdrew a small paper sack, then came back to retrieve the cellphone. Using the point of a pen, he switched the phone on and held it up for Rebecca to see.

"That's Thomas's. Is the ringer on?"

Brody checked, then dropped the phone into a bag. "No. I'll have the lab go over this, but my thought is it fell off him when he was dragged."

"I agree. But what if someone called him out to this location? Lured him here. It would mean this was attempted murder."

"We'll check everything on it. Fingerprints. Calls."

Rebecca took the reins of her horse, then mounted. Having been a prosecutor and now a judge who presided over murder cases, she'd seen the worst in human beings. It tended to shade her view of life—especially when her husband was killed. She needed concrete answers. She spurred Angel Fire toward the place where this all had started.

Brody, with his father right behind him, quickly caught up with her. "Slow down. We might miss a piece of evidence if we rush. If you found the cellphone, think of what else we might find. About all the sheriff found last night was Thomas's hat."

She pulled back on the reins. "Sorry. I know impatience doesn't help an investigation."

"Son, I'm going to the left to check the ground." Sean traveled in a back-and-forth pattern to cover an area more level and not as rocky as the rest near the gully.

"I'm going to the right. We'll make a sweep on horseback and foot." Brody headed in the opposite direction from his father, leaving Rebecca to check the middle section.

From her height on Angel Fire she had a good vantage point. She poured all of her concentration into inspecting every inch of the ground, trying not to think of Thomas lying in the hospital bed, hanging onto life. But the image of his battered body wouldn't leave her mind. Making a zigzag pattern toward the gully and outcropping of rocks, she saw nothing other than an occasional bootprint or hoofprint where the earth wasn't as hard as stone.

When Brody approached from the right, his expression told her that he'd come up empty-handed, too. "What few prints I found could have been from Jake, Gus, the sheriff, or his deputy."

"That's what I was thinking."

Sean joined them. "Nothing. You two?"

Brody shook his head while Rebecca said, "No. Just some prints."

"That's the problem with this." Brody swept his arm wide. "The more people search the area the more damage is done to the original scene."

"Not to mention the elements and what animals can do. I'll cover this section. Meet you at the gully." Sean started to dismount.

"No, Dad. You promised. If you came, you wouldn't tire yourself. Getting up and down on a horse and walking over rough ground is too much. I shouldn't have even let you come out here. Cover what you can on horseback. Rebecca and I will check on foot."

Again, Rebecca took the ground between father and son and examined the rocky surface with an occasional bush or cactus popping up through the cracks in the hard earth. Then to her right she spotted smears of blood staining the stony surface, and her step faltered. Here, the wind blowing dust over the ground didn't obscure the path her brother's body had taken.

A rock with red stained into its pores riveted her attention. What injury had it caused? One of the gashes on Thomas's head? Or his back? Along his arm? Visualizing the path her brother had been dragged made a band contract about her chest. How long was he conscious? An invisible force yanked the band until she couldn't draw a decent breath. She forced air into her lungs, determined to see this to the end. In the heat of the sun rising higher in the sky, she shivered.

Brody came up behind her—so close that all she had to do was take a step back to encounter his solid body, full of warmth.

She didn't step back, but she wanted to. "I can't lose Thomas, too. I've lost too many lately."

"Your brother is a fighter. You aren't going to lose him." He grasped her arms.

She looked over her shoulder into those gray eyes, like molten pewter. "How do you know? What if he never regains consciousness and stays in a coma? People stay like that for years and just waste away. I don't want that for my brother."

"I can't predict the future, but I do know that worrying about it won't change anything except your stress level. Pray instead of worrying. Much more productive." Brody shook his head. "A wise man told me that recently, but don't tell Dad I said that."

"You make it sound easy." She turned to face him.

"Easy? No. Necessary? Yes. When Dad had his heart attack, I thought I was going to lose him. I stewed for days, my stomach tied in such huge knots that I felt like a hot poker had been thrust through it. I finally went to God. I should have done that from the beginning. He gave me the peace I needed to get through those tough days when Dad's doctors weren't sure he would pull through."

"I didn't realize it had been that bad. Thomas didn't tell me that. I should have been there for you."

He glanced away. "I didn't let others know how bad it was."

"Why?"

"It's not easy sharing that with others."

"You mean letting someone get close to help you?"

"I'm used to handling it by myself. With the Lord."

"Sometimes God sends others to help you. You have to be open to those others. If something like that happens to you again, you'd better let me know, or else."

He arched a brow. "Or else? I'm afraid to ask what that would be."

"My wrath. And you know how wrathful I can be."

"I can remember a couple of times when we were growing up, and you got so angry with Thomas and me."

"Yeah, anyone who disrupted a thirteen-year-old's sleepover deserved my wrath."

"Ah, but what I learned about how girls think was very interesting." His eyes twinkled as he stepped back from her.

"Eavesdropping is wrong."

"That didn't stop you from listening in on Thomas and me."

"I was paying you back."

"An eye for an eye?"

"Exactly." She planted her fist on her hip.

"Hey, you two, what's keeping you?" Sean called from the edge of the gully.

Rebecca glanced toward the older man, a smile crinkling the lines at the corner of his eyes. For a few minutes, she had forgotten why she was here. That surprised her. She peered back at Brody. They hadn't seen each other in ten years, and all of a sudden it was as if those ten years hadn't existed. That she hadn't married, become a widow, lost her father, and now, might lose her brother.

She backed away. "Coming. We got sidetracked." *That won't happen again.*

༺ༀ༻

Rebecca entered the back door into the kitchen with Brody and Sean behind her. The scent of frying bacon infused the air, vying with the aroma of baking bread and coffee. "You need to bottle this smell, Hattie."

At the stove the housekeeper finished taking the last piece of bacon from the frying pan, then prepared it for scrambled eggs, Hattie style. "Did y'all find anything?"

"No, but I sure worked up an appetite. I'm hoping a certain pretty lady will ask me to stay for breakfast." Sean removed his Stetson and set it on a peg by the door.

Blushing, Hattie dumped her egg mixture into the hot skillet. "You have a standing invitation here. No need to ask."

"Are the girls up?" Rebecca crossed the large kitchen, over to the door that led into the hallway.

"They're getting dressed. They both asked where their dad was."

Rebecca paused in the entrance. "Have you said anything to them?"

"No, it's not my place to tell them, and Tory is still sleeping. She may be their stepmother, but it needs to come from you."

"I know," Rebecca whispered and went in search of her two nieces.

But the closer she got to their upstairs bedrooms the slower her pace became. She didn't know what she was going to say to them.

I don't want to do this. I want time to turn back to yesterday at this time. Have a second chance to redo the day.

Then she remembered the trial she was hearing, the long road ahead on the Petrov trial. What would Dmitri Petrov think he could accomplish by killing her brother? She wasn't a witness against him. Yes, she controlled how the trial proceeded, but a guilty verdict could be appealed if she didn't conduct the trial according to the law. Ultimately, nothing they saw at the scene today had confirmed that it was attempted murder. Everything at the moment pointed to an accident. Unless the cellphone revealed something or Thomas woke up and said otherwise, she had to accept that it was an accident.

Before she could knock on Kim's door, it was flung open and her older niece stood in front of Rebecca. "Aunt Becky, when I woke up, you were gone. I thought you had left the ranch." Her niece's voice wavered, and her bottom lip quivered until she bit down on it.

Rebecca drew Kim to her. "Have I ever left you and Aubrey without telling you?"

Kim shook her head against Rebecca's chest.

"I came up here to talk with you and Aubrey about what happened yesterday and to answer any questions you two might have."

The door across the hall opened, and her younger niece raced out of her room and straight into Rebecca, pressing herself against the two of them. "I heard you talking."

"Let's go into Kim's room and talk," Rebecca said, hugging both girls to her as she moved forward. Sitting between them on the bed, Rebecca wrapped her arms around their shoulders. "First, I want you to know your dad is being taken care of at Mercy Memorial. They have an excellent staff."

"We want to see him." Kim shifted around to look at Rebecca, her large blue eyes wide and fringed with long dark lashes.

"Yes, Daddy needs us."

"He's recovering from having surgery late last night. If the doctor allows him visitors, I'll take you tomorrow. Okay?"

"Why not today?" Kim lifted her chin, determination in her expression.

"Because he's been through a lot and he's sleeping. He needs the rest to help his body recover."

"But we need to see him."

"Yes, Aunt Becky, please." Aubrey clung to her, burying her face against her.

"This afternoon I'll talk with the doctor and see what he says. We have to do what is best for your dad." She didn't want the children to see their dad's battered and bruised condition, but maybe it was better if they did. Their imaginations might come up with something worse—although she wasn't sure what it could be.

"What happened to Daddy? Hattie couldn't tell us much. No one is telling us anything."

"It was an accident. He was trying to save a calf and got caught in the rope." Muffled sobs from Aubrey intruded into Rebecca's train of thought. She stopped and grasped for the right words to say. She couldn't lie in order to try to protect them, but the truth was hard to tell them. "Rocket was spooked and ran with your dad behind him."

Kim's mouth fell open. "Dad is alive?"

Rebecca smoothed her niece's hair behind her ear then turned Kim to look at her. "I won't ever lie to you. He is alive but seriously hurt. He'll need you two to be brave and to pray for him."

Aubrey wrenched herself away from Rebecca. "We need to pray now."

"That's a very good idea. Do you want to?"

Aubrey folded her hands together and bowed her head. "God, make my daddy all well. Please."

"Kim, do you have anything to add to it?"

She shook her head, tears running down her cheeks.

"I understand. I think Aubrey said it all." Rebecca hugged both her nieces closer. She would protect them at all costs. "I love you two."

⋯⋙⋰

Brody took a sip of his coffee and glanced at the doorway where Rebecca had disappeared twenty minutes ago. Each moment she was gone solidified his gut into a hard rock until he could only eat a few bites of a delicious meal that at any other time he would have wolfed down.

"Mmm, Hattie, this hit the spot." Sean lounged back in his chair at the kitchen table and patted his stomach. "I'd forgotten how good you cook."

"You have a short memory, Sean Calhoun. I brought you several casseroles while you were recuperating."

Sean laughed. "Oh, that's right. My only defense is that I wasn't myself back then. But I'm fit as a fiddle now, even if my son doesn't think so."

"I can see, Brody, that you've got your hands full with this old coot."

"Old? I'm wounded," his father said with a frown, but a sparkle danced in his eyes and before long a smile broke out on his face. Brody had missed seeing that expression from his dad.

A movement out of the corner of his eye caught Brody's attention, and he shifted his gaze to the entrance into the kitchen. The girls stood there with Rebecca right behind them.

"We smelled the food and got hungry," Rebecca said as she ushered her nieces into the room. "You remember Mr. Calhoun and his father?"

"Sure. Mr. Calhoun went with us to Sea World and had lunch with Dad and me." Kim sat in the chair across from Brody. "And we visited you in the . . ." She swallowed hard and hung her head.

"That's right," Sean said immediately. "I remember you and your sister coming with your dad right before I got to come home. I sure appreciated those cards you two made for me. I still have them on the dresser in my bedroom."

"You do?" Aubrey took the seat next to Sean.

Hattie scooted her chair back from the table. "It won't take me long to whip up some scrambled eggs for you. I have the mixture already to go. Rebecca, there's some orange juice in the fridge."

The tired lines on Rebecca's face spoke of a sleepless night. Brody wished he could take her pain away. After seeing the scene at the gully, he hadn't found any evidence that pointed to anything hinting at foul play. But he still had to talk with the medical staff attending to Thomas. Were there any injuries that seemed suspect to them? Then there was the possibility of his friend waking up and eventually remembering what had happened. With the head wounds Thomas had sustained, Brody wasn't going to count on that, though. Even when Thomas came out of his coma, chances were he wouldn't recall anything about his accident.

"Brody?" Rebecca's voice penetrated his musing, and he blinked, looking at her.

"Would you like more coffee?" She held up the pot.

"I can always use a cup." He met her gaze, trying to convey his support from across the table where she sat.

After she poured the brew into his mug, she refilled his father's cup, too. "I hope y'all can spend some time here."

The plea in her gaze pulled at him, and he noticed her hand shook as she put the coffeepot down. "I have to go into Dry Gully, but, Dad, you can stay if you want. I'll be back in the early afternoon."

"You can come with us to the hospital. Aunt Becky is taking us this afternoon." Kim downed half of her glass of orange juice.

Rebecca shot her niece a look.

"Well, after she talks with the doctor and gets his okay," Kim added quickly.

"That sounds like a good plan. How about I drive everyone when you're ready to leave?" Brody said. Emotions she tried to suppress—sadness, fear—flitted across Rebecca's face, and Brody wished they were alone so that he could discover what she was thinking. He cared about her as a friend, but any chance they had for a relationship beyond that had passed ten years ago. She'd moved on; he'd moved on.

"I would like that." Relief spread across Rebecca's face as she took the bowl with the scrambled eggs from Hattie. After spooning some onto her plate, she handed the bowl to Kim.

"Where is Tory? Will she be going with us?" Aubrey asked, then shoved some eggs into her mouth.

Rebecca shot a glance at Brody. "I'll check with her. She wasn't feeling well last night."

"I should go tell her I'll pray for her, too." After taking another huge bite of her breakfast, Aubrey pushed back her chair.

"Honey, I'll talk with her. You need to eat. Let's give Tory some extra time to sleep. That'll make her feel better."

Aubrey settled back onto her chair, bowed her head, and whispered loudly, for everyone to hear, "God take care of Tory, too. Make her feel better."

"Amen," Rebecca added, followed by everyone else chiming in.

Aubrey looked up. "She'll be better now."

There had been a time when Brody had wanted a family—a wife and children—but that time had passed. He was thirty-seven and now dedicated to his work. Being with Thomas's girls, however, made him wonder what his life would have been like if he'd married and had children. He'd even thought he would get married after leaving San Antonio and dating a woman named Emily, but that hadn't worked out.

Brody's cellphone rang. He rose and said, "Excuse me," then walked into the hallway. "Calhoun here."

"You told me to call you first if there were any problems on the ranch."

Hearing the urgency in Jake's voice, Brody quickened his pace and walked onto the porch. "What's happened?"

5

$\mathcal{B}$rody moved toward the far end of the porch, where he could see the stables and barn in the distance.

"Some cattle in the far north pasture are missing," Jake said, anger filling his voice. "Probably went missing yesterday. One of the guys went out to check on the herds early this morning."

"How many are gone?"

"About eighty. I'm heading out there now. Wanna come?"

"Yeah, I'll be down there after I tell Rebecca what's going on." Brody started toward the front door.

"Do you think somehow this is connected to Thomas's accident?"

Jake's stress on the word *accident* brought Brody to a halt. He scanned the yard and the pastures nearby. "I don't know. They could be two different incidents. Or it's possible the cattle rustlers heard about Thomas's accident and saw an opportunity. They would be counting on things being chaotic for a while, especially since Thomas is a hands-on owner. Have there been any problems with cattle rustling in the area?"

"Not for the past few years. We patrol our herds almost daily."

"In any sort of pattern that someone watching the ranch could figure out?"

"No. We'll take the Jeep to that part of the ranch. I'll swing by and pick you up in a few minutes."

Brody slipped his cellphone back onto his belt. As he surveyed the ranch, he couldn't rid his mind of the question: Did the cattle rustling have something to do with Thomas being injured?

❧

Where's Brody? Rebecca took her dishes to the sink, then excused herself for a moment to go look for him. *What if it's something to do with Thomas?*

Brody had gone down the hall. To the foyer? When she reached the entry hall, there was no sign of him. Her stomach clenched. What if the sheriff had discovered something concerning Thomas's accident?

As she glanced into the living room, the front door opened and Brody stood in the entrance. A frown creased his face. "What's wrong?"

He stepped into the foyer and grabbed her hand, then tugged her out onto the porch, closing the door behind them. "I don't want the kids to overhear. They're worried enough."

Dread captured her next breath, to the point where she couldn't speak.

"Jake called to tell me that about eighty head of cattle have gone missing from the northernmost pasture."

"When?"

"He thinks sometime yesterday afternoon or night."

"Could Thomas have caught them and . . ." She couldn't finish her question. She would have helped the cattle thieves take the whole herd if that meant Thomas would not now be lying in a hospital, fighting for his life. "I—I—No amount of cattle are worth what has happened to my brother."

Brody took her hands and held them in his. "Listen, Rebecca. The cattle rustling might not be related to what happened to Thomas."

"But they happened at the same time." Although he clasped her hands, they trembled from the force of her anger at the phantom rustlers.

"News travels fast around here, especially since so many outsiders who were here last night heard about Thomas. Someone might have taken that opportunity to steal your cattle."

She opened her mouth to protest his logic, needing someone to blame for her brother's accident. But she didn't. Instead, she clamped her teeth together and tried to see the recent events from a calm perspective—as she did when reviewing evidence during a trial.

"Is Jake going to check the north pasture?"

"Yes, and so am I. I can go to Dry Gulch to see the sheriff later." Brody peered at the Jeep coming from the barn toward the house. "I'll be back to take you to the hospital."

"I'm coming with you two."

"Don't you think you should stay here and be with the girls and Tory? They need you right now."

"I want a report when you get back."

Brody gently squeezed her hands and then released them. "I will." When the Jeep came to a stop in front, he hurried to the passenger side and climbed in.

Rebecca watched Jake and Brody leave, heading north. When they disappeared from view, she went back inside and ascended the stairs to the second floor to check on Tory. She knocked on her sister-in-law's door and waited for a long moment. As she turned away, the door swept open to reveal Tory dressed in navy blue linen slacks and a white silk blouse, her long blonde hair pulled back in a severe bun at the nape of her neck. Dark circles, barely hidden by makeup, drew Rebecca's gaze to Tory's green eyes.

"I was worried about you. Are you all right?" Rebecca asked to break the silence that had fallen between them.

"What do you think? No. Thomas is in the hospital. He might not make it. He might be permanently disabled. He might never wake up." Her voice rose with each sentence.

"Shh. The girls might overhear." Rebecca wouldn't put it past Kim to eavesdrop if she thought it would get her some information about her dad.

Tears immediately welled up in Tory's eyes. "What am I supposed to do? I don't know how to handle this. I—I—" She snapped her mouth closed.

Rebecca quickly guided Tory backward into her bedroom, shut the door, and led her sister-in-law to her bed. Scanning the area, Rebecca saw touches of her brother—one of his cowboy hats, a tan one, on a table; his dress boots by the chair; a wallet on the dresser. But mostly the room reflected Tory, from the pink and green bedspread to the pictures of ballet dancers on the walls. Tory loved ballet. She'd even talked Kim into taking some lessons that would start soon, which had surprised Rebecca, since Kim had always been a tomboy, devoted to riding.

Rebecca sat on the bed beside Tory and laid her hand on Tory's shoulder. "You'll take it one step at a time. We don't really know anything yet. Thomas hasn't even been out of surgery twelve hours. They're keeping a close eye on him, and we haven't heard anything bad. That's a good sign. If the doctor says it's okay, I'm taking the girls to the hospital to at least see their dad."

Shrugging away from Rebecca, Tory blinked, and one tear ran down her pale face. "Do you think that's a good idea? Seeing him like he is might scare them."

"Maybe. But if we don't allow them to see him, they'll imagine worse things than the way he looks right now. Believe me, both Kim and Aubrey have very creative minds."

"I agree." Tory pressed her fingertips into her forehead. "I just hate to see them so upset. I don't know if I can take that on top of everything else."

"We'll be there for them."

Tory took a deep breath, then released it slowly. "I'll try my best not to . . ." she turned toward Rebecca, "not to let them see me cry." With a quick brush of her fingers across her cheeks, she erased any evidence of tears. "I don't want to do anything to make it harder for them. Can you give me a half an hour to get myself together a little better? Touch up my makeup so they don't," she waved her hand at her face, "see my dark circles."

Rebecca stood. "You take all the time you need. It would worry them if you didn't go with us. We can wait. Besides, Brody is driving us, and he has gone to the north pasture with Jake."

"Why?"

"Some cattle are missing."

"What?" Tory bolted up from the bed.

She shouldn't have said anything, but Tory would find out soon enough. "Nothing to worry about. They're going to check the situation out."

"But—but—"

"Tory, while Thomas is injured, I'll take over running the ranch. Jake's a wonderful foreman. I can handle it. I'm going to stay here for a while to help the girls and you. You won't have to worry about the ranch."

"I appreciate that. I don't know anything about running a ranch. So that's one thing I won't have to deal with. If you're sure . . ."

"I am. I grew up on this ranch and used to help my dad and Thomas. It's second nature to me." She hoped. It had been years since she had worked on the ranch, but it was half hers so she was the most likely one to take over. "See you downstairs when you're ready."

Rebecca left her sister-in-law's bedroom and escaped to hers to make the call to the doctor. She didn't want the girls overhearing what she said to Dr. Henderson. When he came on the linee, she asked, "How's my brother doing?"

"He didn't have a good night. We've been keeping a close eye on him, but his blood pressure is high. I'm afraid on top of everything he'll have a stroke."

"The girls need to see their dad. It doesn't have to be long. Just a few minutes."

"That's all I'll allow. We have a lot of machines hooked up to him. You might prepare them for that. And of course, he hasn't woken up yet. This first twenty-four hours will be tough. I don't want too many people visiting, and the ones who do can only stay for a short time. Okay?"

"Yes, I understand." *No, I don't. I want to be with my brother, hold his hand, talk to him.* "We'll do whatever is needed."

∽୬

"I've got some hands coming out here to repair the fence. It looks like the rustlers cut the barbed wire and then brought their semis through here." Jake indicated the tire tracks in the softer dirt of the north pasture.

"This isn't too far from the highway. Probably one of the better locations if you're looking to steal cattle. Isolated. Easy to get to." Brody walked his horse in the direction of the tire tracks until they stopped. All around were hundreds of hoof prints. "They led them right up a ramp into the truck. Modern-day cattle rustlers."

"Yeah, there were two semis. If they'd had more, we would have lost the whole herd in this pasture."

"I would suggest you bring the cattle closer to the center of the ranch, away from easy access to the highway, and then post a guard, out of sight. I would like to get these guys if they decide to come back."

"That should take care of them stealing the Circle S cattle. Can't speak for our neighbors. I've already made some calls to alert them."

"If the cattle rustlers are smart, they'll leave the area."

Jake took off his cowboy hat and smacked it against his leg. "Until we let down our guard again."

"True. We'll just have to make it more difficult for them. Let's head back. I'll let Rebecca know."

"I'll drop you off at the house, then start moving the cattle."

As Brody climbed into the Jeep, he surveyed the pasture. Had someone been casing the ranch out? Could there be a connection between the missing cattle and Thomas's accident? Logically, he didn't think so. The two areas weren't near each other. But he didn't like coincidences—two unusual events happening the same day—not many hours apart.

❧

The noise of the machines beeping, the sight of the blinking numbers, the antiseptic scent that dominated all other smells meant nothing to Rebecca. The tears of Aubrey and Kim as they looked at their dad in the hospital bed in the ICU overrode every other sense. She wrapped an arm around each child.

"Honey, I told you he was bandaged and bruised." Rebecca's teeth dug into her lower lip as she too tried to control her sorrow at seeing Thomas so helpless and vulnerable. He was her older brother—her protector, the one person she could go to with a problem and he would be there for her. "You heard the doctor say he was doing okay." Which translated as Thomas was holding his own. He hadn't deteriorated, but he hadn't improved either.

"Why doesn't he wake up?" Kim asked, turning her gaze, shiny with tears, on Rebecca.

"He needs to sleep to get better. His body is doing what it needs to do. He'll wake up when he's ready." *I hope.*

"I want him to wake up *now.*" Aubrey reached out slowly and touched his hand.

So do I. "No matter how much we want something, it doesn't always happen when we want it to. We have to be patient and let his body repair itself."

The nurse came into the ICU cubicle. "It's time for y'all to leave. We have some tests we need to run."

"But—but—" Kim moved closer to the bed.

Aubrey clasped her dad's hand. "I don't wanna."

"We'll visit him every day we can. But we'll need to leave when the staff asks us to. Okay?" Rebecca grasped her nieces' shoulders and gently tugged them back.

Kim came with no resistance, but Aubrey clung to her father, tears running down her face.

"Go outside, Kim. I'll get Aubrey."

The nurse stood to the side while Rebecca took Aubrey's arm and swung the child toward her. She knelt and grasped Aubrey's hands to keep her niece from turning away. "Aubrey," she waited for the child's attention, "I know this is hard, but if we want to come back to see your dad, we have to do what the nurse says. You do want to see your daddy tomorrow, don't you?"

Tears streamed down her cheeks. The five-year-old stared at her father for a long moment, then nodded.

Rebecca took out a tissue and wiped the girl's face. "I know it's hard to understand why you can't see your daddy anytime you want, but the staff is working hard to make him better." Rising, she hugged the child to her, then left with Aubrey dragging her feet but moving slowly forward.

Outside the ICU Tory and Brody were waiting. When Brody saw them, he pushed off the wall and came toward them. "I bet the girls could use an ice cream cone. They have a cafe across the street that serves delicious ice cream, or so the nurse told me."

Aubrey brightened. "Can we, Aunt Becky?"

Rebecca looked toward Tory. "Do you want to come? They're running some kind of test, so it may be a while before you can go in."

"You all go ahead. I'm not very hungry. They may get through before you're finished, and then I can go in and see Thomas."

"Can't we go back in with Tory?" Kim asked.

"Yeah, Aunt Becky. I don't hafta have ice cream."

Tory smoothed Aubrey's hair back from her face. "Baby, you go with your aunt. You can come back another time."

Crossing her arms over her chest, Aubrey dropped her head.

Brody started for the elevator. Both girls followed.

"Rebecca, can you wait a moment?" As soon as Aubrey and Kim were out of earshot, Tory continued. "I'm staying here at the hospital. I know the doctor said there isn't much we can do right now, but I need to be here. Can you take the girls back to the ranch? I heard Aubrey crying. It's hard for them to understand what's going on."

With a protest on the tip of her tongue, Rebecca mentally counted to ten. "I can take them home, then come back and stay with you."

"I'd rather you watch the girls. They love you and need to know you're there for them. They shouldn't be at the hospital until Thomas is much better. As a child I went through something similar with my mom. No matter how much my father tried to explain what was happening to Mom, I didn't understand, and it was very hard on me seeing her every day, hurt, wasting away. I don't want that for Kim and Aubrey."

There was some wisdom in Tory's request, but Rebecca wanted to be the one staying by Thomas's side.

"The girls and I are getting closer, but you three have such a special relationship. They need you right now. Thomas needs me."

"I told them if the doctor said it was all right they could see their dad each day for at least a few minutes. I'll bring them."

"What about school? What about your trial?"

"We can work it out."

"I think the girls need as normal a schedule as possible. I could pick them up from school and bring them to the hospital, then you can take them to the ranch when you get off work."

Aubrey waved to Rebecca to come. The elevator dinged and the doors opened. "I've got to go. I'll talk to you later about what schedule we'll have concerning Thomas."

Tory's eyelids slid halfway closed, and she stared at the floor. "Fine."

Rebecca hurried to the elevator, which Brody held for her. "I think I'd like a double dip. No diet today."

Aubrey scrunched her mouth up. "Diet? Tory talks about that. What do you do?"

"Deny yourself all the food you love to eat." Rebecca caught Brody's amused glance.

The five-year-old tilted her head to the side, which was what she did when she was trying to figure something out. "I wouldn't like that. Why would you do that?"

"So you'd be thin, dummy," Kim said with a huff.

"I'm not dumb. My teacher says I'm smart."

"You're in kindergarten. What's there to learn?"

Aubrey rushed her sister and pounded her with her fists. "You take that back."

"Why?" Kim locked her arms around Aubrey to keep her sister from hitting her. "All you're learning is your letters and numbers. Wait 'til you have to do math and read."

Rebecca folded her arms over her chest. "Aubrey. Kim. We're in a hospital. This is no way to behave. Ever."

"She started it." Kim shoved Aubrey away.

Brody caught the five-year-old and steadied her. She tried to go after Kim again. He clamped his hands on her shoulders.

Kim stuck her tongue out.

"I hate you, Kim. You're mean."

"Stop it. Right now. I certainly can't bring you two back to the hospital if you're going to act like this." Rebecca tightened her grip on Kim to keep her from going after her little sister.

Both girls quieted and looked away from each other.

"Maybe Brody needs to take us home now."

"No, we'll be good." Her head tilted up, Aubrey squinted and stared at Kim.

Kim nodded.

As the doors at the lower level swished open, Brody's cellphone rang. He stepped off the elevator and to the side to take the call. His voice pitched low, he turned away as he talked.

Rebecca stood between her nieces. They usually didn't fight, but she knew they hadn't slept well the night before. Aubrey had come into her bedroom several times and ended up sleeping with her while Kim paced her room before finally coming into Rebecca's room, too. She'd lain awake the rest of the night, alert to any movement from her nieces. Except for Aubrey crying out a couple of times, both of the girls finally went to sleep about four in the morning.

Brody swung around. "The doctor can see me now. Can you all go on without me to the cafe?"

"Are you sick, too?" Aubrey said, her bottom lip trembling.

"No. This is about a case I'm working on. Nothing for you two to worry about. I'll come to the cafe when I'm finished, so I hope you save me some ice cream."

"We can't. It melts too fast. Unless you hurry." Aubrey took Rebecca's hand while Kim hurried ahead of them.

"Just don't eat all the ice cream they have at the cafe," Brody called out, then headed down a hallway to his right.

Aubrey glanced back. "I won't."

Rebecca rushed toward the exit; her niece was already outside. "Kim, wait for us."

The girl stopped at the curb, looked both ways, then stepped into the street as though she hadn't heard Rebecca.

A screech filled the air as an old white pickup sped around the corner, heading right toward Kim. Rebecca opened her mouth to scream "stop," but nothing came out.

6

"Dr. Henderson, thanks for seeing me." Brody shook the man's hand. "I have some questions about your observations of the condition of Thomas's body when he came into the emergency room. I'm investigating his accident to make sure that was all it was."

"Yes, Rebecca told me about that, and I've been reviewing his records. I've thought back to last night, and I can't think of one wound that probably wasn't caused by being dragged. No bullet holes or knife cuts. There were several deep gashes in his head—the kind caused by contact with a rock. I suppose someone could have hit him on the head, then tied him up. In which case he either knew the person or he was surprised."

"That area on the ranch is rocky ground."

"Which accounts for all the bruising and ragged cuts on his backside."

"So you didn't see anything that made you suspect something other than his being dragged by a horse?"

Dr. Mike Henderson rubbed his chin and thought a moment. "I don't see too many injuries caused by a horse dragging its rider. His body was a bloody mess when he arrived. If there was something else, it was obscured by the dragging injuries."

"In other words, nothing stands out to you, but there's a possibility it could have been caused by another person. Did you run a tox screen on him?"

"No. I had no reason to. Besides, we were busy saving his life. He's still not out of the woods."

"Can you run one now?"

"Yes, if you suspect someone tried to murder him. You think by incapacitating him, then tying him to the horse?" A frown marred the doctor's craggy features.

"I need to rule it out."

"Thomas has enemies who might want him dead?"

"Yesterday some cattle were rustled from him. Possibly around the same time."

"You think he came upon them and they did this to him?"

"It doesn't seem likely since the incidents occurred in different parts of the ranch—a ranch of twenty thousand acres. That's a lot of ground."

"Is Rebecca worried? His wife?"

"Tory hasn't taken the news well. She hasn't said much of anything. Rebecca wants to make sure it was an accident—nothing more. The governor has asked me to look into what happened to his cousin." Mike Henderson was a Sinclair family friend. His father had been the Sinclairs' doctor until he'd retired, when his son had taken over. He moved in the same circles as the Sinclairs. "You haven't heard any rumors about someone having a grudge against the Sinclairs, have you?"

"No. In Dry Gulch everyone loves them. Their neighbors appreciate their cooperation and helpfulness. Do they know about the cattle rustlers?"

"Yes, Jake is informing them."

"I wish I had some concrete evidence or a definite answer for you, but what I saw fits with an accident."

"That's the way it's looking right now, but if you think of anything that contradicts that, please let me know. Thanks." Brody touched the tip of his tan cowboy hat and left the doctor's lounge.

He'd already talked with the emergency room nurse who attended Thomas, and she hadn't had anything different to say. He had another ranger checking Thomas's cellphone and the calls he'd made and received. Unless something turned up there, he would inform the governor it appeared to be an accident. But his gut clenched each time he thought that. Was he missing something?

❧

"Kim, stop," finally shot out of Rebecca's mouth as she ran toward her niece, who was a few feet from the curb of the two-lane street.

The child slowed and glanced back at Rebecca. The truck kept coming toward Kim, still speeding.

Rebecca dove the remaining distance to push her niece out of danger. At the last second, Kim saw the truck and scrambled for the sidewalk on the other side of the street. Rebecca fell down onto the asphalt, pain shooting up her knees.

The careening pickup was only ten feet from Rebecca.

❧

As Brody neared the front entrance to the hospital, a loud sound like wheels peeling out echoed through the lobby. He hurried his pace, hitting the glass door with his palms as he raced outside.

Rebecca launched herself at Kim in the middle of the road and shoved her toward the sidewalk.

As a white truck with darkened windows came toward Rebecca.

He darted forward, adrenaline pumping through his body. Passing Aubrey, he yelled, "Get inside the hospital."

❧

When Rebecca clambered to her feet, someone tackled her, shoving her out of the way of the pickup as it sped past her. Inches away from her. Her thundering heartbeat overwhelmed all other sounds. A young man helped her stand. He was saying something, but she didn't hear.

Her gaze latched onto Kim, frozen, all color washed from her face, her mouth hanging open.

"Lady, are you all right?" she finally heard the twentysomething man ask, his face now looming in front of her.

"Rebecca, what happened?"

Brody.

She sank to the sidewalk, all the strength was siphoned from her legs. Her hands began to tremble, and the trembling quickly spread throughout her body.

"Rebecca? Are you hurt?"

The urgency in Brody's voice compelled her to look at the young man who had saved her and then at Brody, his gray eyes shadowed with fear, his mouth pulled into a tight line. He put his hand on her arm and tried to help her up.

She shook her head, dragging both hands through her hair. "Let me sit here for a moment."

Twisting around, she found Kim and motioned for her to come to her. The child didn't move; shock held her immobile.

Rebecca scanned the street, her eyes widening when she couldn't find her younger niece. "Where's Aubrey?" she asked as she bolted to her feet, a light-headed rush causing the world to swirl before her eyes.

Brody took hold of her again and supported her. "I sent her inside the hospital. I'll go get her. You stay here."

"I'm not going anywhere except to check on Kim."

As Brody jogged toward the hospital entrance, Rebecca slowly swung around and moved toward her niece.

"Ma'am, if you're all right, I'll leave you."

Rebecca made it over to Kim and hugged the child against her, the ten-year-old burrowing her face in the crook of Rebecca's arm, while she turned to face her rescuer. "Thank you. Those words sound so inadequate at the moment. I'm Rebecca Morgan, and this is Kim."

The brown-headed man grinned. "You have a pretty daughter. I'm glad I could help. She needs her mother. Thank you is all that is required." He wore a dark brown cowboy hat and tipped it toward her. "Have a good day."

"Wait. Who are you?"

"Rob Clark."

"We were just going into the cafe for ice cream. Please join us. If you don't want ice crea—and it's great here—then I'll treat you to whatever you want. That is, if you have the time. My niece and I won't take no for an answer." Rebecca managed a smile that quivered at the corners of her mouth. The residue of fright from the near hit-and-run still pinged through her body at a dizzying speed—much like the speed of the pickup truck.

"Well, ma'am, I hate to disappoint two pretty ladies, but—"

Kim peeked at the young man. "Please. You saved Aunt Becky."

Rob Clark blushed a deep shade of red, and he lowered his dark eyes. "You don't have to do that."

"Yes, I do. Please." Rebecca spied Brody approaching with Aubrey in tow. "Brody, I'm trying to talk Rob into joining us for some ice cream."

Brody made eye contact with the young man. "I hope you can. I couldn't reach Rebecca in time, but you did."

"You were so brave." Aubrey bent her head back to stare up at Rob, who stood over six feet tall. "I'm having peppermint ice cream. But they have all kinds."

"Well, in that case, how can I refuse?"

Ten minutes later Rebecca settled into a chair between her nieces, with Brody and Rob across from her. Still quiet, Kim dug into her banana split while Aubrey talked nonstop to Rob, except when she shoveled ice cream into her mouth.

"Honey, give Mr. Clark a chance to answer one of your questions before asking him another one." Rebecca nursed a tall glass of sweet tea.

"Are you a cowboy?" Aubrey repeated her last question.

"I've ridden broncos and steers on the rodeo circuit."

"Are you in town for the rodeo now?" Not having taken her eyes off Rob since he sat down, Kim licked her spoon and absently tried to scoop up some more of her banana split. Some plopped onto the table.

Rebecca pressed her lips together. The girl didn't even notice as Rob answered, "No, I'm here visiting some friends before heading back to Dallas."

"Do you live in Dallas?" Rob had brown hair that curled at the nape of his neck and dark, chocolate-colored eyes, and Rebecca could see why her niece, who had discovered boys in the past year, was enthralled with him. It wouldn't be long before she discarded her tomboy ways totally and became boy crazy like so many of her girlfriends were.

Rob took a bite of his pecan pie with a scoop of vanilla ice cream on top. "Yes, ma'am. I grew up in the area north of the city. I ain't had something this good in a long time. Pecan pie is one of my favorite desserts, that and carrot cake."

"It's mine, too," Kim said, her gaze locked on Rob's face, a dazzled look in her eyes that had nothing to do with her near miss with the pickup.

"Since when?" Aubrey finished her peppermint ice cream and swiped a paper napkin across her face, managing to smear some on her cheek. "I thought you loved banana splits."

Dragging her gaze from Rob, Kim focused it on her little sister. "I like banana splits, but I like pecan pie better. I've never had carrot cake, but I bet it's good, too."

"It is." Rob's grin dimpled both of his cheeks.

"I recently moved from Dallas. What part do you live in?" Brody asked, amusement twinkling in his eyes as he took in both girls.

"Plano."

"I lived closer to Garland, where I worked."

With only crumbs left, Rob placed his fork on his plate. "I sure thank you for this pie."

"It was nothing compared to what you did." Rebecca shuddered when she thought about seeing the banged-up front end of the truck coming toward her like a train barreling down a railroad track straight toward her—a recurring nightmare she had a few times a year. She never knew what happened next because she would wake up before she got hit.

Rob ducked his head, his cheeks red. "Ain't nothing. Anyone would have done it."

"But they didn't. You did."

"Speaking of the truck, I'd like to have a few words with you about what you remember seeing." Brody set his coffee on the table.

A confused expression crinkled Rob's forehead. "What do you mean? It was white. I don't remember much of anything else. Are you thinking of calling the police?"

"I am the police."

Rob's eyes grew round.

"Not the local police. I'm a Texas Ranger. And yes, I'm reporting the incident. The person behind the wheel was speeding, not to mention driving recklessly."

"I certainly agree with you. Thanks, ma'am, for this little taste of heaven. Reminds me of my mom's pie." Rob rose. "I best be going. I'm late to meet up with my friends." He gave each of the girls a big smile, then turned away.

As Rob ambled toward the exit, Brody looked at Rebecca. "I'll be back in a few minutes," he said, then scraped back his chair and went after the young man.

"Aunt Becky, he's so cute. I wish he'd saved me." Elbow on the table, Kim put her chin in her palm and stared at Rob's disappearing figure. "And he smiled at me. Just for me."

"No, he didn't. He smiled at me." Aubrey knocked Kim's arm, and she nearly fell forward.

Kim glared at her little sister. "What's gotten into you, brat?"

"I'm not a brat."

"Girls, I know you two are worried about your dad, but you need to get along. Remember, I'm here for you. We need to stick together, not fight."

Kim's dreamy expression evolved into a frown and unshed tears glistened in her eyes. "I know, but what if Dad—"

"Worrying about what might be isn't good. Chances are it won't happen, and then you've done all that worrying and getting upset for nothing. When your dad wakes up, it'll be our job to cheer him up. A deal?"

"I can do that." Aubrey raised her hand for a high five.

Rebecca gave each girl one. "I know you two can. And we'll have to help Tory, too. She's upset right now."

"Yeah, she hardly said anything to us this morning. Aubrey, let's make her a card when we get home."

❧

"Other than the vehicle being a white pickup, you can't remember anything?" Brody asked Rob outside the cafe. His gaze skimmed over the spot where Rebecca could have been run down if this young man hadn't gotten to her in time.

"No, sir. I can't. I saw it and reacted. I've got good reflexes. Have to on the rodeo circuit."

"I'm glad you do. Could you tell if there was one person in the truck or two?"

Rob shook his head. "The window was tinted dark, and the sun reflected off the chrome—nearly blinded me."

Brody handed Rob his card. "If you remember anything at all, please give me a call."

"I do think that the way the truck took the corner the driver was probably drunk or on something. Just my opinion. He should have been able to avoid Ms. Morgan."

"Sometimes our gut feelings and opinions are right on. I would like a contact number for you, in case I need to ask you any more questions. I doubt I will. I did get a license number except the last digit. It had mud over it. I also have a make and model."

"What?"

"Dodge Ram, probably 2003 or 2004."

"Good. I'd just as soon not be out on the road with whoever was driving that truck," Rob said, then gave Brody his cellphone number.

Brody shook Rob's hand. "Thanks for being at the right place at the right time."

As Rob crossed the street, Brody took out his phone and called one of the detectives he had worked with in the San Antonio Police Department. "This is Brody Calhoun. There was a truck at the main entrance of Mercy Memorial Hospital that nearly ran down Judge Rebecca Morgan."

"I think trouble seeks you out," Detective Moore said, a dead-serious tone in his voice. "Is she all right?"

"Yes, scrapes on her knees and shaky but otherwise alive and well. It was a white Dodge Ram, beat-up and obviously driven a lot. Something you would see used on a cattle ranch. I got the license number," he rattled off the letters and numbers, "except the last one."

"I should know something for you by the end of the day. With Judge Morgan on the Petrov trial, I'll let Detective Nelson know. This could be connected."

"That was what I was thinking. I haven't said anything to Rebecca, and I'll stay with her until I hear from you or Nelson."

"That's good. The Russian Mafia is ruthless."

Brody pocketed his phone as Rebecca and her nieces came out of the cafe. "Are y'all ready to leave? I thought I would rescue Hattie and Jake from my dad." *And make sure Dad's all right. He isn't used to doing much during the day.*

"Let's check on Thomas and see what Tory wants to do."

"Sounds like a plan." He would feel better when he got Rebecca back to the Circle S Ranch—and he wouldn't feel completely at ease until he knew who had been driving the truck. Another consequence of her being in the wrong place at the wrong time, or something more. Either way, she needed protecting.

J. R. paced in front of his blue Malibu in the hospital parking lot. The ranger had left with the judge and her nieces. Probably going back to the ranch. Was there someone else trying to kill her? If the driver of the pickup reached her a second later, she would have been hurt at the very least. He didn't like this one bit.

As he placed a call, he leaned back against the hood of his car, staring at the street that ran in front of the cafe. "She almost got run down by a pickup today."

"What happened?"

"She and one of her nieces were crossing the street to go to the cafe." J. R. described the incident, then finished with, "She's lucky to be alive. I could swear the person driving meant to run her down."

"No one is going to steal my revenge. Keep an eye on her. She's mine."

"I had to give the ranger my cell number."

"The throwaway phone?"

"Of course. I might not have graduated from high school, but I ain't an idiot."

"I know that. Just another thing she needs to pay for. You know what you have to do next." The phone went dead.

J. R. shoved off his hood and climbed into his Malibu. How in the world was he supposed to keep an eye on the judge and case his next target, too?

～⳽～

"It's good to get away from the courtroom for a couple of hours, and I love to eat here," Rebecca said as she took a booth at the back of the diner on Monday.

Laura, her law clerk, slid into the place across from her. "This is a dive, even by my standards, which aren't as classy as yours. How in the world did you find this?"

"This dive has the best burgers in town, and the French fries are to die for."

"Please don't say that after your weekend." Laura glanced at the man standing near them, his back against the wall. "Should we ask the marshal to join us? He wasn't too happy we came here. Maybe the burger will put him in a better mood."

"He declined when I asked him earlier. He'd rather keep his attention focused on protecting me. It feels so strange having someone following me around. As a judge, I've never had this happen before."

"You've never had this kind of trial either."

The waitress stopped at the booth, and Rebecca ordered her usual while Laura went with a chef salad.

After the waitress left, Laura leaned forward. "I hope the salad is as good as the burgers I'm smelling."

"You should have gotten one."

"I'm on a diet."

Rebecca laughed, surprised at how nice it felt to do that after an intense morning of jury selection—still not completed. "You're always on a diet."

"I don't have your slender genes."

"Is there such a thing as a slender gene?"

"I don't know, but no matter what I do I can't seem to lose much weight. I think it has to do with the fact that I sit at a desk or in a courtroom all day."

"That might have something to do with it. You need to go for a walk when you get home in the evening. It's getting cooler now."

"You do that?"

"No, I use a treadmill, which will keep my bodyguard," Rebecca nodded toward the marshal behind her, "happy."

"Around-the-clock protection?"

"Yes. Deputy U.S. Marshal Randall Wentworth arrived at the ranch yesterday while Brody was there. Between him and Detective Nelson, I'm stuck with someone following me all the time. Not a feeling I like."

The corners of Laura's mouth drooped. "But necessary. I think this Brody and Detective Nelson are right. Something's going on."

"I agree, especially after the police found the white pickup abandoned several blocks away from the hospital. No prints. Stolen."

"And no one saw anything?"

"At least no one who'll say they did."

"Do you blame them?"

"No. This whole trial is about intimidation and revenge. These gangs are good at that."

"I'd be so scared right now. You don't seem to be. Aren't you worried?"

Rebecca shrugged. "I'm in the Lord's hands. I can't let these people intimidate me, or I couldn't function at all. What kind of life is that?" At least she was trying desperately to approach her situation in that manner. But at night the fear crept into her mind, robbing her of any peace.

The waitress placed their food in front of them. "Would you like anything else?"

"No, this smells great." Rebecca smiled at the young woman who must be new at the diner.

When she left, Laura stabbed at her salad. "I thought when your brother had his accident that you would delay the trial or step down."

"No way. Although I think my brother's accident was just that, especially after his cellphone didn't reveal anything suspicious, I won't let others see any kind of weakness in me. They would circle me like the vultures they are and go in to tear me apart when they thought I'd given up. I'm not going to let the Russian Mafia win. Thomas is in excellent hands. Tory is staying at the hospital a lot and is keeping me up-to-date. And I'm seeing him when I can." Rebecca bowed her head and said a prayer over her food.

Midway to bringing her fork to her mouth, Laura stopped. "How do you do it? Keep such a positive attitude when everything is falling apart?"

"Because if I don't, then I've lost. I can't always control what happens to me, but I can control how I react. Not always easy but something I keep working on. My brother needs prayers, good medical attention, and positive thoughts around him. I can give him those at least. I can't give him his health back." Frustration churned Rebecca's stomach.

Laura took a swallow of her coffee. "Yes, but doctors can't always fix everyone."

"Doctors can't, but the Lord can. It's in His hands now."

Laura lifted an eyebrow. "Just as you are?"

"Yes."

"I don't get it."

"Why don't you come to church with me on Sunday?"

Laura shook her head. "I don't think so. It's a little late for me."

"Late? You're forty years old. Has that stopped you from recently applying and getting into law school?"

"No, but that's not the same thing."

"I agree. It's much more important than what a person's job is. But it's your call, Laura."

"You mean you're not going to try and persuade me?"

"I'm here to answer questions if you have them. The decision is yours."

"I'll think about it." Laura took another bite. "Tell me about this Brody Calhoun. You haven't mentioned him before, other than that he and your brother were best friends growing up. It sounds like he's taking a personal interest in you. Calling a couple of times this morning to make sure you're all right."

"He's a friend of mine, too." But as Rebecca said the words, they didn't quite sound true to her. He'd been at the ranch all weekend, except when he took his dad back home and made sure his niece came over to stay with his father, despite Sean's protestations.

"What does he look like?"

"Short, dark hair. Gray eyes that gleam like sunlight striking silver. In good physical condition. He's nice to look at."

"I've got to meet him. Have him come by the office sometime."

"I thought you liked Detective Nelson," Rebecca said with a chuckle.

"Doesn't mean I can't look at other men. Besides, Detective Nelson doesn't know I like him."

"Maybe we need to change that."

"How? I'm certainly not going to tell him how I feel, and you'd better not either."

Rebecca held up her hands, palms out. "No. Never. But you get all flustered when he comes by."

"That's because I like him. I don't think that's going to change."

"Let me think on it. Maybe I can come up with something."

"Rebecca Morgan, you may be my boss, but don't forget we're friends, too."

"Never." Rebecca finally took the first bite of her hamburger, juicy and delicious. Closing her eyes, she savored its rich, grilled favor. And for just a moment she could forget about all that had happened in the past few days. It was just Laura and her, having one of their lunches, talking about life and men.

A crash sent her heart pounding against her rib cage. Her eyes flew open. The busboy had dropped a tray full of dishes. Her peaceful moment vanished, and everything that had transpired lately came crashing down on her, reminding her of the Deputy U.S. Marshal sitting at the next table.

Late Friday afternoon, Rebecca sank into the chair behind her desk in her office and covered her face with her hands, tired from the week of selecting jury members and then hearing opening arguments. But at least the trial would proceed with the witnesses on Monday. Finally.

She could now spend some quality time with Aubrey and Kim at the ranch for two whole days. Laura had even said she would like to go to church with her on Sunday. And, best of all, Thomas was being moved to a regular room this morning. Although he hadn't woken up, his condition was stable and the doctor was more optimistic about his recovery than he had been at the beginning of the week.

A knock sounded at her door. Rubbing her hands down her face, she lifted her head and released a long sigh. What now?

She pushed to her feet, crossed the office, and opened the door. "Come in, Charlie." As Detective Nelson of the San Antonio Police Department entered, she leaned out of the entrance and said to Deputy U.S. Marshal Randall Wentworth, who was still guarding her, "I want to leave as soon as I'm through talking with the detective."

"Yes, ma'am."

After shutting the door, she turned toward Charlie Nelson. "What's happening? Lately I don't hear from you unless something is wrong."

"Goes with the trial you're on." His frown carved deep lines into his face. "One of our witnesses has slipped away from the safe house."

"Willing or unwilling?"

"We think willing. There was no indication otherwise. The officers protecting him said he'd been talking about the trial a lot. Agitated. Pacing."

"So someone got to him and scared him enough to leave. How did that happen?"

"Don't know, but believe me, I've launched an investigation into it."

"Who was it?"

"Ben Fuller."

"One of the key witnesses."

"But not the only one. I've tightened security around the other two witnesses. We can't afford to lose another one." The grooves in the detective's craggy face spoke of his exhaustion. This case had taken up most of his time—and had done so for all the people involved.

Rebecca longed for life to return to normal—if it ever would. If Thomas didn't regain consciousness, she didn't see how it could. She was the girls' guardian. She'd always wanted children, but when Garrett died, she'd given up on that dream. Becoming permanent guardian to the girls was unthinkable because that would mean Thomas was in a coma or . . . No, she wouldn't think about that.

"I have something else to tell you, but Laura asked me to wait until the trial was over for the day."

"Obviously it isn't to tell me you found out who was driving the truck that nearly hit me."

"I wish. We do have a couple of leads. One man, an older gentleman, could describe the person he saw fleeing the truck."

"When did he come forward?"

"Yesterday, but I wanted to check him out before I said anything to you. He owns a shop near the vacant lot and was putting some things in his window when the pickup drove into the lot and the man left it. I have a sketch artist with him and will have a picture to show you soon. I'll drive it out to the ranch."

"That sounds like some good news for a change. Why would Laura want you to keep it from me? I could have used that earlier."

"That isn't what I needed to tell you." He drew in a deep breath. "Thomas received a bouquet of dead flowers this afternoon."

7

$\mathcal{T}$he box of dead roses was on his bed. It was waiting for him when he was moved into his room. The box of dead roses was on his bed. Your sister-in-law was very upset and demanded answers." Detective Nelson sat across from Rebecca, who sank into a chair in front of her desk.

"How could that have happened?" she whispered more to herself than to Charlie.

"It had to have happened in the twenty-minute window between preparing Thomas's room and bringing him up to it. Your sister-in-law saw the box and hurried to take it off the bed while the orderlies transferred Thomas to his bed. The nurse was settling your brother in when Mrs. Sinclair opened the box and screamed. On top of the bouquet, like the one you received, there was a note with a skull and crossbones on it—the symbol of the Dos Huesos Cruzados Gang. It was written in blood."

"Human?"

"Yes. There was a severed finger in the box, probably what was used to draw the symbol."

"Is DNA being run on it to see if it matches anyone in the system?"

"Yes, but it will take some time. Mrs. Sinclair called the governor. We should get the test results back by tomorrow. It pays to know people in high places."

"This doesn't make any sense. I could understand if it was from the Russian Mafia. But a note from the Dos Huesos Cruzados Gang?"

"Maybe we'll know more if we have a DNA match. The severed finger is a signature of the Russian Mafia we've been dealing with."

"You think someone is out there, dead?"

"Yes."

"From which group—the Dos Huesos Cruzados Gang or the Russian Mafia?" Rebecca's head pounded from stress and exhaustion. It just kept getting worse with each passing day.

"I don't know. The message is confusing."

Another knock cut through the quiet, causing Rebecca to flinch. She stiffened.

Charlie rose and moved quickly to the door. Before he reached it, Brody pushed it open. The tense set to Charlie's stance relaxed.

"I just came from the hospital. A guard is being put on Thomas, and the number of people who go and in out of his room will be limited." Brody came to Rebecca and touched her shoulder. "You okay?"

"Yes . . . no." The touch of his hand on her calmed the racing of her heart, but weariness still clung to her like a second skin. All she wanted to do was sleep, though she doubted she would be able to.

"The governor has asked me to be in charge of Thomas's and your protection. I'll be working with the U.S. Marshals and the local law enforcement agencies. He wants to send a message to these thugs that in the state of Texas intimidation will not be tolerated. He doesn't want us to go through another trial."

"What does all this mean?"

Brody's gaze linked with hers. "It means I'll be staying at the ranch with you. My niece will take care of my dad. Although he says he doesn't need anyone to look in on him, I'll feel better if someone does. Samantha won't mind."

"I can't have that. You came back to San Antonio to be with him and take care of him. Do you think he would mind coming to the ranch?"

Brody grinned. "Dad? I don't think he'd mind at all, especially since he loves Hattie's cooking. He'll think he's on vacation. He doesn't have to eat any of my food for a while. Will Tory be all right with it?"

"You'll be there for everyone's protection. I can't imagine her minding. Don't worry. Half the house is mine, not that I think we'll be drawing a line down the middle and confining you to only that half of the house."

Brody threw back his head and laughed. "That would be interesting." He turned his attention to Charlie. "I've talked with your captain. We're forming a task force concerning the targeting of the judge and the apparent connection to the trial. I specifically asked for you. Are you okay with that?"

"It would have been hard to keep me off the task force."

"Good. We need to find the driver of the pickup and see if there's a connection to either the gang or the mafia. Also we need to find where the flowers came from."

"Not to mention who the finger belongs to." Charlie started for the door. "A Blooms and Such box was used to send the dead roses to Judge Morgan. The flower shop didn't know anything about it. I'll try them first. Good thing I'm not married. It looks like a long evening ahead."

"Also Detective Zed Moore is at the hospital going through the security tapes to see if he can find the perpetrator behind the bouquet of flowers."

As Charlie left, Laura entered Rebecca's office, blushing as she passed the detective, and mumbled a few words Rebecca couldn't hear. She hid her smile behind the hand that she rubbed across her chin.

"I'm sorry to interrupt your meeting, but before I go home, I wanted you to know that your sister-in-law called. She was extremely upset and needed to make sure you stop by the hospital before going to the ranch."

"When did she call?"

"Right before I took the papers over to the DA's office before he left for the weekend."

"Thanks." Since Laura was focused on Brody—rather blatantly—Rebecca coughed and decided to appease her law clerk's curiosity. "Laura Melton, this is Texas Ranger Brody Calhoun, an old friend."

"It's so good to meet you finally," Laura said, pumping his arm up and down in a handshake. "I've heard Judge Morgan mention you."

One of his dark eyebrows rose. "She's talked about you, too. Maybe we should get together and compare notes." He winked at her.

Laura grinned and ducked her head, her cheeks flaming. "Do you want me to meet you at your church on Sunday?"

"Yes, how about ten forty-five? Service is at eleven," Rebecca answered.

"I'll be there. If your plans change, just let me know and I can go another time. It was nice meeting you, Ranger Calhoun. I'm heading home for an evening of old movies and popcorn."

When Rebecca and Brody were alone in the office, she said, "I'll get my things, then we need to go to the hospital. You just came from there. Do you know what Tory wants? Did something else go wrong that Detective Nelson didn't know about?"

"I hope not. When I left, Tory was sitting in Thomas's room, huddled on the couch with a blanket. I asked the nurse to check on her when she looked in on Thomas. Tory seemed exhausted. About how you look."

"Thanks. I'm glad to know I look the way I feel." She made her way to the closet to grab her purse and umbrella. The weather forecast had predicted rain, but it hadn't come. Dry, as usual. Not even the weather was cooperating lately. The area needed the rain.

Brody opened the door for her. "After we go to the hospital, do you mind if I stop by my house and see about bringing Dad to the ranch?"

"No. Maybe we can take him something to eat. Hattie will have fed the girls by the time we get to the ranch. They might even be in bed by then. They had been sleeping a lot lately, but Kim is starting to have nightmares. She was up twice last night. I didn't get much sleep either."

"Up with her?"

"Yes. In fact, the second time she got up I had her come in and sleep in my room with me."

"I'm glad your nieces have you."

"Thomas and the girls are my only family, other than distant relatives I don't see much."

"It seems like the governor is on top of your situation."

"Since he became governor, we haven't stayed in touch as much. Foster is destined for a great future. He has what it takes to go all the way."

"President of the United States?"

"I think so." At the elevator, Rebecca punched the down button while Brody and Deputy U. S. Marshal Wentworth followed her into the elevator, which took them to the lower level.

The marshal escorted her to Brody's SUV, then said, "I'll see you, Judge Morgan."

As per a Memorandum of Understanding signed between the agencies, Brody handled the protection detail during the night while the U.S. Marshals took the detail during the day.

Inside Brody's car, Rebecca laid her head against the cushion and closed her eyes. The throbbing ache behind her eyes still pulsated through her skull. She sighed.

"A bad day with the trial?" Brody switched on the engine and pulled out of the parking space.

"What do you think?"

"I think when this trial is over you should take a month-long vacation on some beach, where the only thing you have to do is turn over to tan the other side."

"Sounds wonderful. I haven't had a real vacation in years. Since before Garrett was killed. He always insisted on going somewhere away from here once a year."

"Why haven't you taken a vacation?"

"Work. The court docket is overcrowded as it is."

"As a judge you don't get vacation time?"

"Well, yes. I have taken long weekends to spend time at the ranch. But there was no reason to go away by myself." She couldn't bring herself to do that. She found work kept the demons at bay, but lately her work pace had been catching up with her. She should consider Brody's suggestion once the Petrov trial was over.

"How about with a friend?"

"Maybe I'll see if Laura would like to go somewhere after the trial. She's been putting in extra-long hours lately. But a lot of it will depend on Thomas."

"I have no concrete evidence pointing to Thomas's accident being anything but that, but I'm treating it as though it could have been intentional, especially in light of your near-miss and the flowers delivered to him today."

"I hope my being the judge on the Petrov trial isn't the reason Thomas is lying in a coma in the hospital. I—I . . ." Her words stumbled to a halt. The very thought dragged her down into a dark abyss she might not be able to claw her way out of.

"I hope not either. But you've got a reputation for being tough on crime. Must be your prosecutor's background. There are judges Petrov could have on his case who would make it easier for him to walk away without a conviction."

Brody wasn't telling her something she hadn't already thought of. She had been eager to prove the system worked— that people like Petrov wouldn't get away with murder. Putting herself in danger was one thing, but at the cost of harm to a loved one? A tremor rippled through her.

"When I found out that you would preside over the trial, I applauded your selection at the same time I dreaded it for you. These kinds of trials are hard on everyone."

"I know. As a prosecutor, I wanted cases like Petrov's, but when I was through, I was totally drained for weeks. Poor Garrett. He had to put up with me and my moods."

"I'm sure he didn't mind. It comes with the territory when you marry a dedicated prosecutor or judge."

"No, he didn't mind. He saw what I did as completing his job as a police officer. Nothing is worse than seeing someone guilty go free to prey on others."

She remembered Garrett's frustration when that happened, and she had pledged that when she was a judge she would do her best to put the guilty away as a tribute to her husband. Sometimes her hands were tied—when there wasn't enough evidence to convict, for example—but she never wanted to see a criminal go free because of a technicality.

Ten minutes later, Rebecca stepped off the elevator and walked toward Thomas's private room, complete with a police officer standing guard. The sight both comforted her and upset her. He had done nothing wrong but be her brother. She hoped the person who sent her flowers only did the same with her brother to mess with her mind—not because he had a vendetta against him, too.

When Rebecca went in to see Thomas and find out what Tory needed, her heart ached and her throat felt parched. The idea she might be responsible for this tore a hole through her stomach.

Guilt riddled, she stared at her brother for a long moment, repeating all the prayers she'd uttered today. His battered face—mostly on each side as though it had been tossed back and forth across the ground—would haunt her and was now added to the picture of Garrett's last minutes before he slipped away from her.

"Rebecca, where have you been?" Tory rose, the blanket around her falling to the floor. "Did you hear what happened here? Some maniac was in Thomas's room." Her voice was pitched high, which only reinforced Rebecca's assessment of how fragile her sister-in-law was at the moment.

She made her way to Tory and gathered her close. "Yes, but he's got a police officer outside the door and an order for restricted visitors. Only the immediate family."

Tory pushed away. "But is that enough?"

Brody moved toward them. "The officer knows which staff has access to this room. All others will not be allowed in without my approval."

"How could this happen here? Why to Thomas? I thought his injuries were an accident." Tory stepped back farther from

Rebecca, waving her arm wildly toward her husband. "Did someone try to kill him?"

"We don't know. There is no evidence that points to anything but an accident." Rebecca consciously lowered her voice to a calm level, repeating almost in a rote tone what she was trying to convince herself was the truth.

"Who would have done this? Everybody likes him." Her shoulders hunched, Tory folded her arms across her chest and stuck her hands under her armpits.

"We don't know."

"You don't know anything," Tory retorted in such a savage voice that Rebecca backed away.

Anger highlighted the dark shadows under Tory's eyes, then suddenly her expression dissolved into a pain-filled one. "I'm sorry. You aren't to blame for what's happened to Thomas." She pulled her fingers through the long strands of her hair, almost as if she were going to tear it out. "I need rest."

Rebecca tried to ignore what her sister-in-law had said. She tried to tell herself that no one knew for certain what was going on with Thomas. "I agree, Tory. You need to come home with us. I don't want you to drive as tired as you are."

"What about my car?"

"I'll bring you back tomorrow when the girls come to see their father."

"No, I'll bring you both back here tomorrow. No driving by yourself until we figure out what's going on." Brody moved to Rebecca's side, a look of sympathy on his face as though he knew what she was feeling—guilt.

"Why do I need a guard? What is going on here?"

"It's possible someone is targeting my family because I'm the judge on the Petrov trial."

Tory's eyes widened until that was all Rebecca could focus on. "You are the reason?"

"I don't know, but it's better to be safe than sorry." The words she uttered to her sister-in-law did nothing to appease the guilt she was feeling. "You shouldn't stay here all the time. When Thomas wakes up, he's going to need you to be there for him." Rebecca took Brody's hand, needing the connection at the moment.

The color leached from Tory's face. She opened her mouth, then snapped it closed. A half a minute later she finally said, "I need to be here. I want to be here when he does wake up."

"The staff will let us know."

Tory shook her head over and over. "No, I'll be fine. I know you need to be at the ranch so you can be there for the girls." She lowered her gaze to the floor between them. "I'm sorry I made it sound like you brought all this on Thomas, on us."

The apology only reinforced Rebecca's fear about what she might have caused. "How about we talk it over tomorrow? Let's go home."

Tory stared vacantly at the foot of the bed, chewing on her bottom lip. "Okay. I do need some sleep. The doctor gave me something to help." Her glistening gaze swept to Brody. "But if someone did do this to Thomas, I want you to find him."

"I will. That's a promise."

While Tory gathered her sweater and purse, Rebecca paused at Thomas's side and kissed the small patch of his cheek that was not scraped or bandaged. "I love you, Tommy. I'm so sorry you're lying here. Please wake up. I pray every day for you." *Please, Lord, take this guilt away.*

As they left through the main entrance of the hospital, Rebecca spotted Rob entering through the sliding glass doors. Smiling, she caught the young man's attention. "What are you doing here? Visiting someone?"

His gaze skimmed over Brody and Tory before it settled on Rebecca. "A friend. An accident with a bull. The rodeo can be brutal on a person's body."

"Rob, this is my sister-in-law, Tory Sinclair."

Touching the brim of his cowboy hat, he nodded at Tory, then said, "What are y'all doing here?"

"My brother was in an accident."

"Rob is the one who pushed me out of the way of the pickup Monday," Rebecca said to Tory.

"Kim told me all about it. You're her hero. I don't know what I would have done if either Kim or Rebecca had been hurt, too. If you stay long in San Antonio, you should come out to the ranch. I know Kim would love to see you again."

"Mrs. Sinclair, that's right neighborly, but I'll probably not be around much longer. Have a nice evening, folks." Rob sauntered into the lobby.

"He seems like a nice young man," Tory said as she went outside.

"He's one of those guys who plays down what he did. But I'm sure grateful." If he hadn't acted, Rebecca might have been in the hospital, like her brother, or worse.

⊷⊶

"Thanks, Aunt Becky, for letting me sleep in here." Kim threw her arms around Rebecca's neck and kissed her cheek. "I love you."

"I love you, honey." She tucked her niece in and smoothed her hair away from her face. "I'm going to check to make sure everyone has what they need, but I'll be back later. Are you okay with that?"

Kim hugged her ratty stuffed polar bear against her chest and curled up. "Yep."

"If you need me, I'll be downstairs making sure Brody and his dad get settled in."

"I like them being here. Mr. Calhoun's dad is funny."

"Did you say your prayers before I came in?"

She nodded. "I asked God to watch over Dad, you, Aubrey, Hattie, Tory, and Mr. Clark."

"Mr. Clark? We saw him tonight at the hospital."

"You did? I wish I could have been there to thank him. Something bad could have happened to you."

"It didn't. You don't need to worry about me. Good night, honey."

As Rebecca reached the door, Kim called out, "It's a good thing that Dad is in his own room, isn't it?"

With her hand on the overhead light switch, Rebecca glanced back at her niece and said, "Yes, very good. Before we know it, he'll be home." Then she flipped the light off and left.

In the upstairs hallway, she savored the quiet now that Kim and Aubrey were in bed. If only she could feel the peace she so desired. But since Thomas's accident—or whatever it was—even when praying she hadn't experienced the peace she usually did when spending time with the Lord. She was losing her focus, her thoughts always going to the trial and to her brother.

And she still had to see Jake tonight. She'd had little time this week to find out what was happening concerning the cattle rustling. Glancing at her watch, she couldn't believe it was only nine. It felt like midnight. Between the trial, spending time at the hospital, and being with the girls, time crawled by.

Trudging toward the staircase, she breathed deeply, over and over, but the tension that knotted her shoulders and neck wouldn't release her. By the time she came into the den, Jake had joined Brody and his dad. Their voices went silent when she appeared.

She put her hand on her waist. "Okay, what has happened?"

Jake dropped his gaze, rubbing his forefingers against his thumbs.

"There's been another incident of cattle rustling. At the Double T Ranch." Brody sat forward, elbows on his thighs, hands clasped.

Rebecca collapsed onto the couch next to him. "How many? When?"

His jaw clenched, Jake stared into her eyes. "Probably sometime last night. They didn't have a chance to check all their herds until late this afternoon. Sheriff Overstreet called me a while ago. Around a hundred cattle. Two semis. It looks like the same outfit that stole ours."

"But we haven't lost any more cattle?"

"No, I've added some men on to keep an eye out, especially at night."

"What's the sheriff doing?"

"Doubling the patrol cars on the roads around here. They'll be stopping any semis they don't recognize and checking for cattle."

"The rustlers would be stupid to stay now," Sean said.

"The only good thing about this is that it means it isn't connected to the Petrov trial. They wouldn't bother stealing from another ranch. They would want me to know it was them making my life difficult." *Like the flowers.*

Jake swung his attention from Rebecca to Brody. "You think what has been happening is connected to the Russian Mafia?"

Brody lifted his shoulder. "It's a possibility we have to consider. The task force I'm on is looking into the situation." Touching Rebecca's arm, he locked gazes with her. "That means keeping you safe so we can put this Petrov away for a long time."

"If the witnesses aren't scared away. They made it through one trial, but the longer it takes, the more opportunities someone will have to get to them. Already one has gone missing."

Sean pushed to his feet. "I think the girls have it right. Time for bed for me, too. Jake, if you need any help with the rustling situation, I'd be glad to give you any I can, especially with security issues."

"Thanks, Sean. We'll talk tomorrow." Jake waited until the sound of Sean's footsteps had faded before he continued. "Is it okay if your dad helps? I'd like him to look over what I've done. See if he sees any flaws in my security measures."

"If I said no, he'd try anyway. The worst part of his heart attack is the recovery period, where he's had to curtail his activities. After his retirement, he was doing some consulting work to tighten security at several businesses. So all I ask is to keep him from overextending himself as much as you can. I realize he can be a stubborn man."

"So you came by that honestly," Rebecca said with a laugh.

Brody covered her hand on the couch between them. "Stubbornness can be a good thing. I don't give up when there's something that has to be done. I think of my stubbornness as perseverance."

"Like a dog guarding his bone?" The warmth of his palm against the back of her hand spread up her arm and throughout her body.

Jake chuckled. "I think I'll leave you two to argue which is it, stubbornness or perseverance. I'll keep an eye on your dad, Brody. See y'all tomorrow."

When her foreman left the den, silence descended. The sound of the Big Ben clock on the mantle resonated through the room. She relaxed back against the cushion, the long day felt in every taut muscle. "I'm glad you're here. I feel safe with you." As she said those unexpected words, she realized she did feel safe whenever Brody was around, and lately that was a nice feeling to have. Even the Deputy U.S. Marshal protecting her didn't give her that sense of safety. Although she was sure he was good at his job, she didn't really know that deep down. She did with Brody.

He lounged back, his arm inches from hers. "I'm glad you're okay with me being here."

"I'm not knocking Randall and the other marshals, but I know what you've done. The cases you've worked on. The people you've protected."

"You do?"

"Yes. Thomas was always talking about your exploits. You've protected some important people."

"I was trained for situations where it was called for. I've become one of the Texas Rangers with expertise in protecting dignitaries. In a few cases I've worked, I needed to oversee the protection detail, usually with U. S. Marshals or local police officers or deputies."

"I'm glad we're friends. It makes it easier for me."

He tensed.

"What's wrong?"

"It makes it harder for me. If something happened to you, Thomas would never forgive me. Not to mention that the governor wouldn't be too happy either."

"I guess you've got a point. I promise I'll follow your directions. I won't run off by myself or try to slip the detail." She lowered her voice. "I won't blame you for what others do."

He turned toward her, the look in his eyes intense, all-encompassing. "I've known you since we were children. If anything happens to you, I won't forgive myself."

"But I'd much rather have you overseeing my protection than some stranger. That's because I have known you *forever*. I know what type of person you are. You're a detail person, and I have a feeling that can come in handy when providing security."

One corner of his mouth quirked. "A few times."

"I wonder if that's why Thomas had his accident. He's always looking at the big picture. Dives into a situation without regard to the details. He probably saw the calf down in the gully, panicking, and all he could focus on was getting the animal up. Mix that with trying to hurry and get back for the party. I can see it the more I think about it."

"You sound like you are trying to convince yourself it was an accident."

"You said there is no concrete evidence saying otherwise."

"No, there isn't, but something is still nagging me, especially with what happened today at the hospital."

"But that was a message for me. Like the one they sent me when the trial began. But now we know what was really behind it. Charlie hasn't said if he discovered anything at the Blooms and Such. Do you know? A dead end?"

"They're missing a couple of boxes, some roses and a delivery uniform. But this didn't happen until the middle of this week. After you received the flowers."

"No leads on who?"

"Nothing. It was a professional job, which was strange to the officer investigating it considering what little was taken. The money wasn't stolen."

"Why a delivery uniform?" A throbbing behind her eyes made it difficult to comprehend all that was occurring.

"On the security feed at the hospital, the only person seen was a medium-sized man with a ball cap, pulled low, wearing a brown uniform going into that room carrying a long white box."

"Did the officer looking at the tape ever see a face?" Lots of questions—no answers. Rebecca rubbed her temples with her fingertips, but the ache continued to pulsate against her skull.

"No, not on that tape, or on any of the tapes in the hospital. He was avoiding the cameras."

"Have you discovered anything about who was driving the pickup?"

"We've got the man's composite from the one witness, and we're circulating it, especially in the area where the truck was abandoned. Nothing so far."

She angled her body so she was completely facing him, with one leg drawn up on the couch. "What did he look like? Can I see a picture of him? In case I've seen him around."

"I have it on my phone." He unclipped it from his belt, found the photo, and gave her his cellphone.

Rebecca studied the man, probably in his late twenties, with short brown hair, a scar on his right cheek, small eyes, and a nose that must have been broken at some time. "This is pretty detailed."

"The man is vigilant about what's going on in his neighborhood. He kept talking about the young punks who were ruining the streets."

"So many people won't come forward, which makes it hard for the police to crack down on those young punks. I'm glad he did."

"I haven't released the man's name. I'm protecting his identity."

"What if it comes to trial?"

"We'll build a case without him. All he really saw was this man getting out of the stolen pickup. We wouldn't get far with that as our only evidence. There were no fingerprints to back up the man's description of the would-be assailant."

"True. If I were the prosecutor, I wouldn't go to trial on that." She noticed the crinkles at the sides of his eyes, as if he smiled a lot. His dark eyelashes were long, framing his gray eyes and highlighting their silvery color.

"Exactly. But hopefully, once we ID this man, we can build a case."

It took her a few seconds to realize he'd said something to her. So entranced by his perfectly formed mouth, the lips not too full or too thin, she wouldn't have known he was speaking if she hadn't seen it moving. She dropped her gaze to the cleft in his chin. "Do you think he's part of the Russian Mafia?"

"I have a couple of police officers who work in the gang division checking with their resources, but none of them recognize the man."

"Then it could have been random. Like Rob said, someone drunk or on drugs and behind the wheel of the truck. We've seen that enough times."

"I investigated my share of car wrecks as a highway patrol officer."

Thomas had kept her informed of what Brody was doing through the years, but she really didn't know a lot. She'd used to know so much about him. That he could outride her, out-shoot her, but couldn't beat her at a game of chess. "What is it about your job that you like the most?" She thought she knew the answer, but she wanted to find out if she was right.

"To help people in need."

"For years I thought you would become a veterinarian, then suddenly you decided to join the San Antonio Police Department. That surprised me." She'd been in her second year of college when Brody graduated and made the announcement to Thomas and her. "I thought you didn't want to do what your dad did."

"I changed my mind. I love animals, but I thought I could make the most difference being a police officer." He laid his arm along the back of the couch.

"Then why didn't you stay with the police in San Antonio?" He'd been so much like her, wanting to help others, especially with getting justice.

"Because I wanted to be a Texas Ranger. You do that by becoming a Texas Highway Patrol officer."

"Why that?"

"Because Dad had tried several times and didn't make it. Finally, he quit being a Highway Patrol officer and joined the San Antonio Police Department, but I don't think he was ever satisfied with himself for not making it. I wanted to do it for him." He grinned. "And because as a kid I was always the Texas Ranger when Thomas and I played cops and robbers."

"Ah, I vaguely remember that. You tried to tie me up to a tree once."

"I was capturing the bad guy—girl." His eyes sparkled with amusement. "Of course, you were the only person around we could use as the robber."

"Until Kenny moved close."

"Yeah, poor Kenny. We never let him be the cop."

Reminiscing with Brody brought back some fond memories. He and Thomas had barely tolerated her presence, but usually they would include her in whatever game they played. Until they became teenage boys—everything changed then. They started going their separate ways. Then she married Garrett, and Brody moved away to Amarillo. And now, ten years later, they were together again—playing cops and robbers, sort of. But in this case she was the victim—not a role she wanted to play.

"I want my life back. I want Thomas to wake up tomorrow, tell you what happened, and leave the hospital as soon as possible."

His hand slid down the back cushion to grasp her shoulder. "I know. You and I have both dealt with many people whose lives were disrupted by a crime or an accident."

"Now I can sympathize with them because I've walked in their shoes? Is that why the Lord is doing this?"

"Whoa. Where did that come from?"

"From my anger. I've prayed for the past week, and nothing has changed. Thomas is still in a coma."

"But he's alive. A prayer being answered doesn't happen on our time schedule."

"So I can't rail at the Lord for what's happening?"

"Yes, you can. He wants us to come to Him with the good, the bad, and the ugly. He won't love us any less if we are angry with Him. But when this is all over with, you might want to ask yourself what insight you gained from this ordeal."

"Most of the time I'm able to manage my anger, but sometimes it slips out."

"Then let it. Do you think when you're managing it that you're keeping it from God? He knows everything and still loves us regardless."

"How have you kept your faith so strong? You've had to have seen some terrible things."

He kneaded her taut shoulder muscles with his fingertips. "Because if I didn't, I wouldn't be able to deal with those terrible things. And someone has to."

The relief from his massage robbed her of a reply. His strong hand worked the tension out of her, and she closed her eyes to savor it for a moment.

"Turn around."

Her eyes popped open. "What?"

"Turn around. I'd like to rub both your shoulders. They're very tense."

"This is where my stress settles in my body. I have a special chair to sit in when I'm in the courtroom. One that's comfortable to sit in for eight hours at a stretch. That has helped some."

Brody worked his fingers into the muscles along her shoulders and at the base of her neck. All she wanted to do was lean back into him and let him support her.

"You're hired," she whispered, contentment drenching each word.

Close to her ear, he said in a husky voice, "All you have to do is ask me. I'd be glad to accommodate you."

His lazy drawl heightened her awareness of him—his hands massaging her shoulders, his breath tickling her neck, his scent, with a hint of lime, wafting toward her. For a few moments she surrendered herself to the pure, pleasurable sensations—as knot after knot unraveled.

Her eyelids started to close until the blast of his cellphone jerked her straight up.

"Sorry." He answered the call. "Calhoun." As he listened to the person on the other end, his relaxed expression tightened into a tense one. "I'll be there."

When he disconnected the call, Rebecca twisted toward him. "Where are you going?"

"The suspected driver of the white pickup has been found."

"Oh, good. That's a break."

"Dead."

8

"Dead! How? Where?" Rebecca balled her hands, any relaxation she'd enjoyed while Brody had been kneading her shoulders was gone.

"Interestingly, in the middle of the area the Russians have moved into. He was propped up against the back door of one of their businesses."

"A message to them. Great. Now I'm being protected by the Dos Huesos Cruzados Gang. Just what I want—to be the reason there's more violence. Possibly more innocent people being killed."

Brody stood. "I'll let Ranger Parker know I'm leaving for a couple of hours so he'll post someone inside."

"We've got to stop this. Now the Russians will seek revenge. Then the Dos Huesos Cruzados Gang will retaliate."

"I know, and it doesn't mean they'll stop coming after you. But what really has me interested is why they went after the guy. It's not like the Dos Huesos Cruzados Gang has any love for the authorities."

"Especially with my stance on crime." She rose, stretching and rolling her shoulders. "I'll wait up for you. I want to know what happened."

"I'll fill you in tomorrow morning. It may be late before I get back here. You know how crime scenes can be. I'm meeting Charlie over there. You need your rest."

"But this is about me. I want—"

He put his forefinger over her mouth. "It may be, but if you don't take care of yourself, you'll be no good for your family or for the trial." He tugged her toward him and kissed her forehead. "Go to bed, Rebecca."

Trying not to react to the casual touch of his lips on her brow, she leaned back and fixed her gaze on his. "If I wasn't so tired, I'd argue with you."

"So all I have to do is get you exhausted to get you to agree with me?"

"Don't bet on it." She stepped back, her heart thumping against her chest. The tenderness in the gesture wrecked her composure, and the last thing she wanted him to see was how much the kiss—if a person could call it that—had affected her.

When he left, she made her way up the stairs, lured by the rest she hoped she could get. But when she opened her bedroom door, a scream split the air.

⌘

Careful not to breathe too deeply of the odor of death, Brody approached the crime scene near the back of the pawnshop door. A man—one who fit the description their witness had given the sketch artist—sat slumped against the tan clapboard with a large symbol of the skull and crossbones spray-painted nearby, one of its black lines going over the man's body as though to shout to the world the murder and the symbol were tied together. Taunting whoever saw it.

The glare of the spotlights illuminated the terror on the victim's face. His gutted remains announced the brutality of the murder. It fit others he'd seen committed by the Dos Huesos Cruzados Gang. But what riveted his attention was the fact the victim was missing his left forefinger. Probably the one that was delivered to Thomas's hospital room in the dead roses.

Charlie spotted Brody and he pointed to the ground behind some trashcans. "Someone threw up here recently and tried to clean it up. Didn't quite succeed or was scared away before he could finish."

Remnants of vomit splattered the asphalt, seeping into the cracked surface. "Someone found the victim. Who reported it? It could be that person, especially if it was someone who is not involved in the mafia and isn't used to the violence."

"It was an anonymous 911 call. According to the medical examiner over there, the man hasn't been dead long."

"Someone who witnessed the murder?"

"Whoever did this was either fearless to do it on the doorstep of the Russian Mafia or an idiot and who doesn't realize how close he came to being caught."

"Maybe he had no choice."

"An initiation? Could be." Charlie waved to the crime scene tech to take care of the vomit. "I'm having the leaders of the two groups brought in. I wouldn't put it past the Russians to make a statement about this guy failing to do the job he was sent to do and also pointing a finger at their rivals."

"When will the leaders be at the station?"

"One's already there. Serpiente was quite easy to find. Get this, the officers who picked him up said he was surprised."

"Yeah. Surprised he was found so soon. Or maybe he was practicing his acting skills."

"Whichever, let's have a little talk with him and Sasha Alexandrov. I have officers canvassing the area, not that I expect much."

"Who owns the pawnshop?"

"Alexandrov. You know, it was rumored that he was actually the killer of the man Petrov is on trial for."

"So Petrov might be a fall guy."

"Yes, and his brother-in-law."

"Wonder what that's doing for Alexandrov's family life?"

As Brody headed back to his SUV, the stench of blood and garbage infused the air to a gagging point. It didn't matter how many times he'd been to a violent crime scene, he couldn't get the smell of death out of his mind for hours. This would be no different.

Rebecca flew through the doorway to her bedroom, quickly found the light switch, and flipped it on.

Kim sat straight up in bed, her eyes wide, a pallor to her face, her long brown hair a wild tangle about her head.

Rebecca rushed to the bed and scooped the child up. "Another nightmare?"

"No, I thought someone was in the room."

"I didn't see anyone leaving." Rebecca smoothed her niece's hair back behind her ears and then cupped her head. "Are you sure it wasn't a bad dream and you woke up thinking it had really happened?"

Kim blinked rapidly, confusion skittering across her face. Her forehead scrunched. "I didn't think so." She leaned around Rebecca and surveyed the bedroom. "I guess it was a bad dream. It seemed so real."

"I know it can. Occasionally I think the phone is ringing, and I wake up. But it isn't. And yet it seems so real to me. I even check caller ID to make sure someone hasn't called."

Kim threw her arms around Rebecca and plastered herself against her. "Are you coming to bed?"

"Yes. You won't be alone. Okay?"

Her niece nodded against Rebecca's chest.

She kissed the top of Kim's head. "I'll tuck you in. I'm going into the bathroom to get ready. I'll leave the door partway open. If you need me, let me know."

When Kim settled down in the bed again, Rebecca stared at the child, who was not taking her dad's injury well. She and Thomas were very close. She often followed her father around the ranch, trying to learn how to run it. She was determined to run the ranch when she grew up. Rebecca's throat swelled. As tough as Kim tried to act, she wasn't. She held everything inside until it erupted out.

"I'm here for you, honey," Rebecca murmured and then strode toward the bathroom.

She gripped the counter's edge and leaned forward to examine her image in the mirror. Blue eyes with a tired vacancy peered back at her. Her hair framed her pale face in wild disarray from repeatedly running her fingers through it.

What a day! More than a few times during the trial she'd discovered Petrov drilling her with an intense gaze meant to unnerve her. She'd steeled herself and returned his look, but inside, her muscles knotted and her stomach roiled. All she could think about was what that man was responsible for. A member of the jury from the first trial was still missing.

Suddenly a thought struck her full force in the chest, snatching her breath. *What if the finger in the bouquet box belonged to the missing juror? Or belonged to the missing witness who had slipped away from the police protecting him earlier today?*

⸱⸱⸱

Lounging against the wall in the interview room at the police station, Brody crossed his arms over his chest and lowered his head as he stared at Serpiente while Charlie interrogated the leader of the Dos Huesos Cruzados Gang, who was slouching, with one arm slung over the back of the chair.

"I'm gonna do you a favor, Dee-tect-ive Nel-son," the black-haired man with most of his visible body tattooed said, a taunt behind each word.

"You're going to confess to one of the unsolved murders?"

Serpiente smiled, slowly revealing a front tooth with a diamond in it—or at least something that was supposed to look like one. Knowing the illegal activities attributed to his gang, Brody didn't doubt it was real. The man's outfit of frayed jeans and a white sleeveless T-shirt gave no indication that he ran a successful gang of thugs who were into anything that could turn a profit—from drugs to assassinations.

"My good dee-tect-ive, I was thinking I'd chat with you without my highly successful lawyer here, since I have nothing to hide."

"So you do think some of the time." The sneer in Charlie's voice made Brody grin. "A dead body was found by the back door of Alexandrov's pawnshop."

"Man, why would anyone risk dropping a body off at the door of the pawnshop? Pure *loco*, if you ask me." The expression on the gang leader's face seemed genuinely confused.

"Somebody did, so why would they?"

Serpiente examined his fingernails, pushing his cuticles back. "*Loco*, as I said. I'm just a businessman with some car shops. I don't know why you think I know anything about a murder."

"Murder? I didn't say that. All I said was that there was a dead body in the alley."

"Oh, my mistake. If he wasn't murdered, then why am I here?" His almost black eyes bore into Charlie then fell on Brody. He straightened, put his hands on the table, and stood. "I'll be going then."

"Sit." Brody came forward and positioned himself across from the gang leader. His gaze bored into the man, in a silent skirmish between them. "You're a person of interest in this murder."

Serpiente bent across the table, his eyes narrowing. "Book me or let me go. I know nothing about this murder." He started for the door. "I have an alibi."

"You do?" Brody didn't move, although the man was at the door, his hand on the knob. "How do you know when it happened? We don't even know that yet."

"Because I've been with—my employees at the shop for the past half a day since noon. I know for a fact that body hasn't been there long. There is no way it could have been. Alexandrov knows what happens on that street."

"So you think he killed the man and placed him at his own back door?"

Serpiente shrugged. "I would never do something like that, but the man is *estupido*. Why else did he come to San Antonio, my town?"

"To move in on your territory. Unless you sent him an invitation."

Serpiente punched his fist into the door, the sound reverberating through the small room. Turning to face Brody, he pointed his finger at him. "They're scum. They've made a big mistake." Anger slashing across his face, he moved a couple of feet closer to Brody. "But I'm in a good mood today. One of Alexandrov's *esbirros* has been taken care of by a good Samaritan. If I meet the man, I'll give him a reward."

As the gang leader turned to leave the room, Brody said, "You'd better get some ice for your hand. We wouldn't want it to swell."

Serpiente kept walking. Brody and Charlie followed him. At the end of the corridor, a police officer with a man in his early forties rounded the corner, another, younger man right behind him. Serpiente came to a halt, his chest puffing out, his hands clenched at his sides.

"I'll escort Serpiente out of the station. You take Alexandrov." Brody strode to the gang leader and gestured toward the exit.

Alexandrov slowed his step when he neared Serpiente. Brody tensed, poised to act if he needed to. The rage on the Russian's face homed in on the gang leader with such force Brody was sure the two would have killed each other if they weren't in a police station, unarmed.

"You will not get away with murdering one of my men," Alexandrov muttered, then kept going to the interview room.

"*Estupido.*" Serpiente started toward the exit. "He must be guilty. He brought his lawyer."

When Brody returned to the interview room, he couldn't shake the feeling that the Dos Huesos Cruzados Gang wasn't responsible for the dead man in the alley behind the pawnshop. By the time Alexandrov left, Brody felt something wasn't right about the whole situation, and yet he couldn't figure out what was bothering him.

"That was certainly fruitful," Charlie said, coming back into the room after escorting the mafia leader out.

"It would have been nice if one had confessed, but we knew that wouldn't happen. From the show in the hallway, though, Alexandrov thinks it's Serpiente." Brody stared at the place where Alexandrov and his lawyer had sat a few minutes ago.

"So do I."

"I'm not so convinced. Why would Serpiente care about Rebecca? Besides, he seemed surprised by this death. I know he's got a reputation in town, but I don't think it includes acting."

"Well, we *know* Alexandrov doesn't care about Judge Morgan. So why would he kill his own man and prop him up behind his pawnshop? If he had a beef with the man, I don't see him leaving the guy in the alley, especially with the heat Alexandrov is under right now."

"In the hall he said to Serpiente something about murdering one of his men, but in the interview room, he acted like he didn't know the man when you showed him a picture of the dead guy."

"Maybe he thought it was one of his men until I showed him the picture. I suppose the man might not be involved with the Russians, or maybe Alexandrov doesn't know everyone working for him."

"If he doesn't know now, he will by tomorrow. But then he might not be telling us the truth. He could know who the man is but not want us to know. It's not like he wants to make our life easier. Both groups are under a lot of scrutiny." Brody glanced at his watch, noting how late it was. He hoped Rebecca had gone to bed and wasn't waiting up for him. She needed the rest; he did, too. "If they're smart, they'll both lie low for a while."

"But they haven't necessarily been smart in the past."

"Then they'll make a mistake, and we'll be there."

"That hasn't been the problem. We've caught them. They just aren't getting convicted. At least the ones in positions of power."

"Petrov can be our start. We need to run DNA on the victim to see if it matches our finger from Thomas's room." Brody crossed to the interview room door. "I'm heading to the ranch. Let me know what forensics says about the crime scene."

"You'll be the first."

Outside, Brody walked toward his SUV, fishing for his key and then clicking the remote to start the engine.

An explosion rocked the parking lot. A mushroom of fire shot up into the sky. The blast knocked Brody back. He slammed into the asphalt like a ball being flung to the ground.

9

The air swooshed out of Brody as he struck the pavement next to the police station parking lot. Bits and pieces of what had been his SUV pelted the area around him. A jolt of pain flashed through his body. His ears rang. Mind swirling, he rolled over to push himself to his feet. Halfway up, the world spun before him. He closed his eyes and sank to the asphalt.

Someone knelt next to him and placed an arm on his back. He jerked away, going for his gun. Charlie's grim face swam into his vision. The detective's lips were moving, but Brody could barely hear what he was saying. Brody pointed to his ears.

Charlie bobbed his head once, then stood as more people invaded the parking lot.

Brody's arm throbbed. He looked down and saw a tear in his long-sleeved shirt, with blood spreading outward from it.

Charlie bent down and snagged his attention with a note that said, "Okay?"

He nodded. Although disoriented, he'd sustained worse injuries than a gash on his arm.

Again he tried to stand, needing to find out what was happening. The scent of burning gasoline and the scorched stench of smoke assaulted his senses. A siren penetrated the haze in his brain, and flashing red lights made him dizzy when he looked at them. Turning away, he used the wall of the building to support him as he rose. His rubbery legs barely held him upright, but he managed to remain standing.

While the firefighters swarmed the scene, Charlie assisted him back out of the way. As he moved, his attention was glued to what used to be his SUV, now a ball of fire.

Someone wanted him dead. Because of Rebecca's case?

❧

Not able to sleep more than a few hours, Rebecca finally got up and went downstairs. Something was wrong, beyond what had been going on. She could feel it deep in her bones.

When she put her foot on the tile floor, a Texas Ranger came out of the living room into the foyer. "Is everything all right, Judge Morgan?"

"Couldn't sleep. Has Brody Calhoun returned yet?"

"No, ma'am, not yet. From what I heard from Ranger Parker, Detective Nelson is bringing him back to the ranch."

"Why?"

"His car isn't working."

"Oh," Rebecca started toward the kitchen. "I'm going to make some tea. I can put on a pot of coffee if you would like some."

"That's all right. I'm fine. I'm going to make my rounds in the house."

"I'll be in the kitchen."

Strange. What had happened to Brody's SUV?

After preparing a cup of tea with caffeine because she knew she wouldn't sleep any more tonight, she sat at the table and nursed her drink. She wanted to make sure to tell Brody about who she thought the finger might belong to. To have him run a DNA match.

She spied the calendar on the wall and realized it had only been a week since Thomas's accident. It seemed much longer than that. An eternity. So much had happened—possibly life-changing. The implication of Thomas's injuries left so much up in the air. She couldn't plan anything beyond this moment. She never knew when something would happen and things would go in a different direction.

"Ma'am, Ranger Calhoun and Detective Nelson are arriving," the other Texas Ranger said from the entrance to the kitchen.

"Good." After placing her mug on the table, she made her way toward the foyer.

As the door opened, calmness descended on her. Brody was finally back. In that moment she realized why she had been agitated earlier. He'd been gone longer than she thought he would be. Most of the night. In just a few days she'd come to depend on him to make her feel safe. This surprised her.

Charlie entered first. When Brody came into the entry hall, what calmness she'd experienced fled at the sight of him.

"What happened?" She hurried to Brody's side, noting the bandage around his arm and the scrapes and cuts on his face, hands . . . and where else that she couldn't see? For a few seconds she was flung back to the moment when she found her brother, bloodied and barely hanging on to life.

Brody touched her face, ran his finger along her jawline. "I'm fine. I was checked out and taken care of by a doctor at the hospital." He lifted one corner of his mouth. "Charlie wouldn't bring me home until I agreed to go by Mercy Memorial."

"Why?"

His eyes guarded. "Why, what?"

"Why are you hurt? What happened? You haven't told me a thing."

His gaze slid to the side. "My car blew up."

Rebecca stiffened, then she turned toward the ranger. "Is that what you meant by his car wasn't working? I think it's a tad bit more than that." Turning back to Brody, she continued, "I'll put on some coffee, and you can fill me in on what happened. You left to go to a crime scene, and it sounds like you ended up being in the middle of a new crime scene."

Charlie exchanged glances with Brody. "I'd better head home. I'll be back later."

Rebecca raked her narrow-eyed look from Charlie to the ranger. "You do that. I expect a full report about what happened, and I won't accept anything less than full disclosure from each of you in the future. A car not working is a little different than a car blowing up."

She turned away from Brody and marched toward the kitchen, not even waiting to see if he followed her. Anger vibrated through her. She would not be kept in the dark about any aspect of something that involved her, and she would make that very clear to Brody Calhoun or she would ask her cousin for another ranger to protect her.

But as soon as the thought came to her, she rejected it. She knew Detective Nelson, but she wasn't as comfortable with him as she was with Brody. A stranger coming in would be even worse. And with all that was going on, she needed to feel safe.

Seek Me for your safety, Rebecca. I will always be here for you.

The realization that she'd forgotten the most important One who could give her the peace she was so desperately sought halted her step just inside the kitchen. She bowed her head. *I'm so sorry, Lord. I'm looking for solutions without You. Please guide me in what to do. In how to help Thomas. Keep my family protected. Put these murderers behind bars. I need You.*

Although she didn't hear Brody approach, she felt his presence behind her—it was as though he had the ability to set her nerve endings on fire. She moved a few paces further into the room and swung around to confront Brody, but the words died on her lips when she saw the look on his face.

One of concern. One of—passion. Her pulse quickened. She took a step toward him.

His mask quickly fell into place, and he strode past her toward the stove. The fleeting look caused her to doubt what she thought she saw in his expression. They were friends—childhood friends. Just a week ago they hadn't seen each other in ten years.

She cared for Brody, but he was a cop. Never again. The sight of his injuries only hammered that home. She shook away any feelings she imagined she saw in him and said, "Go sit down. I'll fix the coffee. I may not drink it, but I'm capable of preparing it. Garrett was a heavy coffee drinker like you." Why had she mentioned her deceased husband? To reinforce her determination to never marry another cop?

Brody gave her a look she couldn't decipher, his body held rigidly in place for a long second before he sat at the table. A sigh escaped his lips, and he rolled his shoulders before kneading the back of his neck, as if he hadn't quite shaken off the effects of the bomb blast.

He could have died tonight.

Brody's massage last night intruded into her thoughts, which were spiraling out of control. She latched onto the memory as she spooned the coffee into the basket, and filled the coffeemaker with water, and then switched it on to brew. She couldn't handle Brody dying because of her. She was carrying around enough guilt concerning what was going on lately.

"Okay, it'll be a few minutes before this is ready. You've got time to fill me in on what happened after you left here." She took the chair across from him, needing to put space between them.

"A body was found behind Alexandrov's pawnshop, propped up next to the back door with the Dos Huesos Cruzados's symbol painted around the dead man."

"Who was he?"

"We think he was the man who was driving the white pickup that nearly ran you down. He was missing a forefinger, like the one found in the box of dead roses for Thomas."

The news stunned her, driving all else from her mind for a long moment. It confirmed that she'd placed her brother in danger. Who else was in jeopardy? Brody?

"We'll check the DNA to make sure it belonged to the man in the alley."

"I had a thought tonight that the finger might belong to the missing jury member from the first trial or the witness who left his protection detail."

"Not a bad idea, but I'm 90 percent sure it is the driver of the white truck. We'll know for sure later. Whoever killed him made it appear that the gang murdered him."

"You don't think they did?"

"Not according to Serpiente."

Rebecca wrapped her cold hands around her warm mug. "And you believed him?"

Brody frowned. "I know it sounds crazy, but I do. I don't think his gang killed the man. But what little evidence there is at the scene points to them. Alexandrov certainly believes it. I think Charlie does."

"Then why don't you?"

"A gut feeling is about all I can give you."

Rebecca bolted to her feet and headed for the coffeemaker to pour Brody some coffee. His injuries obviously had addled his brain.

When she brought his mug to him and set it down in front of him, he grabbed her hand. "I'm not crazy. I know that's what you're thinking."

"Explain to me why you aren't."

His eyes widened for a few seconds. Then he chuckled. "I guess I don't blame you. It's the look Serpiente gave me when we were talking about it. It's what the officers who picked him up said. The man was surprised by the news."

"People fake emotions all the time. You know that."

"Yes, and because I'm in the business of figuring out if a person is lying or not, I've gotten quite good at telling the difference. I don't think Serpiente was lying about this. About a lot of other things, but not this."

"Then that leaves Alexandrov. Why would he kill his own man?"

"We don't know who the man is for sure. He might not be Alexandrov's hired gun. And for the record, I do agree that Alexandrov doesn't have a reason to have killed him and staged the body outside his door. It's not like he has to strike terror into the people around him. I think they're sufficiently scared of the man. This wasn't about proving himself to anyone."

"Then what's it about?"

"Good question. I don't have an answer. If I did, I wouldn't be so upset."

"Okay." She took her chair again. "What happened to your SUV?"

"There was a bomb connected to the ignition. When I hit the start button on my key chain, my car exploded. Thankfully without me inside. But I was nearby and was knocked to the pavement. It took a while for the ringing in my ears to stop. At least now I can hear you clearly."

"Where did this happen? At the crime scene?"

"No, the police station parking lot."

"That's bold. That sounds like either the Russians or Dos Huesos Cruzados. You still don't think they are behind the dead guy in the alley?"

"I can't shake the feeling someone is wanting all this to look like it's one of them behind it."

"Why stir up these two groups? They're already at each other's throats. What is accomplished by doing that?"

"I don't have an answer, but we can't rule out that someone else has an agenda here."

"But also you can't rule out that it's one of them doing it."

Brody raised his mug to his mouth and sipped. "No, a good detective has to keep all his options open. So we'll continue to investigate all possibilities. The task force is taking over the murder of the guy in the alley. First order of business is to find out who he is. Alexandrov wasn't forthcoming on the man's ID." Yawning, he took another drink of his coffee. "I think I'm going to need the whole pot to stay awake."

"Why are you staying awake? Go to bed. You look like you need it."

"How about you? Have you been up since I left?"

"No, I slept for four hours. More than you have."

"Four hours? That's not enough for you. You want to be fresh for the trial next week."

"Sleep is overrated."

"Sure. If you say that enough, maybe you can convince yourself it's true. Tell you what. I'll go to bed if you'll go back to sleep."

She glanced toward the bay window near the table, but the blinds were closed. "It'll be morning soon."

"So, sleep in late."

"With Kim in my room, I doubt that will happen."

He rose, took his mug and hers to the sink, then came back to her. Clasping her hand, he tugged her toward the hallway. "C'mon. I'll walk you to your bedroom, then I promise I'll crash in mine."

As she mounted the wide staircase next to Brody, she kept her hand within his grasp, enjoying the connection. "Are you really okay?"

"I will be, with some sleep. I have a few stitches and a headache, but nothing that time won't take care of."

At her door she shifted around to look at him. She ran her finger lightly over a cut on his cheek and then over another on his brow.

He caught her hand and held it still. "Flying debris. It could have been worse."

"Yeah, you could have been blown up. I don't want anything to happen to you because of me. I couldn't live with myself if it did."

He pulled her closer, flat up against him, and cradled her head between his palms. "It's my job, Rebecca, and I'll do what has to be done to keep you safe."

His fervent words caused a shiver to run down her. "Why would someone put a bomb in your car in the police station parking lot?"

"Don't know. Before I went to the hospital, Charlie and I viewed the security tapes from the parking lot. A medium-sized man was seen hanging around, but he wore a ball cap, pulled low, and his face wasn't visible on the tape."

"Like in the hospital."

"He knew where the cameras were and made sure he wasn't caught on tape. I'm sending the tape to the lab to see if they can pull anything off of it, but I think it's a dead end."

"At least we know a medium-sized man is involved."

"So we're looking for a man about five feet nine or ten inches. That narrows it down to a few hundred thousand," he said with a laugh.

"And if he was hired to do the job, it still doesn't tell us who is behind it."

He ran his fingers through her hair. "Your optimism overwhelms me."

She sighed. "Sorry. I'm usually a regular Pollyanna. I'll do better next time."

His chuckle died on his lips as he stared into her eyes. A fire blazed in their gray depths, which drew her even closer. He tilted his head and placed his mouth over hers. The kiss started gently but quickly evolved into a fierce possession. Brody wrapped his arms around Rebecca, plastering her against him.

For a few seconds she couldn't believe Brody was kissing her, but soon that thought fled, to be replaced with a building desire for the kiss to continue. She gave into the sensations rampaging through her—heady ones—feelings of safety, of femininity . . . of love. Suddenly, she remembered the danger in continuing.

Rebecca pushed away from him, her chest rising and falling rapidly. Drawing one deep breath after another, she tried to compose herself as she put some space between them. She tried to grasp onto a thread of sanity, logic. All she had to do was look at his bandaged arm and the cuts on his face to know that there could never be anything between them. Ever. She had lost one man to this kind of job. She couldn't again.

"I could tell you I'm sorry I did that, but I'm not. I've wanted to do that for a while now. I've always wondered if things had been different eleven years ago, what—"

She laid two fingers over his mouth. "I can't love another cop." Grief hardened each word—firming up her determination. She quickly fled into her bedroom, quietly closing the door behind her.

She checked the bed, the slit of light from the bathroom illuminating the room to let her know that her niece was still sleeping. Sighing, she settled into a chair nearby, just before her legs gave out.

Her hands shook. She laced her fingers together to still the quivering. But she couldn't. It took over her whole body. Clasping her arms across her chest, she relived that amazing kiss. Feeling his need in it. Feeling a part of her defenses crumbling. Feeling her life shift again.

∽⧔∾

Brody lay in bed, staring up at the ceiling. He replayed yet again the scene in front of Rebecca's door an hour ago. Why did he kiss her? To satisfy a youthful fantasy? To see if he felt anything for her other than friendship after all these years? The reason wasn't important anymore. He couldn't imagine being anything but an officer of the law. She'd made it clear this evening she could never be involved with someone who was. End of story.

But the realization he wasn't protected from falling for her inundated him, stirring his anger. He wasn't going to let her hurt him a second time. He couldn't change who he was. Maybe eleven years ago, when they flirted with dating before Garrett entered her life, he could have. They were two different people now.

He would do his job and guard her. After that he would move on. Maybe there was someone out there who would accept him for what he was. He'd been a fool to think it might be different this time. Rolling onto his side, he punched the pillow several times then tried to sleep.

Mid-morning on Saturday, Rebecca followed the scent of sausage cooking and coffee brewing to the kitchen, where Tory, Brody, and Sean sat at the kitchen table while Hattie finished making breakfast. "I thought everyone would be long gone by now. I haven't slept to ten in years."

"You weren't the only one. My son did, too, this morning. But not me. I've been out with Jake checking the security." Sean went to the coffeemaker, brought back the carafe, and refilled his and Brody's mugs. Tory indicated she didn't want any by covering her cup.

"Where are the girls?" Rebecca walked over to the kettle of hot water and fixed herself some tea.

Hattie handed her the sugar bowl. "They're in the den working on another card for their dad. Tory is heading to the hospital in a while."

"I'm surprised Kim didn't wake me when she left my room this morning."

"She said you were dead to the world."

Rebecca flinched when Tory said that word.

Her sister-in-law's eyes grew round. "I'm sorry. That probably isn't the right word to say under the circumstances, with all that's happened. Brody was telling us what happened last night. The man who tried to run down you or Kim or both of you was murdered. Frankly, I'm glad he's been taken care of. One of you could have died if that young man hadn't saved you. What was his name?"

"Rob Clark." Rebecca sat at the far end of the table from Brody. His kiss last night had surprised her. Years ago she'd thought they might date, but nothing ever came of it and then she had met Garrett.

"Ah, yes, Rob Clark. Kim has mentioned him a couple of times."

"She's been talking about him?" Rebecca sipped her tea, her gaze sliding to Brody and catching him looking at her. Her pulse rate kicked up a notch.

"Just this morning she wanted to make him a card and write him a thank-you note." Hattie set the platter of sausages and pancakes on the table.

"She told me he was cute." Tory took a couple of pancakes and passed the plate to Sean.

"Who's cute?" Kim asked as she came into the room with Aubrey right behind her.

"That young man who saved me."

"You think so, too?" Kim put a card on the counter and came to sit at the table. "I want to make him a card. I started one, but I don't know where to send it. Mr. Calhoun, can you call him and get his address?"

With his gaze linked to Rebecca's, Brody said, "Sure, if it's okay with Rebecca and Tory."

"Aunt Becky? Tory?"

"Of course you can. He did a good deed that day. So many people nowadays don't. They don't want to get involved." Tory grabbed the pitcher of orange juice and poured herself some. "I'm so grateful he did. I think that's a nice gesture. If he's still in town, I think we should see if he'd like to come to dinner one evening."

"That's a good suggestion." Rebecca drenched her pancakes in syrup, trying not to look at Brody anymore.

Kim clapped her hands. "I like that. Hattie could help me make a cake for him."

"I don't know if that's a good idea," Brody said, producing a pout on the ten-year-old's face.

"Why not? We've got to eat. He has to, too." Hattie added another batch of pancakes to the platter.

"Well . . ." Brody scanned the people staring at him. "Sure. I can extend an invitation to him. Which night?"

"I've got a better idea. You give me his number and I'll invite him. This time I won't accept no for an answer." Rebecca went to the counter, where a pad and pencil were kept.

"That's great, Aunt Becky. And we won't need his address. I can give him the card in person. We can show him around the ranch. Maybe he likes to ride."

The enthusiasm in her niece's voice made Rebecca smile. She had been having nightmares about nearly getting run down by the pickup. Seeing Rob and treating him to dinner might help her put the incident behind her. "Honey, let's take it one step at a time. First I need to get him to agree to come to dinner. There probably won't be a lot of time to go riding."

∽≫

For the past few weeks J. R. had been watching his target, waiting for the opportunity to make his move. She usually didn't do things during the week in any kind of order so that he could predict where she was going to be and be there before her. But the past two Saturdays he'd found that she did have a routine on that day. He was counting on it. It was time he set up the next part of his plan.

Sitting at a game table in the nursing home, he let the old man across from him win at checkers.

"Beat ya again." The man cackled and reset the board.

J. R. grinned. "I told ya I wasn't too good at this game. Sure I'm not boring you?"

"Nah. I like winning." Vinnie made his first move.

J. R.'s disposable cellphone rang. There was only one person who had the number. The Texas Ranger. He scooted his chair back and said, "Excuse me. I have to answer this. Hang on, and I'll be back in a sec."

As he walked to a corner that afforded him some privacy, he glimpsed Laura Melton coming into the rec center, heading right for Vinnie, who was the woman's grandfather and who had dementia.

His smile grew as he answered the phone. "Hello."

"Is this Rob Clark?" a female voice asked.

"Yes," he said, a bit leery.

"This is Rebecca Morgan, the lady you saved last weekend."

J. R. relaxed and leaned a shoulder against the wall. "You've been keeping yourself out of trouble, I hope."

"Yes, and if you'll agree, I'll be able to make a young girl happy. Kim would really like you to come to the ranch for dinner next week. Actually, I hope you'll come, too. We both owe you more than a thank-you. How about a home-cooked meal by one of the best chefs in Texas?"

"You?"

"Oh, no. That'll never be, but my brother's housekeeper is great."

"Which night?"

"That depends on you. We can work around your schedule."

J. R. slanted his glance toward Laura, who was sitting with her grandfather. This was turning out to be a great day. "How about Wednesday? I have some free time."

"Great. Is six o'clock okay with you?"

"Fine, ma'am. Where do you live?"

Rebecca gave him directions to the ranch, which he was very familiar with, having cased it for the past month. He'd even seen the cattle rustlers checking the place out.

"I'll see you at six on Wednesday. By the way, what's your favorite cake?"

"Cake?"

"Yes, Kim wants to make you one. Don't worry. She'll have Hattie's help. Is it carrot cake?"

"Yes." He couldn't remember the last time someone had baked him a cake. His twelfth birthday?

After disconnecting, he covered the distance to the table where Vinnie and Laura were seated. He paused between them. For a few seconds he remembered that cake his sister had baked for him on his birthday, before everything fell apart. The icing had been runny and the cake too dry, but he'd loved every bite.

Laura Melton glanced up at him while Vinnie gave him a confused look.

"Can I help you?" she asked, one brow lifted.

"I was playing a game of checkers with Vinnie. He wanted to beat me again." J. R. gestured toward the checkerboard set up on the table.

"Who are you?" Vinnie's forehead wrinkled.

"I'm Jim Howard. I'm a volunteer here." J. R. swung his attention from Vinnie to Laura, flashing her a smile. "I've volunteered on Sundays but needed to change my day." To make his cover story ring true, he had actually come the last two Sundays for an hour and played checkers with Vinnie, though he never remembered him from week to week. "Do you usually work with Vinnie at this time?"

"Usually. Vinnie is my grandfather. Have you played checkers with him before?"

"Yes, ma'am." He lowered his voice and leaned toward her to say, "Every week, but he forgets."

She bent closer to him. "I know. On good days he remembers me." Then sitting back, she said more loudly, "Jim, please join us. Grandpa loves to play checkers. He has all his life."

"Thanks, ma'am."

"Please don't call me ma'am. It makes me sound so old."

"My mama always told me to say that as a sign of respect. It has nothing to do with age, especially in this case." His gaze captured hers and held it.

"I'm Laura Melton." She presented her hand.

He shook it. "Nice to meet you—Laura."

Her brown eyes twinkled. "Much better." For a few extra seconds she held the visual connection before turning to her grandfather. "Grandpa, Jim wants to play checkers. Are you up for a game?"

Vinnie cackled and rubbed his hands. "When am I not? I'm the champ."

"Yes, Grandpa, you are." Laura moved to the chair between Vinnie and J. R.

He took his seat again, sliding a glance at Laura. For forty, she wasn't too bad. He could certainly romance her until he gained her confidence. *Revenge is best savored slowly, according to Mama.*

10

Sunday afternoon, Rebecca sat on Angel Fire, staying off to the side of the rest of the group riding. Tomorrow, the first witness who had been in protective custody would testify. At this point the two main witnesses for the prosecution were ready to go. But anything could happen between now and when they testified. Every precaution was being made, but just thinking about the next couple of days knotted her stomach into a hard mass.

"Thanks for talking me into going riding with you, the kids, and," Laura peered over her shoulder, "your protection."

"Ranger Parker is a good rider," Rebecca remarked.

"So is *your* Texas Ranger."

"Mine?"

"Isn't he a long-time friend?"

"Yes, but that's all." Pulling her cowboy hat lower, she looked sideways at Brody, who was talking to her nieces. The girls enjoyed being with him. He took time for them and never tired of answering their hundreds of questions about his job.

"It's okay to be interested in a man again."

Laura had married her high school sweetheart, who had died five years ago, serving his country. That was one of the reasons Rebecca and she had become such good friends. Laura knew what she had gone through when Garrett was killed. "I know. Has anything come of your flirting with Charlie?"

"No, I don't think the man even realizes when a woman is coming on to him. Too focused on his work."

"Garrett was like that when he had a tough case. Maybe when this Petrov trial is over you can catch his attention."

Laura grinned. "May not have to."

Rebecca twisted in her saddle. "Why not?"

"I met a man yesterday when I went to see Grandpa."

"How old is this man?"

"He isn't a resident at the nursing home. He was volunteering there. And he certainly isn't old. In fact, he's younger than I am."

"How much younger?"

Laura shrugged. "I didn't ask. Age has nothing to do with a relationship."

"In other words, no comments about cougars."

"You're brilliant. Jim said to Vinnie he would be back for a rematch of checkers on Tuesday evening. I think I'll visit Grandpa then. Is it okay if I leave work a little early that day?"

"Since you usually stay late most nights, I don't see why not. But on one condition: you tell me what happens on Tuesday with this Jim."

"No comments if you see me wear a new dress Tuesday."

"Mum's the word." Rebecca zipped her fingers across her lips and twisted her hand.

"That I've got to see. You being quiet."

"I like your taste in clothes. I live vicariously through you. I never have time to go shopping, and that isn't going to change anytime soon."

"I don't know how you do everything and still have time to take your novice law clerk on a tour of the ranch." As Laura turned more fully toward Rebecca, she shielded her eyes with her hand.

The sun slanted across the pasture and was almost down behind the hills to the west. The terrain glowed with a golden hue. Rebecca sighed. "I wish I could come out here every day. But with the trial, visiting Thomas, and taking care of the girls, there's no extra time during weekdays. The weekends aren't going to be too much better. The longer Thomas stays in the hospital, the more trouble the girls have understanding why their daddy hasn't come home. When I take them to see Thomas, Aubrey gets upset that her daddy can't talk to her and Kim is super quiet. But Tory has been a trooper. She spends hours with Thomas every day. She's hardly at the ranch."

Laura nodded toward Ranger Parker. "How does she feel about having this place patrolled by Texas Rangers and deputies?"

"She refuses to believe that anything other than an accident happened to him and she's right. Thomas is well liked. There are no disgruntled ex-employees or people he's swindled in a business deal. He's one of the good guys."

"How do you feel about all of this?"

Rebecca studied Texas Ranger Parker and Brody. "We're being guarded by the Texas Rangers and the U.S. Marshals. They are splitting the duties. Brody insisted on it, and Foster agreed. At least I know Brody. That makes this bearable."

Brody reined in his horse next to Rebecca. "Are you ready to head back? I think we've left Dad and Hattie alone long enough. He's trying to talk her into baking his favorite pie for him."

"I thought she refused because of his diet." Rebecca turned her horse in a half circle, facing home—the ranch house, stables, and barn visible in the distance.

"That isn't going to stop him from trying."

"I need to leave. It's almost an hour back to my apartment, and tomorrow will be a big day." Laura spurred her horse into a trot and caught up with Kim and Aubrey.

Smooth, Rebecca thought. She knew exactly what her friend was doing. Leaving her alone with Brody.

"What's happening tomorrow?"

"The prosecutor has left the main witnesses to last. He wants to leave an impact on the jury. The first one testifies tomorrow."

"I'll be picking you up tomorrow. I should have some tests back by then. I've been promised the DNA results on the finger."

"Having the governor involved does help get results back *a lot* faster than usual."

"Yeah, it's gonna spoil me on my next case."

His cowboy hat shaded his eyes, but she felt them taking in every inch of her face. The memory of the kiss edged its way into her mind. She pushed it away. "Any progress IDing the man in the alley?"

"Yes, he's from back east, New Jersey. Peter Ivanov. No arrests or record, but the police are delving a bit deeper into the man's life. He wasn't a tourist looking for Sea World."

"A hit man?"

"Probably. Possibly a new one. He was only twenty-three. Before we're through, we're going to know everything about him."

"Have I told you thank you lately?"

"Not in the past few hours."

She smiled at him, their pace slowing while the others rode ahead. "I know you didn't want us to go for a ride, but the girls need to do some of the things they are used to doing, and besides, I wanted some fresh air."

"And to show Laura the ranch."

"Yes, she's been here before, but she's never gone for a ride. I was thrilled she came to church this morning."

"I thought you were angry with God."

"*Angry* might be too harsh a word. *Not sure what's going on* is more like it."

"Honing your faith."

"You think?" She had to admit this last week had made her rethink her faith, which she had been taking for granted.

"When I've gone through difficulties, I find my faith deepening. Sometimes that's the only way I can get through the problems."

She had weathered her husband and father's deaths and had come out still believing, but was she really putting her trust in the Lord to be there for her when she needed Him? Had she put God in the center of her grieving—was He the one she depended on to get her through it? No, not really. Instead, she'd thrown herself into her work to the point of not even taking vacation time. As though she was afraid to be by herself to think about what she was really feeling. "You've never questioned your faith?"

"Yes. I think most people do at one time or another, but without the Lord what do I really have? He hasn't caused the problems. We do. But He's there for us."

"So my anger should be directed at the people causing all the troubles—the Russian Mafia, the Dos Huesos Cruzados Gang, the cattle rustlers."

"Anger is definitely a stage we go through in dealing with our problems, but hopefully not the last one."

"Are you angry at the person who put the bomb in your car?"

His eyebrows rose. "I haven't had time to think about it. I've been busy lately." He cocked his head. "I guess I feel more inconvenienced. I have to get a new car. And it's another aspect of everything going on that has to be investigated. It makes me wonder what the point was behind the bombing. I'm just one person on the task force. I certainly don't feel close to breaking the case. Killing me would only intensify the investigation into both groups. So why the bomb?"

"Maybe you should ask Alexandrov and Serpiente."

"I think I'll pay them another visit this week. We do know that whoever delivered the dead flowers to Thomas probably put the bomb in my car—at least they were the same build, height, and wearing the same color and type of ball cap. Also bold."

"I know this week will be the turning point in the trial. The prosecutor will make his case or not with his two witnesses."

"We're tightening security around everyone involved. Including you."

"Meaning?"

"I'll be by your side, or Randall will. We're increasing the security around you. You'll have very little privacy."

"I'll be glad when this trial is over. I value my privacy." Riding into the yard in front of the stables, Rebecca halted Angel Fire. She didn't want the girls to overhear any of their conversation about what was going on with her or with Thomas. "But I'm afraid it may be weeks before it ends."

"Then we'll deal with it while putting pressure on both groups."

"I feel that, whether Thomas's injury was an accident or not, my job has put him in jeopardy. He would never have received those dead flowers if I hadn't been the judge on this trial. What if the cattle rustling is also a direct result of this trial? Just another way for the Russian Mafia to harass me?"

"I can't answer your question about the cattle rustling. Dad tells me the cattle have been secure since Jake has made the changes. Nothing else has happened since the two incidents—the one at your ranch and at your neighbor's."

"I'm having Jake run a head count on our herd. I've wondered if we've lost smaller amounts that wouldn't be obvious without checking numbers."

"That's good. When will you know?"

"Your dad and Jake were working on it yesterday and today with the cowhands. It's quite an undertaking." *As is everything on the Petrov trial.*

"Dad didn't mention it to me. But now that I think about it, he has been unaccounted for a lot this weekend. I don't want him overextended."

"I told Jake that. He'll make sure your dad doesn't do too much. But did you know he's eager to help? I think that's a good thing." Rebecca urged her horse toward the entrance to the stables.

"Are you telling me not to worry about my dad?"

She threw a glance over her shoulder. "I wouldn't presume to do that. I know you'll worry no matter what I say. That comes with loving someone." The second she said that last sentence she realized how much she worried about Brody. *I can love a friend. That's all this is.*

As Rebecca dismounted and one of the cowhands took Angel Fire for her, Jake and Sean emerged from the stables, where Jake had his office. Their sober expressions didn't bode well for her.

"We're missing more head than we know were taken by the cattle rustlers?" Her heart sank as Jake nodded. "How many?"

"Another hundred and twenty spread out over all the different herds. The most are missing from the herds on the fringes of the ranch. A couple from the herds that had been kept closer to the ranch house."

"When did we do the last count?"

"Middle of the summer. Two months ago."

"So we've lost over two hundred head. With the price of beef, that's quite a loss. Call the other ranchers and let them know. It may have happened to them." Or not. If it hadn't, the implication was that the Circle S Ranch was the main target.

Jake went back into his office, leaving Sean, Brody, and Rebecca facing one another. Rebecca's two nieces ran toward the house, dragging Laura with them. Ranger Parker was right behind them.

"What if it's only this ranch?" Rebecca finally asked out loud. "Only one neighbor has been rustled besides us."

With a grimace, Sean pivoted and started for the office.

"Dad, why don't we go up to the house and wait for Jake to make those calls? It'll take a while and even then we still won't know much."

Sean stopped, his shoulders lifting and then falling as if he'd taken a breath to compose himself. "Sure. I am tired."

The pale cast to Sean's features worried Rebecca. Seeing Brody's expression corroborated her concern. She looped her arm through the older man's and together they headed toward the main house. "I know what you mean. We were supposed to rest this weekend. It hasn't turned out quite like that. I plan to go to sleep early tonight." She slowed her step to keep pace with Sean.

"But not until I've had Hattie's prime rib roast. She said she was fixing that tonight. I've been thinking all day about that." Sean gave her a smile that didn't linger on his face.

Rebecca squeezed his arm. "I know—it melts in your mouth. After that ride, I'm starved. How about you?" she asked Brody, who was very quiet as he walked beside Sean, his intense gaze fixed on his father.

"Sure," Brody mumbled.

"After that, I thought I would take a ride in my car alone. Okay, Brody?"

"Sure."

"Brody Calhoun, you weren't listening to a word I said."

He blinked. "Sure I was. You're hungry."

She shook her head. "Sean, do you care to tell your son what he agreed I could do?"

"My pleasure. After dinner, Rebecca is going for a ride by herself. In her car."

"Okay. I wasn't listening as carefully as I should have been." Brody halted at the back entrance into the kitchen and rounded on his father. "You don't look good. When you get inside, you should lie down until dinner. I don't want to hear—"

"Sure."

"a word about how you're not . . . What did you say?"

"I agree. I'm tired. Lying down sounds like a good plan. That's what you do when you're tired."

Sean trudged up the steps and went into the house, heading straight for the hallway. At the entrance to the kitchen, he released Rebecca's arm. "Thanks, my dear, for escorting this old man into the house. I appreciate it." He leaned down and gave her a peck on the cheek. Pulling back, he drew in a deep breath. "Ah, what a wonderful aroma. Hattie, you sure know how to tease a man."

The housekeeper paused in stirring something in a pan on the stove. "Flattery will get you far. An extra slice for you tonight, Sean Calhoun."

He chuckled. "Yes, ma'am. You've twisted my arm. I'll eat a second piece."

As he shuffled down the hallway toward the downstairs bedroom, Rebecca exchanged a look with Brody. "Go ahead and check on him."

He took off after his father, who turned around and grumbled at his son, but kept walking to his room.

Hattie crossed the kitchen. "Is he okay?"

"I think he overdid it today."

"I knew it. I tried to tell him earlier, but he wouldn't listen to me. Men. Don't they know women know best?"

"I don't think so." Rebecca walked to the sink and washed her hands. "Can I help you?"

The scent of the prime rib vied with the aroma of garlic and onions simmering in butter in a large skillet. "What else are we having?"

"Zucchini and yellow squash along with rice and—"

The back door opened, and Jake entered. "I'm not sure if you'll consider this bad news or good news. All but two ranches told me they made a count of their cattle when the rustling started. No cows are missing. The other two will get back to me. But it's looking like we're the main target."

"Jake, you want to join us for dinner?" Rebecca asked.

"You don't have to ask twice. Where's Brody?"

"With his dad. I'll let him know you're here."

After she told Brody about what Jake had found out, she needed to rescue Laura from Kim and Aubrey. The door to Sean's bedroom was open. Rebecca stepped into the entrance to catch Brody's attention.

He walked back toward the doorway. "I'll be sure to get you."

Sean stretched out on his bed. "If you forget, you'll have me to answer to."

"I know. That's why I won't forget." Brody shut the door and turned to face Rebecca. "I wanted to make sure he'd taken his medicine. When he gets busy, he doesn't."

"Had he?"

"He said he has."

"Jake's in the kitchen. It looks like we're really the only ranch affected, except for one neighbor. So why would we be deliberately targeted? I'm starting to think this might be connected to Thomas's accident."

"He has an enemy? A rival ranch? Someone he's ticked off?"

"We've gone through this. It doesn't make sense. Our neighbors aren't like that."

"That you know."

"What are you implying?"

Brody kneaded the back of his neck. "I don't know. Something else is going on here."

"I'm getting a headache. How do you do it with your cases—try to outthink people?"

The corners of his mouth tilted upward. "I've had a headache since yesterday."

Reaching up, she rubbed his temples. "A car bombing will do that to you. I thought you were better this morning."

"I'm better than I was yesterday, but—"

The door to Sean's room opened. He appeared in the small gap, clutching the doorframe. "I'm not feeling too well, Son. My chest hurts. I thought if I lay down I'd be better, but the pain isn't going away."

Brody rushed toward his dad. "Rebecca, call 911."

11

*B*rody came out of the room where his father was being treated in the ER. "It's indigestion. This time," he clipped out tersely.

Rebecca leaned back against the wall across from the room. "They ran all the tests they needed to?"

"Yes." He glanced toward the sliding glass doors into the hospital, darkness greeting him. "You need to get some rest. It's going to be morning before you realize it. They'll be releasing Dad in a few minutes."

"Before we leave, I'd like to go up and see Thomas."

"It's three in the morning."

"He's in a coma. I don't think it's going to disturb him. I may not get back later today. If I only get a few hours of sleep, I may not be in any shape to do anything other than to go to the ranch and go to bed early tonight after the trial."

He caressed her cheek with the back of his forefinger, his gaze searing her. "You shouldn't have come with me."

"And have you come by yourself? No." She captured his hand and held it cupped between her two palms. His touch distracted her. "I don't know where I would be right now if you hadn't come back into my life. You have made the past week bearable."

"I aim to please, ma'am. So while they're finishing up with Dad, let's go see Thomas." As Brody strode to the elevator and punched the up button, he tried to forget the near panic he'd experienced when his father had clutched his chest earlier, pain etched into his face. He didn't want to lose his father. Since he'd come back home, their relationship had deepened, although they certainly had their differences of opinion, mostly on how his dad should take better care of himself.

On the ride to the fourth floor, he propped himself against the back wall of the elevator, tired enough to sleep standing up if given half a chance. Normally, he welcomed a challenge in a case, a test of his abilities, but not this one. Too much was at stake. The lives of people he cared about were in jeopardy. Especially Rebecca.

She stood slightly in front of him. Her posture, with shoulders slumped, attested to her exhaustion. He'd cared so much for her while they'd grown up together. But at her wedding, he'd known he had to move on. The hardest thing he'd had to do was watch her marry another man. That day at the reception, as Rebecca and Garrett toasted each other, he'd sealed his heart against getting hurt again. He had left San Antonio, made a life for himself, dated, and even got engaged. His job had interfered with that relationship, and he and his fiancée had ended up deciding not to get married.

The doors slid open, and he pushed away from the wall and placed his hand at the small of Rebecca's back as they exited the elevator. At the end of the corridor, the police officer sat in a chair outside Thomas's room. The lights in the hallway were dimmed. Quiet reigned, except for two staff members talking behind the counter at the nurses' station.

At least he didn't have to admit his dad tonight.

Rebecca stopped at the counter. "How's Thomas Sinclair been doing? I'm his sister and thought I would stop in to see him. I know it's in the middle of the night, but I was with a friend in the ER."

The older woman set aside a chart she was holding. "I recognize your picture from the news about the Petrov trial. I hope he's put away for good. Your brother's status hasn't changed. Holding his own."

"Thanks. I won't be long."

After they both showed proper ID to the officer, Brody held the door open for Rebecca. Although the young man knew who she was, Brody was glad he asked for identification.

Inside, only one light illuminated the area, but machines continued to monitor Thomas, who lay in the bed, cocooned in a white sheet and blue blanket. Seeing his childhood friend like that made his throat tighten. What if he woke up and couldn't walk again? What if he never woke up? Thomas had always been so full of life. He was a good man who loved the Lord and tried to live as Christ would want him to, giving a helping hand to others when they needed it.

Was that why he couldn't bring himself to believe this wasn't anything but an accident?

Rebecca stood next to the bed, her face in the soft shadows created by the dim lighting, her long auburn hair pulled back in a ponytail, the way she liked to wear it when she wasn't in court. "He looks peaceful. The doctors assure me he isn't in any pain. That makes the waiting a little better." She looked up at Brody, her eyes shimmering. "But not much."

Brody came to her side and took her hand. "I know it seems we can't do much for him, but we can pray."

"I need to do more than that. My prayers haven't helped so far."

"How do you know? He's alive and stable. A week ago we thought he would die."

"You're right. That's my frustration talking."

"And the fact is, you haven't had much sleep." Lifting her hand, he placed it against his chest. "Father, please heal Thomas and make him whole and well again. He is in Your capable and loving hands."

With her head bowed and eyes closed, Rebecca whispered, "Amen."

A tear leaked out from between her eyelashes and ran down her cheek. The sight of it constricted his chest until it was difficult to draw in even a shallow breath. He hated seeing her hurt. He hated being helpless to change the situation.

He turned her toward him and brushed his finger across her cheek. Their gazes locked together, he cradled her face between his hands. "It's hard having to stand back and let God do His work."

"I'm used to being in control. As a judge. As a prosecutor. But with this situation, I have no control. Not with my brother. Not with what's happening around me. It makes me sympathize with the people whom these gangs have terrorized and have robbed of control over their own lives."

"You think you have control? Really? What about three years ago?"

She frowned. "When my life fell apart?" She dropped her head for a few seconds.

When she looked at him again, he glimpsed fear in her expression. "How much time do you spend worrying about that control—planning your life down to the smallest detail?"

"I've always been a very organized person," Rebecca replied.

"I'm not talking about organization. I'm talking about setting down plans and getting uptight when they don't work out the way you want."

Her mouth quirked into a grin. "Lately—this past week—not much at all, especially with Kim and Aubrey. It's not easy with children around."

"I can imagine. Why didn't you have children? You're good with your nieces."

"My plan," her chuckle full of derision filled the air, "was to wait until after I was thirty, then the judgeship came up and I wanted to get settled in the job before we started a family. I thought I had all the time in the world."

"Do you want children?" he asked and regretted the question the second it left his mouth.

"Yes. How about you?"

"I haven't thought about it much lately."

"But you used to?"

"I was engaged in Amarillo. We talked about having a family."

"You were engaged? Thomas never told me that."

"Because I didn't tell him."

"Why not?"

"We were engaged a month and decided to break it off. Or rather I decided." The tense set of his shoulders made them throb with pain. He didn't want to get into this conversation with her.

"Why?"

He'd known she would ask and he still couldn't come up with an answer he wanted to give her. Her gaze was fixed on him, demanding the truth. "She wasn't you."

Rebecca's mouth fell open.

He gently closed her mouth and gave her a smile, meant to reassure her that it was all right. "It was a year after I left here. I dated Emily on the rebound. I thought I'd accepted your marriage and the fact that you didn't want to date me because we were good friends."

"I could talk to you about anything. I didn't want to ruin that. I didn't . . ." Her voice came to a quavering halt. "I'm sorry. Your friendship meant so much to me. I didn't want to change it."

"I get it. You couldn't control me."

She stepped back. "What do you mean?"

"I saw how you wrapped Garrett around your finger. Everything had to be your way."

Her cheeks flamed. "That's not true—okay, maybe. But I've mellowed over the years. I was young, had just finished law school, and was ready to take on the world."

And he'd been there the whole time. Until he had realized he wanted more than friendship. The best thing he'd done was to move. He'd focused on his career and become a Texas Ranger on his first try.

"Don't worry. All those imagined feelings I had died a natural death. I moved on with my life and haven't regretted what I've accomplished. I realized I don't want to get married. I like my independence. The ability to do what I need to do without answering to someone else. So you did me a favor."

Liar. He thrust that word from his mind. No, he was content.

"We're still friends?"

"Of course. That will never change. You were right. That was the best thing for both of us."

"Yeah, right." She shifted toward the bed and took her brother's hand. "Tommy, please get better. I want to hear you laugh. I miss your teasing."

Thomas flinched, his hand falling from her light grasp.

"Did you see that? He moved." Rebecca pressed the nurse's call button. "Maybe he's waking up."

Thomas's eyes opened wide for a second, then closed.

"He is!" Rebecca punched the button again. "Maybe they can do something to help him come out of it."

As the nurse came into the room, Thomas twitched again.

Rebecca pointed at her brother. "He's moving. He's coming out of the coma."

The nurse stood on the other side of the bed, checked the monitors, and then took his pulse, and blood pressure. Several minutes later, she said, "Sometimes patients in a coma will move but don't wake up. We'll monitor him, and if he does wake up, we'll give you a call right away."

When the nurse left, Rebecca touched her brother's face. "I don't want him to wake up and no one be here for him. I'm going to stay for a while."

Brody clasped her arms from behind. "Let's at least sit down on the couch. I know you're exhausted. You know the saying, a watched pot won't boil, or something like that. Rest, and if something happens, we'll be here."

"You don't have to stay. I have the officer outside if something goes wrong. You have to take your dad home."

He tugged her toward the couch and set her down, then settled next to her. "I'm not going anywhere. His job is to protect Thomas. Mine is to protect you. If you stay, I'm staying. I'm calling my sister to pick up Dad, and he can stay with her until I'm free. I'll let them know down in the ER."

She gave him a tired smile. "I'm glad you're staying. At least go downstairs and bring your dad up here until your sister arrives. I'll be fine for that short amount of time."

"How about you come with me? We won't be gone more than ten minutes." Brody pointed toward Thomas. "He's quiet right now."

"You really are taking this bodyguarding seriously."

"That's my job, ma'am."

Rebecca snuggled closer to the warm body next to her. Visions of Garrett morphed into Brody as she tried to surrender to a deeper sleep. A woman's voice penetrated the haze that clouded her mind. She opened her eyelids up halfway.

She saw Thomas lying in his bed, sunlight streaming through the slits in the blinds behind the couch. Suddenly the reason she was in Thomas's hospital room and the awareness of who was with her caused her to bolt straight up.

"Has he moved anymore?"

"No. Not a twitch." Brody reached behind him and pulled open the blinds.

She blinked, trying to adjust to the light that poured into the room. "What time is it?" she asked, as she fumbled to push back the long sleeve of her sweater that covered her watch. "Eight! The trial starts in an hour. I've got to change. Get ready." Panic with a hint of disorientation overwhelmed her. She surged to her feet, looking around for her purse and for her shoes, which she'd taken off sometime last night—or rather, early this morning. "Why didn't you wake me up?"

Brody rose. "Because you needed the rest more than a change of clothes. You wear a black robe. No one is going to care what you wear underneath. They might care if you nod off while listening to the lawyers and witnesses."

Heat scored her cheeks. "I care. I need at least to swing by my house. We should have time to do that before going to the courthouse." She started for the door. "I need to talk to the nurse in charge, and I'm going to call Tory to let her know about Thomas moving. If he wakes up today, I want to be notified as soon as possible."

Brody caught her before she went out into the hallway. "Rebecca, you have to prepare yourself for the fact that he might not wake up anytime soon. Movement happens with coma patients. It doesn't mean they're going to wake up for sure."

"He's going to wake up." The pitch of her voice rose several levels. If she said it enough, it might come true.

"That's what I'm hoping, too. We're on the same side here."

She began to yank the door open but stopped and peered back at Brody. "I know. Sorry. Even though I got some sleep, it was obviously not enough."

"Let's go. The traffic will be heavy, and I don't want you late for the trial. The sooner this trial is over, the better for you."

After she talked with the head nurse and left instructions about how to reach her if Thomas's status changed, Rebecca headed to the parking lot with Brody. Once in the car, she retrieved her cellphone from her purse and called Tory.

Her sister-in-law answered on the second ring. "Why didn't you come home last night? Is Brody's dad all right? Hattie told me you went with Brody to the hospital and that he had called to let her know his dad only had indigestion. She was expecting you to come home."

"I was going to but decided to stay because I went up to see Thomas and he moved. He even opened his eyes."

"He did?"

"Yes, only a second but surely that means something. I wanted you to know. I hate for him to wake up and not have someone there."

"I'm on my way there right now. I'll talk with his doctor and find out what's going on."

"The trial will start at nine, so let Laura know if he wakes up."

"I will," Tory murmured in a lackluster-sounding voice.

"Are you okay?" Rebecca shifted the cellphone to her other ear.

"Tired."

"I hope you got more rest last night than I did."

"I wish I could say I did. I haven't slept well since Thomas's accident."

"I know. Maybe this is the beginning of his full recovery."

"Yeah. I'll let Hattie know what's going on."

"You might not say anything to the girls yet. I'd hate to get their hopes up and nothing happen for a while."

"I agree." Tory hung up.

Rebecca relaxed against the seat. "I know what happened last night is a good sign."

"I hope so." Brody turned into her subdivision.

A minute later, he had parked in Rebecca's driveway. In this upscale area of town, her medium-sized adobe home with a tile roof fit in with the surrounding houses and their manicured yards.

Rebecca climbed from Brody's rented car and hurried toward her front door. "It shouldn't take me more than ten minutes."

"Great. That's probably all you have if you're going to make it on time."

Inside, as Rebecca hurriedly set her purse on the table by the entrance, she abruptly perceived the scent of rotting meat. *Did I leave some meat out? I wouldn't be surprised, with all that has happened lately. I've got to remember to throw it away before leaving.*

She made her way toward her bedroom, her pace slowing as she neared the entrance. *I didn't turn off my alarm. I'm sure I set it when I left the last time. I think. I know . . .*

She stepped into the doorway while looking back down the hall toward her control panel. An unpleasant scent accosted her nostrils at the exact moment she scrunched something beneath her shoe. Her gaze swung to the chaos before her.

Then she saw the man and screamed.

12

Rebecca froze in the entrance to her bedroom.

Blood everywhere. The scent of rotting meat stronger, nauseating.

Nothing left untouched.

A man propped up on her bed, his death-filled eyes staring right at her.

A hand clamped on her shoulder and dragged her out of the doorway. "Go into the living room. I'll take care of this."

"No, I'm not leaving your side."

"Then stay right there." Brody picked his way across the room to the bed and examined the body carefully staged on top of her rumpled sheets. "Do you know this man?"

She had avoided looking at him after the initial few seconds. Slowly she ran her gaze up the length of the man, flinching at the blood covering him. Then she spied his gutted stomach, and her own stomach roiled. She swiveled away. Bile rose in her throat, and she covered her mouth to keep from getting sick. She couldn't. She raced for the bathroom down the hall and barely made it to the sink before throwing up.

She couldn't rid her mind of the picture of the mutilated dead man in the very bed she slept in. But his face had been left intact—enough, at least, that she knew who it was.

The witness who had given his protection team the slip.

Or had he?

"Rebecca, I'm so sorry you had to see that." Brody wrapped her in an embrace.

She burrowed deep into the shelter of his arms for a moment. As a prosecutor, she had witnessed horrible crime scenes, but nothing like what she'd just seen in her own home. The body, not of a stranger, but of someone she had interacted with in the courtroom. *So much death. When will it end?*

"C'mon. I'll call it in and get you out of here."

She pulled back. "Give me a sec."

He backed out of the bathroom and gave her some privacy. She rinsed the sink out, then splashed some cold water onto her face before brushing her teeth, each action done as though on autopilot. She wished she could wash the memories away as easily. But she would never forget what she'd seen.

When she left the bathroom, Brody stood right outside the door. He finished a call and put his cell away. "I'm checking the rest of the house. The man has been dead for a while, so I doubt anyone else is here, but I want to make sure."

"I'm tagging along."

"That's what I thought you would say." Brody quickly moved through the rooms, examining any place a person could hide.

When they ended up in the living room, she sank down on the couch. The short survey left her drained. She'd half-expected to find someone in the house, waiting. "That's the missing witness. One mystery solved."

"And another opened."

"Isn't it obvious who killed this man? Why else put him in my bed for me to find? A loud and clear message has been sent."

"This man was killed in the same manner as the one left in the alley behind Alexandrov's pawnshop."

"So the same man killed both of them. One a traitor to the Russian Mafia. The other not competent in doing his job. But I'm still alive." A bubble of hysteria swelled inside her, coming toward the surface. She couldn't fall apart. Too many people depended on her.

"As much as I would love to pin this on Alexandrov and his men, I don't know if they did it. Some things didn't add up at the other crime scene."

"How long do you think the man has been dead in my house? I haven't been back here in three days."

"Less than eight hours. I'll let the ME narrow that down some more, if he can."

"So, last night." She shivered and hugged her arms across her chest. Her gaze fixed upon the grandfather clock. "It's almost nine. I've got to get to the courthouse."

When she started to rise, Brody placed a hand on her arm. "No, you don't. Call Laura and let her know what's happened. Delay the trial a day. I need to wait until the police come."

She settled back on the couch. Her head throbbing, she squeezed her eyes closed, but immediately the scene in her bedroom filled the screen of her mind. She never wanted to go in there again. How could she, after what she'd seen? "I can't delay it more than an hour or so. I won't let Petrov and his pals win. If I delay it a day, no telling what they'll do to get me to do it again. May I use your cell?"

He unclipped the phone from his belt and gave it to her. "I can't get anything from your room. It's a crime scene, and I need to leave it as is."

"These clothes don't seem so bad at the moment." Rebecca punched in her office number.

Laura answered on the first ring. "Brody, where's Rebecca?" Her voice sounded frantic, rushed.

"It's me. I'm using his phone," Rebecca said, realizing her law clerk would have known it was Brody's cell by the caller ID. "I'm at my house. I'll be late. The trial will be delayed until ten o'clock."

"Why? What's wrong? You're never late."

"The witness who disappeared has been found—in my bed, dead. Is Randall there?"

"No, I thought he might be bringing you in."

"I'll call you when I'm on my way."

"Hey, you can't leave me with a dead man in your bed. What's going on?"

"That's about all I know. The police haven't even arrived yet."

When she hung up, Brody took the phone. "I called Randall right away. He's on his way here so he can take you to the courthouse."

"You're staying here at the crime scene?"

"Yes. I want to make sure every clue is collected and every possible person is interviewed. Although it occurred in the middle of the night, someone might have seen something and not realized it. If there is some way to tie this to Alexandrov, the federal government would be happy. Before moving here, he was involved in all kinds of schemes in Maryland. When things got hot for him there, he packed up and came here."

"Aren't we lucky?"

"Randall told me the FBI talked with Alexandrov this morning concerning the body found at the pawnshop. They want to put the screws to Petrov, see if he'll turn against Alexandrov."

Rebecca sat up straight. "Why didn't you tell me? Don't you think I need to know that?"

"I'm telling you now. This morning was the first I heard about it."

Tension gripped her and squeezed. Lowering her head, she rubbed her eyes to ease the pounding behind them. "I'm leaving with Randall, and believe me, I'm going to have him repeat the whole conversation to me. I want Petrov to pay for his crimes."

"The person behind Petrov is his brother-in-law, Alexandrov. He is not a nice man. Not one we want running around San Antonio."

"And you think Petrov is a nice man?" She glanced out the large window behind her couch as a couple of squad cars pulled up in front of her house.

"He's a minion, only following orders. We want the man giving those orders." He stood. "The thing we need to ask is how the killer got inside. You have an alarm system. Was it on when you left three days ago?"

"I thought so, but I'm not 100 percent sure."

"We'll check the system and all entry points." Brody headed toward the foyer to meet the police.

She rested her back on the couch cushion, staring up at the ceiling, trying to compose herself before she went to the courthouse and tried to act as if nothing had happened at her house. She didn't want the defendant or his cohorts to think they'd gotten to her. Voices drifted to her, along with the sound of men tramping toward her bedroom. But she couldn't deny she felt violated—her home invaded first by a killer and now by the police. Running her hands down her face, she tried to block the noises coming to her and the stench of death that seemed to follow her from her bedroom, and for a few moments she visualized what it had been like right before everything fell apart on Thomas's birthday. When she'd been chosen to be the judge for Petrov's second trial, she'd known her life would be difficult, but not like this. She felt like Humpty Dumpy when he fell off the wall and cracked into hundreds of pieces. All the king's men couldn't put him back together.

Will I be able to piece my life back together when this is over? Will Thomas? Doubts that she or her brother would be able to make things right again engulfed her.

※

"When are you going to buy something new to drive?" Rebecca slipped into Brody's rented SUV.

His chuckle rang in the cooling air. "In between working several murders and protecting you," he tapped the steering wheel, "this will do until things settle down."

"What if they don't?"

As he pulled out into traffic, he flicked a glance at her. "They will. We caught a break with the man who was found in your house."

"What?"

"The witness fought his attacker. There were two blood types found at the scene. One could be the killer's. The lab will run DNA on the samples. Maybe the murderer is in our database. They're rushing all tests in this case, but it will still take time. Also, on a closer comparison of the two murders, Charlie and I aren't as sure that they were done by the same person."

"Two different killers?"

"Possibly."

"Well, at least I have some good news. The witness's testimony today went well. He came across as credible and convincing. If the other one does, too, Petrov is going to have a hard time getting off."

"I know Petrov didn't want to make a deal beforehand with the government, but this may persuade him. Randall told me they moved Petrov to a more secure area."

"I want him to pay for what he did to the man he murdered. I don't care if the murdered man was in the wrong place at the wrong time and his death wasn't intended. Petrov has made my life a mess. He went into that building to murder someone. It doesn't count if it wasn't the right person."

"But to get Alexandrov would be huge for the government."

"Where's the justice for the victim?"

"It's sometimes a hard question to find the right answer to." Brody pulled onto her street.

Rebecca spied her home, with yellow tape strung up out front, announcing to the world that a crime had happened there. "I appreciate your taking me by my house. I have some papers and a few items I want to take with me to the ranch. I'm going to stay at the ranch for the time being. I don't know if I'll ever be able to live here again." She and Garrett had bought the house a few years after they got married. They'd fallen in love with it when they first saw it. Now her memories would always be tainted by the witness's murder in her bedroom. A lid had slammed shut on that part of her life. She didn't like change, and suddenly her life was a series of changes, one after the other.

"Did you find out how the killer got in?"

"He disabled the alarm system and came in through your back door. The door will need to be replaced. The lock on it wasn't as good as the one on your front door." Brody parked at the curb.

"How did he disable my alarm?"

"He broke the power by circumventing the circuit using aluminum foil. You might check into other alarm systems, too."

He grasped the door handle. "The house has been processed, but we won't release it right away. Maybe in a day or so."

"That's okay. I don't intend to come back—at least not anytime soon. With Thomas in the hospital and Tory focused on him, I need to be there for the girls."

"You'd make a great mother."

His statement surprised her. All she'd been centered on lately were murders, the Russian Mafia, and crimes. The idea of having a family still appealed to her. She'd wanted children, but she might have to be satisfied with loving her two nieces. "Well, I don't see that happening anytime soon, and I'm certainly glad right now that I don't have a child. I wouldn't want any child of mine to be subjected to what's going on."

"It's an unusual circumstance."

"Doing my job?" She shoved open the door and headed into her house.

Brody caught up with her and stopped her. "I'll go in first, or have you forgotten what happened here?"

She rounded on him, the frustration and fury she'd kept bottled up inside the whole day pouring out. "How could I? Oh, don't worry. I'll let you do your job."

"Listen, Rebecca, I know this isn't an easy situation."

Her anger poured out, as though someone had uncorked a stopper. "I'm sorry. You aren't responsible. Alexandrov and his thugs are."

"We'll get him, and whoever has done this."

"You say that with such confidence."

"Because I believe it. When someone comes after a friend of mine, it becomes personal. I won't give up until justice has been done."

"We've been around long enough to realize that doesn't always happen, even with the best of intentions."

"C'mon. Let me check the house, and you get your stuff, then we'll go by and see Thomas before going to the ranch."

"I'd like that. I kept hoping I'd get a call today that Thomas was awake. I need to see him and the girls. They are what keep me going. When I'm sitting up there on the bench, listening to the testimony and the evidence submitted, I feel so alone."

He faced her. "You are not alone. You have me. You have the Lord. You have a lot of people who care about you. Friends. Family."

His nearness comforted her. She laid her palm flat against his chest. The beat of his heart thumped against her hand and soothed her even more. "I don't usually throw myself a pity party. Just ignore my most recent outburst."

He covered her hand with his. "I'd be worried if you didn't have an outburst or two."

"Oh, good. I get to have another one, and you won't think I'm falling apart." Her last words reminded her of how she'd felt this morning—as if she'd cracked and fragmented into hundreds of pieces.

"Tell you what. Next time you want to have an outburst, find me. I'll listen to you."

"That's a sign of a true friend. It's like those ten years apart hadn't happened."

A shadow clouded his eyes. "They did. They honed us into the people we are today."

For all they had shared today, a barrier stood between them. She didn't want that. She needed him. "I know we aren't the same two people we were growing up. What has happened to us since we parted has changed us, especially with all the evil we've seen in our jobs. But nothing is going to change our friendship. I won't let it this time."

"Do I have a say in this?"

"Of course. I know it takes two people for a rela—friend-ship to work." The word *relationship* had come so easily to mind, but she didn't want to send the wrong signal. No matter how hard it was, friendship was all she would allow herself to feel—after Garrett. She wouldn't go through losing another man the way she had lost her husband.

～❧～

"Aunt Becky, where have you've been?" Kim threw her arms around Rebecca the second she stepped into the house, later that evening. "I missed you."

"Honey, I missed you, too. Where's Aubrey?"

"She went to bed. I told Hattie I wouldn't go to bed until you came home."

"I'm sorry it took so long today."

"Have you two eaten yet?" Hattie asked from the entrance into the back hallway.

Rebecca threw a look at Brody. "We went to see Thomas, then because it was so late, we went on and grabbed some-thing at the hospital cafeteria."

"You should have called." Reproach roughened Hattie's voice.

"I'm sorry. I left a message on the answering machine when I stopped by my house to get some things. I thought maybe you were outside with the girls."

The rigid set to the older woman's shoulders relaxed. "I was. It was a beautiful day, so I took them to the stables to see the animals. They get tired of staying inside so much. The young officer here was fine with that."

"Yeah, Aunt Becky, I want to go riding again. Can we go this weekend?"

"Sure. I could use a good ride myself."

"Hattie took Aubrey and me to see Dad right after school. She said you would be working longer today."

"The trial didn't start until late, so we stayed longer at the end of the day." Because she wanted it finished as quickly as possible. She wanted her life back.

"Okay, Miss Kim, you have seen your aunt. It's time for you to get ready for bed."

"Do I hafta?" Her niece swept her pleading gaze from Hattie to Rebecca.

"Sorry, you have to. You have school tomorrow. Did you do your homework?"

"Yes, and Mr. Calhoun checked it."

"Where is my dad?" Brody secured the lock on the front door, then strode toward Hattie and the back part of the house.

"He's in the den with Tory. She was here in time for dinner this evening." Hattie shot Rebecca an irritated look before turning on her heel and making her way down the hall.

"She usually checks the messages on the machine. I guess she forgot," Rebecca said with a long sigh. "I'm not used to having to account for myself."

"I think it's more from worrying than anything else. A lot has happened."

"You don't need to remind me. I'll talk to Hattie later."

When Rebecca entered the den with Brody, Sean and Tory stopped talking and looked at them. Hattie stood frowning in the center of the room.

"We were wondering where you two were." Sean took a sip of his drink.

"Don't you start, Dad. We had things to do."

"That you couldn't tell us about."

"Rebecca said she left a message on the machine." Hattie went to the phone and checked. "There's no message here."

They all stared at Rebecca. She settled her fist on her waist and looked at each one of them. "I left a message. I guess I could have called a wrong number. You should personalize your answering machine."

"Rebecca is right." Tory rose. "I'll make sure to do that before I go to sleep. Are the girls in bed?"

"Aubrey is already asleep according to Kim, and Kim went upstairs a few minutes ago."

"I'll say good night to her, then, and check on Aubrey." Tory crossed the room to the door. "I haven't seen them much lately, and I don't want them to forget who I am."

"They understand you've been busy with Thomas." Rebecca noted the dull sheen in her sister-in-law's eyes. This had taken a toll on her, too. Thomas was Tory's husband, and Rebecca knew all too well what it was like to have one's love in the hospital, fighting for his life. Garrett hadn't made it, but from what the staff had said tonight, Thomas was out of danger. Now the big question was when he would wake up and how affected he would be by the ordeal he had gone through.

"I can remember when I was a child," Tory said. "You understand to a point, then you begin to wonder why your needs aren't being met."

Before Tory left, Rebecca asked, "How was Thomas today?"

"No movement. I was hoping the whole day I'd get to see what you did. But nothing. When the doctor came, he didn't seem too excited about what happened during the night. Actually, when he left, I cried. I'd gotten my hopes up."

"I'm sorry, Tory. I didn't mean to make it worse for you. It could still be something."

"I hope so," Tory said on a heavy breath. "Good night. It's been a long, emotional day. After I see to the girls, I'm going to bed."

When her sister-in-law left, Rebecca looked from one person to the next, her gaze finally resting on Hattie. "Should I go talk to her?"

"I did earlier. This has been hard on her, especially all the unknowns. Will Thomas wake up? When? How will he be? What will he remember?"

"I know what she's going through. I've been there . . ." She refused to go back to three years ago and relive Garrett's death.

Brody slipped his arm around her and whispered in her ear, "You are not alone."

Her eyes blurred, and she dropped her head forward. *I will not cry. I will not cry. It doesn't change anything.*

Brody drew her to a wingback chair and sat her down. Then he took a seat across from her. "I didn't want to tell you over the phone, but today Rebecca found a dead man in her bed at her house."

"What! When?" Sean sat forward, clasping his hands together. "Why didn't you let me know right away?"

"There wasn't anything you could do. The San Antonio police are taking care of the crime scene."

"Who was it? Why?" Hattie mirrored Sean's position on the couch, her knuckles white from her tight grip.

"The 'who' is the witness who left the protection provided for him, refusing to testify. It didn't make any difference. He ended up dead." Brody removed his cowboy hat and put it on the coffee table near him.

"I guess the Russian Mafia don't care that you aren't going to testify." The picture of the man posed in her bed flashed into her mind. Chilled, she hugged her arms to her.

"So the why is the Russians are mopping up every loose end they can." The fierceness in Sean's voice blasted the air. "Do they consider Rebecca a loose end?"

"Dad, calm down. We're doing everything we can to make sure she's safe. A lot of guys on the police force are taking this personally. They won't let anything happen to one of their own."

Hattie's forehead furrowed. "Rebecca isn't a police officer."

"But she was married to one—a cop who died in the line of duty. Her security has been doubled."

"I just want this trial over with. It's difficult at the best of times, but with Thomas hurt, and my having to commute back and forth from the ranch, I'm left with little time to think." The chill embedded itself deep in the marrow of Rebecca's bones.

"This is when I wish I was back on the force. I was sitting here resting today when you were dealing with a murder in your very own house. Rebecca, I'm so sorry that this is happening to you."

"Thanks, Sean. I know we have deputies and rangers covering the ranch, but I still feel better knowing you're here."

"How are you feeling, Dad?"

"Yes, Sean. Any more problems with indigestion?" Rebecca sagged back against the chair, wanting to focus on something other than the trial she was overseeing.

"Don't you spend a second worrying about me. The ER doc said I was fine after running a ton of tests, and he's insisted I go see my doctor."

"Are you going?" Brody asked.

Hattie swung her attention to Sean, their gazes meeting. "I'm going to see that he goes to his doctor tomorrow morning. I sat and listened to him make the appointment, and I'm driving him, unless you want to."

"No, you'll have a better chance of getting him there without his complaining the whole way."

"That's why I volunteered for the duty." Some of Hattie's tension left her face.

"You make it sound like I'm not cooperative." Mock indignation grooved lines into Sean's face, while a twinkle sparkled in his eyes, his attention totally centered on Hattie.

"This Christmas you're getting an extra-special present, Miss Hattie," Brody said, exaggerating his Texan drawl.

She laughed. "I'll start making out my list."

Rebecca yawned, trying to stay up with the conversation, but her thoughts jumbled together in her mind until she stopped listening to what the other three were talking about. The comfort of the chair was luring her toward sleep.

Standing, Brody held out his hand to her. "You've got another long day tomorrow."

"How did the trial go?" Sean asked, lounging back on the couch at the same time Hattie did.

Another yawn escaped from Rebecca as she fit her hand within Brody's. "Actually I saw some hope today. I can see the end of the tunnel."

"Great! That coupled with Thomas opening his eyes last night is wonderful news. This family needs to get its life back."

Sean chuckled. "Says the mother hen."

Hattie playfully jabbed him in the arm.

"Ouch! I'm a sick man. You've got to be careful with me."

Hattie rolled her eyes while Brody tugged Rebecca to her feet.

"We'll leave these two to fight it out. After I walk Rebecca to her room, I'll be checking with the security detail outside."

"I can walk myself to my room. I've been doing it for years."

"Humor me after the day I've had."

"The day you had? You didn't find a dead man in your bed."

Brody guided Rebecca out of the den to the chuckles of the couple left in the room. "But I had to process the crime scene and start running down leads."

"Children, play nice," Sean called out.

Rebecca looked at Brody and burst out laughing. Her laughter unknotted the tense set of her shoulders and lightened the burden she'd been carrying all day.

At the staircase, she blocked Brody's path. "I'm going to see if Kim is still awake. Then, after I check on Aubrey, I'm going directly to my room. I really can do this by myself."

"Even as a young girl you used to give me grief for trying to help you."

She wanted to smooth the lines of worry from his face, but instead she curled her hands into fists to keep from touching him. She didn't want to spoil their friendship. They were starting to revive it after the years apart; it was as though they had been estranged. She couldn't risk any more than friendship with Brody. What if he'd been in the car when the bomb went off? She would be attending the funeral of another fallen officer.

Against her better judgment, she leaned toward him and planted a peck on his cheek, quickly pulling back before it evolved into something more. "Good night."

She spun around and mounted the stairs to the second floor. Pausing in Kim's doorway, she surveyed her niece's bedroom, noting the pile of clothes on the floor, tubes of lip-gloss and eye shadow out on her dresser. Rebecca had totally disagreed with Tory about getting Kim the makeup to play with, but Thomas had given in to his wife. What next? Heels? She wanted Kim to stay a child as long as she could. There was enough time later for her to grow up. But since Tory had come into Kim's life, she was less a tomboy and more a young girl who mimicked what Tory did. At least her niece was bonding with her stepmother. That had made her brother happy.

In the dim light, Rebecca saw one of Kim's eyes pop open, then quickly shut. "You can quit pretending, young lady. I know you aren't asleep."

Kim sat straight up, her hair a mess about her shoulders. "I can't sleep. Tomorrow when I come home from school, Hattie is gonna help me make the carrot cake from scratch for Rob. That's what Hattie said. What does that mean?"

"It isn't going to come out of a box. You'll put all the ingredients together. No shortcuts."

"Why?"

Rebecca closed the distance between them. "Because it's usually a lot better from scratch."

"Good. Then I'm glad I'm doing it that way. That's why Hattie wanted to make it tomorrow. She said we might not have enough time before he arrives on Wednesday."

Rebecca sat on the bed beside Kim and tweaked her nose. "Did you recite your speech for your dad today?"

"Yes. I'm ready to give it tomorrow." Kim cocked her head. "When will he wake up? I miss my daddy."

"I miss him too, but he's here with us. He just can't say anything right now. His body is mending itself while he gets a lot of good rest."

"I'm gonna tell him tomorrow he's had too much rest. It's time for him to wake up."

"Sweetie, he will, but in his own time." *Like with the Lord, I sometimes have to wait for His timing. Not always easy.* "Let me tuck you in, and, this time, go to bed."

As Rebecca left, she peered over her shoulder and winked at Kim, who immediately squeezed her eyes closed. Rebecca started to close the door.

"Leave it open. I promise I'm going to sleep."

"Good night, honey. Love you."

"Love ya, Aunt Becky."

In the hallway Rebecca slowed her step, her heart swelling with the love she had for her nieces. *Please, Lord, watch over them, and help them deal with what's going on with their dad. And help me deal, too.*

⋘≶⋙

J. R. perched on top of the ridge, with a view of some of the pastures on the Circle S Ranch as well as the house in the distance. Flattening himself against the hard, dry ground, he propped his elbows up and brought the night vision binoculars to his eyes. Not far below him, two men he'd hired over the phone crept along the fence line where a fourth of the herd was being kept. The men doused the brush with gasoline—exactly as he'd told them. The night was perfect for a little wildfire. The wind blew at about twenty miles per hour toward the main house and barn. With frightened cattle charging and trying to flee, the fence on the other side of the pasture wouldn't hold, not with fire eating its way toward the animals.

If the two guards didn't move fast enough, they wouldn't be able to get out of the way of the stampede. Collateral damage—a price they would pay for working for Thomas Sinclair.

The glee he felt from the prospects of tonight's work widened his grin. This plan had been years in the making, but it was worth every moment they'd had to wait.

Revenge is sweet, especially the longer I have to savor it. Mama had the right idea about this. I wish she was here to see all this.

⋘≶⋙

Brody stepped out onto the decking that wrapped halfway around the Sinclairs' two-story adobe house, which blended so well with the landscape of the ranch. When he was growing up, this place had been a second home to him. After his mother walked out on him and his father, he spent many a week out here when his dad was working long hours, especially in the summers. Although Rebecca was two years younger than he and Thomas, they had hung around together a lot in those days. Before they cared about the differences between a male and a female. Before they discovered the opposite sex. That was when everything began to shift into something different, something he'd not always known how to handle.

He lounged against the post. There was a part of him that wished things had never changed. But he knew that wasn't really possible. Children grew up. Life changed. What didn't in life.

With a sigh, he went to find the ranger in charge of patrolling the grounds. Before he turned in for the night, he'd check with Jake to make sure the guards on the cattle had reported in. They were instructed to do so every thirty minutes. What Jake and his dad had set up had so far kept the cattle rustlers away. One of the two ranches Jake had finally talked to reported some losses. Other than that, nothing had happened for a couple of days. Brody hoped the rustlers had moved on to fresh territory.

He strolled around to the yard between the house and the stables and found Ranger Dan Parker stationed there. "Quiet?"

Parker nodded. "I heard the trial went well today. Everything okay inside?"

"Yes, most have already gone to bed."

"I can imagine Judge Morgan is exhausted with all that has been happening."

"It was a long day, but hopefully the trial will be winding down soon. One more witness, then the defense presents its case."

"What case? Petrov's wife will testify her husband was home with her, the sister of the man running everything." Parker searched the darkness beyond the yard.

"I imagine they'll be emphasizing there's no forensics to support the state's case."

"The weapon was Petrov's, a witness identified him at the scene of the crime right after it happened, and another heard the man arguing with the victim minutes before."

"But by the time he was brought in there was no gunpowder residue on his hands."

"He wore gloves, and they were never found."

"Maybe." Brody lifted his shoulders in a shrug. "I'm going to check with Jake. Knowing Jake, he's still in his office."

"I haven't seen him go to the bunkhouse."

Brody strode toward the stables, noting that some of the lights were still on. The door to Jake's office stood ajar. When Brody entered, he found the foreman with his head down on the desk, his arms serving as a cushion. He hated waking him up, but he was sure the man hadn't wanted to fall asleep here.

Jostling his shoulder, Brody said, "Jake," then louder, "Jake, wake up."

The foreman shot straight up, blinking his eyes. "What's wrong?"

Brody leaned against the desk. "Nothing. I just thought you would be more comfortable sleeping in your bed."

"I still have another hour until one of my men comes and relieves me."

"When are the hands checking in again?"

Jake glanced at the clock on his desk. "Five minutes."

"I take it there haven't been any problems."

"No more cows are missing. It's been peaceful."

"With the sheriff doubling up on patrols in this area, the rustlers would be stupid hanging around here."

"Yeah, but I want to give this vigilance at least another week. And even then I'll keep the cattle close to the house even if I have to bring in more feed because they have grazed the ground bare."

A call came in, and Jake quickly answered. It was the team in the south pastures. As soon as he hung up the phone rang again. Replacing the receiver after listening and replying to his cowhand, he said, "East herd is okay."

Brody had discovered that his dad had made Kathy bring him to the ranch instead of having him stay with her. "I appreciate you not letting Dad go out with you today. He needed to rest."

"He didn't give me too much of a hard time. To tell you the truth, I think he was relieved I didn't need his help."

"He was up most of the night at the hospital, and although he won't admit it, he was worried he was having another heart attack."

Jake grinned, tipping his chair back and resting his boots on the desk. "Miss Hattie made it easy for me. She'd already asked him to help her in the house."

"She did?"

"She needed a taster. She was trying out a couple of new recipes to serve the guest Wednesday night."

"Rob Clark? I'd almost forgotten about him coming Wednesday. So much has happened since Rebecca asked him." Brody shook his head. "But my dad agreeing still surprises me. He bought the food taster ploy?"

"Not really. I think he's sweet on Miss Hattie. I can tell she is on your dad."

"Yeah, you'd have to be dead not to see the glances they give each other. I never thought I would become a chaperone for those two."

"No, you thought you might need one for you and Rebecca."

Brody's mouth dropped open. "I'm sure I didn't hear what I thought I heard."

"Yes, you did. I've been working for the Sinclair family almost as long as Miss Hattie. I remember you as a teenager, trying to act like you didn't care about Rebecca when it was obvious to everyone you did."

Not to Rebecca. "Thomas never said anything."

"He wouldn't. He was rooting for you two. I never did get to ask you what happened."

"She got married."

"No, before that."

"It just never was the right time. We were such good friends, and we didn't want anything to ruin that. She'd be dating someone. By the time she broke up with that guy, I was dating someone. Then Garrett came along and instead of breaking up with him, she married him." He was better off not loving someone. He could remember how hard his dad took it when his mother left and would only talk with him through her lawyer.

Jake glanced at the clock again. "The team in the north pasture should have reported in by now. Which shouldn't surprise me, really. Both of them are my newest hands. Not as invested in the Circle S as the rest of us."

"How new?"

Jake laughed. "You do have a suspicious mind. One was hired two years ago, and the other two and half years ago. Thomas treats his cowhands well, and they know when they have a good gig."

"I'm paid to be suspicious."

"For Rebecca's sake, I'm glad you are, and that you're here. Thomas would be."

The reminder of his friend, still lying in a hospital bed in a coma, made Brody tense up until his muscles ached. "C'mon, I'll ride out with you to see why your two men aren't checking in on time."

"No, I'll rouse Gus from bed. He's relieving me anyway in thirty minutes. I'll have him take my place early, and I'll go alone. Your job is to protect Rebecca. Mine is the ranch."

"But—"

"I know these two guys. I shouldn't have teamed them up. They get to jawing and forget the world around them."

"Call my cell if there's a problem."

"Yes, Mr. Texas Ranger." Jake accompanied him out of the office and went toward the bunkhouse.

Back on the front deck, Brody looked north. It was probably nothing, but just in case, he decided to go upstairs with his binoculars and survey the area. Striding to his rented car, he popped the trunk and took out his night vision binoculars, then made his way inside and up the stairs.

At the far end of the hallway, he switched off the overhead light and opened the blinds to check the north pastures—at least as far as these high-powered binoculars would allow. He swept the expanse outside the north window once, then again more slowly.

"What's going on?"

He whirled around to face Rebecca, her hair finger-combed, her feet bare, her short terry cloth robe on. "Nothing. Jake hadn't heard from the two cowhands out in the north pasture. He's going out there to check on them. I thought I would check from here."

"That's pretty far away. Did you see anything?"

"Yeah, Jake driving the Jeep toward the area."

"Should I be worried?"

Brody closed the distance between them. "No, you need to go back to bed. That's an order."

She arched a brow. "Oh?"

"Yes, ma'am. I'm in charge of your protection, and I'm protecting you from yourself."

Her laughter floated on the air. "It's more like I need to be protected from your he-man ways."

He turned her around and prodded her forward. "I'll escort you to your room."

"That could be dangerous for me."

His movements stilled. The vision of them kissing in the doorway of her bedroom days ago drenched him in a sudden sweat. He slammed the door on that picture before he could decide that kissing her once wasn't enough. She needed her sleep. He needed his. No telling what surprises tomorrow would bring.

At her door he leaned forward and lightly brushed his lips over her forehead. "Good night. I'll be ready to take you to the courthouse at seven-thirty tomorrow."

As she went into her bedroom, he started for the stairs. Through the slats in the window at the other end of the hallway, which faced south, a glow like the sun rising streamed into the house. He ran toward the window and pulled the blinds up. He didn't need his binoculars to know that there was a fire and, with the wind blowing from the south, that it was coming this way.

13

*T*he pounding at her door brought Rebecca straight up in her bed. Brody? She whipped back the covers and snatched up her robe, tying it as she rushed toward the door. When she opened it, Brody filled her vision. The chiseled stone of his expression alerted her to his having spent another night without much sleep.

"Get the girls and Tory and get out of the house. There's a fire in the south pasture, and it's coming this way. You should have time to get dressed. If there's a change, I'll let you know. I've called 911, as well as Jake, who is rounding up the men to fight the fire."

"What do I do after that?"

"Stay with the two rangers. I'm getting Hattie and Dad out, then going with Jake to survey the damage. He also saw it and called me. He's coming back from the north pasture."

"Have Hattie ring the bell to let everyone know there's an emergency." Rebecca shut her door and rushed to throw on some clothes.

A couple of minutes later, spurred by the sight of the fire out the south window, she quickened her pace toward her nieces' rooms. She woke Kim up first. "Get dressed. Two min-utes. There's a fire in the field."

Frowning, Kim rubbed her eyes. "Are we going to lose our home?"

"Don't know. I'm getting Aubrey up. You go and wake up Tory after you get dressed."

Five minutes later, carrying what she could, Rebecca emerged from the house with Kim and Aubrey flanking her, their arms full of their most prized possessions. Immediately, the two rangers surrounded them and guided them toward their SUV. Tory was sitting in the backseat. Sean and Hattie stood next to the car.

After the two girls climbed inside, Aubrey going into Tory's embrace, Rebecca turned toward the rangers. "I'm not going anywhere, but you need to take them somewhere safe."

"No, ma'am. My orders are to take everyone, including you."

"Whose orders?"

"Ranger Calhoun."

"Well, he isn't here. I can't leave here."

"And neither can I," Sean said, stepping forward. "I can help fight the fire."

Rebecca pivoted toward him, her hand on her waist. "After your hospital visit last night, there is no way I'm letting you exhaust yourself trying to fight a fire. Hattie, make sure he leaves."

"I'm going to follow in my car. There isn't enough room in that SUV and I need company." Hattie pointedly looked at Sean.

"Where are you going?" Rebecca asked Texas Ranger Parker.

"Brody offered his house. The U.S. Marshals are meeting us there. Even if the hands and the firefighters put the fire out, it will be chaotic around here. Not a safe place for y'all." Ranger

Parker opened the back door. "Please climb in." His glare challenged Rebecca to defy him.

"Please, Aunt Becky," Kim said over the blare of sirens coming down the road toward the house.

Rebecca stared south. In the distance, she could see the flames dancing along the ground, sparks caught on the wind and spreading closer. The scent of smoke saturated the air.

"Ma'am?"

"Oh, all right, but I don't like this one bit." Rebecca scrambled into the backseat and sat next to Kim, who clung to her.

As two more fire trucks from Dry Gulch arrived in the yard, Ranger Parker drove out to the highway.

"What's happening, Tor-eee?" Aubrey asked, a sob escaping at the end of her question.

"There's a wildfire out in the field. We're getting out of the firemen's way so they can put it out."

Kim lifted her head and peered out the window, and then whispered, "What about the animals?"

Rebecca hugged her niece to her so she wouldn't see the red inferno consuming the ranch. "They'll run away. They'll be all right." She prayed they would be—that they had a place to run to.

⌘

Both cowhands watching the herd in the south pasture galloped into the yard ahead of a stampede of cattle not forty feet behind them. The frantic sounds of the animals reverberated through the smoke-thick air. Firefighters and cowhands mobilizing to fight the fire scattered and tried to find a safe place to be as the cows charged through the wooden fence on that side of the house.

Brody hopped up on the back deck, with Jake right behind him. He saw a man trip and go down. Brody jumped down from his perch and raced toward the older ranch hand. The man got to his knees, looked at the wall of animals coming at him, and faltered. Brody flew toward him, picked him up, and kept going, pushing the man under a truck parked out back, then diving in behind him as the pounding hooves of the cattle churned up dust and chaos.

❧

With the children finally in bed and asleep, Tory paced from one end of Brody's living room to the other. Her sister-in-law's trembling hands and nervous flitting from one person to the next heightened Rebecca's panicky feeling. She wanted to shout at Tory to sit down but realized that wouldn't resolve the pent-up tension they'd all felt for over a week—as though waiting for the next catastrophe to strike. And it had tonight.

They could lose their home—a home built by their grandfather and added on to by their father. The place she'd grown up in gone, not to mention the memories stored inside—the pictures, the treasures.

"I'm just going to say what we're all thinking. There was no lightning storm tonight, so most likely the fire was arson." Sean put his arm around Hattie and pulled her close.

Tory paused in her pacing and faced them. "Will we know for sure?"

"Probably. That'll be for the arson expert to determine, but you can bet that my son will have someone out there looking for the source of the fire."

"Arson, Thomas's accident, cattle rustling. What's going on?" Tory's voice rose to a shrill pitch.

"Don't know for sure, but we've got help to figure it out." Rebecca bit her bottom lip and wished she had answers to all that was going on.

"Is this connected to that trial you're on?" Tory clutched the back of the chair near her, her hands digging into the leather so hard her fingertips reddened.

"I can't imagine cattle rustling having anything to do with the trial." She hoped it wasn't another thing to be piled on top of all the other reasons she had for feeling guilty.

"How about Thomas's accident or the fire?" Tory came around and sank into the chair across from Rebecca.

"I guess it could, if Thomas's accident wasn't really an accident, but there's no proof it was deliberately done. And if the fire was set, I could definitely see Alexandrov having someone do it."

"Alexandrov, the Russian mob guy?" Tory twisted her hands together, over and over.

Her sister-in-law was close to the edge. Concerned about Tory, Rebecca kept her voice even and soothing. "Yes, he runs the Russian Mafia in San Antonio and the surrounding area."

"Arrest him. Get him off the street."

"I wish we could. Knowing something and proving it are two different things."

"So this could be happening to us because you're the judge on that Russian gangster's trial. Step down. Get as far away from it as possible. Then maybe our life will go back to normal." Tory's voice gained volume as anger took hold of her. Her glare drilling into Rebecca, Tory grasped the arms of the chair.

"It's not that easy. The trial should be over by next week. How long the jury will deliberate, I can't say."

"Thomas shouldn't be . . ." Tory snapped her mouth closed and averted her gaze. Pushing herself to her feet, she stomped toward the hallway. "I'm going to try to get some sleep. I'm sure tomorrow will be long and difficult, even if the house is still standing."

Rebecca waited a good minute after Tory left before drawing in a deep, fortifying breath, which helped to ease the constriction about her chest. "Have I done this to everyone?"

The question hung in the silence for half a minute before Sean frowned and shook his head. "If the Russian Mafia is behind what happened at the ranch or to Thomas, they are the ones who are responsible. Not you. Do you understand?" His fierce tone and expression hammered home who he felt was the guilty party.

But still the guilt nibbled at her composure, snatching breath from her lungs. Her chest rose and fell as she gulped in oxygen-rich air.

Hattie left the comfort of Sean's loose embrace and knelt in front of Rebecca, taking her hands. "You are not responsible. Tory is exhausted and will feel a lot different when she gets the rest she needs. She needs to get some rest, to sleep for a good long while, and to focus on herself. Not spend all her time at the hospital, or she won't be any good to Thomas *when* he does wake up."

Sean spoke next, "The same goes for you, Rebecca. I've seen you drag yourself home and try to act like everything is the same as before. I know you're doing it for your nieces. But maybe you should talk with them. You've been so busy avoiding the subject of their father being in the hospital that I'm afraid the girls are scared to bring up the subject."

Rebecca gazed at Sean, his words sinking in as she thought back to the times she spent with Kim and Aubrey. Even when they went to visit their dad with her, she tried to keep everything upbeat, and any time one of them wanted to know how Thomas was really doing, she focused on the fact that his body was healing and that he'd wake up when he was better. She really didn't say much else. She didn't want the girls to continue to have nightmares, especially Kim. But she still did.

"If we're talking about Thomas, when the girls come into a room, we usually clam up. Kim's a smart girl. She knows what we're doing. She needs to feel she can freely talk about her father." Hattie patted Rebecca's arm, then rose. "I've done the same thing."

"But shouldn't we keep their life as normal as possible?" Rebecca's gaze skipped from Hattie to Sean and then back to the housekeeper.

"Yes, to a certain point, but we have to acknowledge the change, too." Hattie settled next to Sean as though she'd never left his side.

"You two are right. I'll have a talk with Kim tomorrow."

"Oh, no." Hattie covered her mouth, her eyes round.

"Rob is supposed to eat with us Wednesday night, and we might not have a place to do that." Rebecca didn't want another problem that needed solving.

"I know this is Brody's home, but I'm sure my son wouldn't mind if we had dinner here if we can't at the ranch. Kim has been looking forward to seeing him."

"Yeah, we can always make the cake here tomorrow, or even Wednesday. Before we start worrying about what to do, let's see what happens at the ranch."

Rebecca checked her watch. "I'm calling Brody. I can't stand not knowing what's going on."

❧

"What's going on, Brody?" Rebecca asked the second he answered his phone, holding it in one hand while using a shovel to keep any sparks that were landing in the yard around the house from catching on fire.

"Some of the cowhands and I are making a stand at the house, trying to keep the fire from spreading to it. The fire-fighters are out in the field directly to the south, trying to stop the fire, but with this wind some of the sparks are jumping the line."

"What happened to the cattle in the south pasture?"

"They came through here. Jake and a few other ranch hands are rounding them up and settling them down. We don't need another stampede."

"Anyone hurt?"

"No, not yet." The scent of smoke filled the air. "Gotta go."

When he hung up, he put his bandana up over his nose and went after another spark that had flared into a small flame when it landed on the grass. He pounded his shovel into it, extinguishing it before it became a raging inferno. With the wind, it wouldn't take much for that to happen.

In the glow from the fire in the nearby field, he looked around at the holes that he and the other men had created trying to put out the sparks, and it was as though they had gone treasure hunting and didn't have the exact location, and so they had dug everywhere.

"Over here," one of the cowhands yelled over the crackling of the fire. "I can't stop it."

Brody raced to help the man, trying not to suck in too much of the smoke-laden air.

❧

Wearing the same clothes she had on when she left the ranch last night, Rebecca rolled out of the bed she shared with the girls and stood next to them for a moment to see if her movements had disturbed either one. They still slept.

In the dim lamplight, Rebecca watched her nieces sleep. Her heart swelled at the sight. The king-sized bed had easily held her and the two girls. Brody's bed. His smell on the pillow. When she'd finally lain down three hours ago, she hadn't realized she was sleeping on his pillow, but waking up a few minutes ago, his musky scent surrounded her as if he were there holding her through the night.

She wished he were.

Had he come home yet?

With it still dark outside, Rebecca tiptoed from Brody's bedroom, passing the other two closed doors. She must be the only one up. She hoped the others slept better than she had. As she made her way toward the kitchen, the scent of coffee perfumed the air. Hoping it was Brody who was up, she quickened her step.

Entering the room, she found him standing at the counter, his hands clutching the edge, his head dropped down.

"Brody," she whispered, not wanting to startle him.

He didn't move for a long moment.

Worry pushed to the foreground. What was wrong?

Then he shifted around, black smudges on his face, his expression solemn, his eyes filled with weariness.

She hurried to him. "Are you hurt?"

He shook his head. The coffee behind him on the counter finished perking. He poured himself a mug and shuffled toward the table as though he were too tired to even pick up his feet. He plopped down onto the chair.

She needed caffeine and was desperate enough to drink the coffee. After filling her cup, she sat next to him. Brody reeked of the odor of smoke. But she didn't care. He was here and not hurt. That was the most important thing to her.

She laid her hand on his arm. "Was anyone hurt?"

"A couple of guys were treated for smoke inhalation, but other than that, no." His voice roughened with each word he spoke. Coughing, he continued, "We lost a few cattle that were caught in the fire. It's too hard to know the full extent of the damage since it's still dark, but men are guarding the area. I'll be back out there with the arson specialist. I doubt this was an accident."

"Me, too. Today is another important day for the trial. Short of something happening to me, I'll be at the courthouse on time. I want this trial over with as soon as possible. The prosecutor will rest his case after this last witness."

"I called Charlie to let him know what was going on. He was letting the detail on the witness know and telling them to add a few more men. This trial needs to end."

"How did Charlie feel about being woken up?"

"Someone had to let him know what was going on at the ranch. He was getting dressed and going to head in to work early."

"Early? I'd say that was an understatement. What time is it?" She scanned the kitchen, searching for a clock. On the stove the digital time proclaimed 4:45 a.m. "You know you shouldn't drink that coffee. You should get a few hours of sleep at least."

"This caffeine drink won't stop me when I finally lie down. I don't think anything will, but I want to take you to the courthouse and see Charlie, then I'll come home and crash until I have to pick you up."

"You don't have to. Randall can."

"No. I'm going to. Did you get any sleep?" His finger caressed the skin beneath her eye.

"A few hours. I was worried about you and everyone else at the ranch."

He brushed his fingertips across her other cheek. "Go back to bed now that you know we're fine. The house is still standing. The stables and barn, too." One corner of his mouth hiked up for a second before it fell back into place as though the effort to smile was too much. "I promise I'll wake you up in time to go to the courthouse."

His palm curved along her jawline. She pressed it against her face, relishing the feel of his touch. "Thank you, Brody, for all you've done for me. For us."

"I couldn't do anything less. We go way back. You're a—friend."

When he paused at the word *friend*, her lungs seized her breath and held it for a few seconds. "You've gone beyond the call of friendship or duty. How do I ever repay you?"

His features tensed into a frown. "Repay me? You don't. I'm glad to help you."

She smoothed her fingers over the lines at the side of his mouth, trying to coax a smile out of him. "I'm sorry. I know that. It's just that when I think of this past week you're always foremost in my thoughts."

He reached across and caught her face between his large, roughened hands. "I care for you, Rebecca. I'd forgotten how much until this past week, but . . ." He swallowed hard, his eyes shimmering.

"But what?"

"Nothing." He pulled her to him while at the same time leaning toward her.

His arms gathered her against him, and his mouth slanted across hers. The kiss started as a gentle mating, but soon it evolved into a possession that threatened her peace of mind, breaking down all the barriers she'd erected. Tired of fighting her feelings, she surrendered to his kiss. She let herself enjoy the pure pleasure of the tender feel of his lips against hers.

When he pulled back slightly, his breathing heavy, he laid his forehead against hers, his eyes closed. Linked together in an embrace, she savored the moment for what it was. Soon real life would intrude and all her defenses would go back up. But for the few minutes she reveled in the femininity he provoked in her. They were just a man and a woman—no past history, no people trying to harm them.

He sucked in another deep breath, his chest swelling. "You need to go back to bed."

"It would be nice to have my life back."

"Yes. Back to normal."

She chuckled. "I'm not sure that will happen." Normal? When he had disrupted her life emotionally? If he pursued a romantic relationship, she might give in and want more. Then what? She would have put herself in the same position she'd been in when Garrett was killed three years ago. Garrett's job had been dangerous. So was Brody's. Someone had already tried to kill him because of his involvement in this case. What if they succeeded? How could she live with that?

He pulled away from her, giving each of them the space they needed to remember what was happening around them. His gaze linked with hers. In the smoldering depths of his eyes, she glimpsed wariness. They had had their chance at love once, but at the time she couldn't see him as anything other than a best friend. Now she didn't know how she saw him. Everything in her life was in flux. She didn't trust her emotions, not when she was a target for the Russian Mafia.

"Good night, or maybe I should say good morning. I need to be at the courthouse by eight thirty." She turned away from him, but the whole way out of the kitchen she sensed his intensity boring into her back.

What I'm feeling isn't love. It's friendship. It's the by-product of the danger I'm in right now. Nothing is real, nothing is to be trusted, especially my emotions.

❦

"He's here," Kim said as she ran into the kitchen at the ranch. "He just pulled up to the house. What should I do?"

Rebecca pressed her lips together to keep from laughing at the perplexed expression on her niece's face. "Go let Rob in when he rings the doorbell."

"Yes, I can do that."

"I want to." Aubrey put the spoon with the leftover icing into the bowl and hopped down from the chair. She rushed after Kim.

Hattie looked at Rebecca and chuckled. "I don't think the fact we had a fire and stampede has affected them one bit. They're going about a hundred miles per hour."

"It helped that we were able to return to the house almost immediately and the ranch hands have been working to get everything back to normal."

"Where's Brody?"

"He went with Jake out to the south pasture to make sure there aren't any hot spots and to check out where the fire started."

Hattie removed the brisket from the oven. "To think someone used gasoline and deliberately set the fire. What's the world coming to? That wildfire could have spread to the other ranches and hurt even more folks and livestock."

"That might have been the intent. With the cattle stampeding, they created mass confusion. Thankfully our cowhands have been trained in what to do in case of a fire, and the fire department from Dry Gulch got here in record time."

"Has Tory returned from the hospital?"

"She'll be here in fifteen or twenty minutes. Thomas was restless for her today. She called me at lunch all excited, but she wanted to be here for Rob's visit. She wants to thank him for what he did for me." Sounds of voices coming from the foyer drifted toward Rebecca. "I don't know how much Kim slept last night. She had sugarplums dancing in her head. All she talked about was Rob."

"She has a crush on him. He's a hero to her."

"He is to me, too. I could have been seriously hurt if he hadn't been in the right place at the right time."

"Let's go meet this young man. I'm anxious to thank him, too."

≈੦≈

Brody studied the burn pattern, the stench of gasoline still evident almost two days later. "They must have used a lot of gasoline."

"They didn't care that we knew it was arson. They left the gasoline cans at the scene." Jake gestured toward the area where the firefighters had found the evidence.

"I would say that could have been a mistake, but we didn't find one fingerprint on any of the cans. Now that you've accounted for the cattle, how many did you lose?"

"No more than seven, so I don't think it was the cattle rustlers. Why would they burn the cattle instead of stealing them? We've found most of the cattle, or rather, their dead carcasses."

"I agree the intent wasn't to cover taking more cattle. The intent was to burn down the house and other buildings." Brody walked back to the Jeep and hopped in on the passenger side. "How are the two cowhands?"

"Embarrassed, angry, and suffering nasty headaches."

"But they're alive. They should be thankful for that."

Jake started the engine and headed back toward the house. "They survived only because one of them recovered consciousness and managed to drag the other out of the way of the cattle. If they'd stayed where they went down, they would have been trampled."

Or at least that was what the two cowhands said when they were found. Sheriff Overstreet was checking into their lives. Was there any connection to either the Russian Mafia or the gang? Although he didn't think the Dos Huesos Cruzados Gang was behind this, Brody was covering all his bases. The Russian Mafia had had a clear motive.

As Jake drove past the burn line, where the fire had finally been put out, the main house stood only thirty yards away. Too close. What was the motive for the fire? With all the security in the immediate area of the house, it would have been hard to get close enough to actually burn down the house. Setting the fire in the pasture gave everyone a chance to get out of its way. Pretty risky as a harassment statement for the Russians, but maybe they didn't think everyone would get out in time. The wind had been strong that night.

Brody's gut burned as though a spark had taken hold and flared into a wildfire that was out of control within him. He didn't have a good feeling about this. There was something he was overlooking. If he couldn't figure it out, someone else might die.

"It looks like your company has arrived." Jake came to a stop at the front door, noting the dusty white pickup parked not far away and two rangers at the front door checking the visitor for any weapons. "Poor Clark, he probably didn't realize what he was getting into when he accepted the invitation to dinner."

"Yeah. Thank God Rob Clark was able to get to Rebecca in time."

Brody remembered watching the near hit-and-run—too far away to do anything—with frustration and helplessness. He would never have been able to forgive himself if something had happened to Rebecca that day at the hospital. She had been under his care. He owed this Rob a debt of gratitude.

❧

Kim led the way to the stables to show Rob her horse, and Aubrey had insisted he see hers, too. Rebecca smiled at the small battle between the two sisters for the young man's attention.

Rob paused at the first paddock, nearest the stables where Dusty, Kim's pinto, was kept. Leaning against the fence, he watched the horse approach Kim, then nuzzle her hand for the treat she had brought for her mare. Rebecca came to Rob's right side, and Tory flanked him on the left. Ranger Parker stood in the background, his gaze sweeping the surroundings.

"Ma'am, you have a nice spread. I've dreamt of settling down one day and getting myself a ranch. Not this big, though. A small one, to raise horses." Rob looked from Tory to Rebecca.

"Not cattle?" Rebecca asked while Aubrey drew her small horse to her by presenting the flat of her palm, which held pieces of carrot.

"Let me show you the stables. We have two—a small one and another, larger one, where our more expensive horses are sometime kept. With all that has been happening, most of them are inside their stalls." Tory started for the large stable, where Jake kept his office. "The cowhands use the smaller one when needed."

"Why are the horses in their stalls?" Rebecca heard Rob ask her sister-in-law as they strolled toward the twenty-stall stable. She was surprised that Tory knew anything about the horses. She always stayed away as if she were afraid of the animals.

Thomas had been toying with breeding quarterhorses, but had not yet fully committed to the idea. Rebecca didn't know what would happen now. Until Thomas was conscious and his health stronger, she would have to run the ranch with Jake's help because Tory knew next to nothing about it.

Rebecca wanted to be involved. She watched until Kim and Aubrey had finished feeding treats to their horses, then joined them to follow Tory and Rob inside. Rebecca glanced back and found the ranger trailing about three yards behind them.

Aubrey took Rebecca's hand, while Kim skipped ahead to catch up with Rob and Tory. "Why didn't Mr. Calhoun come with us?"

"He got a phone call he needed to take. He may be down here when he's through."

"I like him."

"So do I, sweetie."

"He likes you."

"Why do you say that?"

"He's always looking at you."

"That's because he's making sure nothing happens to me." She'd wished she didn't have to say anything to either girl about what was going on, but she'd had to explain the protective detail at the ranch. Members of the detail even drove her nieces to school.

"Cuz he doesn't want anything to happen to you like happened to Daddy? When will Daddy be home? I miss him putting me to bed, reading me a story."

Rebecca swallowed hard, not sure how to answer Aubrey. "I can read you a story."

"Not the same, Aunt Becky. When you do, you don't use the voices like Daddy."

"Why didn't you say anything? I can try to do that."

Aubrey stopped just outside the large stable and turned her face up to Rebecca. "It still wouldn't be the same. Daddy's always happy. He makes me laugh. You're sad."

"Oh," was all Rebecca could say.

"But I love you anyway," her younger niece quickly said to reassure Rebecca.

"I guess I'm going to have to have your dad teach me how when he gets better."

"I've been praying every night for Daddy to wake up. Why isn't God listening to me?"

Rebecca knelt in front of Aubrey and clasped her arms. "He's always listening to us. He has His reasons. Maybe your daddy needs more rest. Sometimes we don't always know what's best for someone, but the Lord does. Keep praying."

Aubrey bent over and kissed Rebecca on the cheek. "I won't stop."

"Good. We'll shower heaven with our prayers."

"You pray?"

"Every day."

Aubrey whirled around and raced toward Tory, Rob, and Kim. Rebecca rose slowly, watching them. She was glad to see Tory smiling and the girls laughing at something Rob had said to them.

A tingling sensation skimmed down her body. A grin came to her lips. Rebecca didn't have to look over her shoulder to know that Brody was behind her. She sensed him as though she was able to home in on him. Even when they were children, she'd always known where Brody was. When they'd played hide-and-seek, she'd always found him.

"Is everything all right?" she finally asked with a glance behind her.

"The DNA results came back from the crime scene at your house. We got a match."

"You did? Who?"

"Alexandrov's bodyguard, Nicholas Saldat."

Rebecca stiffened. "Do you think Alexandrov was in my house?"

"We're showing your neighbors his photo, along with the bodyguard's."

"Do you have a BOLO out on Saldat?"

"Yes. I want to move fast before Alexandrov finds out. Charlie thinks he has a location on the Saldat. If they get him, I'm going to the station to have a little conversation with him."

"Ask him about both murders."

"I will, but I don't think he murdered the guy found behind the pawnshop. When I compared the scenes, I could see that although they were similar on the surface, there were too many differences in method and weapon."

"He could have used a different weapon and method."

"Yes, and I'm not totally ruling that out. But I'm leaving it open that there are two killers, not one." Brody's cellphone rang, and he answered the call with, "Calhoun here."

He listened to the speaker on the other end, then said, "I'll be there."

When he disconnected the call, he grinned. "They've found Saldat. They're bringing him in. I'll let the security detail know where I'm going."

"I've noticed them around more than usual."

"The fire was a bold move. They don't want to be caught unaware."

"We all were caught unaware with the fire."

"I'll let you know what happens."

As Brody walked toward Ranger Parker who stood not far away, Rebecca's phone interrupted the quiet with the old-fashioned ringtone of a phone from forty years ago. When she answered, the caller identified himself as the prosecutor on the Petrov trial. She knew Barton well, having worked with him for a couple of years before she became a judge.

"Is there a problem?"

"No. In fact, the opposite. Petrov wants to cut a deal. He'll testify against Alexandrov for immunity from prosecution. We're drawing up the papers and want to make sure you're on board. He can give us dates and information to place Alexandrov at the scene of several unsolved murders. Petrov's trial can be over tomorrow."

14

*Y*ou're going to have to have more than that to bring Alexandrov in." Rebecca swung around to see if she could catch Brody before he left, but he was already gone.

"He's kept an account of the hits. The voice on the recorder will match Alexandrov's, or so he says. If the information doesn't give us enough to convict Alexandrov, the deal is off the table. The Feds really want Alexandrov. Petrov is nothing compared to his brother-in-law, who ordered the hits. That innocent businessman Petrov killed wasn't innocent. Petrov is giving us information on his involvement."

"So why is Petrov doing this?" She asked the prosecutor on the phone.

"Alexandrov told him he would take care of him. That he wouldn't see any prison time. After the prosecution presented its case, Petrov has seen that that's not going to happen."

"What do you want?"

"We'll reduce his charge down to manslaughter. He's been in jail almost a year since this began. When he goes into the Witness Protection Program, he'll be under house arrest for the remaining years of his sentence. He'll wear an ankle monitor.

If he breaks any part of his sentence stipulations, he'll go to prison to finish his term."

Rebecca began walking away from the stable as Tory, Rob, and her nieces started for the exit. "Where he will most likely be killed."

"Yes, and he knows that."

"Send me the agreement first thing tomorrow morning. You do realize this will start all over with Alexandrov." The thought of going through this again, especially when they were close to a possible conviction of Petrov, didn't sit well with the prosecutor in her. But she also realized Alexandrov had to be stopped. He ruled with fear and intimidation and was quickly getting a tight grip on the area. They needed to stop him now and send a message.

"The Feds will be taking over his case. There are charges that go across state lines. In the short time Alexandrov's been here, he has expanded quickly, even into some of the surrounding states and Mexico."

"No wonder the Dos Huesos Cruzados Gang is so upset. They saw what was coming."

"Yeah, a total takeover by the Russian Mafia."

The girls hurried toward Rebecca. She lowered her voice and said, "I'll see you first thing in the morning," then clicked off before Kim and Aubrey were in earshot. The Petrov trial had already disrupted their lives far too much. She didn't want it to intrude any more.

"Rob has to leave," Kim said when she skidded to a halt. "I told him he could take home what was left of the carrot cake."

"That's a great idea." Rebecca took the hand of each girl and fell into step with Tory and Rob.

For the first time in weeks the weight she had carried was lifted from her. Hope nipped at the edges of her mind.

Just maybe things would return to normal soon, especially if Thomas awakened.

⁓

J. R. paced the floor of his rented house, waiting for the call. He should have heard something an hour ago. When the cellphone finally rang, he yanked it out of his pocket and flipped it open.

"It's about time." J. R. bit back the impatience surging through him. He wanted this over with.

"It's all true. The Petrov trial is over. Petrov made a deal. Judge Morgan signed off on it and sent the jury home."

"That means we go on to the next part of our plan." Anticipation replaced his earlier impatience. Finally the end game.

"Yes, you know what to do. She thought her woes were because of the trial. She doesn't know what heartache is. She will soon."

"I've enjoyed throwing her off what is really going on, but I want her to know why in the end."

"She will, but we'll be out of the country with all the money by that time."

When he disconnected, he placed a call. "Laura, this is Jim. I enjoyed our time together a few nights ago. How about going to dinner tomorrow? I found a nice restaurant I think you'll like."

"How about I treat you to dinner at my house? I love to cook and don't get to that much. Living alone and cooking for one isn't fun."

J. R. grinned. "This guy isn't gonna turn down a home-cooked meal. What time?"

"Seven."

Perfect. This is going better than I thought it would. In the background he heard voices. A man said something about a job well done. Cheers followed his statement. "Where are you?"

"A few of us who worked on the Petrov case are out celebrating."

"Have fun. See you tomorrow."

When he ended the call, he sank onto a nearby couch, his smile growing. *Because soon you won't have any more fun.*

⁓⁓

"Who was that, Laura? You're blushing," Rebecca said. They were sitting in the Blue Bonnet Cafe not far from the courthouse.

"Jim. We've got a date tomorrow night."

"What is this, the third date?" Detective Charlie Nelson scooped up some dip with his chip and popped it into his mouth.

"I didn't realize you were keeping track. How did you know?"

Charlie tapped his temple. "I'm all-knowing. How do you think I solve my cases? You can't keep much from me."

Laura's blush deepened, and Rebecca decided to come to her friend's rescue. "What about you, Charlie? Who are you seeing?"

"No one. Who has time with all that's been going on?"

Brody lounged back in his chair at the table for six. "I have to agree with Charlie."

Deputy U.S. Marshall Wentworth sighed and pushed to his feet, tossing down some money. "Which reminds me, I have a wife who hasn't seen a lot of me lately. Y'all continue this celebration without me. I'm going to have my own celebration with my wife."

Rebecca gave the marshal a mock look of fright. "You mean I'm not going to have you following me around? I was just getting use to you or one of your men always being nearby."

Randall laughed. "I think you'll adjust. Alexandrov is in jail. Petrov is somewhere safe. You won't have anything to do with Alexandrov's trial. That'll be federal. And in the last two days, the FBI has rounded up quite a few members of his mob. It's Friday. Enjoy the weekend."

As the marshal walked away, Charlie signaled to the waitress for the check. "This is on me. My life is going to be so much easier now."

But before the young woman could lay the bill on the table, Rebecca snatched it out of her hand. "No, it's my treat. I owe each one of you. No telling what would have happened if not for you all."

"Our lives will be easier until the next big case or trial comes along." Laura lifted her iced tea in a toast. "Here's to people getting what's coming to them. May Alexandrov spend many years in prison contemplating what he has done wrong."

"More likely he will be trying to figure out where Petrov is. I understand Petrov's wife won't be going into Witness Protection with her husband. Petrov's choice, not his wife's." Charlie downed the rest of his coffee.

"He doesn't trust the woman. What kind of marriage is that?" Laura shook her head. "I'd rather be single."

Rebecca laid down the money for the bill, then stood. "People give up being able to trust others when they decide to go into that line of work. It certainly makes me glad I'm on the right side of the law."

Brody scraped back his chair. "Power and money is everything to them. Good night, Laura, Charlie."

As Rebecca weaved her way to the exit, she glanced at Brody. "This is the last day you have to take me home. I don't know what it's going to feel like driving myself around."

He chuckled. "It's only been a couple of weeks. I think you'll get the hang of driving yourself soon enough."

"I imagine I will. I like my independence."

Outside in the warm September evening Brody guided her toward his new gray SUV. "I know I appreciate my own wheels."

"Ah, so you know what I've been going through."

At the SUV, he opened the passenger door for her. "The one I'm worried about is Dad. He's been enjoying himself at the ranch, especially with Hattie."

Rebecca waited until Brody had rounded the front of the car before saying, "I was going to say that about Hattie. I've never seen Hattie so dressed up just to stay around the house to cook and clean. I'm constantly catching them looking at each other. It's not that they didn't know each other before."

"True, but Hattie was married until five years ago, when her husband died."

"She deserves to be happy. She's given so much to my family. When the girls' mother died, she was there for them, especially when Thomas was so distraught."

Brody pulled out of the parking lot and into traffic. "What are you going to do now? Go back home? Stay at the ranch?"

"Definitely stay at the ranch. I've decided to sell my house. Eventually I'll get an apartment when my nieces are more settled. Hopefully because Thomas has come home. I think Tory appreciates me being there."

"I have some more leads to run down on the fire. If you're okay with it, I'd like to stay at the ranch over the weekend."

Rebecca angled toward him. "What aren't you telling me?"

"I want to be satisfied you and the ranch aren't in anymore danger from this cattle-rustling ring. An informant has come forward about a slaughterhouse that isn't totally aboveboard. We're raiding it tomorrow to see what we can find. Sheriff Overstreet is getting the warrant first thing in the morning. I'm going along on the raid."

"So this might be the end of the cattle rustling, too. How glorious. When I spoke with the doctor today, he seemed more optimistic about Thomas for the first time. The swelling in his brain has gone down. He's been restless. I know he's going to wake up. If we aren't there, the staff will notify us immediately. I told them to call even if it was in the middle of the night."

"That's great news."

"I'm going to spend tomorrow afternoon taking the girls to see their dad, then on a special outing. You're always welcome to tag along. I may have withdrawal symptoms without my bodyguard around."

"Ma'am. I can accommodate you after the raid," Brody drawled, then gave her a wink.

She blew a long breath out. "For the first time in weeks, I can finally relax. I'll probably sleep for twelve hours."

"We have about forty minutes. Take a little nap. I have a feeling that when you get back to the ranch you'll have a couple kids hanging off you, wanting your attention."

"So true, but their aunt doesn't mind." She laid her head on the back cushion, her eyelids closing.

❦

Brody entered the interview room at the sheriff's office and plopped a folder down on the table in front of the suspect. "We've been busy gathering lots of evidence against you and your men this morning. Your place of business was very accommodating to us." Across from the husky man whose weathered face aged him ten years, Brody leaned forward, towering over him. "You *will* be convicted of cattle rustling, especially since one of your crew was forthcoming with us."

Ethan Johnston sat stiff in the chair, his thick, dark eyebrows crunched, his glare glued on a spot to the left of Brody.

"Why did you come back to the Circle S Ranch and set fire to the south pasture?"

Not a muscle moved—it was as if Johnston was paralyzed. No indication he had heard the question.

Brody settled into the chair across from the suspect. "I can make this easy for you, or hard. We're interviewing your three men as we speak. One has already admitted to what you all are doing. It won't be long before he or one of his buddies cops a plea. I want to know about the fire. I want to know who you're selling the meat to. I'll be generous to the person who gives me that information."

Johnston's glare swung to Brody. "I don't know what you're talking about. You can't pin something on me that I didn't do."

Brody spread the papers they had gathered at the slaughterhouse. "Your own papers tell us otherwise."

The man flicked his gaze at the evidence. "I'm talking about the fire. I didn't have anything to do with that. I want my lawyer."

"Fine. I'll be glad to give you a phone to call your lawyer. No information, no deal." Brody shoved his chair back and rose, snatching up the folder.

When he left the interview room, Sheriff Overstreet turned toward him. "Good thing we don't have to depend on him. The case is coming together quite nicely. His crew isn't very loyal." The corners of his mouth dropped down. "But all of the other suspects are saying the same thing. They don't know anything about a fire at the Circle S Ranch. They said their boss is the only one who knows where the meat is going."

"That's what Johnston said. They didn't set the fire. Otherwise, nothing else."

Sheriff Overstreet massaged the back of his neck. "I'm beginning to think they didn't do it. Someone else is responsible for the fire."

His gut churned. "You may be right. If that's the case, then it is mostly likely Alexandrov's minions. It'll certainly be something I'll be chatting with him about. As I dig into his businesses and life, I'll be looking for evidence to support his guilt."

"At least the cattle rustling will stop. I know some ranchers who will be glad to hear that."

"Rebecca will be. I'm heading to the Circle S right now. I'll let her know we've caught the rustlers."

But as Brody left the sheriff's office, that nagging feeling he got when something didn't quite fit together kept bothering him. He kept running some of the facts from the crimes committed recently through his mind, trying to make some kind of sense out of them. It had been a long shot that they could get DNA from the vomit found in the alley near the pawnshop, and they hadn't been able to. Although at first glance similar, the murder of the witness found in Rebecca's bed had a different feel than the guy killed behind the pawnshop as if someone had heard about the man in the alley and had tried to copy the murder with the witness, blaming the Dos Huesos Cruzados Gang, or at the least had tried to throw off the police to what was really going on. They might have the witness's killer, but he thought there was another killer out there. Another member of the mafia or the gang? Or someone entirely different?

What if everything goes back to Thomas and his "accident"?

"Why all these questions about Thomas?" Rebecca asked Brody as they got off the elevator later that day at Mercy Memorial Hospital. She glanced down the hall toward her brother's room. "Why is the officer still outside of Thomas's room?"

"I'm taking another look at the things that happened to Thomas and his ranch."

She stopped and moved to the side to allow an orderly pushing a wheelchair to go by. "The cattle rustlers struck a couple of other ranches. Not just the Circle S. We found no evidence that Thomas's accident was anything but that. Nothing in his blood work. No wounds that don't fit with what happened to him."

"But as I told you earlier, the fire wasn't started by the cattle rustlers."

"Because they said so. How many criminals have denied doing something?"

"I'm still trying to link them to the arson, but I'm also looking at other possibilities, including Alexandrov's ordering the fire. But to tell you the truth, something isn't adding up."

She wanted it over with. "Is this your cop instinct on overdrive?"

"Humor me. I want you safe."

"Alexandrov is in jail, along with a lot of his men. There's no reason for him to go after me now that the trial is over."

"Why was Peter Ivanov killed? We can't link it to either the Russian Mafia or the gang."

"Exactly. If someone was after me, they certainly wouldn't have any reason to kill Ivanov."

At the end of the corridor where Thomas's room was located, a flurry of activity drew her attention. A nurse went in, and soon the staff doctor was striding toward the same destination.

"Let's go. Something is happening with Thomas." Rebecca hurried toward the room, and the officer opened the door for her.

Inside, Tory stood off to the side with an arm around each stepdaughter. They had come to see Thomas while Rebecca waited for Brody to return from the sheriff's office.

Kim stretched her neck and leaned around the nurse to look at her dad. Rebecca shifted her gaze to her brother. He lay there with his eyes closed just as he had the past couple of weeks.

The doctor tested the reflexes on the bottom of Thomas's feet. His toes curled down.

Rebecca moved closer. "What's going on?"

"Dad jerked when I hit Aubrey, and she screamed. I was sure he opened his eyes."

The doctor lifted her brother's eyelid, shining a light into his eye. "His pupils react to the light. That's good. His reflexes are normal."

Using his knuckle, the doctor pressed into Thomas's breastbone. Thomas flinched as though trying to get away from the doctor.

"Good. He's feeling pain. Mrs. Sinclair, I think your husband is coming out of his coma."

Aubrey and Kim cheered—loudly.

Thomas shifted, attempting to roll toward the sound. Rebecca's breath seemed trapped insider her lungs. Then her brother went still. Slowly, she released her breath and nibbled on her thumbnail.

"He's gonna wake up. He's gonna wake up." Kim jumped up and down, clapping her hands.

"Child, this is a hospital. People are trying to rest," Tory said, putting a restraining hand on the ten-year-old.

Her niece peered up at her stepmother and wiggled from beneath the grip. "Sorry. I'm just so excited."

Tory smiled at Kim, the corners of her mouth quivering. "So am I, but it may take a while before he's fully awake. Right, Doctor?"

"Yes, it could. But hold on to the news that he is much better." The doctor started for the door with the nurse. "If anything changes, let us know."

For the next hour, Rebecca sat on the couch, sandwiched between Kim and Aubrey. Tory paced the room, stopping by the bed every few minutes to see how Thomas was doing. But there was no change.

"He hasn't moved in a long time," Aubrey cried out, sticking her thumb into her mouth and sucking on it. She pressed her face against Rebecca.

A knot of emotions jammed Rebecca's throat. She swallowed several times before she replied, "It will take time."

Tory came to the child, knelt down in front of her, and took her hands. "The waiting is the hardest. Why don't you let your Aunt Becky take you home where it won't seem so long? I'll call the minute anything changes."

"I don't wanna go." Aubrey hunkered down closer to Rebecca. "Do I hafta?"

Rebecca looked at Tory, whose eyes held a dull shadow and whose hair was not its usual well-coiffured style. Instead, it fell in messy waves about her pale face. Rebecca remembered the agony of waiting to hear about Garrett. Not knowing what was going to happen. Praying for the best.

"We'll wait a little longer, then we'll have to leave. What do you think, Tory? Half an hour, tops?"

Relief fluttered in her sister-in-law's eyes. "Yes, that sounds fine."

"That way we'll get back to the ranch and you two will still have time to tend to your horses. You know how much they look forward to seeing you all." Rebecca hugged the girls to her.

"Yeah, I bet Princess has missed me," Aubrey mumbled around the thumb still in her mouth.

Rebecca stared at Brody sitting in a chair on the other side of Thomas's bed, with his legs stretched out in front of him, his cowboy hat pulled down low, veiling his expression. This whole time he'd been unusually quiet. She wouldn't be surprised if he'd fallen asleep. She'd gotten up in the middle of the night, and he'd still been downstairs, prowling the rooms as though on guard. She wasn't sure how much rest he'd gotten, but it couldn't have been much because he'd been up when she went to the kitchen in the morning. He was at the table nursing a mug of coffee, and seeing the half-empty pot, she could tell it wasn't his first cup.

When half an hour had passed without any kind of movement from Thomas, tears filled Aubrey's eyes. "I want my daddy to wake up."

"I know, Sweetie. We all do. Remember, God has picked the perfect time for him to wake up. His body is healing while he sleeps."

"Why is God being so mean to us?" Kim asked—the first words out of her mouth in over an hour.

Aubrey burst out crying. "God hates us."

Brody sat up straight, pushing his hat up on his forehead.

His and Rebecca's gazes touched briefly before she pulled Aubrey closer to her and patted her back. Aubrey's wails resonated through the room. "Honey, God is love. He would never hate you. Ever."

"How do you know?" Kim asked, a wet track streaking down her face.

"In here I know," Rebecca placed her hand over her heart. "He's always with us even when we're hurting."

Aubrey turned her face up to Rebecca. "Why does he let us hurt? My heart aches, Aunt Becky. I don't want it to."

"Neither do I, but God lets people make their own choices. Sometimes when they do, they get hurt. But he doesn't abandon us, or get mad that we didn't make a better choice. He's there, loving us through the hurt."

"Rebecca," Brody called out.

She looked toward him. He pointed at Thomas.

When her gaze lit upon her brother, he was staring straight at her.

15

Tory rushed to the hospital bed before Rebecca could get up from the couch. "Thomas, you're awake!" Clasping her husband's hand, she hovered over him.

Rebecca let the girls run to their father while she hung back, tears coursing down her face. Brody came to her side and held her against him.

"Daddy, we missed you." Kim grasped Thomas's other hand while Aubrey tried to climb up onto the bed.

Tory stopped her. "You might hurt him."

Thomas blinked, his gaze roaming from one person to the next. When it fell on Rebecca at the end of the bed, his forehead wrinkled.

"Honey, do you need anything?" Tory pushed the call button.

He mumbled, "Water," in a dry, raspy voice.

Tory poured him a glass from the pitcher on the bedside table, then held the straw up to his mouth for him to drink. He took a couple of sips before his eyes closed, his head rolling to the side.

"Daddy," Aubrey cried out.

Kim shook his arm. "Wake up. Don't go to sleep."

Tory set the drink on the table. "I've been reading up on patients coming out of a coma. This is perfectly normal. They still need rest and will go in and out for a while. We need to let him get the sleep he needs. Okay, Kim? Aubrey?"

Both girls nodded their heads but still held onto their father. Rebecca settled her hand on each niece's shoulder. "Let's go home and take care of the horses. I know Angel Fire could use a good ride. How about yours?"

"But what if Daddy wakes up again?" Kim swiped at the tears that flowed down her cheeks.

"We'll be back tomorrow. Each day he'll get better and better and be able to stay up longer. But only if he gets the rest he needs, like Tory said." Taking their hands, Rebecca moved toward the door, with Brody following.

Out in the hall the girls wrapped their arms around Rebecca. Her heart expanded, and her throat closed with emotion. Over their heads she stared into Brody's eyes, knowing exactly how her nieces felt. She wanted Thomas awake, reassuring them that he would be all right.

Brody gave her a lopsided grin and said, "I hope I'm invited to go riding with y'all. I could use the break."

Kim peeled herself away from Rebecca and twisted around, leaning her head back to look up at him. "I'll show you my secret place. It's so peaceful. I like to go out there to think."

"That sounds perfect." Brody held out his hand and Kim took it.

As Brody and Kim walked toward the elevator, Rebecca fought back the tears that were threatening. Hope that Thomas would be all right blossomed within her. With Aubrey in tow, she started after the pair. More than anything she wanted to stay, but the girls didn't need to spend hours at the hospital waiting for their daddy to wake up again.

The sound of giggles drifted to Rebecca as Kim and Aubrey played in the stream, trying to catch fish with their hands after Brody showed them how.

Sitting under the shade of an oak, Rebecca twisted around toward Brody. "We should have brought towels to dry them off with."

"It's unusually hot today. I bet it doesn't take too long for them to dry in the sun."

"I don't think I've ever seen either one stand still so long, waiting for a fish to swim by."

"Good training in patience. Dad taught me. Can't say that I caught very many while I was growing up."

"But you did today."

"I've learned to wait when I want something." His gaze held hers.

Suddenly breathless, she asked, "What do you want?" Her heartbeat kicked up a notch from the intensity of his look.

"That's changing."

She finally lowered her gaze. "What's that mean?" Her pulse beat even faster.

"My life has changed since I move back to San Antonio. For one thing, I have my dad to think about."

"Oh." For a few seconds she'd thought he meant something else—something involving her. "I know I've enjoyed renewing our friendship. I hope you won't be a stranger. The girls talk about you a lot. 'Mr. Calhoun did this.' 'Mr. Calhoun showed me how to do that.'"

"Thomas was my best friend. He still is. We may not have seen each other a lot in the past ten years, but that friendship is still there. I intend to be in his life and in his daughters' lives. They're special."

"Yes, they are." Glancing toward the girls, who trudged out of the stream and plopped down on the grass a few yards away, Rebecca remembered the times she and Garrett had talked about having children. She still wanted them. Being with her nieces only reinforced that.

Kim held up a medium-sized turtle. "Look what we found in the water, Aunt Becky."

Aubrey took the reptile and put it in the thick grass, sunlight streaking the lush green carpet. She offered the turtle something to eat. "He likes leaves."

"I recall when we used to come out here and play. That's probably a baby of a baby of the same turtle we captured. Dad wouldn't let your daddy and me keep it. We had to come back and put it on the bank."

"So can we keep it?" Kim propped herself up on her elbows.

"No, they belong here."

"Then can we visit him?" Aubrey got down low to watch the turtle eat a leaf.

"Sure."

As the girls took the turtle back to the water's edge, Brody said, "I seem to recall one you named Spot."

"Yep, you were with us that day. Remember that it had spots on its back?"

"I remember how you carefully cradled it as you rode back to the stable."

"He hid in his shell the whole way."

"Do you blame him? Here is a huge person picking him up and carrying him around. He didn't know what to expect."

She laughed. "The second I put him down on the bank, he moved faster than he probably ever did. He would have beaten the hare into the water."

Brody watched the girls return to the grassy patch after letting the turtle go. "We had some good times playing, in spite of the fact that you were a girl."

"I made the perfect damsel in distress."

The laugh lines at the corners of his eyes deepened. "Let's see. We rescued you from robbers. The bad man who had kidnapped you. A cougar. A burning building. And in real life we saved you when you climbed up the cliff and got stuck."

"Trying to follow you and Thomas. To this day I don't like heights. Clinging to the side of a mountain will do that to you."

"It wasn't a mountain. Maybe a hill."

"I had to be sixty or seventy feet off the ground."

"That's right—a hill."

She'd forgotten how much they used to banter back and forth. She'd missed that. For years she could tell Brody anything and then one day, when she was sixteen and he was eighteen, things began to change. No more shared confidences. Secrets sprang up between them. Slowly they drifted apart. They went to different colleges. She became busy with her life, he with his.

"I'm glad you're back in San Antonio. I know your dad is."

"You wouldn't know it, the way he gripes sometimes, but yes, I do know Dad appreciates me being here. This heart attack scared him. He won't admit it, but I've seen it in his eyes. In the past he would dismiss most pain like the indigestion he had. Now he realizes it might cost him his life." Brody cocked a grin. "He keeps telling me he's waiting around for more grandchildren. One just isn't enough."

"You would make a good father. Like I said, the girls love you. It didn't take you long to win them over."

His gaze drifted to Kim and Aubrey, now lying in the grass, peering up at the clouds and pointing at them. "Ah, I see they've got the right idea."

"The hectic way their life has been going I won't be surprised if they fall asleep."

"Sleep. A commodity that lately we have been short in." Leaning back against the tree trunk, Brody wound his arm around her. "Take a nap. I'll wake you before it gets dark."

She cuddled against him. "I'll rest my eyes for a little while. But I doubt I'll fall asleep."

"That's fine, too. It's nice just slowing down for a bit. Did I ever tell you about the time Thomas and I went camping in Big Bend National Park and had a run-in with a bear?"

She shook her head. He began telling her the story, but instead of listening to what he was saying, she focused on the sound of his deep voice, its cadence, the Texas drawl.

Before she knew it, a soft whisper tickled her ear with, "Wake up, Rebecca. We need to get back before dark. The girls are still asleep."

Her eyes popped open. Somehow she'd managed to turn over and cushion her head against his thigh. Looking straight up into the amusement in his expression, she zeroed in on the slight curve to his full lips, the cleft in his chin. Then their gazes met, and she couldn't look anywhere else but into the bright silver of his eyes. Smoldering. Totally intent on her.

Slowly he bent over and touched his mouth to hers. And everything else faded but the feel of his lips on hers, the taste of him, and the sense she had come home in his embrace. She wrapped her arms around him and held him against her. Connected for a moment. At peace as she'd not been in years.

"Aunt Becky," Aubrey cried out.

Rebecca jerked up, pulling herself from Brody's embrace. Raising her hands to her hair, she smoothed it into place and rose to her feet.

Aubrey sat straight up in the grass, looking around as if she didn't know where she was.

She hurried toward her niece. "I'm right here, honey. You're okay."

"Where am I?" Aubrey blinked over and over.

Kim rubbed her eyes and looked around. "We're at the ranch, silly."

The five-year-old screwed her mouth up into a pout. "I had a bad dream. A fire was trying to get me."

Rebecca enveloped Aubrey in an embrace. "It's not real, sweetie. You fell asleep by the stream." Leaning back, she captured the child's attention. "Ready to ride back to the stable?" Aubrey nodded.

Brody scooped Aubrey into his arms and carried her to her mare. After he set her on the horse, she kissed him on the cheek.

Rebecca and Kim untied their mounts, and Brody gave Kim a leg up, then Rebecca. She glanced down at him and said in a low whisper, "You've already gotten your kiss from me."

He tipped the edge of his cowboy hat, said, "I'm always open for more," then sauntered toward his gelding. In one smooth motion, he swung up into his saddle. "Ready?"

"Can we race?" Kim asked as they reached the open pasture.

"We'd better not. It's getting dark."

"Ah, Aunt Becky, it's not that dark."

"Kim Nicole, no faster than a trot."

"C'mon, Aubrey, let's leave the old folks behind."

As her nieces took off across the pasture, the sun dipped down near the western horizon. Orange, rose, and purple mingled with the blue sky, fingering their way outward from the bright yellow ball. The fresh outdoors scent and the soft breeze brushing across her added to the tranquility of the day, a welcome reprieve after the past couple of weeks.

"I need a few more days like today to feel normal again. I'm glad we did this." She slanted a look toward Brody, whose gelding moved in perfect harmony with her mare. In sync. Like she and Brody were. In that moment, she realized if she gave into these feelings growing inside of her, she would fall in love with him and be right back where she had been with Garrett, involved with a man who had a dangerous occupation.

Except now she knew about the very real possibility that one day he wouldn't come home. That she would receive a call from one of his colleagues to meet them at the hospital.

By the time they arrived at the stables, Rebecca was glad that the case she and he were involved in was over. After this weekend, they wouldn't have to be together much, certainly not every day as they had been recently. Somehow she would keep her distance. That, or she would end up brokenhearted again.

◈

Monday morning, before Rebecca needed to be at the courthouse, she entered her brother's hospital room to find him awake and talking with the nurse. He spied her in the doorway, and his eyes brightened.

The woman swept around toward Rebecca. "Mr. Sinclair has been up for a while. Each time he wakes up, he's more alert and stays up longer. I'll leave you two to talk."

As the nurse left, Rebecca moved to the chair at the side of the bed and sat, her gaze never straying from Thomas. She smiled. "It's so good to see you this way." Her throat constricted, memories of the past couple of weeks tumbling through her mind. "I thought I was going to lose you."

"Me. No way. Someone has to be here to keep an eye on you," Thomas said in a raspy voice that grew stronger as he spoke.

"I'll have you know I can take care of myself. I've been doing it for thirty-five years. Well, maybe not so much the first five or six years, but after that."

His chuckles turned into coughs. "That's why I love you. You won't take my grief," he finally said when he got his coughing under control.

"Where's Tory?"

"I told her to go home and get a really good night's sleep." He glanced toward the window through which the sunlight poured into the room. "I know it's morning, but she was practically falling asleep in the chair you're in. Every time I wake up, she's been right here."

"She didn't want you to wake up without seeing one of us. I was here yesterday some to give her a break, but she insisted on being here most of the time herself. She's been devoted to you." Rebecca scooted the chair closer and took his hand. "Thomas, can you tell me how you ended up getting hurt?"

His eyebrows bunched together. "Tory asked me the same thing. I don't remember anything but seeing the calf in the gully, carrying on. I think it was hurt, but I'm not sure. Everything else is blank until I woke up here." He yawned, wincing when he opened his mouth wide.

"The calf had a big gash on its backside. I'm surprised it didn't break a leg or two in its fall. But it's with its mother now, happy."

"Its carrying on was what drew me to it in the first place."

"Do you remember getting your rope and hitching it to Rocket?"

"No." Thomas's eyes closed for a few seconds.

"Do you want me to get you anything? Something to eat, drink?"

"That's—okay. I'm tired. I think . . ." His voice faded into silence.

Still holding his hand, Rebecca waited for ten minutes, hoping he would open his eyes again, but his healing face evened out into the peace of sleep. She let go of him and sat back, drinking in the wonderful sight of her brother, alive, out of his coma, making sense when he talked. She wasn't going to kid herself. The next few months to full recovery would be a hard road. The doctor said he didn't think Thomas was going to be paralyzed, but with his leg fractured severely in two places, he would need a good deal of physical therapy after the breaks healed.

As she started for the door, it opened and Brody came into the room. "Does he remember anything about the accident? Tory told me he hadn't yesterday. I was hoping to catch him awake."

"He was for a while but fell asleep about ten minutes ago. He's more responsive and talkative today, but, no, he didn't remember anything other than seeing the calf in the gully." Rebecca tried to look any place but at Brody's mouth. Each time her gaze brushed across his lips, she remembered the kiss they'd shared late last Saturday afternoon.

"He remembers seeing the calf? That's a little more than what he said to Tory yesterday. I can't seem to get here in time to talk to him."

"Tory and I decided not to tell him much about what has been going on at the ranch. He doesn't need to worry. He needs to totally focus on getting better. I haven't mentioned that you have been staying there, either. He'd want to know why." Brody wouldn't be staying at the ranch anymore, which would give her some time to distance herself from him emotionally. Seeing him confirmed she needed that. She had missed him and Sean last night and this morning. In a short time she'd come to depend on him, and she had to stop that. Now. She had her life back and could move forward.

"Good to know. I'll hang around until I have to go back to speak with Ethan Johnston about his meat-packing company. I have to wait until his lawyer can come. Yesterday I discovered the man has ties to New Jersey, where Alexandrov is originally from. Then this morning, I found out he had a large gambling debt that has been paid off recently."

"So it's looking like Alexandrov might be behind the cattle rustling." She stepped to the side to let Brody go past her, but he didn't move. He remained close, making the small area shrink even more.

"That's what I'm thinking. He was using the company for laundering money. With the high cost of beef, he was also using the cattle that were rustled from various places in Texas as a way to make some money overseas. We're just starting to unravel it all. But if I can get Johnston to turn on Alexandrov, we can get him on a number of additional charges. Especially since Nicholas Saldat refuses to say anything about the murder of the witness. The case is building against him, and he won't cut a deal."

"I guess there's loyalty among the bad guys after all. Closer to the trial, he may change his mind. His DNA at the crime scene is hard to refute."

"Alexandrov and Johnston weren't too smart going after cattle near their operation. Harassing you may be the man's downfall. Although ranches lose millions of dollars every year to cattle rustling, there was more than just local law enforcement investigating the people who were working your area. The task force we formed put a lot of effort into catching them. An unmarked car followed a semi to the meat-packing plant the same night your neighbor lost his cattle—the night before the fire."

"Since he sent the cattle rustlers, Alexandrov has to be behind the fire."

"Yeah, that's what I'm thinking. I'm going to give Johnston a deal he can't turn down. Getting Alexandrov is our primary objective."

"Sometimes the good guys do win." She looked toward her escape route. "I'd better go."

Rebecca hurried from the room, glancing back at the place where the officer had stood for so many days guarding Thomas. The empty space, coupled with Brody not escorting her everywhere, affirmed she really did have her life back. So why didn't she feel happier about it?

On the drive to the courthouse, she wrestled with the question and in the end knew the only reason was that she would miss Brody. She never wanted to repeat the last few weeks, but Brody had reminded her of the relationship they'd once had. They could have that again. Just as soon as she could put a halt to anything beyond friendship.

When she arrived at her office, she put up her purse and went in search of Laura. But when she didn't find her at her desk, she checked for a note left by her friend about some errand she needed to run. When she didn't find one, she listened to her three messages. None of them were from Laura. Strange. Come to think about it, she should have heard from Laura about her big date on Saturday night. With all that had been going on, it wasn't until now that she realized she hadn't.

Before she went into the trial that was beginning that morning, Rebecca made a call to Laura. After the fifth ring, the answering machine came on, and she left a message. Maybe she was sick and hadn't gotten up yet to let Rebecca know she wouldn't be in to work. *Wait 'til she hears the good news about Alexandrov and the cattle rustlers.* Rebecca could hardly wait to tell her friend.

In the interview room at the sheriff's office, the FBI agent said, "If you agree to testify against Alexandrov about the money laundering, cattle rustling, and arson, you'll be put into Witness Protection and won't do jail time. It's your call, Mr. Johnston. I suggest you talk it over with your lawyer. Time is of the essence if you want assurances of safety."

Brody stood back, lounging against the wall, his arms folded over his chest. Watching.

Johnston whispered to his lawyer. The older man frowned, then said to the agent, "He can testify on two of the charges but not the arson one."

Brody stepped forward. "It's a package deal. Why wouldn't he? He'll have immunity."

Johnston pinned Brody with a hard glare. "Because I didn't do it. I told you that. I don't know anything about a fire. I'm a businessman. Not an arsonist."

"So if Alexandrov told you to set the pasture on fire, you would have refused."

Johnston jumped to his feet. "He didn't ask. The fire wasn't our doing."

"Sit down, Mr. Johnston," the agent said in a steely voice.

The lawyer put his hand on Johnston's arm and pulled him down into the seat. "The deal needs to be amended. Believe me, it's to my client's advantage to take this deal as is, but he insists he didn't have anything to do with the fire. Why would he lie about something like that?"

"Very well, Mr. Johnston. We will drop the arson charge, but if I find out that you were involved, you'll be prosecuted to the full extent of the law on that crime."

Johnston looked right at Brody. "I'm not guilty. Someone else set the fire."

The man's body language reinforced his words concerning the fire. So if it wasn't Johnston doing the bidding of Alexandrov, then who set the fire and why? The direction Brody's thoughts were going sent a white-hot poker through his gut.

Rebecca may still be in danger.

At the end of the day Rebecca prowled her office, waiting for Brody to arrive. Here it was only eight hours since she'd seen him, and she'd had to phone him to come over. Laura never called her. Something was wrong. At lunch, when she'd tried Laura's house line as well as her cellphone again, she started calling people who were Laura's friends, neighbors, and family. No one had seen her since Saturday.

This isn't like Laura.

Her nerves tightened. Pinpricks danced on them. Something was wrong.

Someone knocked on her door. She quickly walked over and opened it. Relief fluttered through her at the sight of Brody. "I'm so glad you could come."

"What's this about Laura being missing?"

Rebecca whirled around and crossed to her cabinet to get her purse. "We're going to her duplex. She didn't come to work or call in sick."

"People have been known to forget to do that."

"Not Laura. She's in trouble. I know where she keeps her spare key. With her landlady. She lives in the other side of the duplex. Let's go. You can follow me to Laura's."

"Why do you think she's in trouble?" Brody asked as Rebecca locked her office door.

"Because Laura is the most conscientious worker I've ever had. Because she's a good friend and I know her. She would never do something that would make me worry, especially with all that has been happening."

"What if she impulsively went to Las Vegas to marry this new man in her life?"

"She isn't impulsive, and she would have had me vet him before she did something like that."

"You make falling in love sound like a rational, logical decision. Sometimes it isn't."

"Yes, it is. If you let your emotions take over, you can get hurt." If she said that often enough, she would believe it and not get hurt by letting herself fall for Brody.

"Okay, you've convinced me. Something might be wrong." He headed for his SUV. "I'll follow you."

Twenty minutes later Rebecca parked her car in Laura's driveway with Brody parking in the street. She strode to Laura's door and rang the bell. Several times. Finally, when her friend didn't answer, she skirted around Brody and headed toward the landlady's side of the duplex.

"Mrs. Norris, I hope you're doing okay."

"I was until you called and told me about Laura. I hope she's all right."

"I'm afraid something might be wrong and would like to check out her place to make sure she isn't unconscious in her house."

"Oh, my dear. I thought you would have found her by now." Moving slowly on her cane, Mrs. Norris hobbled toward Laura's front door, giving Brody a once-over. "You really do think something is wrong. You brought your own Texas Ranger."

"He's a friend."

Brody nodded. "Nice to meet you, ma'am. I'm Ranger Calhoun. May I open the door?"

"Sure, young man. It sticks some of the time."

Brody inserted the key in the lock and turned it, then pushed into the small foyer of the duplex. Holding up his hand, he said, "You two wait out here. Let me do a walk-through."

The fact that he wanted to check Laura's house first heightened Rebecca's fears. What if Laura had slipped and fallen in the bathroom, hitting her head? Or what if someone had broken in and . . .

Brody returned, scowling. "Mrs. Norris, thank you for letting us in. You never saw Laura leave?"

"No. I saw her young man come to see her Saturday night, and she must have let him in because he went into the house. When I went to bed, he hadn't left yet. But his car was gone when I got up early Sunday."

"When?"

"Four in the morning."

Rebecca's heartbeat accelerated. She balled her hands so tightly her fingernails dug into her palms. Brody was questioning the landlady as if a crime had been committed.

"When did you go to bed?" Brody stepped out of the house and started walking the older woman toward her side of the house.

"About nine. He came right after the local news was over at six thirty."

"I'm going to keep the key for now. I'll return it later."

Mrs. Norris's lips pursed together. "What has happened to Laura? I've watched a lot of crime shows and can take the truth."

"I don't know what's happened. She isn't here." Brody waited until the woman had trudged into her house and closed the door before turning to face Rebecca. "I want you to walk through the house with me. I think something bad has happened to Laura. Nothing is obvious. Just a gut feeling. I want your take on it."

She wasn't consoled by the fact that Brody wasn't sure about a crime having been committed or the lack of obvious evidence. Brody had been a law officer for over fifteen years. His instincts were good, from all she'd seen and heard about him.

As she approached the open front door, he peered down at her, quickly veiling the sadness in his eyes. But it had been there. Hesitating, she shoved her hand through her hair and finally hooked some strands behind her ear.

"You don't have to go inside."

"I'm going inside. Laura is a good friend. She has been an invaluable law clerk." Rebecca took a step into the foyer.

Nothing was out of place that she could see from that vantage point, but then, all she glimpsed was the living room to the left—neat as usual. Brody moved past her, indicating that she follow.

When she entered the dining room, she saw the table set for a dinner for two. She'd known that Laura was fixing a meal for Jim on Saturday night. But the dishes and utensils were clean. The roses in the centerpiece were beginning to wilt, the only evidence of imperfection in the scene before her.

"They never ate dinner Saturday," she murmured, the tightness about her chest beginning to build again.

"It doesn't appear so. C'mon. I want to show you the kitchen and the bedroom." Brody tugged her toward the entrance to the kitchen.

When she stopped a foot inside the kitchen, she knew that something was very wrong. She walked slowly around, peeking into pans on the stove filled with partially cooked food, the burners off. A half-made salad, the lettuce wilted, sat in a large red bowl on the counter, with a chopping board next to it. A knife and a cucumber, sliced through about a third of the way, lay on the chopping board.

Using the edge of a towel, she opened the oven and found a roast in a deep pan, not totally cooked, starting to smell rancid. Closing the door immediately, she whirled around. "What happened here?"

"That's a good question. I want you to look at the bedroom. Then I'm calling Charlie."

As Rebecca approached the room, the clamoring of her heartbeat filled her with dread. Afraid to go inside, she slowed her pace. There was no body, but something cautioned her about looking inside. Cold burrowed into her bones.

She stepped into the entrance and couldn't go any further. She didn't need to enter. She saw what Brody wanted her to see. A brand new dress of turquoise and white, with the tags still on it, was lying on the pink and green bedspread. Next to it was white lacy lingerie. Three-inch white high heels lay on the floor.

Rebecca backed out of the room, pivoted, and hurried to the front door and out of the duplex. Gasping for air, she bent over and sucked in what oxygen-rich breaths she could. The image of the clothes Laura was probably going to wear on Saturday night flashed in and out of her mind like a strobe light.

Brody put his hand on her back. "I called Charlie. He'll be here soon."

She straightened. "Something has happened to her. And it's not good." Goosebumps snaked down her spine.

"Let's sit in the car and wait." With his touch at the small of her back, he escorted her toward the SUV and waited until she was settled in the passenger seat before going to his side and getting in.

"Did you see any signs of a forced entry?"

"No. But Charlie and his forensic team can go through the place."

Rebecca turned toward him, her attention zooming in on Laura's closed front door. "So she let the person in."

"Her car isn't here."

"Then she left everything here and went somewhere else. Why?"

"No, remember what Mrs. Norris said. Her date came and she let him inside. What time was he supposed to arrive?"

"Seven." She could still hear the excitement in Laura's voice about the date she was going to have with Jim. She loved to cook, and she was going to prepare him a special meal. She hadn't heard her friend that excited about a man in a long time.

"Then he was early, or at least someone Mrs. Norris thought was her date came around six thirty."

"It may not have been Jim."

"But the man who came stayed at least until after Mrs. Norris went to bed at nine. I think it was probably him. Besides, she never saw anyone else."

"What if it was Jim, and they did go somewhere?"

"From what you tell me about Laura, she wouldn't be gone this long without at least letting you know she wouldn't be at work today. Unless something was wrong and she couldn't call."

Brody said aloud the words she'd been thinking. "Then why is her car gone?"

"They drove somewhere in separate cars? But that can't be right. Why did she have the meal almost prepared and they never ate it?" Pain throbbed against her skull. "None of this makes sense."

"Not yet. I'll have Charlie put a BOLO out on Laura's car. Maybe we'll know more when we find it."

What if Laura is in it—dead? What if her car is never found? Laura is never found? Question after bleak question rolled through her mind like tumbleweeds across the ground.

"What is this Jim's last name?" Brody asked, cutting into the awful place where Rebecca'a mind was quickly going.

"What?" She shook the questions she couldn't answer from her thoughts.

"Jim's last name?"

"I don't know. She never told me. I never thought to ask. I'd been so preoccupied with all that was going on, I didn't ask the questions I usually would."

"I'll talk with Mrs. Norris after I take you back to the ranch. I'll have an officer follow us in your car."

"No. I'm staying, and I'll go with you to talk to her. I know her, but mostly I know Laura. I might be able to help you when you talk to Mrs. Norris."

His gaze probed her as though weighing his options for how to reply to her.

"I'm not leaving. This is my friend."

"Fine. But after that I'm taking you home."

"I'll drive myself." She squared her shoulders, lifting her chin.

"I don't know what's going on, but I'd feel better if you let me drive."

"Are you in your protective mode again?"

"Yes. This may not be connected to you, but until we know . . . After all that has occurred, I don't want to take a chance with your safety."

"Why would Alexandrov go after Laura? It doesn't make sense. At the moment, I'm the least of his worries. I'm not involved in his case. It's federal."

"Maybe some warped sense of revenge. Whatever it is, it's better to be cautious."

"Fine," she clipped out, hating the sense that she was the one who was in prison.

"Good." Brody peered behind his car. "Charlie has arrived."

⁓♋⁓

"Thank you, Mrs. Norris, for talking with us. I just have a few more questions." Brody sat in a chair across from the older woman, who had arranged her hair in a bun at the nape of her neck and had put on a different smock—bright yellow.

Rebecca stood behind Brody, her nerve endings jangling. She gripped the back of the chair to keep from pacing.

"Anything I can do to help Laura. I suspected you'd want to ask me a few questions."

"Why is that, ma'am?" Brody removed his cowboy hat and set it on the floor beside his chair.

"More police officers have arrived. That means the possibility of foul play. Y'all don't come in full force unless you have a good reason."

"You're very astute. I'm glad to hear that."

"Yes, indeed. I know what's going on around here."

"Can you describe the man?" Brody took out his pad and pen.

As Mrs. Norris tapped her chin and stared off into space, Rebecca tried to remember anything that Laura had said about Jim. "Laura told me he had the prettiest eyes she'd ever seen—blue."

Mrs. Norris chuckled. "He ain't bad-looking either. I couldn't see his eyes behind the sunglasses he was wearing, but he had a strong jawline and when he smiled at Laura, two dimples appeared in his cheeks. His hair was blond and I think kinda long, but his cowboy hat covered most of it."

"This is good. How tall is he?"

Rubbing her chin, Mrs. Norris frowned. "Maybe half a foot taller than Laura."

"That's about five ten, five eleven," Rebecca interjected.

Laura's neighbor snapped her fingers. "Yep. That's about right."

"What was he wearing?"

"Jeans, black cowboy boots, and a white long-sleeved shirt. He had a fancy silver buckle on his belt. Couldn't tell what exactly it was, but definitely silver."

"How about the car he was driving?" Brody glanced back at Rebecca, his look silently asking her if she was all right.

She nodded.

"I'm glad you ask. Now, cars I know. My husband loved different cars and was always going on and on about this car and that one. When he died a few years back, I continued it as a way to keep connected to him."

"What kind was it?"

"It was a blue Malibu, 2006 or 2007."

"Are you sure?"

"Yes, I'm positive. Like I said, I know my cars. Laura drives a red Camaro. I even know her license number. B32 WHL."

Brody sat forward. "Did you see the license of the Malibu?"

Mrs. Norris's shoulders sagged. "Sorry, I couldn't. I did notice a pine cone freshener hanging from the rearview mirror."

Rebecca rounded the chair Brody sat in, restlessness storming through her. "Mrs. Norris, did you hear anything unusual from the time the man came to visit to the time you went to bed? Like the radio or TV turned up too loud."

"Ah, like to cover up a crime?"

"Anything out of the ordinary." She tried to dismiss the image of Laura fighting off an attacker and prayed she was overreacting.

"No," the older woman began, then paused and frowned. "Come to think of it, not long after the man arrived I heard a crash like Laura dropped a plate or something like that on the tile floor. That really isn't that unusual necessarily, but otherwise it was very quiet." She ran her hand along her chin. "Which is kinda unusual. The walls between the units aren't the thickest. I can usually hear her TV going, but Laura is very good at keeping it down. I do the same for her. She is the ideal tenant." Her eyes watered, and she blinked as a tear rolled down her wrinkled face.

Brody finished writing something on his pad. "The sound came from the kitchen?"

"Yes."

Brody threw Rebecca a glance before returning his attention to Mrs. Norris. "Anything else?"

The neighbor thought for a moment, then shook her head.

Brody rose. "Thank you for your help. If you remember something later, you can reach me here." He withdrew a card and gave it to the woman. "Don't get up. We can find our own way out."

Putting down the footrest on her lounge chair, Mrs. Norris struggled to the edge and pushed off, using her cane to steady herself. "No way am I leaving my front door unlocked. But thank you kindly for thinking about me. I have a friend directly across the street that keeps a good eye out for the people around here. You might ask her if she saw anything."

"I will, ma'am."

Mrs. Norris pointed to a one-story, red brick house. "She isn't home right now. Her car is gone. I can call you when she comes home."

"I appreciate that." Brody waited until the landlady closed her door and the lock clicked into place before starting for his SUV. "I'm taking you home."

After she climbed into the passenger seat, Brody took out his phone and made a call while walking to the driver's side.

"Who did you call?" she asked as he got in.

"Charlie. I told him to look and see if anything was broken in the kitchen."

"You think that's important?"

"Probably not. But you never know. If it was something like a glass or plate, that gives me an idea of how thin the walls are between the two units."

"Which means Laura didn't put up a struggle or Mrs. Norris would have heard it."

"Exactly."

"I'm glad you're looking into Laura's disappearance."

Brody waited until an officer approached his SUV. After giving the man Rebecca's car keys, Brody pulled away from the curb. "I hope you don't mind me being your guest again for a while."

"It's fine. But I don't want anyone else. I don't see how Laura's disappearance has anything to do with me directly. My family needs their life back. I don't want to ever go through again what we've been through these past few weeks."

"How about Dad? He's going to insist if he thinks you might be in danger."

"I love having your dad around. He's been great for Hattie and the girls."

"To tell you the truth, last night he complained the whole way back to my house about not being at the ranch. I think he misses his ranch."

"Why did he sell it?"

"It was too much to keep up with and be a full-time cop, too, plus driving back and forth from the ranch into town was taking up so much of his time. Sometimes when he was really into a case, he would stay at a motel close to the station. He hated that."

"But now he's retired, and I think from what I've seen lately, he needs a purpose."

"I hadn't thought of encouraging him to get a small spread, but I think you're right. Since I've been back, I've seen how restless and unhappy he has been. He isn't the type to sit around all day and watch TV or play golf four or five times a week, or even read much beyond the newspaper."

"I know of a ranch Jake was telling me about a couple of miles from the Circle S. Maybe he should take a look at it while he's staying with us. I'll bet he could talk Hattie into showing it to him. She knows the owner, who is moving to Florida to be near his aging parents. I've seen Sean's interest in Hattie. She'd be down the road from him if he bought the ranch."

"Are you matchmaking, Rebecca Morgan?"

"Yes, they would be good for each other."

At a stoplight, Brody angled toward Rebecca. "When things settle down, you and I need to have a serious discussion about what's going on between us."

His gaze scorched a path over her face, but the urge to break eye contact was overridden by the need to stay connected. She wanted to say that there was no future beyond friendship, and even that was becoming risky. But the words wouldn't form. The silvery gray of his eyes bound her to him until the person behind them honked.

As Brody turned to face forward and drove through the intersection, she lifted her hand to her hot cheek. Surely, when her life got back to normal, she wouldn't feel so drawn to this man, who offered her protection.

J. R. fought his way out of a deep sleep. He jerked upright in the lounge chair in front of the TV, some inane show on, and grabbed his cellphone sitting on the table next to him. "Yes, what's taken you so long to call?"

"Obligations. It's time. Make your move tomorrow."

"Good. I want this over with." He disconnected the call and picked up the remote to turn off the TV. What he'd done this weekend hadn't been as easy as he thought.

He dragged himself out of the chair and headed for bed. Tomorrow would be a long day. But he doubted he'd get much rest tonight. He wasn't looking forward to what he had to do next, but the woman deserved all the pain they could give her for what she'd done to his family.

16

"What are you doing here? Taking me to lunch?" Rebecca said the next day when she let Brody into her office, not wanting to stay in there one second longer than she had to. Whenever she went to get something from Laura's desk, she quickly retrieved what she needed and hurried back into her office. Laura's empty chair and desk taunted her with a sense of helplessness concerning her friend's disappearance.

She faced Brody in the middle of her office and stiffened. His grim expression told her what she didn't want to hear. "Laura? You've found her?"

"No, not yet, but we found her car."

Rebecca took a step back and reclined against her desk. "Oh, good. She could still be alive. I thought—"

"Rebecca, the police discovered her car in your driveway."

She gripped the edge of the desk. The galloping of her heartbeat matched the pounding of a horse's hooves in a full run. "Was—was she in the car?"

"No. I came to get the key to your house. I could have broken in, but I felt I owed it to you to let you know."

"You think she's inside?"

"I don't know. Charlie is waiting there. We checked around the house and couldn't find anything to indicate that someone broke in, but we still need to search your place before we expand the perimeter."

"I fixed the back door but hadn't had a chance to get a new security system." She straightened. "I'm coming with you."

"I figured you would say that." He closed in on her and caged her against her desk, his hands on her upper arms.

"She may be inside," chilled and trembling, she swallowed the knot in her throat and continued, "like that man."

"That's why you shouldn't come."

If that's the case, I'm the reason. I can't run from that, but the person responsible will pay for it. "If she is inside, then I'll need your protection because that means someone is after me, and I don't think it has anything to do with the case I was presiding over."

"I've brought an officer to guard you."

She shook her head. "Not the same thing. I trust you and right now I'm not sure who to trust. This feels very personal."

"Yeah, I agree. And that is something we're going to have to talk about. Who wants you to suffer?"

That question stayed in Rebecca's mind the whole way to her house, a place she never wanted to see again. When she saw Laura's car, that notion was solidified—she would be putting the place up for sale as soon as possible. There was no way she would stay another night in that house. Shivers skimmed over her body, and she quickly got out of Brody's SUV and into the warm early afternoon sun, but it did nothing to heat her cold insides.

Charlie approached Brody. "If this is a crime scene, I can have some men here quickly. As is, the crime scene techs are coming to process Laura's car, then have it towed to police impound. I'm sorry we have to meet again under these circumstances, Rebecca."

"Let's get this over with." She marched toward her front porch, took out her key, and put it in Brody's palm. "I'm not staying out here."

He slid a look her way that warmed her insides a little. "I know. But you're to stay put just inside the door. You don't need—"

"I won't move," she cut in. If Laura was found in her house, she didn't want her last image of her friend to be anything but that of the alive, vibrant woman that she knew her to be. The second she stepped inside and the decaying scent of something dead accosted her, she knew Laura was somewhere in her house.

As Charlie and Brody began their room-by-room search, Rebecca stood so straight her muscles locked into place, tension in every fiber of her being. The seconds—minutes—crawled by as she waited for the confirmation. Knowing it was coming. Wishing she was anywhere but here. The sound of footsteps alerted her to Brody's approach. He didn't need to say a word. Grief marked the planes of his face and darkened his eyes to a stormy gray.

"Where did you find her?"

He swallowed hard, tearing his gaze from hers. Again his Adam's apple bobbed up and down. "In your bedroom, on the bed, like the other victim, except dead roses are scattered all over."

A picture of the witness on her bed, blood everywhere, invaded her thoughts. But this time Laura was the victim. Trembling started in her hands and spread through her body. She clutched her hands together to try to keep them from shaking so much.

Brody laid his hand on her shoulder.

She yanked away, saying in a bare whisper, "No, not Laura. Not like that."

The sound of footsteps barely penetrated her mind. But seconds later, Charlie appeared in the foyer.

"Rebecca, we need to get you out of here. I'm taking you back to the ranch." Brody hung back, but concern clouded his eyes.

"I have—I have a trial." She couldn't remember what case she was hearing, but work might keep her from thinking about . . .

"I'll let them know you're ill and won't be there."

She finally locked eyes with Brody. "Fine."

She headed for Brody's SUV, Charlie and Brody flanking her. She lifted her chin and tried to present a facade of composure. If for some reason the person behind this was watching to get his jollies, she was not going to let him think he had won.

Taking a deep, fortifying breath, she murmured, "I want you to come back and find the person responsible. He will pay."

"Rebecca, we can arrange for another security detail," Charlie said.

"No, so much manpower has already been used. I want those people on the case trying to find out who is behind this. I can have the ranch hands patrol, and with Brody or his dad guarding me, I'll be fine, but I do want someone on Thomas and an officer to pick up the girls from school. Until this is over with, they'll be staying at the ranch and not going to school."

"But you need . . ." Charlie stopped when he caught Brody shaking his head. "You two work it out. I'll be processing the scene."

As they left, more cars arrived, bringing home how real this all was.

"Hattie's cell is going to voicemail. She's already gone to pick up the girls." Rebecca dropped her phone onto her lap.

"Sheriff Overstreet sent a deputy to pick up the girls. He'll follow them home." At a stop sign, Brody reached over and wrapped his hand around hers for a few seconds. "When I get back later today, you and I need to talk about who would be after you if we rule out Alexandrov. Make a list of everyone you can think of. What cases have you presided over? You're at the center of all this."

"You don't think what happened to Thomas was an accident?"

"I'm going to look at it as an attempted murder in light of what happened with Laura."

"Your car bombing?"

"Maybe tied to this, but could still be part of the Petrov trial."

"What about the witness who was murdered and put in my bed? That has to be Alexandrov."

"With the tie to his bodyguard, yes, but to prove it may be hard." Brody blew out a long breath. "But the guy who tried to run you down who was found behind the pawnshop might not be connected to Alexandrov. If it wasn't Alexandrov, then why was Peter Ivanov killed?"

"The gang?"

"I don't think so. The staging of the man's body points to both groups. Why would either one do that?"

"Then the killer was watching me. What if he didn't want someone else to kill me because he wanted to?" Faces of people she'd seen in the last day scrolled through her mind. Some familiar. Some not. Was one of them the murderer?

"Revenge?"

"That can be a hazard of our job. A criminal not liking what happened and coming after us as payback."

Brody turned onto the highway that led to Dry Gulch and the Circle S Ranch. "When making your list of suspects, think of that. Who wants revenge on you? Who would go to these lengths? This has been carefully orchestrated."

The thought that someone hated her that much shook her to her core. Hugging her arms, she folded in on herself, wanting to escape to a place where none of this could happen, where peace would reign.

I'm here for you, Rebecca.

But all she wanted was to shout at God: *Why is this happening to me? What have I done to cause this?*

Parked on a dirt road off the highway that ran from Dry Gulch, J. R. spied the car coming toward him, then checked to see if anyone was following behind it. Timing was crucial if this were going to work. As the vehicle passed him, he tugged on a ski mask, then pulled out onto the road, matching its speed while he scanned the area to make sure there was no traffic. The second he determined they were the only vehicles on the road, he accelerated and pulled around the PT Cruiser. When his truck was even with the car, he swerved into it. The driver jerked the wheel to the right, veering onto the shoulder of the highway and then into the drainage ditch.

He slammed on the brakes, jumped from his pickup, and ran toward the PT Cruiser. The front end was smashed, and the vehicle sat at an odd angle, partway in the gully. As he yanked open the driver's side door, he retrieved the syringe from his pocket and before the moaning woman could turn toward him, he plunged the needle into her neck.

The older woman in the front passenger seat screamed. He raced to the other side as she opened the door and tried to stand. When he reached her, he hit her in the face with his fist, knocking her back into the car, her head striking the console.

In the distance, he spotted a car coming toward them. He dragged open the back door near him, unsnapped the seatbelt, and grabbed the crying girl. The other one sat beside her in shock, her eyes round, her body stiff. No time for her. He hurried up the small incline with the child in his arms, wiggling and twisting. Her arms were flailing, but he managed to grab them. She screamed, an ear-piercing sound that shot pain through his skull.

At his truck, he glanced back. The car was about three hundred yards away. He tossed the girl into the front, fumbled for the cloth soaked with chloroform, and managed to hold it over her nose and mouth long enough to knock her out. She slumped down, and her body slid onto the floor. He hurried to the driver's side and floored his truck as the other car slowed at the scene of the wreck.

He stared at the bloody scratches on his hand that the girl had inflicted. Great. He didn't like things to go wrong. There was only supposed to be the driver to deal with. Why had that changed?

In the foyer at the ranch house with his cellphone to his ear, Brody started walking away from Rebecca and his father. He shoved open the screen door and stepped out onto the porch. "What do you mean the kids and Hattie weren't at the school?"

His question rooted Rebecca to the floor for a moment until she couldn't hear anything else he said. Then she charged forward to find out what was going on. Sean followed.

"They were picked up?"

Brody's scowl riveted her attention, and she tried to discern what was happening. "Is something wrong with the girls?"

He held up his finger and said to the deputy on the other end of the line, "We'll try both of them again. Thanks."

When Brody lowered the phone from his ear, he looked at Rebecca, his expression evening out into a neutral one. "The deputy missed Hattie by a couple of minutes. He's driving toward the ranch, trying to make up time. He should overtake them soon. Here. Try Hattie and Tory. They both picked up the girls today."

Rebecca tried Hattie's phone, and it went to voicemail again. Then with a trembling hand she punched in Tory's number, and on the fourth ring, a man answered.

"Oh, sorry, I must have the wrong number."

She started to disconnect when the man said, "Were you calling a woman with long blonde hair?"

"Yes?" Sweat coated her forehead.

"I just pulled up to a wreck. There's a little girl in the back, not saying a word, just sucking her thumb and rocking, an older woman out cold in the front seat and a younger blonde lady behind the wheel. Unconscious, too. I called 911."

She barely heard anything beyond the word *wreck*. It took half a minute for the meaning to sink in. "Where are they?" Her mind ached, as though it were on overload and couldn't process anything else. What was she missing?

After the man gave her the location, she thanked him and clicked off. Both Brody and Sean hovered nearby, staring at her. "Tory, Hattie, and Aubrey were in a wreck outside Dry Gulch, driving toward San Antonio the back way at the one-mile marker."

Brody moved closer and took his phone. "Where's Kim?"

"Kim? She wasn't in the car. She might have gone over to a friend's house. She'd been wanting to. Or . . ." The implication of what might have happened flooded her mind, halting any further words.

"Let's go. Dad, please stay here in case Kim is at a friend's house and she calls or is brought home." As he strode to his SUV with Rebecca right behind him, he placed a call to Sheriff Overstreet.

No, Kim's at a friend's house playing. Rebecca had left early this morning and didn't know exactly what her niece's after-school plans were. *That has to be it.*

But on the short drive to the scene of the wreck, Rebecca still couldn't speak the words to reflect the doubt bombarding her from all sides. Her mind went blank until she saw the wreck a few hundred yards away. The ambulance was already there along with a car from the sheriff's department.

When Rebecca stepped out of Brody's SUV and approached the PT Cruiser in the ditch, she saw that one paramedic was checking Hattie who sat in the passenger side front seat, while the other was seeing to Tory, lying on a gurney near the ambulance. Rebecca was striding toward Hattie to find out what had happened when her gaze latched onto Aubrey, sitting in the sheriff's patrol car, the back door open, her feet dangling out, her thumb in her mouth, her chin touching her chest. Rebecca changed direction and hurried to Aubrey.

"Honey, are you all right?"

For a long moment, Aubrey kept her gaze and head down. Rebecca laid her hand over her niece's. "Aubrey?"

When she glanced up, the blank expression on her face scared Rebecca more than if the child had been hysterical.

"Sweetie, tell me what's wrong."

Tears began to well up in her niece's eyes. "He—took her."

"Who?"

"Bad man took Kim."

"So your sister was with you?"

Aubrey nodded, tears spilling from her eyes. "He hurt Hattie and Tory."

Kim kidnapped. No! If someone wanted revenge against me, then they should come after me.

Overwhelming rage possessed Rebecca to the point where she was afraid to say anything to her niece. Her body quaked, her hands opened and closed.

"I—I didn't—know what to do, Aunt Becky."

Aubrey's pain-filled voice penetrated the haze of anger surrounding Rebecca. She blinked, making an effort to focus on the child who needed her. "Baby, I know. You did fine." She scooped her niece into her embrace and clung to her as though she would vanish if she let go of her.

"Rebecca, may I have a word with you?" Brody's husky voice seeped through the wall she was trying to erect between Aubrey and her and the world.

Rebecca leaned back. "Honey, I'll just be a few feet away. I won't take my eyes off of you." As she rose, her niece hung onto her arm for a few extra seconds. Finally, though, she released her grip but watched Rebecca's every move while sucking on her thumb.

Her gaze trained on her niece, Rebecca turned Brody away from her and whispered, "Kim has been kidnapped. Aubrey said it was one man."

"I figured as much. Hattie told me Kim was with them. Hattie didn't come around until the deputy arrived. She thought the child could have wandered off, but the officer said Aubrey pointed to the road when he asked her where her sister was."

"What happened to Tory and Hattie?" Rebecca saw Aubrey push herself off the seat and stand by the patrol car, glancing around, then begin sucking her thumb again.

"It looks like Tory was drugged and is still out. The deputy found a syringe on the ground by the driver's side. I talked with Hattie. She should be okay, but the paramedics are taking her to Mercy Memorial to have a doctor make sure. The assailant who ran them off the road punched Hattie in the face, and when she fell back, she hit her head on the console. She might have a concussion. She tried to tell me what happened but was agitated and vague."

Rebecca covered the distance to her niece. "Aubrey, honey, can I help you?"

"Bad man has Kim," her niece said with her thumb still in her mouth.

"I know," was all Rebecca managed to say. Her throat closed around those two words and although she was desperately trying to hold it together for Aubrey, her composure fragmented.

Because of me, Kim has been taken.

The hand she settled on her niece's shoulder quivered so badly that Aubrey peered up at Rebecca, pulled her thumb out of her mouth and said, "I'm scared. He had a black mask on. Bad, bad man."

Brody approached and knelt in front of Aubrey. "Can you remember anything else about the bad man?"

Chewing on her bottom lip, Aubrey shook her head. The tears began streaming down her cheeks. "Black mask. Mean eyes."

"What color?" Rebecca asked, realizing how little they had to go on. This stretch of back road into San Antonio, liberally littered with potholes, wasn't used as much as the main highway, but it was a shorter route to the hospital and reduced the time it took to get there if the driver managed to dodge the potholes.

"Dark."

"Dark brown?"

"Dark." Aubrey clamped her mouth around her thumb and sucked.

"I'm following the ambulance to Mercy Memorial. The deputy will take you and Aubrey back to the ranch. Sheriff Overstreet will meet you there while the scene is processed. I've called in another Texas Ranger." He pulled Rebecca a few feet away and whispered close to her ear. "He'll set up a command post at the ranch in case there is a ransom demand, and Ranger Parker will check out this crime scene. I'll be there as soon as I can."

Rebecca gripped his arm as he turned to leave. "Don't say anything to Thomas. I need to tell him."

"I won't. I'll check to make sure his security is in place and won't go in to see him."

As Brody walked away, an EMT helped Hattie into the ambulance and then shut the doors. Another patrol car came from the direction of Dry Gulch. This deputy would drive them to the ranch. The officer first on the scene escorted her and Aubrey to the vehicle.

She sat in back, with Aubrey glued to her side. They drove through Dry Gulch and toward the ranch. The landscape blurred as she stared out the window, not really seeing anything but a man in a black ski mask dragging Kim toward a . . . What kind of car was the man driving? How big was he? Did he say anything? Suddenly the onslaught of questions an investigator/prosecutor would ask came to a halt. She wasn't that person anymore, and her career as a judge was probably the reason her niece had been taken.

As her eyes glistened with tears, the terrain faded totally from view. She felt the tears roll down her face. She kept her head averted. Aubrey was already upset enough.

I'm always the one in control. Somehow I have to hold it together. But I don't want to. I want to scream, sob, lose control.

❧

Brody paced the hall in the ER as he waited for the doctors to release Hattie. Tory, still a bit groggy, was upstairs visiting Thomas; who had expected to see her. She had agreed not to say anything to Thomas until they had a better idea about what was going on, but she understood that he would have to be told soon. Once Hattie was ready to leave, Brody would take her back to the ranch and bring Rebecca here to support Tory while she told her husband about Kim being missing.

Hattie appeared in the doorway of an ER examining room, pale, her eyes lackluster, her face beginning to show bruising. Brody hurried over to her and took her elbow to guide her to his SUV. "I'm taking you back to the ranch. Dad is there to help make sure you follow the doctor's orders to take it easy. In fact, Dr. Henderson may still be there. Rebecca asked him to check on Aubrey."

"This isn't the time for me to rest. What's being done to get our baby back?"

"Everything we can do. There hasn't been a ransom demand yet, but hopefully there will be."

"What if there isn't?"

"We'll continue doing what we're doing. Searching and following every lead we have."

"What leads?"

"That's what I want to talk to you about. The crime scene techs are processing the PT Cruiser for fingerprints, and the syringe used on Tory, but if you can—"

"That won't help probably. The guy had on black gloves."

Brody helped her into his SUV, closed the door, came around to the driver's side, and slid behind the steering wheel. "Okay. That's good to know. I want you to think back to what happened from the beginning, until you passed out. Take your time. Anything you can think of might help us."

With a deep sigh, Hattie rested her head on the seat cushion. "It's fuzzy, but I'll do what I can. It would be better if it didn't feel like a herd of cattle were stampeding through my mind."

"I know. Been there recently."

She massaged her temples. "Did Tory tell you much?"

"A description of the pickup. No license number."

"I didn't get as good a view as she did. I know it was black and what I would call a clunker. A big one. That made it easy to run us off the road. Sorry I wasn't paying much attention until it hit us. Then I was trying to calm the girls while Tory tried to avoid the ditch. Kinda hard when it was the truck or the ditch." Pausing, she closed her eyes and continued to press her fingertips into her temples. "I do remember when we passed it on the highway. There wasn't a license plate in front. I don't know about the back."

"There may not have been any plates since this was no accident. Tory's description fits yours. She thought it was a Dodge Ram."

"Could have been. I wasn't paying attention."

"How about when he got out of his truck and approached the car? What can you tell me about him—height, weight?"

"I didn't even see him coming toward the car. The airbag went off. That knocked the breath out of me. The next thing I know, he pulls the driver's door open. It looked like he was doing something to Tory. I thought at first he was checking her vital signs. Now I know he was injecting her with something. I tried to get out of the car to stop him, but he came around to my side so fast that the next thing I know he's punching me in the face. Kim is carrying on in the back seat. Her crying is the last thing I remember."

A surge of protectiveness overpowered him, and for a few seconds rage filled him to the point that he lost focus on the road ahead of him.

"Brody!"

The tires crunched along the shoulder of the road. He quickly righted the SUV. "Sorry. I was thinking of what I would do when I find this man." He'd allowed his professionalism to slip and his emotions to take over. He couldn't do that and still do his job the way it needed to be done. "Tell me what you remember about the man." He dug deep inside himself for the calm and composure he needed to be effective.

"Not quite as tall as you are. It was hard to tell about his muscles. He was wearing a long-sleeved white shirt and jeans. He wasn't skinny, but I don't think he had much fat on him. I have no idea about his weight. Like I said not fat, not skinny. So what would that be for a man about six feet tall—180 pounds?"

"What color were his eyes, his hair?"

"Couldn't tell on the hair because of the black ski mask but his eyes were dark blue." Hattie gave him a small smile. "I'm not a very good witness. Sorry."

"You've done fine. Every little bit helps. Anything else that might distinguish him?"

"No. If I think of anything, you'll be the first to know. Maybe if I rest, something else will come to me."

"It's about twenty more minutes to the ranch. Rest."

Quiet ruled for the next fifteen minutes until his cell rang. To free his hands for driving, he pressed his Bluetooth-connected cellphone. "Calhoun."

"I've interviewed the couple who were first on the scene and called in the wreck," Ranger Parker said. "Carl and Betty Hanson. They are retired and usually use that back road when they go into San Antonio, to avoid the traffic on the highway. They live in Dry Gulch. In fact, they know Hattie and the Sinclairs."

"Could they give us anything about the man, the vehicle he was driving?"

"Betty was useless as a witness, but Carl described the truck as black, a Dodge Ram maybe six or seven years old and with no license plate in the back."

"That fits what Hattie told me about the front license plate. It might be a stolen truck. Check the reports of stolen trucks for the past few months. This has been planned, maybe for a while." Brody glanced toward Hattie whose eyes were still closed. A bruise was starting to show around her right eye.

"The description of the man was vague. They were several hundred yards away. Medium height. The woman thought he was skinny. The man didn't. That's about all they could say other than that he was wearing jeans and a white shirt. Oh, and the black ski mask."

All information that supported Hattie's, Tory's, and Aubrey's statements. "I think the best thing at this time is to find the truck. It's been stolen, most likely, which means it will be dumped once its usefulness is finished. Start with the turnoffs along the road on the right-hand side, going west. He pulled out of one not far from the wreck. He was waiting for them. If we find the truck, maybe we'll get a viable fingerprint or a witness who can describe the person who left the truck. I'll reinterview the couple tomorrow, after they have had time to think about the wreck." When Brody hung up, he saw that Hattie was beginning to awaken.

"Any news?" Hattie asked with a hopeful ring to her words.

"Nope. Ranger Parker was filling me in on the crime scene."

Her expression fell. "If anything happens to Kim, I'll never be able to forgive myself. I should have been able to overpower him. Protect the girls."

"This isn't your fault. Whoever is behind this is pretty sick to involve children."

"What is going on?"

"I think someone is after Rebecca."

"Why?"

"Not sure, but if we can figure that out, we'll know who to look for."

"This isn't tied to Alexandrov and Petrov?"

"No. This is much more personal." Brody told Hattie about Laura.

"I can't believe this."

"I'm not even sure Alexandrov was behind much of what happened to Rebecca. Maybe he hired the man to try to run her down and had the witness killed, but nothing else really fits his style." Brody turned into the Circle S Ranch.

⚹

"Have you disposed of the girl's body?"

Grinding his teeth, J. R. gripped the cell. "Not yet."

"What's taking you so long?"

"This has to be done carefully. She has to be found, but nothing should lead back to us. That takes planning."

"We planned it. Do it. Our revenge won't be final until you do. You promised. Remember?"

"I've got to go. She's waking up."

"Kill her and it won't be a problem. You messed up with Laura. She was supposed to be killed like the guy behind the pawnshop. Strangling her wasn't enough. Rebecca needs to suffer like we have. Kill the girl."

J. R. cut the conversation off. He didn't need to be reminded of what his part in the plan was. Nor his promise to his mama.

Nor his failure to carry out the plan exactly. His mistake was getting to know Laura.

He stuffed the cell into his jean pocket and stared at the child lying on the couch, her features so innocent right now.

So peaceful.

That would change soon.

He didn't want to be a disappointment again. He had promised, but now he wished he hadn't.

∽❧∾

"What am I going to say to Thomas?" Rebecca advanced toward her brother's hospital room. A few feet from the door, she swung around and walked away. "I can't do this, Brody . . . I . . ."

He stopped her progress toward the elevator. "He has to be told, and you and Tory are the best ones to do it. Your sister-in-law is in there waiting for you. By now, she should be pretty clearheaded. Thankfully, whatever was given to her wasn't long lasting. She needs your help. You know Thomas better than anyone."

"That's just it. I know what this will do to him. He's making progress in his recovery. What if—"

Brody touched her lips with two fingers to stop her words. "I know what it's going to do to him. His girls are everything to him. I'll be there for you. C'mon. We need to get back to the ranch in case there is a ransom demand."

"There isn't going to be one. Isn't that what the dead flowers all over Laura and my bed meant? This isn't about money. It's about hate. About revenge."

"I agree. At least the ME didn't think she suffered."

"A small consolation, but I'll take it," she choked, tears closing her throat. She pushed the guilt that swamped her into the background. She couldn't afford to deal with her emotions when everyone needed her to be strong.

"I haven't had a chance to tell you that a bouquet of dead roses was found at the side of the road where the truck was parked at the wreck."

"What!" *What have I done to cause all of this?* The guilt she tried to keep at bay surged forward.

"In my defense, I just found out not long ago."

She thrust her fingers through her hair, clenching a handful for a few seconds before releasing it. *Calm, in control. Don't let him get to me. He can't win.* "I didn't see it at the accident scene," she finally said in what resembled a composed voice.

"That's because the ambulance blocked your view of it. The deputy told me about it as I was leaving for the ranch to bring you here."

"So there are four instances where dead flowers were left. All roses. Remember, Laura had that arrangement of roses on her dining room table where she was going to eat with Jim. He has to be the man doing this. Everything is connected. He wants us to know what this is all about."

Brody took her hand and strode toward her brother's room, where an officer stood guard outside. "And that will be his downfall."

She wished she could believe it. Kim had been missing for five hours. An Amber Alert had gone out, every law enforcement officer had her niece's picture, and it had been blasted over the airwaves to the public. There was little she could do but wait—something she had never been good at.

Pulling in a deep breath, she pushed the door open and they entered her brother's room.

Tory sat by his bed, relief flooding her face when she saw Rebecca. She relaxed her stiff posture and slumped back in the chair. "Thomas, you've got visitors."

Rebecca wanted to tell her not to wake him up on her account, but her brother's eyes opened immediately.

He gave her a weak smile. "Hey Brody. Hey, Rebecca. I was just resting my eyes. Tory said you were coming to see me. It's about time. I was wondering if you had forgotten your brother."

"Never. Today has been a busy one."

"Yeah, my big, important little sister, the judge."

"I see you're getting better. You're becoming your usual obnoxious self."

"Who? Me? I'm wounded." Her brother put his hand over his heart.

"That's why you're in the hospital."

Thomas chuckled. "Love you, too."

Tell him. Quit putting it off. In that moment, she wanted to whirl around and flee the room. She looked at Tory, who dropped her gaze. She didn't want to say anything, either. Rebecca didn't blame her sister-in-law. That was how she felt. If she knew for certain they could get Kim back soon, she wouldn't tell Thomas to save him heartache.

Brody drew a chair to the opposite side of the bed from Tory and indicated that Rebecca should take a seat. She sat before her legs gave out on her. The next few minutes would be the worst in her life. Brody stood behind her with his hands on her shoulders. From his touch, she sensed his support and it shored her up for what she had to do.

Rebecca glanced at Tory. "We have something to tell you." She pointed to Tory and to herself, then waited to see if her sister-in-law wanted to continue. The look in Tory's eyes told Rebecca otherwise. Her sister-in-law had cried over the phone when they had talked earlier about how to tell Thomas.

Tory sat forward and took Thomas's hand. "The reason I was late earlier is that—" she swallowed hard "—Hattie and

I were in an accident. I was run off the road. The car crashed into a ditch. It wasn't my fault but . . ." Her voice disappeared as though it were a wisp of smoke caught on the wind. She gulped and opened her mouth to say something, but instead pressed her lips together.

"Is Hattie all right?" Thomas frowned.

Tory nodded, looking down at their clasped hands.

"I don't care about the car. That can be fixed—just so everyone's okay."

When her sister-in-law lifted her head, her eyes shone with tears.

Rebecca waited a few heartbeats, her chest so tight she could hardly breathe. When Tory couldn't continue, she said, "Thomas, Hattie and Tory picked up the girls from school, and they were coming here to surprise you."

Thomas turned his attention to Rebecca. "Are the girls hurt?"

The urgency in his voice compelled Rebecca to finish this ordeal. "Aubrey is fine, but Kim has been kidnapped." The words tumbled out of her mouth in such a hurry even she could hardly understand herself.

But her brother got the gist of what she had said. Yanking his hand from Tory's grasp, he flipped back the sheets and labored to sit up. "How long were you going to keep this from me? I've got to get out of here."

Rebecca and Tory stood at the same time and tried to stop Thomas from getting up. He resisted, pushing their hands away, then struggled to swing his broken leg, which was in a cast, off the bed. He couldn't do it. He collapsed back onto the bed, groaning at the effort.

Brody moved to Rebecca's side. "Every effort is being made to find Kim. So far there hasn't been a ransom demand, but if we get one, Rebecca has made arrangements with the bank to put together whatever money is needed. We're on this, as are the local law enforcement agencies."

Thomas tried to change position and winced. "FBI?"

"They have been informed, but I'm taking the lead on this. Since I know the area and what's been going on, Sheriff Overstreet asked the Texas Rangers for help. Believe me, Kim is our top priority right now."

"What kinds of leads do you have?" Thomas closed his eyes, his face pallid and his hands twisted at his sides, attesting to the control he was trying to maintain.

"A couple of promising ones. We're tracking down the truck used. The license plates were found on a gravel road where the kidnapper waited for your car to pass on the highway. We discovered the truck was reported stolen earlier today. The man who owns the truck reported the theft to the San Antonio police around the time the kidnapping occurred."

"Could he be involved in any way? Covering his tracks?" Thomas reached out to take Tory's hand.

"No, he has an alibi, but we'll look into his background to see if he might be an accomplice. I know you'll say something if you remember anything about your accident, but I need you to concentrate on trying to remember."

Thomas frowned. "Is there a connection?"

"I don't know, but so many things have happened lately, and some of them are starting to tie together."

The furrows on Thomas's forehead deepened. "You think someone is after me? First my accident and now Kim's kidnapping?"

The pressure in Rebecca's chest increased. "No, we don't think it's you." She shot Brody a narrow-eyed look. "I think the person is after me," she whispered, her voice thready.

"You? I thought Alexandrov had been taken care of."

"He was, and he may have been responsible for a few things that have happened, but not all of them. Several things have occurred lately that indicate there's a totally different person involved."

Closing his eyes, Thomas pinched the bridge of his nose. "You'll be the first to know if anything comes to me. Right now it's a blank. I was looking down at the calf carrying on in the gully. I felt a sting and started to slap the bug on my neck when everything went black."

"Bug? What bug? This is the first you've said anything about being stung." Excitement lit Brody's eyes and infused each word.

"I've been stung by a wasp before. I never thought much of it. But a wasp sting wouldn't cause me to black out."

"But someone shooting a dart gun at you might."

"How's this going to help my daughter?"

"I don't know if it will, but it might. If someone drugged you and then set up that accident, that same person could be behind Kim's kidnapping."

"I have to go home. I can't stay here with my baby out there somewhere." With a fierce determination to get up again, Thomas pushed himself up.

Rebecca saw blood on his sheet where he'd been lying. She pressed the call button and said, "You've opened a wound. You aren't going anywhere if I have to have you drugged to keep you here. We're getting Kim back, but you have to take care of yourself. She will need you. There's nothing you can do at the ranch."

The nurse came into the room, and Rebecca gestured toward her brother's back. While the woman took a look at Thomas's reopened wound, Rebecca said, "I'll keep you informed about what's going on every step of the way."

"So will I," Brody added, as the nurse called for the doctor.

"If y'all can step out of the room, we need to tend to Mr. Sinclair."

Rebecca kissed Thomas's cheek. "We have to get back to the ranch. I love Kim like my own daughter. I'll do everything I can to get her back and find out who is doing this to me and the people I'm close to. I'm so sorry."

Rebecca started to turn away before she cried in front of everyone when her brother grabbed her arm and stopped her. "This isn't your fault. I don't blame you for what some maniac is doing to us."

She glanced back at him, tears swimming in her eyes. "I love you, Tommy." He let go, and she hurried from the room, Brody and Tory following. He might not blame her, but she did.

"I'm staying here tonight. Thomas will need me. I'll be okay with the officer outside the room." Tory leaned against the wall, stifling a yawn. "Y'all need to go. I'm sure there's a lot for you to do."

Rebecca hugged her sister-in-law, who stiffened. Rebecca stepped away, noticing that her sister-in-law's mouth was pressed in a thin line. "I'm sorry about what's happening."

"You should be. You've put your family in danger." Tory's eyes narrowed.

"It's not her fault—"

"I don't blame you for being upset," Rebecca said, interrupting Brody's protest. "I never meant for anything like this to happen."

"I'm sure you didn't, but it did." Tory glanced at the doctor, who was going into the room. "Now if you'll excuse me, my husband needs me."

Brody took her hand. "I'm sorry, Rebecca. She doesn't mean that."

"Yes, she does. Her husband is injured and her stepdaughter is missing. She has a right to be upset."

"But you didn't do this."

"No," Rebecca turned and started for the elevator, "but I'm going to do everything humanly possible to get my niece back." On the ride down to the first floor, she started going through the cases she had presided over the past year. Someone out there hated her enough to go after her loved ones. Why?

17

Rebecca collapsed into the overstuffed chair in the den and put her feet up on the ottoman. "Alone at last." Her head pounded from all the commotion and noise made by a packed house of law enforcement officers, who were setting up a command post, which included putting a tap on the phone in case there was a ransom demand.

"Sorry for the invasion, but you need to be protected, and I need to work on the case. Best if the command center is here at the ranch house." Brody settled onto the ottoman. "How's the list coming? Any more people you can think of who might want to do this to you? We're running down the three you've already given us."

She rested her head on the cushion and stared at the ceiling. "It's sad that my life has come down to figuring out who hates me enough to murder a good friend and colleague, to try to kill my brother, and now to kidnap my niece. In law school, I don't think I took a class that would prepare me for the crazies of this world."

"Revenge is a powerful motivator."

"What about to forgiving our fellow man?"

"In theory, that's great. In practice, many people don't know how to do that. When we catch this person, and we will, can you forgive him for what he's done?"

"If the man responsible walked through that door right now, I would be greatly tempted to snatch your gun and shoot him. I know God wants us to forgive, no matter what. But, frankly, I don't know if I could forgive him. Ever."

"Focus on that feeling. Who in your life might feel that way toward you? A family member of someone you put away? A person who is finally out of prison?"

She kneaded her forehead with her fingertips. "What if I overlook the person for some reason?"

"I'm not depending totally on you. There is a countywide search for the truck. I'm taking another look at the arson, and the murder victims that we're not sure Alexandrov was responsible for."

She caught his gaze. "Tell me you've got a solid lead."

"I can't. The roses are a dead end. No fingerprints on the syringe or on the white pickup that we can't rule out."

She handed him the sheet of paper in her lap. "Here are two more names."

"Have you gone back to when you were a prosecuting attorney?"

"Not yet. I'm going through my notes on the cases I presided over. I'm up to my first year as a judge. Almost through, then I can start on my cases as a prosecutor, but that was five years ago."

"A person can hold a grudge a long time. Or maybe something changed to make him come after you now. I've got a couple of officers looking into all the people whose cases you've presided over." He peered at the paper. "Who stands out the most?"

"The top name I gave you earlier. Zeb Matthews. Very vocal when he was sentenced for a crime he insisted he hadn't done."

"I'll look into him personally. Anyone else?"

Rebecca glanced over at the short stack of folders on the table next to her and tapped the top one. "Owen Smith. He was one of my first big trials. I don't need to review his case to know he's capable of doing something like this."

Brody took her pen and wrote his name on the sheet. "What's his story?"

"He kept saying someone else kidnapped his little girl and murdered her. But all the evidence pointed to him. The jury convicted him. I can remember the last time I saw him. If looks could kill, I'd be dead. As he left the courtroom, he pointed to me and then made a gesture as if he were strangling me." She sank back against the cushion, so tired she could barely keep her eyes from shutting. When they closed, she forced them open again. "And Laura was strangled." She shuddered.

Brody leaned forward, gently traced his finger down her jawline, and then cupped her chin. "You are not to blame. Let your guilt go and turn it over to the Lord. He can handle it."

"It's not that easy."

"I know, Rebecca." The softness in his eyes soothed her for a moment. "Get some sleep first. You aren't going to be good for anyone if you don't."

"I will soon. But I want to review some of my cases as a prosecutor." She waved her hands at the stack of files spread out over the den. "I only have a few hundred."

He stood and pulled her up against him. "I'm escorting you to your bedroom, where you're going to sleep for at least a few hours. I'm serious. You can hardly think straight as exhausted as you are." Taking her face between his palms, he kissed her forehead. "I promise I'll wake you in three hours."

"How about you? You haven't gotten any sleep, either."

"I've done this before." One corner of his mouth lifted up. "Besides, I don't require as much beauty sleep."

"If I wasn't so tired, I'd take offense at that statement."

"Don't. You're beautiful to me inside and out." This time he brushed his lips across hers, lightly, barely connecting with her. Then he rose, drawing her up with him and draping his arm over her shoulders.

As they started for the hallway, she cuddled against him, needing his strength and his assurance that they would find Kim alive. As they passed the living room, she spotted another Texas Ranger as well as two deputies and the sheriff. "They look as tired as I feel."

"They are."

"We've got a spare bedroom."

"We thought we would take shifts."

At the bottom of the staircase, she turned to face him. "I can find my own way to the bedroom. I don't think there's anyone hiding under my bed. Not with all these cops here." She started up the stairs. "Remember, three hours. I still have a lot of files to go through."

"No way do I want to be in trouble with you." Brody glanced at his watch. "I'll give you five minutes to go to sleep. I'll wake you up at four."

❧

J. R. drank another shot of whiskey, stalking from one end of the small living room to the other. Periodically he glanced at the girl on the couch. But the innocent set of her features taunted him. He'd checked her earlier. She was alive, but she still hadn't awakened—even when he tied her hands and feet.

He stomped into the kitchen to pour himself more liquor. He caught sight of the card she'd made him on the desk. He grabbed it and balled it up, then tossed it in the trash. Kim was a means to an end. It was one thing to kill a criminal and, for that matter even Laura. But a child? He'd thought he could do it. Now he wasn't so sure. No, he just needed to drink enough, then he wouldn't feel anything and he could do it.

A scream split the air, and he nearly dropped his glass. He grabbed for the ski mask and pulled it on then ran from the kitchen into the living room. The girl sat up straight, her eyes huge as she wrestled with the rope at her wrists.

Her gaze seized his. "Please don't hurt me. Please." Her bottom lip trembled as she continued to twist her hands, trying to loosen the restraints. "I want my daddy." Tears flowed down her cheeks.

He took a step toward her. Then another. More sobs penetrated the hard casing he had built around his heart. Nobody had ever cared about him—except his brother. He owed him.

A few more paces, and he sat down by the girl. He could remember her looking up at him, her eyes sparkling, a big smile on her face. She'd hung on every word he'd spoken the couple of times he'd seen her.

She finally gave up trying to free herself and instead buried her face in her hands and cried.

He reached toward her to pat her back. The action surprised him, and he yanked his hand back before he actually went through with it. He needed to kill her now. Dispose of the body and then get out of San Antonio as planned.

He looked at her neck, slender, tanned, probably from spending a lot of time outdoors. Curling and uncurling his hands, he listened to the anguish pour out of her.

Kill her. Now.

***

His face loomed before her. His sinister smile seared into her heart, branding her with the threat it held.

I never forget. Behind those words there was an even deeper threat, full of unspoken evil. He had tortured and murdered a teenage girl and been caught taking another on whom to do his will.

His laughter burst forth from his lips, his teeth gleaming. *Never.*

Then his face fragmented into a hundred pieces like a jigsaw puzzle thrown into the air. Then another killer appeared, occupying every crevice of her mind. *You'll regret ever prosecuting me. I'll get out and come after you.*

She started running as fast as she could. But no matter where she went, he was there, waiting for her. Grabbing for her, trapping her.

She fought. But something confined her arms and legs—imprisoning her.

Rebecca bolted up in bed; darkness shrouded her. Except for the lighted red numbers that read 3:42.

She flung back the covers wrapped about her and rose. She knew who could have done this.

⟿

J. R. couldn't stand it a second longer. The girl's sobs tore at his composure.

Anger warred with regret. Anger because he should be able to do this. Regret because he shouldn't have agreed to the plan. Not the part about killing an innocent child.

"Kim, do you want some water?"

Her cries quieted.

"Or something to eat?"

She raised her head and looked at him. Biting her bottom lip, she stared at the black ski mask.

He flipped his hand at his face. "Does this scare you?"

She nodded.

He peeled off the mask. No matter what he did, she wouldn't be returning home.

❧

Rebecca made her way downstairs to the living room, transformed now into the command center where Brody was running the investigation. It was deserted. Where was everyone? Had something happened? What? Panic started in her stomach and zipped throughout her so rapidly it took her by surprise. She'd been able to hold it back. But not anymore. Her palms were sweating. Moisture cloaked her forehead. Tremors shook her.

Then she heard voices coming from her kitchen. She sagged against the back of a lounge chair. Regaining control.

Pushing herself upright, she started toward the kitchen, only to come to a halt as Sean entered the room. "What are you doing up? You need your rest."

"I was going to say the same thing to you. You have about fifteen more minutes to sleep before Brody was going to wake you up, and from the way you look, you need that, and more."

"I'd say that your powers of observation are as keen as when you were a cop. Is Brody in the kitchen?"

"Yeah, he's making another pot of coffee. I took the last cup." Sean held up his mug, then took a drink. "I taught my son how to make a good cup of coffee, at least. A necessity for these long nights."

"I think you taught him a lot more than that. Why are you up?"

"I reckon for the same reason you are. The case. Not being able to sleep. Too much going through your mind. Take your pick. All three apply to me."

"Same here." She continued her trek to the kitchen to find Brody standing at the bay window overlooking the back of the house.

He stared into the darkness blanketing the landscape. "I'm surprised you slept as long as you did."

"I have two more people to add to the list without going through my files as a prosecutor. One was my first big case working for the DA's office. The other was during my last year, but both frightened me—a lot."

The sound of the coffee finishing perking echoed in the silence between them. He slowly turned toward her, his tired gaze seeking hers. "Who?"

"Daniel Watson was the man I convicted of murdering a teenage girl and kidnapping another. Jeremiah Jones killed a family."

"Did you sneak downstairs and go through your files?"

"No, I dreamed about them. Sometimes it's good to let your subconscious work behind the scenes. I would have come across them eventually. But I've done my best to try to forget those two men. Daniel was convicted at seventeen and didn't get the death penalty, but he wasn't going to get out of prison. He was a cruel teen and tried as an adult. The things he did to his victim made me shudder. Jeremiah did get the death penalty, but he hasn't been executed yet. I would have been notified. When I talked to them, I felt as though I was talking to pure evil."

"Then I'll move them to the top of the list, but if one of them is involved, why now?"

Rebecca yawned. "I'll help you look into them. There was a time I knew them well. When I prosecuted a person, I found out everything I could about them. I didn't want any surprises in the middle of the trial."

He walked over to her. "That's why you were such a good prosecutor and moved up rapidly through the ranks."

"You know me. All or nothing. That's the way I approach my job, and life."

"I'll let you help me if you go back upstairs and sleep a couple more hours."

"I could work on it behind your back. I do have contacts, Mr. Calhoun."

"I know. But you'll do a much better job with some rest."

"The same goes for you."

"I'm going to catch a few, too."

She waved her hand toward the coffeepot. "What about that?"

"For Dad. He's manning everything for me. If something breaks, he'll come get me." He continued toward the hallway. "I got a call half an hour ago. A deputy found the truck abandoned in a field between San Antonio and Dry Gulch. Someone notified the sheriff's office and the deputy went out to investigate. That's where Sheriff Overstreet went."

"You didn't?"

"Someone has to stay back and protect you." A smile tilted up one corner of his mouth. "I gladly volunteered for that duty."

The warmth in his eyes suffused her. She was glad he had stayed behind. She trusted him—totally, which wasn't something she did easily. The only others she had ever trusted completely were Thomas and her husband.

"Ranger Parker is meeting them there to process the scene, and then they'll send everything to the state lab."

"The truck, too?"

He nodded, pausing at the stairway that led to the downstairs bedrooms. "A tow truck is on the way. We'll be going over it until I'm satisfied there isn't anything more it can tell us. And as I said before, the governor has stepped in and made this a top priority. I've got carte blanche."

"Yes, Foster called me earlier and told me if he could do anything, he would." Another yawn escaped her.

"Go back to bed. I'll see you at a decent hour in the morning."

"It is morning. It's four thirty. It won't be long before the sun rises."

He cradled her face. "When this is over with," he dipped his head toward hers and claimed her lips in a deep kiss, "we need to talk about what's going on between us that we both keep dancing around."

Not if I can help it. Too dangerous. The words formed in her mind, but she couldn't say them out loud. Not now. Maybe later. "Good night."

He chuckled. "Don't you mean good morning?"

She glanced back at him and grinned. "Yeah, but I'm trying to trick my body into thinking it's night."

She climbed the stairs to the second floor, then moved down the hall to Aubrey's room and eased the door open wider. Hattie lay on the double bed with Aubrey curled up against her. Aubrey had gone to bed early but couldn't sleep. Hattie volunteered to stay with her in her room. But even knowing that, Rebecca needed to check on her niece.

Satisfied they were getting what they needed, sleep, Rebecca crossed over to her room. She stared at her messy bed, the covers balled up with one end dragging on the floor. It looked like she had wrestled with herself and lost.

When she lay on the straightened-up sheets, she thought sleep would descend quickly, if her exhaustion were any indication. But with her eyes closed, her mind filled with the sight of Brody a few minutes ago, when he pulled back from kissing her. The intensity in his expression still had the power to weaken her knees. And to weaken her resolve not to become romantically involved with a man who laid his life on the line every day he went to work.

Then the guilt wormed its way into her thoughts and stayed there while she tried to sleep.

❧

"Daniel Watson is dead." Sitting at the kitchen table in front of her laptop, Rebecca twisted toward Brody, who was at the counter getting another cup of coffee. "There was a fight in the prison yard, and he was killed."

"How long ago?"

"Twenty months."

"He might not be behind what's going on personally, but we'll still look into his family. Do you remember anything about them?"

"I'll look through his file again. It was ten years ago and there have been so many people since. But I do remember his mother was intense. She believed her son was innocent, even with all the evidence presented at the trial. I know a lot of families who profess that their relatives are innocent, but often you can tell they don't really believe what they say. With Mrs. Watson, I felt she believed her son wasn't guilty, even though he was caught with the second kidnapped girl."

"What about his father?"

"Not in the picture. Left the family when the children were young."

"How many other children?"

"I think a younger brother and sister."

Brody sat in front of his computer and turned the screen toward Rebecca. "This is Jeremiah Jones?"

Dark eyes stared back at her, void of emotion, an almost vacant gaze. "Yes. I won't forget that face. Where is he?"

"Still in prison. How about family?"

"His father, who'd be about sixty now, was the only one who acknowledged him. I remember there was a sister who would have nothing to do with her older brother and what he did. She left the area when the trial started. The press kept trying to interview her. She distanced herself as much as possible from the trial."

"Anyone else in his life?"

Rebecca reached across the table and grabbed her working folder of the case. After flipping through the pages, she closed the file. "I wasn't sure, but now I remember he had a girlfriend, and I wouldn't be surprised if she visited him at the prison every chance she gets. I could easily see her being a prisoner groupie."

"I'll check with the warden about the people who have visited Jones in the past couple of years. While I'm at it, I'll check on all the names on the list."

Sean stepped into the kitchen, a big grin on his face. "One of those guys on the list you gave me is out of prison on parole as of six months ago."

"Which one?" Rebecca asked, shivering when she thought of any one of them being back in society.

"Zeb Matthews."

"Dad, see if you can reach his parole officer and find out where the man is. I need to pay him a visit."

"Sure. Owen Smith finished most of his sentence and is out—get this—on good behavior."

Good behavior? Hot-headed, explosive were what Rebecca remembered about him. "When?"

"Six weeks ago."

"Both of them look promising, but if I had to decide which one was behind everything that has been happening, I would say Jeremiah Jones would be at the top of the list."

"You two continue looking into this list and anyone else you can think of, Rebecca." Brody scooted back his chair. "I'm paying Owen Smith and Zeb Matthews a visit."

"Smith might be pretty hard. According to the records, he isn't living in the area. The day he was released, he left Texas for Arkansas. This is Matthews's address." Sean slipped his son a piece of paper.

"What town in Arkansas?" Brody rose, pocketing the address.

"Little Rock. Do you want me to contact the police and have them check on Smith's whereabouts?"

"Yes. It's not that far away and besides, just because he left doesn't mean he didn't turn around and come back." Brody started for the front of the house. "I'll probably be gone for a few hours. I'll even go by and check on Thomas."

"I want to come," Rebecca said, rising to her feet.

"No way. Too risky. What if it's Zeb, or for that matter, Jones's father? Instead, get me the address of his girlfriend. I'm paying her a visit, too."

"But I should fill Thomas in on what we're doing."

"I will, and if we have any time later today, I'll take you over there, along with Aubrey. I have a feeling she needs to see her daddy and her daddy needs to see her."

"That would be great. If you get tied up, I bet I can sweet-talk the sheriff into taking me."

A grin spread slowly across Brody's mouth. "I bet you can, too."

His smile stayed with her after he left. Whenever he turned that smile on her, her resolve to keep their relationship as friends only melted a little more. She was afraid that if they spent much more time together she'd end up proposing to him.

⸺◈⸺

Brody sat across from Mr. Roy Jones as the man expounded on how much his son had changed since he went to prison. "I'm glad to hear that." It wasn't the first time he'd been assured a convict was completely rehabilitated. Sadly, so many times that wasn't the truth.

"You don't believe me." The man, looking a lot older than his sixty years, breathed in oxygen from a tank sitting next to his chair. "Go visit him. You'll see." He took another deep breath. "I used to visit him. Now I hardly leave this house. Takes too much effort."

"Do you ever see your son's girlfriend?"

"Marge? Yeah, she comes by every week and lets me know how Jeremiah is doing. Never stopped loving him. Now, that's true love."

No, it was sick, but Brody kept his opinion to himself. "Do you know where she lives?"

"A couple of months ago she moved into an apartment not far from Mercy Memorial. She's taken me to the hospital a few times when I've needed to go. But I don't know the address. I just remember her saying she lived three blocks away from the hospital so it was no problem to take me to the hospital when I need a breathing treatment."

A knock sounded at his apartment door. "That's my caregiver. She's an hour late. Get the door on your way out."

"I have a couple more questions."

"No, you don't. I'm exhausted and can't think straight. Lack of oxygen will do that to you, young man," Roy said in a raspy voice, then took another deep breath of oyxgen.

Brody debated all of two seconds whether to stay, but one look at Roy Jones's stubbornly set expression told him it would be a waste of time. He'd ask the girlfriend about Jeremiah's friends. Then if he needed to come back, he would.

After he let the caregiver inside, he strode to his SUV, parked right outside the apartment. Once in the driver's seat, Brody punched in the ranch number. Rebecca answered on the second ring.

"Did you get the girlfriend's address?" He shifted the phone to his other hand and started his engine.

"Yes," Rebecca said and recited it to him.

He jotted it down before backing out of the parking space. "I'm heading to Zeb Matthews's place now, then Jones's girlfriend's. Didn't find out anything from Roy Jones except that he couldn't be the one actually doing any of this. He's on oxygen and is physically frail. He might have paid someone, but he lives in a low-income apartment. I'll let you and Dad know if I find anything. How's your computer search going?"

"Slow. I'm glad your dad is as good as he is. There are a lot of people on my list. Until I had to make that list, I never stopped to think about how many people I've angered."

"I know what you mean. I'd hate to make a list of the ones I've made mad. That's the life of a cop." He pulled out into traffic. "I like to think of the good I've done instead."

"Thanks. I needed that reminder."

Thirty minutes later, Brody pulled up in front of a run-down house in a part of town where he hated leaving his new SUV on the street. He studied the one-story house with its peeling paint and a couple of broken steps leading up to a listing porch. As he walked up, the sensation of being watched crawled up his spine—not only from inside the house but from the surrounding houses.

When he rang the bell, the blinds at the window to the left moved. Although no one came to answer the door, someone was inside. He waited a full minute then rapped again. "This is the State Police, Mr. Matthews. Open up."

Finally, a wiry man about five-feet-seven opened the door a crack. "I ain't done nothing wrong."

"May I come in? I need to talk to you about one of my cases."

"Like I said, I know nothing. All I want is to be left alone."

"Either you invite me in or I'll come in. You are on parole. What are you hiding in there?"

Inch by inch Matthews widened the gap to allow Brody into his house. The air reeked of stale beer and cigarettes. He strode into the living room off to the right, furnished with one chair probably found at the dump and an old TV resting on a crate. Another crate, being used as an end table, sat next to the chair and held a lamp without a shade and an ashtray piled high with cigarette butts.

"I'd ask you to sit down, but I ain't got nothing 'cause no one will hire an ex-con."

"So what are you doing with all the free time you have besides drinking and smoking?"

"Looking for a job. Occasionally, I get an odd job here and there."

"Was one of those jobs to scare Judge Morgan?"

"Why would I do that? I ain't going back inside." Matthews picked up his pack of smokes and shook one loose, then struck a match.

"I'd prefer you wait to smoke until I leave. You might not mind inhaling filth, but I do."

The ex-con glared at him, then blew out the match and tossed his cigarettes onto the crate by the chair. "A nasty habit I picked up in the joint."

"Where were you yesterday between two and four in the afternoon?"

"Seeing my parole officer and going on an interview he set up for me—Yellow Rose Diner."

"Who did you see?"

"The owner. She's a tough cookie, but she's gonna give me a chance. More than I can say for most."

"What's her name?"

"Ruth Fisher. She'll vouch I was there. She even gave me a tour of the place—not much, but there was a crowd already there at three. Seems she gives handouts to the homeless in the area. Some kind of Christian. I ain't got any time for religion, but I'm glad she believes in second chances."

"Do you own a truck or car?"

"Me?" He stabbed his finger into his chest and laughed. "Yeah, I may not eat, but I've gotta have my wheels. What do you take me for? A Rockefeller?" His merriment increased.

"How do you get around?"

"The bus." Matthews looked him up and down. "I guess you don't know what that is."

"Have you heard of anyone wanting to get back at Judge Morgan?"

"Only a crazy fool. I don't wanna go back to the joint. That means playing nice." Matthews walked over to his front door. "Now I've got to get ready for my new job. I ain't gonna let you make me late."

His look challenged Brody, who grinned. "I'll be stopping by the Yellow Rose Diner to see how you're doing. Good day." He tipped his hat and left the house.

Again he felt that he was being watched as he made his way to his SUV, all its tires still intact and no visible dents or scratches. Now to see Marge, a woman who definitely needed to improve her taste in men.

❧

"Do you want anything else to eat?" J. R. asked the girl on his couch. Her feet were tied, but her hands weren't, as she ate the peanut butter and grape jelly sandwich he had fixed her.

She chewed the last bite, then drank the rest of the milk. Wiping the back of her hand across her mouth, she said, "More milk, please."

He went into the small kitchen, just off the living room, and opened the fridge, his attention glued to his hostage the whole time. She glanced around, shifting on the couch. "Don't even think it."

She froze, and turned to look straight ahead.

He walked back to her and gave her the glass of milk, then took the chair across from her. What was he going to do with her? It had been almost twenty-four hours since he had kidnapped her, and he still didn't know. Of course, his sister had other ideas. He hadn't minded killing the man and the woman—well, maybe a little—but he wasn't like his brother, he guessed.

I draw the line at children.

The girl gulped down her milk and swiped her hand across her mouth again. "When can I go home?"

The sad, near-tears look she gave him tightened his gut. Not a week ago she'd turned a much different look on him— one he was finding he preferred. He shrugged.

She scrunched her brow. "You've always been so nice to me. What did I do wrong?"

"Your aunt is the prosecutor who ruined my family. She's responsible for my poor mama and older brother dying."

"Not Aunt Becky. She wouldn't kill anyone."

"She didn't do it herself, but her actions caused their deaths. She might as well have pulled the trigger. It would have been faster."

The girl's eyes grew so round that they were all J. R. saw for a few seconds. Eyes that didn't understand. Eyes filled with innocence.

Tears welled up in them, and the girl squeezed them shut for a moment. "She was nice to you. She thought you were a hero," she said between sucking in shaky breaths, trying not to cry. "Rob, you saved Aunt Becky's life. Why did you do that?"

When she called him Rob, he was thrown back to that evening last week when they'd opened their home to him, fixed some of his favorite things to eat, and had talked to him like he was somebody.

"Rob?"

He blinked several times, then stood up. *I could have let Rebecca die then. I wouldn't be wrestling with what to do about Kim now. Why didn't I?*

"The doors and windows are locked. You can't get out. I'll untie your feet and hands if you behave. Understand?"

She nodded, those large eyes looking at him as though trying to find the person he'd pretended to be. He wasn't Rob.

He started to loosen the ropes about her feet but instead said, "You can untie yourself. If you want to watch some TV, go ahead." He flicked his hand toward the set, then hurried from the room.

Sitting at the kitchen table with a clear view of her, he could watch her from a distance until he figured out what was going on with him. He'd never killed a child. He thought he could. He'd killed his fair share of people—mostly men. Laura had bothered him—seeing the trust fade from her eyes and horror take its place when she realized what he was going to do. He rubbed his hands down his face as though to scour it until only raw skin was left.

∼🙚∼

Dressed in a simple, pale blue dress that fell to just below her knees, Marge showed Brody into her small, neat apartment. Jeremiah's girlfriend was nothing like he'd thought she would be. With only a touch of makeup on and her hair pulled back into a ponytail, she appeared demure, almost fragile, like a china doll.

"Please have a seat, Ranger Calhoun. Would you like something to drink? It's officially fall, but the temperature feels like summer."

"No, thank you." He waited until she sat, then took the seat across from her.

"Roy told me you came to see him about Jeremiah. What can I do to help you?"

How can a woman like this be in love with a murderer on death row? Roy tipped her off. Is this an act? It's got to be.

"Who are some of Jeremiah's friends? Does he have any family besides Roy?"

"Jeremiah has a sister, but she left San Antonio years ago. His brother enlisted in the service that first year Jeremiah was in prison. He's traveling the world, I guess. He and his sister don't contact Roy, so I don't know anything beyond that."

"Do they contact Jeremiah?"

"He's never mentioned it."

"How about friends? Does he keep up with any?"

"He's been in prison a long time. All his friends are inside."

"Has he mentioned Judge Rebecca Morgan to you?"

"We don't really spend our time talking about others. Our time is precious together since the state has . . ." She clamped her mouth together, tension exhibited in her jawline. Folding her hands together in her lap, she straightened until Brody wondered if she would snap in two. "Jeremiah was falsely convicted. His lawyer has been working on a retrial. I'm confident he will succeed and then the truth about Jeremiah will come out."

"Ma'am, I've looked over the transcript of the trial, and the possibility of that is remote."

Her dark eyes became diamond hard. "Jeremiah assures me it will. I choose to believe him. He's such a gentle, kind man. He doesn't belong in prison." A thread of steel reinforced the strength behind her words.

Marge was holding herself together—barely. What would happen when her fantasy fell apart? Had it already, and she had decided to strike out at Rebecca?

"Where were you yesterday afternoon?"

She lifted her chin and stared at him. "Why, volunteering at the hospital. I do it twice a week on my days off."

"What do you do to make a living?"

"I transcribe medical records." She gestured toward a desk off to the side with a computer on it. There was no evidence that she had even used it, but then everything he'd seen of her place was like that, overly neat, as if she had to be ready to show the apartment at a moment's notice. The sense that something wasn't right with the woman slammed into him. Rigid. Controlled. Cold . . . Deadly?

"Any family living in San Antonio?"

"No, I'm estranged from my family. They don't understand my love for Jeremiah. But then, I shouldn't have been surprised. They aren't a very loving family." The chill in her voice dripped off each word.

Brody rose. "Thank you, ma'am, for your time."

Marge saw him to the front door, and the moment he escaped into the hot summer, he could feel himself begin to thaw out. This woman could definitely take care of herself. Was she capable of carrying out a plot of revenge?

The irony in the whole situation was that Jeremiah Jones had someone to love him and accept him for who he was. Brody was falling back in love with Rebecca—if he had ever fallen out of love with her—and she couldn't accept that he was a law enforcement officer. That was who he was, and if he walked away from the job he'd always wanted, what would that do to him? How would that affect their relationship?

Striding to his SUV, he placed a call to the woman who confounded him and tied him in knots. "I just got through talking with Marge, and I almost feel sorry for Jeremiah."

"Don't. I shiver when I think about that man." Rebecca sounded tired.

"Have you taken a break?"

"No. Kim's out there somewhere, and it's getting close to twenty-four hours. I know how important the first day or so is in a kidnapping. The police in Little Rock called Sean back. Owen Smith can be accounted for yesterday. He has a job, and his employer, as well as some of his coworkers, vouch for his whereabouts."

"Okay. For the time being we'll set him aside and concentrate on the ones who don't have good alibis. I want you to look at Marge in detail. Also look into her family. She said they don't live in San Antonio, but there was a slight hesitation before she answered me. She could be lying to me. It won't be the first time someone has."

"I know. If everyone was compelled to tell the truth, our jobs would be so much easier."

"Ah, that's the day I'd love to see. I'm wrapping up my interviews and will come get you and Aubrey."

"Your dad said he could take me to the hospital. A deputy will come with us. That'll save you time coming all the way back out here. Okay?"

He thought of the nearly one-hour drive and saw the wisdom of having his father and the deputy drive them. "That sounds good. I have two people to interview connected to Daniel Watson, then I'll meet you at the hospital."

"See you soon. I don't look forward to seeing Thomas and telling him we don't have any more leads. Tory is staying at the hospital. She said she'll come back home with us."

"Does Thomas remember anything else?"

"I only talked to him a few minutes, but nothing else so far. Tory says he's been sleeping a lot. The staff has been in and out a lot today."

When he disconnected, he checked the next address, then climbed into his SUV to head for the home of Daniel Watson's mother, clear on the other side of San Antonio.

❧

J. R. drank his fourth bottle of beer, trying to numb himself so that he could do what his sister expected him to do. He didn't want Kim to suffer. He didn't want to get close and kill her with a knife or by smothering her. Maybe he could shoot her in the back. If he saw her eyes, he wouldn't be able to pull the trigger. Or better, a poison that acted so fast she wouldn't know what hit her. Maybe he could research different poisons on the Internet and kill her tomorrow. He could chloroform her, then go and buy the poison.

With the TV on in the other room, he paced around the kitchen, peeking to make sure Kim was doing what he had told her to do. She was—had been since she woke up. She'd even tried to talk to him from the living room, but he had too much thinking to do to carry on a conversation. Especially when she looked at him—no longer with worship but with distrust. He didn't like that.

He had to do something fast. Sissy was getting impatient. He had never liked making her angry. She could be worse than Mama.

The sound of pounding on the front door jolted J. R. He went rigid. More pounding followed. He hurried toward the entrance, his heart slamming against his ribcage. He wasn't expecting anyone. Parting the blind in the dining room, he checked to see who was on his porch.

Sissy.

18

She hasn't lived here in eighteen months," the older woman, probably about fifty, told Brody.

"Do you know where she moved to?" Brody looked past the woman, whose red hair probably came from a box, and saw a younger woman behind her. The younger woman hung back from the foyer, standing in the entrance to what was most likely the living room, one filled with lots of boxes. The smell coming from the place reminded him of the time he'd spilled milk and hadn't cleaned it up well.

"Yes, she is at the Kennedy Cemetery. Has been there since she found out her son was killed."

"May I come in?"

"What for?"

"I'm working on a kidnapping case and need your help."

"I don't know anything about a person being kidnapped. I never condoned what my nephew did, and I always believed he was guilty. Clare never did. She was a foolish woman when it came to her children." Daniel's aunt stepped to the side. "This is my daughter, Susan. Now, she's a proper daughter— not like Clare's. Evil girl, like her younger brother. Those three just didn't understand that the evidence pointed to Daniel's guilt. No question about it. Then to go and commit suicide because he was killed. Like I said, plain foolish."

Brody followed the rotund woman into the living room. Her daughter remained in the entrance, leaning against the doorjamb.

"Now, Mama, Linda wasn't that bad. They were a close-knit family."

"Linda tried to kick me out of this house, but my sister said in her will I could stay as long as I needed after taking care of her all those years Daniel was in prison. Clare's word meant something. Not Linda's."

"Where is Linda and her other brother?" Brody sat on the edge of the chair, the scent of apples and cinnamon wafting through the air—overpowering, as though to mask the odor of filthiness. Stacks of items littered the perimeter of the room and oozed over toward the middle until there was only a small space available for two chairs, a table, and a TV. The livable space was probably no bigger than eight feet by eight feet. A two-foot stack of magazines—old ones—surrounded the only lamp.

"Don't know. Don't care. I haven't heard from her or her brother, J. R., in over a year. She had better things to do than see to her only close relatives—my daughter and me."

"What better things?"

"Don't know. Don't care."

The piles of possessions seemed to close in on him, robbing him of a decent breath. He took out a business card and gave it to Daniel's aunt. "If you remember anything about where they are or if they contact you, please give me a call. I would like to talk to them."

"What's this about? You said a kidnapping? The two kidnappings were solved ten years ago when they caught Daniel."

"This kidnapping is recent and involves a ten-year-old girl. We're looking into people who might have a grudge against Judge Rebecca Morgan. She was the—"

"The prosecutor on Daniel's trial. She did her job. Is the little girl her daughter?"

"No, niece."

"Oh, that's a shame. I doubt I'll hear anything, but if I do, I'll give you a call."

He stood slowly and turned to make his way through the maze of boxes and piles of belongings, and nearly bumped into the woman's daughter.

"I'll show you to the door."

As he passed an area near the entrance, he thought he caught a whiff of something rotten. He glanced down and saw some food on a plate—black and moldy. Acid churned in his stomach. He hastened toward the exit.

Instead of shutting the door, the daughter walked out onto the porch with Brody. "Mama hasn't heard from Linda, but I have."

"You have? When?"

"At a restaurant a month ago. She was with a man and acted like she'd never seen me before. I tried to say something, but she hurried the man out of the place before I could."

"So she's probably still in San Antonio. Does she go by Linda Watson?"

"That's her name, but J. R. always called her Sissy."

～♋～

"Sissy, what are you doing here? I told you it was too dangerous for you to come here." J. R. blocked the entrance into his rented house. He glanced toward the living room to make sure Kim had done what he'd asked: go to the bathroom.

"Where is she?" His sister burst into the house, shoving him out of the way. Anger had transformed her beautiful features into something he didn't like to see. Losing control usually followed.

When she started across the living room, he grabbed her arm to halt her. "We need to talk about this."

"I'm done talking with you. We agreed to this plan and now you're backing out. I've put more than a year of my life into this, and all I've asked is for you to follow through with what you are supposed to do. Don't forget who's been giving you money." She yanked her arm from his grip and stormed toward the hallway that led to two bedrooms and a bathroom.

He went after her and stopped her again in the corridor. "It isn't that simple. I didn't realize I have a line I won't cross. Killing a kid is that line. I'm not our brother. I can't do it."

"Then I will, you coward. Rebecca Morgan needs to pay for what she did to our family. Daniel was murdered. Mama killed herself because of his death. She used to visit him every week at the prison, and when she couldn't, she gave up on her life. I had to stand by and watch. I couldn't do anything for either one of them. I will not let *her* go about her life as if she hasn't destroyed ours." The rage in Sissy's expression was mirrored in her voice. "Where is she?"

For a few seconds J. R. stood rooted to the floor while his older sister reached for the knob of the bathroom door. Then he moved. "No, leave her be. Keeping her alive could be worse for Rebecca Morgan."

Sissy swiveled toward him. "We talked about this and decided not to. It increases the danger to us. We need to finish this and leave the country. There are places we can go with the money I'm taking from the Sinclairs and live quite well, outside the reach of the law. That's the beauty of my plan. They're paying for everything. They just don't know it yet." She spun around and wrenched the door open.

Kim sat on the floor in the corner, her legs curled up against her chest, her body shaking. The sight tore at J. R. He remembered doing that very thing as a child when his mama and older brother went on a rampage, unable to contain their anger at anyone in their path.

The child stared at her. Hope flared inside the girl for a few seconds before she recognized the expression on Sissy's face—hate. Kim scrambled as far away from her as possible, cowering between the wall and the toilet.

Sissy charged into the room and snatched Kim's arm, hauling her up. As she began dragging the girl from the bathroom, the child cried out, "I don't understand, Tory."

◈

"Which restaurant?" Brody asked the cousin of J. R. and Linda Watson.

"Gill's Steakhouse."

"Do you remember when?"

"Five weeks ago this coming Friday. It was around seven thirty. She was with a good-looking man. Big, had on a western suit with boots and a cowboy hat. Brown hair. I didn't get close enough to see what color his eyes were."

Brody gave her one of his cards, afraid his other one was already lost in the mess in the house. "Please call if you remember anything else. It's very important."

"I will tell you that Linda had a mean streak a mile wide. I once crossed her, and she hasn't ever really forgiven me, so I wasn't surprised she ignored me in the restaurant."

"Do you have a photo of Linda and J. R.? That could help me."

"Probably," she jerked her thumb toward the house, "that is, if I can find it in there. Mama won't throw out anything. She's sure she'll need it sometime in the future. But the reality is, she doesn't. I'll look for some pictures and give you a call if I can find any. Maybe Mama will know where to look. She's probably the only one who might."

"That would be great. Thanks." Brody headed for his SUV, putting in another call to Rebecca. "I may be a little late to the hospital. I have another lead I want to check. I get vibes from the Watson family that there might be something going on with two of them—J. R. and Linda, Daniel's siblings."

"I hope it leads somewhere, because each moment that passes I feel we're losing Kim. I don't know what I'll do if she's killed or vanishes. This is all my fault. This is . . ." Her voice faded into silence.

"Don't go there, Rebecca. You're a victim of someone who wants revenge. You can't control that."

"I don't know if I can let this go." She lowered her voice, a thickness in it. "There's a part of me that realizes I'm not responsible, but a little voice inside me keeps accusing me of being the one who brought this on my family and my friend. Remember what Tory said."

"Take a break. Get away from the computer. Go for a ride. Dad would go with you. Maybe that'll help clear your head."

"I can't. You know that. As long as Kim is missing, I can't rest."

"Clearing your head isn't resting. It's giving you a better perspective on what's going on. That could help Kim."

"I might if I get back from the hospital before it gets dark. See you later."

Tossing his cellphone on the passenger seat, Brody climbed behind the wheel and grasped the warm plastic, tightening his grip on it until his hands ached. *Lord, help me. Please give me* a way to bring Kim home. I can't stand to see Rebecca like this. I feel helpless. And You know how much I don't like that. Anything is possible with You. That even means ending this ordeal.

❧

"Don't call me Tory. I hate that name!" J. R.'s sister screamed at Kim.

The girl stepped back, nearly falling into the tub. But Sissy latched onto the child's arm again and pulled her from the bathroom and down the hallway. In the living room, she shoved Kim onto the couch.

"Don't move." With a savage twist to her mouth, Sissy hovered over the girl, daring her to disobey.

Kim shrank back, bringing her legs up against her and hugging them as though trying to make herself as small as possible.

Satisfied the child was subdued, Sissy whirled on J. R. "This ends today. If you won't do it, I will." She strode around the couch and grabbed Kim's shoulders to hold her still. "Go get your gun."

The color drained from Kim's face. Tears sprang to her eyes.

"No. Hurt Rebecca Morgan in a different way. Didn't you say she was getting close to that Texas Ranger? Go after him."

Sissy's cackle frosted him. "Oh, I will. I'm going to hire someone to take him out since you failed the last time. Some of the problems we're having wouldn't be happening if you had managed to blow him up. He's like a starved dog with a steak. He isn't giving her up." Her fingers dug into the child's flesh until Kim cried out, trying to wiggle away. Sissy hit the girl across the head. "Sit still." Then she drilled him with her razor-sharp look, cutting, burning through his defenses. "You know how much I hate failure. Failure one time I might be able to excuse, but not a second time."

He stood still, his arms at his side as he clasped his hands closed and then opened them again. "I guess I'll be a disappointment to you. I can't do it."

"Then I will. Where is your gun?"

He pressed his lips together.

She yanked Kim off the couch and pulled the girl after her. Moving from one area to the next, searching for the weapon, she shot him a look that unnerved him more than he had ever been. She was intent on killing Kim. At least he wouldn't have to pull the trigger.

As Sissy dragged Kim behind her, he trailed after his sister. He'd hidden it in a good place so that the girl couldn't find it. Although he had planned to tie her to the bed to sleep at night, he had to get some shuteye, too. But now it was a moot point. If he knew his sister, she wouldn't stop searching until she found the weapon.

Finally, in frustration after working her way through the kitchen, Sissy withdrew a butcher knife from the drawer and pulled the girl tight against her. "I don't particularly want to get blood all over me, but I'll slice her to death slowly if you don't give me the gun. How do you want it—quick and easy or hard and painful?"

J. R. ground his teeth. She knew his answer or she wouldn't have asked. He plodded to the fridge and rolled it out, then retrieved his .38 from behind it. Sissy threw Kim to the floor and hurried over to him. After snatching the gun away from him, she faced the child, who was struggling to stand and get away.

Sissy followed the child's movements with the weapon. "If you don't stop and hold still, this will hurt worse. I promise you, brat." Exploding anger caused her voice to be shrill.

Kim froze. No, he thought, the girl. He should never have begun thinking of her as Kim. He had to remember that. She was no one to him. But when he connected with her eyes, so filled with fear, he couldn't look away. Then she turned her full attention to him, a silent plea in her pale blue eyes.

Help me. You're my hero.

No, he couldn't.

Sissy steadied the gun with both hands and aimed it at Kim.

J. R.'s gut twisted into knots, and he couldn't get enough air to breathe. Suffocating. As if someone held him down with a pillow over his head. He sucked in air, but nothing relieved the tightness in his chest.

His gaze glued to Kim's, as though his sister didn't exist and it was just the girl and him. J. R. needed to do something. Her plea drew him toward her.

Help me.

❦

Brody left Gill's Steakhouse, disappointed that they didn't have any security tapes from a month before. Some places kept them a month before destroying them. This place wasn't one of them. The manager had taken pride in stating that they respected the privacy of their customers. Even when Brody talked with some of the employees on duty, no one could remember the couple that Susan had described to him.

Another dead end.

He'd known it was a long shot, but he'd prayed it would pan out. The only other thing he could do is go by the apartment Linda Watson used to live in up until a year ago. Maybe one of the neighbors had a forwarding address.

Twenty minutes later, he pulled up to the office of the apartment complex and made a call to Charlie before going inside to talk to the manager. "I need you to pull a picture of Linda Watson, hopefully from her driver's license. Also one for J. R.

Watson." Then he gave Charlie the only address he had for Linda. "When you get it, please e-mail it to me."

"Will do. Shouldn't take too long."

He hung up and made his way into the office of the apartment complex. A young woman sat at a desk talking on the phone. She held up her hand for him to wait. He walked the few feet to the window and scanned the three buildings for number 145.

"Can I help you? Is there a problem?" the lady at the desk said.

"Yes, I wanted to ask you about a tenant you used to have in apartment 145. Linda Watson."

"No, I'm afraid there wasn't anyone by that name in 145."

"But her cousin said it was 145. Maybe she got the wrong apartment number. Was there a Linda Watson who lived in the complex about fifteen months ago?"

The young woman shrugged. "I'm new. I've only been here nine months."

"Then check your records." His impatience leaked into his voice. The sense of time running out bombarded him from all sides.

❧

J. R. was tired of doing what others told him to do. They needed to respect his decisions. He zeroed in on the .38 his sister held and lunged toward it. "No," he yelled, releasing all his pent-up frustration and rage.

His fingers closed around the metal of the barrel, and he pushed it downward. "Get out of here, Kim." He positioned himself between the girl and Sissy.

"You idiot. What are you doing?"

"What I want."

"She's getting away." Her hand still around the handle, his sister charged him as though to plow through him to get to the child.

He kept his hold on the gun and stood his ground. "She didn't do anything wrong. She's innocent."

Sissy pounded a fist into his arm and back. Bringing her foot down on his, she shouted, "Let go. I'm finishing what Mama wanted us to do."

Anger infused Sissy with extra strength as they wrestled for the weapon. Determined to get his .38 back, he poured everything into their battle, pushing her back against the counter behind her. Using his body, he pinned her.

The action caused his sister to let out a fierce scream, her efforts increasing to get the gun away from him.

Suddenly a blast sounded. Pain ripped through his gut.

His sister's eyes widened. Her body went slack as her hand fell away from the weapon.

Piercing, white-hot sensations flooded his belly. He wavered. All his energy drained from him.

As he sank to the floor, Sissy cried out, "No, I didn't mean to shoot you. Just the girl."

Laying his hand on his stomach, he felt the warmth of his blood oozing through his fingers. His life forces spilling from his body.

Sissy knelt next to him. Through the haze that clouded his vision, he glimpsed her face, emotions flittering across her features so fast he wasn't sure what he was seeing—regret, sorrow, anger, disbelief. It didn't matter now. He rolled his head to the side and looked for Kim.

She's gone. Good.

He closed his eyes. As he surrendered to the darkness, his sister sobbed. Her cries faded . . .

"You don't mind taking me to the hospital?" Rebecca closed her laptop and looked up at Sean, sitting across the kitchen table from her.

"No, not at all. It'll be good to get out for a few hours. The officers in the other room are finishing up their preliminary searches of everyone you've come up with from your files." He sat back in his chair, shutting down his computer. "There isn't much else you or I can do."

"Does it make you wish you hadn't retired?"

He bent forward and lowered his voice, "Don't tell my son, but, no, I don't regret retiring. I don't have the energy to do this nonstop like he does. When a case like this one comes along, you have to keep going until it's solved, if possible. I'm glad I was able to do what little I could."

"Me, too. When we get back, I'm going through the files again. Maybe I missed something." She rubbed her eyes, which stung from exhaustion and from staring at the computer screen for hours with no real result. "I'll get Aubrey and Hattie. They want to go, too. I thought I would go in and talk with Thomas first while Hattie and Aubrey go to the gift shop to find something for Thomas. Aubrey wants to brighten her daddy's room."

"So Hattie is going, too." Sean put his palms on the table, then pushed himself to his feet.

"Yes, the deputy is driving us while Ranger Parker stays back here and coordinates the information coming in."

Sean checked the weapon at his side. "I'm ready. One of the things I can still do is shoot. Haven't lost that ability yet. I won't let anything happen to you, Aubrey, or Hattie."

"Now I know where your son gets his determination." Rebecca left the kitchen and found Aubrey in the den—drawing and coloring a picture for her father. "You ready to go see your daddy?"

Aubrey jumped up. "Yes. Maybe he can help bring Kim back."

"We're working hard to bring her home."

Aubrey ran to her and hugged her. "I miss Kim. I promised God last night I wouldn't fight with my sister if He would bring her home." She leaned back and looked up at Rebecca. "I think He heard me."

"Of course He heard you. He's always with you."

"And Kim?"

"Yes, always. He's making her brave. Just like you are."

Aubrey rushed back to the table and grabbed her drawing of the ranch. "Let's go. Daddy is gonna love this." Tugging on Rebecca's hand, Aubrey dragged her toward the kitchen. "Then when I get back home, I'm gonna draw a picture for Kim. Of her horse. She'll like that."

Aubrey knew what had happened to Kim, having been a witness to the kidnapping, but she really didn't understand what was going on. Rebecca and Hattie tried to keep Aubrey isolated from any discussion about her sister, but that was becoming harder to do.

At the door into the kitchen, Aubrey dropped her hand and hurried over to Sean. "Look what I did for Daddy. I got to use some glitter and new scented markers." She held it up for Sean to smell. "The barn is strawberry. See?"

Sean laughed, brought the picture to his nose, and took a deep breath. "I love strawberries. Maybe I should eat this picture. What do you think?"

Aubrey went still for a second, then snatched the paper back. "Silly. You can't eat the paper." She whirled toward Hattie, cradling the paper to her chest. "Do we have any strawberries for him?"

"I think we do." Hattie's eyes twinkled. "If he behaves, I might fix some strawberry shortcake for dessert tonight." With mock exasperation, she settled her fists on her waist. "Think you can keep your hands off Miss Aubrey's masterpiece?"

"Hey, she gave it to me to look at."

"Exactly. Not to eat." Merriment danced in Hattie's eyes.

Aubrey swung her attention between Hattie and Sean, who were having a staring contest with each other and then burst out giggling.

For a few seconds Rebecca forgot what was happening in the real world as she listened to laughter fill the kitchen. Soon enough real life would intrude.

❦

"These records show that there hasn't been a Linda Watson here in the past two years. Maybe you got the wrong apartment complex. There are some others around here," the young manager said as she closed down the program on the computer.

Brody stood behind her, watching the screen saver pop up, bright colors swirling to form varied shapes. "That's an actual list of your past and present tenants?"

"Yes. You might want to check with some of the other places around here."

"No, the person said it was the Silver Chase Apartments."

"Then sorry. That person is wrong."

"Can you print off a copy of your tenants for the last two years?"

"Don't you need a search warrant?"

"I can get one, but it'll take valuable time. A little girl's life is at stake here."

The manager's mouth dropped open. "The little girl that has been on the news lately?"

He nodded.

The woman turned her attention back to the computer, pulled up the list again, and hit print. "I hope this helps."

"Maybe Linda Watson stayed with someone for a while so her name wasn't on the lease."

"That's possible."

"Is there anyone who has lived here since that time and is home most of the day and aware of the people in the complex?"

"You mean a busybody?"

"That's another way to say it."

She rose. "I can help you with that. Follow me. She lives in the apartment across from 145. If there is anything happening out of the ordinary, Mrs. Peabody knows about it."

"Perfect." Brody crossed the common area and stood to the side as the manager rang the doorbell.

When Mrs. Peabody answered, her face brightened with a smile. "To what do I owe the pleasure . . ." Her gaze fell on Brody, and her mouth formed an O. "Did something happen here? I didn't see anything. Was it about an hour ago? I took a tiny," she indicated an inch with her forefinger and thumb, "nap. Stayed up too late last night."

"Mrs. Peabody, this is Ranger Calhoun. He needs to talk with you."

He moved forward, offering his hand, which the sixtysomething woman shook. "Ma'am, I sure could use your help."

"Sure, anything to help the police. I mean, the Texas Rangers."

"I'll leave you two now. I hope you find her," the manager said, then headed back to the office.

"Come in. I'll assist you any way I can. Do you need a lookout or something? Or do you want to use my apartment to keep watch on someone?"

Brody trailed the woman as she limped into her apartment. "No, I just need information. I understand you're aware of what goes on here at Silver Chase."

She threw back her shoulders. "Yes, if more people kept a sharp eye out for anything unusual, there would be less crime. I'm proud to say Silver Chase has very little."

"That's great."

She waved her hand at her couch. "Sit. Can I get you something to drink?"

"No, I'm on a case and don't have a lot of time." He settled on the edge of the cushion. "I was interested in knowing if anyone other than the tenant stayed in apartment 145 about fifteen months ago. Do you remember seeing anyone coming and going from 145 who wasn't the tenant?"

Staring off into space, Mrs. Peabody stroked her chin. "You know, there was a young lady who stayed there for a while with the woman who lived here. I think she stayed about six months."

"Do you know the young lady's name?"

She thought some more, a frown twisting her mouth. "I think Vickie or Ricky, something like that. I don't remember ever hearing her last name."

"Where did the tenant move to, the one she stayed with?"

"Beats me. She left in the middle of the night. I heard she was late on her rent. I guess she couldn't pay after her roommate left."

"Do you remember anything about Vickie/Ricky?"

"She drove a little sports car—red. The license plate was from Kentucky. I remember, because I always wanted to have a sports car, even an old one like what she had."

"Do you remember the license number?"

"No, sorry. She was a regular, so I didn't think to jot it down. I wish I had more for you."

Brody started for the door. "You were a big help."

"Oh, that's nice. Come back anytime."

As Brody cut across the grass toward his SUV, he unfolded the printout the manager had given him and scanned the sheet for the tenant in 145 at that time. L. W. Larson jumped out at him. Linda Watson Larson?

***

Kim hid behind a clump of bushes on the side of Rob's house, expecting Tory to come out of the house any second. The thundering of her heartbeat clanged inside her skull. Lightheaded, she sucked in air, but she couldn't seem to fill her lungs. The green leaves spun before her eyes.

The sound of a gunshot overrode the clamor of the beating of her heart, sending chills down her body. She covered her ears and squeezed her eyes shut as though she was two again and that was all she had to do to hide.

What should I do? If I run, she'll see me.

Again she saw the gun pointed at her, Tory's face so mean-looking, and she tried to shake the picture from her mind. She began rocking back and forth, her arms hugging her chest, praying no one would find her.

Maybe when it gets dark, I can get away.

Maybe . . .

The screen door banged open. Tory or Rob?

I don't want to look. I don't want to know.

The sound of footsteps pounding down the steps of the porch teased her curiosity. Kim opened one eye halfway and saw Tory race to her car, hop in, and drive off.

Where's Rob? Should I go back inside?

Kim eased partway up to peer over the bushes. There were a few other houses on the street, but they were set back from the road and looked scary—dark, rundown. One had four old cars in different stages of disrepair parked in the driveway and at the curb. Another had tall weeds in the front yard. The last house had broken windowpanes, and the porch leaned to the right. No cars there, or any other sign of someone home.

Should I go to one of them? What if Tory comes back?

Where's Rob? Hurt, dead, or waiting for me? To do what Tory wanted.

She burrowed deeper into the green foliage until it surrounded her. But even then, a sense of safety eluded her.

❧

Outside Mrs. Peabody's apartment, away from earshot, Brody answered his phone. "What's up? I hope some good news."

"We couldn't find a driver's license in our database for Linda Watson with the parameters you gave me," Charlie replied on the other end of the phone.

Thinking back to what Mrs. Peabody had said about the sports car, Brody started for his SUV. "Check with Kentucky's DMV. Maybe she didn't live in Texas until recently and has a driver's license from another state."

"Why Kentucky?"

"Call it a hunch. If that doesn't get a hit, try the surrounding states."

"That's a long shot."

"I'm desperate. I have lots of questions but few answers. Actually no answers."

"So you think everything is connected to Daniel Watson?"

"Maybe. Actually, probably, unless we haven't even considered the real person this revolves around. Also check for an L. W. Larson." A beep indicated another call coming in. "I've got another call. Talk to you later." He switched over to the unknown number, saying, "Calhoun here."

"This is Susan. I found it. I have a picture of both Linda and J. R. The one of Linda is blurry, but J. R.'s is good. He hasn't changed that much since it was taken."

"I'll be back over. Fifteen minutes away."

An urgency prodded him to move fast.

⸎

With the deputy leading, Rebecca held Aubrey's hand as they entered the hospital from the parking lot on the lower level. Sean and Hattie followed.

While riding the escalator to the first floor, Aubrey looked up at Rebecca and asked, "Can I get Daddy something in the gift shop? Something extra special?"

Perfect. Rebecca wanted to talk to Thomas first, before everyone else, and this would be a good opportunity to do that. "Yes." At the top of the escalator, Rebecca shifted around to face Hattie. "Will you take Aubrey to the gift shop? I'm going on up to see Thomas."

The older woman's forehead creased. "Sure," she answered slowly as if she didn't quite understand what Rebecca was doing.

Rebecca released Aubrey's hand and stepped closer to Hattie. Sean moved away to entertain Aubrey while Rebecca whispered, "I want to tell Thomas what's going on without everyone else there."

"Oh, that's a good idea. We'll take our time. Aubrey doesn't need to see him upset."

"Exactly." She gave Hattie her purse. "Use whatever money you need. Aubrey especially likes ice cream, and I know they have some bars in the shop."

"Gotcha. But I can pay for it."

"No, my treat. You do so much for us."

Hattie covered the short distance to Aubrey. "Let's go find your daddy something extra special."

Aubrey took the housekeeper's hand. "Daddy loves chocolate. Maybe a big box of it will make him feel better."

"And maybe some for you. I know a little girl who takes after her daddy." Hattie walked toward the shop with Aubrey.

"Also I'd like to find something for Kim."

Hattie threw a glance over her shoulder. "Sure, baby."

"Sean, you go with them. You, too, deputy."

While Sean started toward the pair, the deputy stayed behind. "Mrs. Morgan, I can't do that. Ranger Calhoun gave me specific instructions to stay by your side."

Nodding, she headed for the elevators. Her keeper could stay outside while she went in to talk to Thomas. It had been over twenty-four hours since Kim was kidnapped, with no ransom demand and no leads to speak of. The news wasn't good, and she wanted Thomas to hear it from her privately.

When the doors swished open on Thomas's floor, Tory was handing the officer on guard duty a cup of coffee before going into the room. Her sister-in-law looked haggard, and her clothes did not have their usual crisp neat appearance. Tory glanced to each side and noticed Rebecca right before the door closed behind her. Actually, she looked more distraught than haggard. Clearly upset.

Has something happened to Thomas? Has he slipped back into a coma?

Rebecca increased her pace, nodding toward the officer as she entered the room, the deputy trailing after her.

Thomas lay in his bed asleep. At least that was what she thought. Moving further inside, she scanned the area.

Where's Tory?

A sound behind her, the bathroom door creaking open, made her turn around. Tory lifted the gun in her hand and brought it down on the back of the deputy's head. He crumpled to the floor.

Rebecca faced her sister-in-law, the gun now pointed at her chest.

19

Will they find me before Tory comes back?

Kim pushed some of the branches aside to peer out into the front yard. No one was outside. Not Rob. Not a neighbor. And Tory hadn't returned.

What if Rob is hurt? He tried to save me.

She backed out of her green cave and rose inch by inch, ready to duck down if she needed to. But quiet reigned, until a dog started barking in the distance.

Finally, she straightened to her full height and crept toward the corner of the house to check out the part of the yard that had been blocked from her view earlier.

Nothing.

She scooted a few feet forward, her gaze sweeping the area. Still no one.

Taking a deep breath that burned her lungs, she scurried up the porch steps. The front door was open. She pressed her face against the screen to see if she could make out anything inside. Her gaze honed in on a phone sitting on a table in the living room, hidden by the couch. She hadn't seen that earlier when she fled the house.

If she could get to it, she could call Aunt Becky for help. She looked around, trying to figure out where she was. She had no idea. In the distance, she could see some tall buildings, but at the end of the block there was a field. She didn't even know if she was in Dry Gulch or—no, not Dry Gulch. It didn't have any tall buildings like she saw. Then, San Antonio?

When she woke up after the accident, she was already here at this house. She could be anywhere.

Her heart raced at the thought.

911!

That was it. She eased the door open. Her chest felt like it was on fire.

One step into the house.

A glance back—still nothing.

She tiptoed toward the phone, her hand trembling as she reached out to make the call. Bringing the receiver to her ear, she started to press the nine, then paused.

No dial tone.

She punched the button up and down several times.

But still no dial tone.

Slamming the receiver down, she examined the phone, only to find there was no cord attached.

She looked around. That was when she heard the sound coming from the kitchen. Panic held her immobile.

Out on the porch of her mother's house, Susan handed Brody a grainy, out-of-focus photograph. "Here's a picture of Linda. See what I mean? It's not a very good one. I think that one is about ten years old, taken right before Daniel went away."

"Blonde hair? I thought you said she was a brunette."

"She is, but she would color her hair blonde." Susan shrugged. "So sometimes she was. Sometimes not."

"How about the last time you saw her?"

"It was streaked, so it was both at that time. But growing up she was a brunette."

"Where's J. R.'s picture?"

"Here." She laid it in his palm.

When he examined it, his muscles tensed. He'd seen this person—recently. "How old was he here?"

"I'm guessing this was taken a couple of years after Daniel went to prison."

"So about seven or eight years ago. What does J. R. stand for?"

"Junior. His real name is Robert Watson."

"Rob," Brody whispered to himself.

"What?"

"Does he go by Rob some of the time?"

"No, never that I know of. It's always been J. R. But he hasn't been in the area for a few years. He was up in Dallas, so I guess he could have started using his first name."

"And you don't know where he is now?"

"No. We haven't heard from him in three years, since he moved to Dallas. He never contacted us. He was upset with Mama. Do these help?"

"Yes. Thanks." He descended the steps to the sidewalk and hurried toward his SUV.

Minus the goatee and sunglasses, J. R. Watson could be Rob Clark. Now to find the man who had saved Rebecca. Had he set up the hit-and-run and changed his mind at the last minute? He shook his head. He still thought that Alexandrov was responsible for that attempt.

He placed another call to Charlie with the new information about J. R. "Look for Robert Watson Jr. He was in the Dallas area for a while. I know for a fact he isn't there now. He's the guy who saved Rebecca from being run down."

"I'm still running down Linda Watson in Kentucky."

"Call me the second you get anything on either one. I'm convinced the Watsons are behind everything."

After hanging up with Charlie, he called Rebecca to tell her he was coming to the hospital. He didn't have any more leads to run down—at least not until he got a line on Linda and J. R. Once he got Rebecca back to the ranch, he'd feel better. There was more than one person after Rebecca. The sister and brother had come back to San Antonio around the same time. Both had a reason to go after her.

On the fourth ring, Hattie answered.

"Where's Rebecca?"

"We're at the hospital. Aubrey, Sean, and I are getting something for Thomas in the gift shop. Just a second." There was along silence then Hattie continued. "I didn't want Aubrey to overhear, but Rebecca wanted some time alone with Thomas to tell him about the progress of the investigation or rather the lack of any."

"She went up by herself?" He tensed, his hand clamping the cellphone.

"No, the deputy went with her."

He sighed. "Good. I don't want any of you to be alone. I believe it is a brother-and-sister team doing this."

"Who?"

"Linda and J. R. Watson. I think the Rob Clark who came to the ranch is J. R. I'm not 100 percent sure, but the man in the photo I've got looks very similar to the man we met." He held the picture up, and the more he studied it the more convinced he was that it was the same person. "I'll be there in twenty minutes."

"We'll probably be upstairs by then. I've delayed Aubrey as long as I can."

*

Another moan sounded from the kitchen, followed by a chair scraping across the tile. Then a loud crash.

Kim backed up against the end table.

Rob?

A noise like a body hitting the floor reverberated through the house. Another moan.

Kim edged closer to the kitchen and peeked in. On the floor lay Rob, blood everywhere, like in a horror movie she'd seen at a friend's house late one night. She hadn't slept well for days after that. She scrunched her eyes closed for a few seconds until another groan came.

She started to back away when Rob rolled his head toward her and fastened his gaze on her.

"Help me." He struggled with something in his pocket, sliding it out. "Help . . ."

Rob's eyes closed, and his hand slipped to the blood-covered floor, still clutching a cellphone.

Her teeth dug into her lower lip. Shudder after shudder rocked her. Cold, so cold. She wanted the phone, but how could she get it?

I'd have to touch him.

I can't . . .

Remember, sweetie, God is always with us. Giving us strength to do what we need to do. Aunt Becky's words poured into her mind, enveloping her like a heavy coat during a winter storm. Just thinking about her aunt and God gave her the courage she needed to take a step toward Rob.

Then another and another.

An awful smell filled her nose. She held her breath. She grabbed a towel off the counter, bent over, and plucked the cellphone from his cupped palm. The sight of blood every-where sent her flying back to the safety of the living room. Forcing air into her lungs, she repeatedly wiped the cellphone until it was clean, then threw the towel away from her.

She punched 911 and inhaled a calming breath. Her hand trembled as she brought the phone up to ear. When the 911 operator came on the line, she said in a breathless rush, "I was kidnapped. Rob has been shot. Help!"

❧

"Get over there with your brother," Tory said, waving the revolver in Thomas's direction.

"Tory, what are you doing? Why do you have a gun?"

Fury twisted her sister-in-law's face, her eyes full of hate as they seared into Rebecca. "You've robbed me of everything, even my little brother now. It ends today. I'm taking your brother away from you and leaving you with the knowledge that your actions caused it."

What does she mean? Rebecca tried to think of a time she had done anything to Tory other than try to support her and be a friend. "My actions?"

"You might not remember Daniel Watson, but he was my brother. You sent him to prison. He was murdered in there, and no one cared. Oh, there was an investigation that lasted a day, but no one was brought to trial. My mother committed suicide when she lost him. My family fell apart because of *you.*"

"He kidnapped and killed a young girl, then tried to do the same thing to another."

"He was sick, not a killer. But no one cared about that." Again Tory pointed with the gun where she wanted Rebecca to stand. "Get over there. I want you to watch as I kill your brother."

"I'll scream before I let you do that. The officer will be in here before you know it."

"By that time, I'll have killed both you and Thomas and be ready to take the deputy out, and anyone else who comes through the door. Do you want to be responsible for that, too? I'm an excellent shot and have no problem pulling this trigger."

Rebecca moved closer to Thomas. *Why didn't I see Tory's true nature? Because I'd tried to leave Thomas, his new wife, and his two daughters alone to bond as a family. Or have I been so involved in my life that I have missed what's really going on around me?* "You won't get away with this. The officer will stop you before you leave."

"He won't be able to react fast enough. I gave him something to slow his reactions and his mental processes, but not put him totally out. Now, that might raise suspicion. And knowing his love of coffee, he has finished the whole cup by now."

Rebecca scanned the hospital room, trying to figure out a way to stop Tory. But there was nothing she could think of short of throwing herself across the bed at Tory.

❧❧

"Have you found anything out about Linda in Kentucky?" Brody asked Charlie, who had called him as he drove toward Mercy Memorial Hospital.

"That's not why I called. There's been a 911 call from Kim. She's talking with the 911 operator. We have triangulated her location. I'm heading there. She told 911 there's a man who has been shot. That's all I know."

When Brody received the address, he made a U-turn. "I'm five minutes away. I'll be there."

Switching off his cell, he floored his SUV, intent on getting there in under five minutes.

Four minutes later Brody was running toward the house, whose front door stood open. Withdrawing his weapon as he mounted the porch, he scanned the area. As he entered, he heard Kim talking somewhere to his right. He moved in that direction, his gaze tracking every inch of the room, his gun up and ready to use if he need be.

He eased around the corner into the living room, following the sound of Kim's voice, telling someone she was all right but scared. He thought about calling out to her, but just in case there was someone else in the house with her, he kept quiet and crept forward.

Kim's alive. That's what's important. Thank You, Lord.

When he swung around in the doorway leading into the kitchen, the little girl turned toward him, cellphone to her ear. A body covered in blood lay behind her. Her eyes widened. She dropped the phone and flung herself at him.

"You came." She hugged him so tightly, she squeezed his stomach.

"Are you alone?"

She nodded. "Except Rob."

That was when Brody's gaze fell on the young man who'd saved Rebecca. His dark blue eyes were fixed on the ceiling. Brody knew a death stare when he saw it, but just to be sure, he disengaged from Kim and said, "Go into the living room. I'll be right there."

After she left the room, he leaned over and felt for a pulse. Nothing. There wasn't anything he could do for Rob now.

He strode into the living room to find Kim standing a few feet away, biting her fingernail. The relief he'd seen earlier was gone, replaced by a look of fear.

Kneeling in front of her, he clasped her arms. "You're safe now, Kim. More police are on the way." In the distance, sirens pierced the air.

"He's Tory's brother. She shot him."

"Tory? Your stepmother?"

Tears glistened in her eyes. She nodded her head. "She hates me."

"Where is she?"

"I don't know. I hid outside when Rob fought his sister for the gun. She wanted to kill me. Rob wouldn't do it."

He grabbed her hand and started for the front door. "Let's go. We're going to the hospital."

As he hurried toward his SUV, a patrol car sped down the street toward them. Kim moved to stand behind him, pressing close to him. One officer stopped behind Brody's car and climbed out of his vehicle, pointing his weapon at him. Brody said, "I'm Ranger Brody Calhoun." Another car—Charlie's—turned onto the road. "Detective Charles Nelson can vouch for me. If you let me, I can show you my ID."

Charlie screeched to a halt and leapt out of his Ford. "Officer, he's a Texas Ranger working the case."

The young patrol officer lowered his weapon.

Charlie came around his vehicle and walked toward Brody, saying to the officer, "Go secure the crime scene."

"There's a dead body in the kitchen," Brody added as the young man walked toward the house. He brought Kim around from behind him. "You remember Detective Nelson."

"Yes." She tore off the tip of her fingernail.

"The person behind this is Tory, Thomas's wife. She shot her brother, the one in the house. She may have gone to the hospital. I'm heading there. That's where Rebecca and the others are."

"I'll stay here and process the scene and get a BOLO out on Tory."

Brody looked down at the girl. "Which car is she driving, Kim? Did you see it?"

"It's white. That's all I know. It isn't one of our cars."

"Charlie, call the officer on duty at Thomas's room and alert him, too."

While the detective made the call, Brody opened the passenger's door for Kim, then rounded the back of his SUV.

Before Brody climbed into his car, Charlie looked toward him and said. "The officer isn't acting right—he's taking too long to answer a simple question. I'm calling for backup."

"I'll be there in ten minutes." He started for the hospital while placing a call to Rebecca's cell, praying that either Hattie or his dad would pick up. He needed to stop them from going into the room until they knew what was happening. The fact that something was wrong with the officer meant Tory was probably there. With Rebecca.

"Hattie, put Dad on the phone." A few seconds later Brody's father came on. "Tory is the one behind this. She and her brother. The brother is dead, but I think Tory is at the hospital in Thomas's room with Rebecca. Stay where you are. Help is on the way."

"Son, I can't do that. We're on the elevator and almost to the fourth floor. I'll keep Hattie and Aubrey at the nurse's station, but I'll go assess the situation."

"Dad, Tory killed her own brother. She is armed. I didn't see the gun at the crime scene."

"Trust me. I've been a cop for thirty-three years."

Brody disconnected, his heart thumping rapidly against his ribcage. He made sure Kim was buckled up, and then drove as fast as he could.

"Is Tory gonna kill my daddy and Aunt Becky?" Kim's voice quivered with fear.

Fear zipped through every part of him. To his very core. *I may lose Rebecca.*

He swallowed the lump in his throat and said, "No, I won't let her." *Please, Lord, make that true.*

⋘੭⋙

Different scenarios flashed through Rebecca's mind. "This is between you and me. Not my brother. I'll go with you. You can use me as a hostage for your escape. You won't make it otherwise."

"Why not? I'll be gone before anyone knows I did it."

Pressed up against the side of Thomas's bed, Rebecca felt his finger poke into her. He was awake and knew what was happening. But what could he do? He couldn't get out of bed without help. He probably was groggy because he was on pain medication.

Tory held the gun with one hand, her finger on the trigger, while she fumbled in her pocket. "I'd planned to kill him after taking care of Kim. J. R. couldn't go through with it. He's weak."

Keep her talking. "Who's J. R.?"

"My brother. He died because of you, too." She withdrew a syringe and flicked off the cover of the needle. "He won't suffer. This poison acts very fast." Plunging the needle into the IV line, she released the solution to do its harm.

"Don't!" Rebecca yelled.

At that moment, Thomas jerked his arm up, knocking the gun away from Tory as a shot went off, throwing Tory off balance. Rebecca lunged across the bed to yank the IV out of Thomas's arm. The door slammed open. Sean rushed in with hospital security while Rebecca dove for Tory, who had raised the gun again.

Tory's hand locked around the revolver as Rebecca focused on turning the weapon away from herself, inch by inch. Tory pulled the trigger again, the sound of the blast temporarily deafening Rebecca. With adrenaline pumping through her veins, Rebecca tightened her grip on the barrel and shoved it around toward Tory.

"Shoot it now," Rebecca muttered through clenched teeth, pinning Tory to the floor.

"I'm here, Rebecca," Sean said, placing a hand on her back while he knelt and put his weapon to Tory's head. "It's over. Let go of the gun."

Looking right into Tory's eyes, Rebecca wasn't sure she would let go, or, for that matter, had even heard Sean. Rebecca kept her grip on the barrel, shifting so that her full weight was on the woman.

"Tory, you can end this. Now. Let go." Rebecca forced her voice to a calm level while, inside, her stomach was a solid knot, her chest burned with the effort of restraining Tory.

In a split second Rebecca saw the finality in Tory's gaze and knew what she was going to do. Rebecca released her grip on the barrel and pulled back just as the shot went off, grazing a path along the upper part of Tory's chest. The bullet lodged in the wall.

In that moment, Rebecca yanked the revolver from Tory's limp hand and sprang to her feet. Her body shook, and she fell back against the bed as Sean and the security guards grabbed Tory and pulled her to her feet, blood streaming from her shoulder.

But alive. Relief flooded Rebecca.

Her brother touched her. "You okay?"

She turned, the gun still in her hand. "Are you?"

"Yes. You must have gotten the IV out in time." Thomas looked past her. "This is too much to take in. Tory? Why?"

"Revenge. Pure and simple," Rebecca said, clutching the side of the bed to keep herself upright. "But I wasn't going to let her kill herself. I won't sink to her level."

Energy draining from her legs, Rebecca tried to steady herself, but what had just happened finally sank in, and she felt herself going down. Strong arms wrapped around her and held her up.

Brody plucked the gun from her hand and cradled her against him. "Thank the Lord you are alive," he whispered against her ear. "I thought I might lose you."

Suddenly she didn't care that his life's work was law enforcement, not when she'd come so close to dying herself. Life was too precious not to cherish every moment God gave her. She turned within his arms and flung her arms around him. "Never."

Epilogue

Rebecca stepped out onto the front porch at the ranch and found Brody leaning against the post, staring into the night sky. As she moved toward him, he turned, the glow from the Christmas lights illuminating his face.

"I heard you escaped from the madhouse inside. Aubrey is excited to be going to her first midnight Christmas Eve service." Rebecca went into his arms, the feel of them about her emphasizing how blessed she was to have found a second love in her life.

"I needed to have a little chat with the Lord."

"About what?"

"About the gift he has given me this year. One I never thought I would have. You." He sampled her lips and then deepened the kiss.

She wound her arms around him. The sense of coming home filled every part of her. If nothing else, last September showed her how important it was to depend on God and not to fight what she was feeling toward Brody. The future was in the Lord's hands and worrying about it didn't change it. She would cherish every moment she had with Brody and be happy for that time. It was so much better than the alternative: being alone.

"I'm glad you brought the subject of you and me up. I want to give you your Christmas present early." She pulled a small wrapped box from her sweater pocket.

"It's not that early. In a couple of hours it will officially be Christmas." He took the gift and unwrapped it. When he lifted the lid, he stared at the ring for a moment, then looked into her eyes. "What's this mean?"

"It's called a wedding ring. Men don't get engagement rings, so I had to settle for getting you that. This is my way of asking you to marry me. Soon. Thomas is getting stronger every day and walking now. The girls are much better now, and I don't want Hattie and Sean to beat us to the altar. They're talking of marrying and settling on that ranch down the road."

Brody chuckled. "Those are your only reasons for getting married?"

"We could sneak a honeymoon in between the trials for Tory and Alexandrov. Two glorious weeks on some beach. Just you and me before we come back to our busy lives."

"So you're okay with me being a Texas Ranger?"

"I wouldn't have it any other way. It's who you are. The more I'm around you, the more I see that." She cupped his jaw. "How about me? Do you think you can handle being married to a judge?"

"It's who you are."

"Yes." Three months ago she might have answered differently, but making sure there was justice in this world was important to her. After taking some time off to help her family mend, she went back to being a judge. She had the Lord on her side.

"But are those the only reasons you want to marry me? Surely there's something else."

Tapping her finger against her chin, she shifted and stared at the sky with its stars glittering bright in the darkness. "Hmm. Let me think." She waited for a good minute, then looked at him. "Oh, there is one more reason. I love you with all my heart."

"You better." His mouth claimed hers. "Because I love you," he whispered against her lips, then pulled back and removed a small box from his pocket. He opened it to reveal a large square-cut diamond ring. "Great minds think alike. I was going to propose after the midnight service tonight, but you beat me to it." He took her left hand and slid the engagement ring on her finger. "Will you marry me?"

"Yes. It only took us twenty-five years to realize we are perfect for each other, so I don't want to wait very much longer. I'm thinking a Valentine's Day wedding."

Discussion Questions

1. Rebecca Morgan is the judge on a high-profile trial of an important member in the Russian Mafia. Scare tactics are being used to affect the outcome of the trial. People are being intimidated not to testify. Rebecca is being intimidated, but she is determined to preside over the trial because justice is important to her. Have you ever had to fight for something you thought was important? Were there obstacles in your path? What did you do to overcome them?

2. Forgiveness is hard to do. When you can't forgive, it can often lead to wanting revenge. Is there someone you can't forgive? Why? Is there a Bible verse that helps you with forgiveness?

3. Have you ever wanted revenge against someone? Why? What did you do about that feeling?

4. Who is your favorite character? Why?

5. Rebecca remained strong through the death of her husband and not long after that her father, but when her older brother was critically injured, she began to question what the Lord was doing. What makes you question God and His plan for you?

6. When Rebecca's husband was killed in the line of duty, she was leery of becoming involved in a relationship, especially when that person was in the same profession as her husband. What makes you leery of a relationship?

7. What is your favorite scene? Why?

8. Brody's dad, Sean, had a heart attack and was slowly recovering, but he felt useless and depressed. Sometimes people who have retired can feel that way. Sean wanted

to feel he was doing his part, valued. What are some things we can do to help people feel important, valued?

9. Brody's job was to protect Rebecca. He was determined to do that and to get her to the courthouse and back home. To what lengths have you gone to protect someone? Where would you draw the line?

Coming soon—
Look for Book 4 in the Men of the Texas Rangers series—

Severed Trust

Prologue

Standing at the gravesite, I stare at the coffin, my mom inside. Dead. I don't understand. Why did she do it? Leave me and Dad?

I glance at my father next to me, tears running down his face, and my own stay clumped in my throat. An ache spreads through my whole body.

Memories of a few days before trying to wake up Mom send the terror through me all over again. I close my eyes, not wanting to remember, only to picture her sprawled on her bed, an empty bottle of pills next to her.

I rub my hands across my face, trying to scrub the image from my mind.

As the crowd thins, my aunt approaches Dad. "I have some ladies from the church lined up to bring food over. Are you sure you don't want Bob and me at your house today? As they bring it, I can take care of it for you. You won't have to worry about anything."

"No. I want to be left alone. Cancel them."

"I know you're hurting. You shouldn't be alone at this time."

My dad leans forward, his face inches from my aunt's. "Don't tell me what I need. I need her."

My aunt pulls my father away a few steps and lowers her voice, but not enough that I don't hear what she says. "Paige was sick. She didn't mean to kill herself."

Dad jerks away from my aunt, grabs my hand and tugs me toward the car. People try to stop him, but he ignores them.

"Mom killed herself?" I ask as he drives toward our home.

He doesn't say anything.

"How?"

Still silent.

"Dad?"

He pulls into the driveway and twists toward me. "She didn't want to be with us. She took sleeping pills so she never had to wake up."

Mom? Leave us on purpose? No, she loved me.

"Go to Tommy's house and play with him." He pushes open his door and stomps to the house.

I don't know what to do. Tears finally flood my eyes. I blink and climb from the car. Instead of going to Tommy's across the street, I trudge toward the porch. I need Dad. I need to understand.

When I put my hand on the doorknob and turn it, a loud blast coming from inside, like a car backfiring, echoes through the air.

1

$\mathcal{F}$ingering the necklace, Jared had given her for her seventeenth birthday, Kelly Winston cracked her bedroom door open. When she peeked out, her mother strode toward the staircase. Releasing a swoosh of air, Kelly snuck down the hall to her mom's bathroom and pulled out the middle drawer where she kept her supply of medicine.

Kelly picked up the first bottle of a painkiller her mother had started taking last winter after her car wreck. Kelly shook one into her palm. She grabbed the next bottle, not sure what these pills were, but she pocketed several of them anyway, then moved on to the next medication, an old one for anxiety her mom had taken when Dad divorced her and moved away. She took three of them.

"Kelly," her mother yelled from the foyer downstairs.

She shot straight up, her heart pounding, but she didn't hear any footsteps approaching.

"Your date is here."

She drew in a deep breath to calm her rapid heartbeat and quickly closed the drawer. "Coming, Mom."

She stuffed the pills she'd taken into her jean pocket and hurried from her mother's bathroom before she came looking for her. When Kelly saw Jared standing next to her mom in the foyer, she smiled and nodded once.

His mouth curving up, a dimple appearing in his left cheek, he winked at her.

"When are you going to be home?" her mother asked as she walked toward the kitchen.

"The party lasts until midnight so after that."

"Don't wake me when you come in. I'm exhausted and hope to go to bed early."

"I won't," Kelly said, right before closing the front door. It was so easy to stay out when her mother took a sleeping pill. Mom would be out until tomorrow.

"What did you get?" Jared rounded the front of his Porsche.

After sliding into the front seat, she dug the dozen pills out of her pocket and laid her palm out flat to show him. "Painkillers, sleeping pills, and an assortment of others. Is that what you wanted?"

"You did great. This will be fun."

"Are you sure your friends will be okay with me coming?"

"You're my girlfriend. We've been dating for over two months." At the stoplight, Jared looked at her, his blue eyes gleaming with male appreciation. "You're the most beautiful girl at Summerton High School. I'll be the envy of every guy at the party."

Though his words flattered her, Kelly's nerves tensed throughout her body. This was her first pill party. She'd heard of them from some of the other girls. She'd always wanted to be a part of the in crowd. Tonight she would be. Finally. All because Jared Montgomery, a hottie and a senior, had started dating her when she became one of the junior cheerleaders—after years of honing her skills and dieting constantly.

When Jared parked behind a warehouse, Kelly glanced at some of the other expensive cars. A few she recognized. "The party is here?"

"Yeah. This place isn't in use right now. Perfect for what we want to do. Ready?"

She nodded, laying her quivering fingers on the door handle.

He clasped her shoulder, stopping her from leaving the car. "Just do what the others do. It's a small group of my closest friends. You'll be fine. This is such a rush. You'll see what I mean tonight."

Peering at him, she fortified herself with the knowledge he told her he loved her last week. All the kids were doing this. What harm could a few prescription drugs really do? They were all prescribed for someone to take. Her mom took several every day. It wasn't the same as taking illegal drugs like meth or crack. Those could seriously mess with her mind.

As they walked toward the back entrance to the warehouse, hidden from the street, Jared grasped her hand, brought it to his lips, and kissed her knuckles. "Stay close and I'll take care of you."

His gaze connected with hers. Her stomach flip-flopped. He could always do that—make her feel so special. She certainly didn't get any affirmation from her mother or her father who lived in Chicago and couldn't be bothered with her.

Before going in, Jared tipped her face up and kissed her, then pushed the door open.

The beat of the music pulsated in the air. Four teens sat or stood around the huge cavernous warehouse—bare of any items as far as Kelly could see, except for a few crates used for the party. Beyond the pool of light, darkness lingered as though a black curtain encircled a small part of the building, cordoned off for the pill party.

Jared retrieved two beers from a cooler and passed one to Kelly. She hated the taste but noticed all the other kids had one. She'd pretend she liked it.

"Let's put our drugs in the bowl. When everyone arrives, we'll grab a handful and take them with the beer." Jared pulled a wad of pills from his pocket.

"Then what?"

"We drink, dance, and wait. For some nothing much happens. Dud pills. Others get a rush, feel euphoric. Either way, we forget our problems and have fun." He released his pills to fall into a large plastic bowl where there were a lot of drugs in various colors and sizes.

Kelly uncurled her hand, and the ones she brought tumbled on top of the others, then she took a swig of beer, suppressing her gag reflex.

Jared tapped his can against hers and then lifted his drink, downing probably half of it. "C'mon. We need to catch up with everyone. We'll be floating in no time. Not a care in the world, especially the English test you have on Monday."

While she tilted the can to her lips, he slung his arm over her shoulder and cradled her against him. His sweet action reinforced why she was here in the first place.

Jared loves me and won't let anything bad happen to me.

っৎ◑

Her throat parched, Kelly swayed in the middle of the lit area with several teens slumped on the concrete floor. The light and dark swirled before her. She searched for Jared and found him where he'd been before she'd gone to see if there was something to drink. The coolers had been empty. To ease her dryness, she'd considered cupping her hands into the melted ice, but she didn't.

Kalvin Majors stumbled and fell into a stand with a light. It crashed to the floor and shattered. He continued wandering around in a circle, shouting every once in a while, "Go Eagles."

Kelly returned to the darker area because the room didn't seem to spin as much. She plopped down and crumpled back against a post. Jared lay not far away, and no matter how much she'd tried earlier to get him up, she couldn't. He'd just batted at her as if she were an annoying fly pestering him.

Another girl, Zoe, was stretched out on the floor moaning, while Luke, who was in several of her classes, vomited. The stench assailed her nostrils, and she almost hurled. She cupped her hand over her mouth and closed her eyes.

This isn't fun. I want to go home.

She crawled toward Jared, afraid to try standing. When she reached him, she shook his shoulder hard. Nothing. At least before, he would mumble or groan, but this time he didn't do anything. Cradling his face between her hands, she intended to yell at him until he woke up.

His skin felt cold, but it was hot in here. How could he be so cold? Her mind fumbled around trying to grasp onto something she should realize. Did she stick her hands into the ice water after all?

"Jared! Wake up!"

Someone—Brendan maybe—said, "Pipe down."

She didn't care. Increasing her volume, she shouted his name over and over.

Kelly lifted his arm to pull him up and get him outside into the fresh air. His limp arm was dead weight, making it hard to budge him at all. Finally, the effort zapped all her energy, her world spinning faster than before. She collapsed on top of Jared. A black veil descended . . .

Someone jostled Kelly, pushing her off her comfortable pillow. She blinked, a harsh light glaring in her eyes.

"He's dead," a frantic female voice shrieked, piercing through Kelly's dazed mind.

Dead? Kelly struggled to focus on the two blurs standing over another blur.

"We've got to get him out of here. This is my dad's warehouse."

"And do what?" the girl screamed.

"Don't know. Can't leave him in here."

Kelly curled up into a ball, the cold concrete against her cheek. She wanted to open her eyes again. To see what was happening but the darkness beckoned. If she slept a little longer, she would be okay.

A scraping sound penetrated the haze in her mind, but she kept moving toward the black.

Slam.

She jerked, then folded in on herself even more. Now running toward the dark void where she could escape . . .

Kelly rolled unto her back, the cold hardness beneath her demanding she wake up. She tried forcing her eyelids up but only managed to open them a slit. Through her narrow vision a face loomed close. The darkness surrounding her made it hard to see who it was. Blue eyes? Jared?

But no matter how much she tried, she couldn't keep her eyes from shutting again. Her mind in a fog, she allowed it to swallow her up.

✑

"Really, Mom, I don't feel well. I think it's something I ate last night." Lexie Alexander drew the cover over her head and hoped her mother would just leave her alone.

Her mom threw back the coverlet and felt her forehead. "You don't feel hot. I hate going to church by myself."

"I thought Uncle Ethan was going."

"He got a call. Some hikers found a dead body."

Lexie's stomach roiled, bile rising up. She jumped from bed and raced for her bathroom before she got sick all over the carpet. Barely making it, she heaved into the toilet.

Her mom handed her a cold washcloth. "Guess you really are sick. I thought you were trying to get out of going to church."

As Lexie hung over the rim, she shook her head.

Her mom filled a cup with water and gave it to her.

Lexie swished the cool liquid around in her mouth then spit it into the toilet. "I really did eat some spicy food that didn't agree with me. I had the Cantina deliver last night while you were out on your date with Cord."

"I'll stay home, in case you need me."

Lexie handed the cup to her mother. "I don't think there's anything else in my stomach. I'll be fine with some rest. I was up a good part of the night."

"You should have come and gotten me."

Lexie rose, glimpsing her wild short hair and pale face. "I know you're a nurse, but what would you have been able to do? Hold my hand while I puked? I know I'm not eating at the Cantina ever again."

Her mother lingered in the doorway into the bathroom. "On the way home from church, I'll stop and get some ginger ale and saltine crackers, in case you want something later."

Lexie waved her away then cupped some cold water and splashed her face. The awful taste in her mouth reminded her of that spicy food that probably was the culprit behind her getting sick. As she heard the bedroom door click shut, she put a glob of mint-flavored toothpaste on her toothbrush and scrubbed her teeth, hoping to get the nasty taste out of her mouth.

She trudged back to bed and fell across the messed-up covers. Her mind started surrendering to sleep . . .

The song "Because of You" blasted the air, startling her wide-awake. She fumbled for her cell phone on her nightstand and brought it to her ear. She didn't feel like talking—even to her best friend.

"Hello." Her answer came out long and drawn out.

"Lexie, I need your help."

"Kelly?" She pushed to her elbows. "Why are you whispering?"

"I'm at a warehouse across town. I need a ride home and bring me that blouse you borrowed last week. Mom has to think I've been up and out with you this morning."

"Where have you been?"

"At a party—all night. I'm scared. Come get me."

Lexie looked around and saw her car keys on the desk by her purse. "Where's the warehouse?"

"At the corner of Sixth Street and Bluebonnet Road."

"That's clear across town in the bad part of town."

"I know. That's why I'm not walking home. I need your help, Lex." Fear laced each word Kelly spoke in a shaky whisper.

Lexie swung her legs off the bed. "I'll be there as soon as I can."

"Pull up in back of the warehouse. I'll be watching. I don't want to leave until you come."

"Okay." Lexie hung up and snatched her jeans and T-shirt off the floor nearby. She stood to put her clothes on, but the room tilted. Plopping down on the bed, she dressed. Remembering the fear she'd heard in Kelly's voice prodded her to move as fast as her shaky body would allow.

"Thanks for coming out on a Sunday morning," the police chief of Summerton said to Texas Ranger Ethan Stone.

"Cord, what happened here?" Ethan stood just outside the cordoned-off area with yellow crime scene tape.

"Two hikers found a car in Summerton Lake with a dead body in it—Jared Montgomery."

Ethan whistled. "Have you told his parents yet?"

Cord Thompson shook his head. "I can't call and tell them over the phone. I need to make sure the crime scene is processed by the book first."

Ethan removed his tan cowboy hat and raked his fingers through his hair. "Agreed." Bradley Montgomery owned the largest ranch in this area of northeastern Texas, and Jared was his only child. "Did the hikers recognize Jared?"

"They are with an officer giving their statements. One of them dove under to see if someone was trapped in the car. He saw Jared and tried to get the door open. He couldn't, but he could see Jared was dead. He hightailed it out of the water to call 911. Hopefully, since only those hikers know about Jared's death, this gives us a little time before the news gets out. I can't mess up this investigation, or I'll be looking for another job."

"What do you want me to do? You know I'm always here to help."

"Considering the potential of this case to be high profile, I'm glad you're the Texas Ranger assigned to this area." Cord rubbed his nape. "I've got a feeling this case will come back to bite me. I don't want Bradley Montgomery to find out from someone else besides the police, but as I mentioned, I need to stay here. Sending a street officer would say to the man his son wasn't important enough to our police department to have someone higher up inform him of Jared's death. Bradley is one of the people whose taxes probably pay a good part of our salaries. He goes to your church. You know him. Would you inform him of his son's death and that you'll be working with us on this case?"

"You and I go to the same church."

"I know, but you two were better friends in high school." A grin skittered across the police chief's face, but only for a second.

"So you're officially asking me to participate in the investigation?"

"Yes."

"Since when have we stood on protocol? We've known each other since childhood, and you know the Texas Rangers are here to help with local cases when needed."

"As I said, we can't make any mistakes with this case. I can already imagine Bradley breathing down my neck, and I won't blame the man when he does. I don't have children, but if something happened to my niece or nephew, I'd be all over it."

"I haven't been here long. What kind of kid was Jared? Like his father?"

"Yes. Jared is a popular guy and well-liked from what I've heard. He's on the football team as the quarterback. This will be a blow to the whole team and school."

Ethan walked to the red Porsche, still dripping water, and studied the boy, his body leaning back, held in place by his seatbelt, his head bent to the right. "Are there signs of foul play?"

"Not that I can see, but the Medical Examiner is on the way. I didn't want to move him from the car until he got here. I'll push to have the autopsy done immediately."

"Suicide?"

Cord frowned. "It doesn't feel right. He has everything going for him. That's why I want to be here when the ME arrives. Nothing about this scene looks like a suicide."

"What are you afraid of? That this is drug or alcohol-related, and Bradley's active campaign against drugs is known all over these parts?"

Cord nodded. "Why here? Yes, I suppose he could have driven into the lake because of the boat ramp here," he pointed at the pavement ending in the water, "but it's set out of the way from the parking lot where the road forks."

"Which brings us back to suicide. He could have purposely driven it into the lake. Or someone else did. So who would have it in for Jared if he's so popular?"

"You see how many questions there are. Bradley will want them all answered and then some. He'll be looking for someone other than his son to put the blame on." Cord removed his trademark toothpick from his front shirt pocket and stuck it into his mouth. According to him, chewing on it helped him think since he'd stopped smoking.

"I'll be back after I notify Bradley. I want to look at his room and check for a suicide note. It's early, he won't have left for church yet. In this region, there have been several deaths in the past couple of months from medication not prescribed to the deceased person found in their system. But no foul play has been determined in those cases."

"Appreciate the help. See you in a while." Cord gestured toward an arriving black van. "Ah, the ME is finally here. I woke him up this morning."

"He got to sleep in. My dog had me up at the crack of dawn to let him out."

"Get a doggie door."

"Can't. That creates a hole in my perimeter in which someone could enter my house. Not comfortable with that."

Cord chuckled. "Ain't police work grand? It makes all of us paranoid."

Ethan began walking toward his blue SUV. "I'd much rather think of it as making us alert and prepared for anything."

Cord's laughter increased. "You keep thinking that."

Ethan climbed into his car and backed away from the scene until he could turn his SUV around and head toward the highway leading to Bradley's ranch. Usually he didn't notify the next of kin about a death, at least not since he'd been a Texas Highway Patrol Officer. That was one duty he didn't miss.

⊷ઙ⊷

Lexie's wheels squealed as she turned onto Bluebonnet Road, her stomach tight with tension. She prayed she wouldn't throw up again. Kelly needed her, and she wanted to be there for her best friend, even if lately they had drifted apart since Kelly began dating Jared Montgomery.

Passing Fifth Street, she began looking for the sign for Sixth. The area around here was creepy, buildings abandoned with several vandalized. Scanning one after another sent a shudder down her length. She hoped Kelly was watching, and she didn't have to get out of her car. Even though her Ford was over eight years old, someone around here might want to steal it, leaving her and Kelly to walk home.

That thought panicked her, and she nearly missed Sixth Street. Lexie slammed on the brakes, and her tires screeched. She fishtailed. Great. If that didn't call attention to her, she didn't know what would short of laying on her horn. She quickly moved her hands away from the horn and turned the steering wheel toward the way she needed to go.

A minute later, she pulled up at the back of a brown warehouse that at one time must have been white. Patches of the color peeked out every once and a while. For a second she contemplated honking, but she took a quick glance around and decided against it. The parking lot was as deserted as these buildings appeared, but beyond them a large, low-income apartment complex backed up to the area.

She'd call Kelly to come outside, but when she rummaged for her cell phone in her purse, she couldn't find it. She'd left it on her bed. Well then, she would give Kelly a few minutes to come outside.

Lexie tapped her hand against the steering wheel, trying to keep rhythm to an imaginary song running through her mind. A beat-up car drove down Sixth Street. Lexie held her breath. Her pulse coursed through her at a maddeningly fast rate. If Uncle Ethan knew what she was doing, he would go through with his teasing threat and really have her frozen until she was twenty-one.

⊸❧

"Mom! A man is here to see you," Sadie Thompson's son, Steven, yelled from the entry hall.

She cringed and wondered how many people in the neighborhood heard that announcement. A man at the door for Sadie Thompson. No doubt one of them would immediately run to her parents and tell them their daughter was seeing a man. She laughed out loud. That was the farthest thing from the truth. After Harris walked out on their short-lived marriage, she hadn't had time for anything but raising her children and trying to make a living.

She finished running a brush through her hair, slipped on some sandals and hurried from her bedroom. When she emerged from the hallway and saw the man standing in her home for the first time in ten years, she stopped, placing her hand on the wall to keep her balance.

Harris Blackburn. What was he doing here? What did he want from her? The last time she'd seen him he'd had the nerve to ask her for money—money she didn't have. He'd left then, like he had right after the twins were born, three years before that, and to her relief she hadn't once seen him.

Until now.

Steven eyed the man who was his father, but she doubted her son recognized him. He then turned to go to the den where he played his video games every waking moment she would let him sit in front of the screen. She gritted her teeth to keep from saying anything to Harris until she heard the door to the den close.

"What do you want?" she asked in a surprisingly civil tone although her first urge was anything but civil.

"To see my kids. I heard you came back to Summerton."

"Who told you that?"

"A friend in town."

"You still have friends?"

He winced. "Yes. In fact, I returned last week. I have a job here. I'm staying for a while so I thought it was a good time to get to know my son and daughter."

She'd so desperately wanted to hear those words from Harris in the past. Now she dreaded them the most. "No."

"Did I tell you one of those friends is a lawyer?"

"Jeffrey Livingston."

"Yes, you remember what good friends we were back in the day."

"You can have visitation rights when you pay me for all those years of back child support. The amount is over a hundred thousand dollars. Come back then and we'll talk." Harris could never keep money for long, so the thought he had that kind of cash was ludicrous.

He stuffed his hand into his jacket pocket, withdrew a wad of money, and tossed it to her. "That's five thousand. The courts will look at it as an attempt. All I want is to see them and get to know them. You can be there."

She unrolled the money, all hundred-dollar bills, and examined them. They looked real, but she couldn't believe it. "What bank did you rob?"

"I've changed over the past few years. I've got a steady job as a private investigator, and I'm good at my job. Been at it for three years. I've settled down. My kids have a right to know their dad."

"Do you even know their names?" Derision dripped off each word. *Lord, I'm trying not to lose it. But it isn't easy.*

"Steven."

"And?"

"I don't know my daughter's name. You know how I am with people's names."

"These *people* are your kids. You call yourself a private investigator? You could have at least found out before showing up here." As much as she could use the money, she put the rubber band back around the wad and threw it at her ex-husband. "I don't want your money. Get out. If you don't leave, I'll call my brother. Just in case you haven't heard, he's the police chief of Summerton."

"I've heard." He snatched up the money and returned it to his pocket. "This doesn't change anything. You'll be hearing from me soon." Stepping back, he rotated toward the door and left, the slamming sound echoing through the house.

Shaking, Sadie finally collapsed back against the wall and slid down. She drew her legs to her and dropped her head on her knees. She'd never thought Harris would come back to Summerton. While growing up here, he'd loathed the town and couldn't wait to get away.

Being a teacher, she still had most of the school year to finish out. She was tired of doing everything alone. She needed her family around her, but she couldn't have Harris in her children's lives.

Can I wait until next May to leave again?

❧

"Is Mr. Montgomery here?" Ethan asked the man who wasn't technically the butler because Bradley would scoff at that term. But the guy was always there to answer the door and bar anyone from seeing Bradley if he thought his employer didn't want to see the visitor.

"He's getting ready for church and—"

"This is official police business." Ethan showed him his badge, staring down the large employee with beefy arms and bowed legs.

"He hates to be disturbed at this time."

"He'll want to talk to me. It's important." Ethan stressed the last word, narrowing his eyes on the gatekeeper as though Ethan could will him to move.

"Very well. I'll ask Mr. Montgomery, but don't be surprised if he tells you to come back another time."

The man escorted Ethan to the formal living room, sterile and stuffy, containing expensive pictures with a western theme on the walls and bronze Remington statues on the tables. There was a time when Bradley would have opened his own door to Ethan. Millions of dollars later his friend kept barriers between him and the townspeople. He missed the days when Bradley and he had ridden a bit recklessly across his family ranch, much smaller in those days.

"Ethan, it's great to see you." Bradley offered him his hand.

He shook it. "I wasn't sure I would get through your man at the door."

Bradley grinned. "I pay him well to keep the riffraff out, but I'll have a word with him about you. I'll let him know you're a longtime friend, even though we've lost touch lately. What brings you here that couldn't wait until church in half an hour?" He waved his hand toward a chair while he fit his long, lean length in one across from where Ethan stood.

"I won't be at church today, and this is something I must tell you in person as soon as possible."

Bradley sat forward, his shoulders thrust back. "What's happened?"

There was never an easy way to inform a parent their child was dead. "Jared was found this morning by hikers in Red River City Park. He's dead."

The color drained from his friend's face. He gripped the arms of the chair and leaned so far forward that Ethan was afraid Bradley would topple from his seat. "No, this has to be a mistake. My son is . . ." His mouth moved up and down, but no words came out.

"I'm sorry, but it's Jared. I saw the body. The police chief ID'd your son. Of course, you'll be asked to make a formal ID."

"How could it be Jared? He should be upstairs." Bradley shot to his feet and strode from the room. "He refuses to go to church, so I haven't seen him yet today, but I'm sure I'll find him sleeping in."

Ethan followed Bradley to his son's bedroom. For Bradley's sake, he hoped Cord was wrong, but the car's registration was to Jared Montgomery.

When the man thrust the door open and stepped inside, he came to an abrupt halt. His hands balled. "No. No. Not Jared. It can't be."

Ethan guided Bradley to the neatly made bed. "Sit. Is Annabelle home?"

"No, she's in Dallas. I'll have to call her." Bradley sank onto the mattress, but he didn't move to get in touch with his wife. "How did this happen? Why Jared?"

"We don't have the answers yet on those questions. Cord stayed to make sure we processed the scene quickly. He knew you would want to know what occurred as soon as possible."

"Was—was he . . ." Bradley brought up a shaky hand and wiped the sweat from his forehead with his palm.

"We don't know the cause of death yet. He was found in his car in the Summerton Lake by the boat ramp." He decided not to mention suicide. Bradley had enough to process at the moment.

"An accident? Why in the world was Jared at Red River City Park? That isn't his normal hangout. And how did he end up in the water? We keep a boat at Monarch Lake."

"Good questions. Ones we will get answers for. Did you see him last night?" Ethan made a visual sweep of the tidy room—nothing like what he'd had when he was growing up.

"Yeah, right before he went out on a date."

"With who?"

"This girl he's been dating for a couple of months. I don't think he was serious about her, but she is beautiful and Jared is always . . ." Tears glistened in Bradley's gray eyes, making them shine like polished silver. He dropped his head. "I don't think I can get used to saying was. He's all I have." Bradley fell silent for a long moment, then he lifted his head and directed his intense, cold gaze to Ethan. "I want you on this case. Actually, I want you to be in charge of the case. If I have to, I'll call the governor. I need to know what happened. Who's responsible?"

"Cord already asked me to assist him."

"No. I want you running it. I want the state lab to run all the tests. I need to know." The urgency and fierceness in Bradley's tone heightened the tension already gripping his friend.

"I'll take care of it. I'm sure Cord will be fine with that." Ethan captured Bradley's full attention. "Understand I will dig until I discover what happened, but I won't put up with you dogging my every step about the case." He knew if his friend called the governor he would have to oversee the case, and he really wouldn't have a say on how Bradley conducted himself. Like Cord, he suspected this was the tip of something big going down in his hometown.

"Fine, but I ask you to keep me informed of any progress."

"I will, but I can't have you hampering my case." *Because you might not like what I find.*

"I understand."

Ethan didn't think Bradley really did. What if it were suicide? Or murder? Either situation brought a whole slew of questions that were hard on a family. "I have a few questions for you before I go back to the scene. Did you see your son return after his date?"

"No. He'll be—would have been eighteen in six months. He didn't have a curfew, but he was always home at a reasonable hour."

"But you don't know if he returned last night and went out this morning or if he was out all night?"

Bradley scowled. "No. He never gave me a reason to question his judgment. What are you saying?"

"Nothing. I need to figure out what he was doing last night. What's the name of the girl he was dating?"

"Kelly Winston." Bradley bit out the words, a nerve in his cheek twitching.

Ah, Bradley had dated Kelly's mom in high school, nothing too serious, but he imagined it didn't set well with Bradley since Mary Lou and he didn't end on a good note. Wasn't Lexie friends with Kelly? He'd seen the girl over at his niece's house a few times in the past month since he'd returned to Summerton.

Bradley pushed to his feet, his gaze fixing on a photo on his son's desk of a younger version of Bradley with someone who looked like Mary Lou. Kelly, the girl he'd seen his niece with. "I didn't want Jared dating her, but I was afraid he would go behind my back if I told him not to."

Like Bradley had with Mary Lou. "So you tolerated him seeing her."

"Barely. Do you think she had something to do with this? Her mother certainly could mess with a guy's mind. I should have listened to my gut and put my foot down concerning Kelly." Bradley began to pace.

Ethan walked to the desk. "Teenagers love to oppose what you think is good for them. Sometimes we have to let them make their own mistakes. You did what you thought was right."

Bradley swung around, his strong jaw line hard. "But Jared is dead."

"Kelly might have nothing to do with this. We don't even know if she was really with Jared last night. Let me do some investigating. Let me do my job."

"My son didn't lie to me. If he said he was going out with Kelly, then he was. Talk to her."

"May I take a look at his computer and this room? See if I can find anything to help me reconstruct his whereabouts last night." A suicide note or an indication someone was mad at Jared.

"Sure, but I can't stay in here. I'm going to call Annabelle." Bradley crossed to the exit, an ashen tint to his tan features. "Keep me informed."

When Bradley left, Ethan began his search of Jared's bedroom. Apprehension nipped at Ethan. Since he'd returned home, he'd only had routine investigations, but he was afraid all of that was going to change with this case.

Lexie eased open the back door of the warehouse, its creaking noise clamoring through her head and the vast building. The sound announced to anyone around that someone was coming in. As Lexie squeezed through the opening, sunlight poured into the place, mingling with the cloudy streams coming in through the dirt-crusted windows scattered along the walls on both sides of her. The stench of stale beer, urine, and vomit permeated the air, nearly gagging her.

Find Kelly and get out of here.

Her eyes quickly adjusted to the dimness while she started to the left, searching for her friend. The beer bottles and cans littered the concrete floor—lots of them. What went on here? The question kept running through Lexie's mind as she moved further into the warehouse.

Then she spied Kelly, or at least it looked like her, curled into a fetal position on the dirty floor, her back to Lexie. Not moving.

Want to learn more about author
Margaret Daley and check out other great fiction
from Abingdon Press?

Sign up for our fiction newsletter at
www.AbingdonPress.com/Fiction
to read interviews with your favorite authors, find tips
for starting a reading group, and stay posted on what
new titles are on the horizon. It's a place to connect
with other fiction readers or post a
comment about this book.

Be sure to visit Margaret online!

www.margaretdaley.com

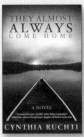

What They're Saying About...

The Glory of Green, by Judy Christie
"Once again, Christie draws her readers into the town, the life, the humor, and the drama in Green. *The Glory of Green* is a wonderful narrative of small-town America, pulling together in tragedy. A great read!"
—**Ane Mulligan,** editor of *Novel Journey*

Always the Baker, Never the Bride, by Sandra Bricker
"[It] had just the right touch of humor, and I loved the characters. Emma Rae is a character who will stay with me. Highly recommended!"
—**Colleen Coble,** author of *The Lightkeeper's Daughter* and the *Rock Harbor* series

Diagnosis Death, by Richard Mabry
"Realistic medical flavor graces a story rich with characters I loved and with enough twists and turns to keep the sleuth in me off-center. Keep 'em coming!"—**Dr. Harry Krauss,** author of *Salty Like Blood* and *The Six-Liter Club*

Sweet Baklava, by Debby Mayne
"A sweet romance, a feel-good ending, and a surprise cache of yummy Greek recipes at the book's end? I'm sold!"—**Trish Perry, author of** *Unforgettable* and *Tea for Two*

The Dead Saint, by Marilyn Brown Oden
"An intriguing story of international espionage with just the right amount of inspirational seasoning."—**Fresh Fiction**

Shrouded in Silence, by Robert L. Wise
"It's a story fraught with death, danger, and deception—of never knowing whom to trust, and with a twist of an ending I didn't see coming. Great read!"—**Sharon Sala,** author of *The Searcher's Trilogy: Blood Stains, Blood Ties,* and *Blood Trails*.

Delivered with Love, by Sherry Kyle
"Sherry Kyle has created an engaging story of forgiveness, sweet romance, and faith reawakened—and I looked forward to every page. A fun and charming debut!"—**Julie Carobini,** author of *A Shore Thing* and *Fade to Blue*.

Abingdon Press fiction
a novel approach to faith

AbingdonPress.com | 800.251.3320